Praise for Shattered Dreams

Sparhawk provides detailed and pragmatic
scientific and military descriptions.

- Publisher's Weekly

Bud Sparhawk's *Shattered Dreams* is a real page turner.
Hard to put down.

- David Sherman, bestselling author of
the *Star Fist, Demontech,* and *18th Race* series

Bud Sparhawk is a natural storyteller, something that's hard to find these days. Reading his work is always a treat, and I have no doubt that readers who are unfamiliar with him will find a new favorite.

- Allen Steele, Hugo
Award-winning author of *Arkwright*

Existential peril. Truly alien aliens. Galactic scope. Bold extrapolation. Plucky heroes. In short, *Shattered Dreams* brims with SF goodness.

- Edward M. Lerner,
Canopus Award-winning author of
the *InterstellarNet series*

Fans of *Starship Troopers* and *Old Man's War* should rejoice!
Both action-packed and thoughtful,
Shattered Dreams sets the standard for military SF!

- David Creek, author of *Chandra's Awakening*

eSpec Books titles including the works of Bud Sparhawk

Dogs of War

Man and Machine

Best of Defending the Future

SHATTERED DREAMS

THE SHARDIES WAR

BUD SPARHAWK

Pennsville, NJ

PUBLISHED BY
eSpec Books LLC
Danielle McPhail, Publisher
PO Box 242,
Pennsville, New Jersey 08070
www.especbooks.com

ISBN: 978-1-942990-72-7
ISBN (ebook): 978-1-942990-73-4

Interior Design: Danielle McPhail, Sidhe na Daire Multimedia
www.sidhenadaire.com

Crystal Icon, Marine Icon, Cover Art, and Design: Mike McPhail
www.mcp-concepts.com

Front Cover Background: Space Scene by Space Creator
www.shutterstock.com

Portions of this novel appeared, albeit in somewhat different form,
in the following publications:

Bright Red Star, *Asimov's*, March, 2005
The Glass Box, *So It Begins*, Dark Quest Books, January 2009
CyberMarine, *By Other Means*, Dark Quest Books, December 2010
Scout, *Asimov's*, June 2012

Hard Choices, *Best Laid Plans*, Dark Quest Books, October 2012

Prologue

THE IMPACT NEARLY DISLODGED LIEUTENANT PINO SILVA FROM HIS SEAT AS something massive struck the cargo hauler, *Provance.* The aft control panel display flashed red, indicating fire. Alarm klaxons shattered the silence. He keyed the bridge. "What's our status?" There was no reply.

Silva glanced at the exterior cameras. He could make no sense of the images. *Provance* was surrounded by something that scattered the bright sunlight as though through a hundred prisms. He switched to another camera. It was dead. A third showed Jeaux's night side. The main settlement glowed with the light of a thousand suns—far brighter than it had any right to be.

Angular objects curved up from the planet, looking nothing like the shuttle he'd expected; all sharp edges and flat planes. Had one of those hit the ship?

He heard the first officer's voice: "Take control, Pino. Get us the fuck out of here." His urgency said the impact had been deliberate—an attack? Could that be what was illuminating the settlement? Silva assumed the incoming objects were hostile. Unfortunately, *Provance* was a defanged former battle cruiser, its formidable weapons removed when it was refitted after the colonial wars.

Flight was his only option.

All this flashed through Silva's mind even as his hands followed emergency actions drilled into him. He torqued the main gyro and fired her side thrusters to rotate *Provance.* He wasn't worried about the ship's stellar orientation or direction at this point; he just wanted to get her away from the hostiles. He prepped the reaction engines to fire and, when the lights blinked green, hit the switch. *Provance* accelerated with head-snapping abruptness, leaving Jeaux's orbit on a tangent. It was dangerous to activate the drive before they'd achieved maximum thrust, but he had to take that chance. He worried as the drive slowly came to life. He realized it may have been damaged and prayed it would still work.

"Come on, come on," he whispered frantically. As the drive indicator inched toward operational range, the impacts on the hull increased. It had barely touched the mark when he activated the drive to send *Provance* on her programmed course to the Morrow colony.

Alarms blared. *Provance* emerged from seven-space and burst into Morrow's system, shaking so violently that Silva feared it would break apart. He heard metal shrieking. The auxiliary board was a field of blinking red, screaming for attention, every light heralding imminent disaster. He could only hope his surviving crew fought to contain the worst of the damage.

The circulation systems couldn't clear the acrid stench of overheated generators and leaking batteries that permeated the compartment. Power was at a fraction of what they needed, barely enough to fire the engine although he couldn't say for how long, given the flickering indicators. It was a wonder that Provance had managed to reach Morrow system at all; so extensive were the flashing damage indicators.

Life support was marginal. There was only enough air to last a few days at best. He didn't know how many of the crew had survived the initial attack. A single fire suppression crewman reported that the drive engineer was severely burned. Silva had heard nothing from the bridge and assumed they'd provide little help and no guidance.

It was all up to him.

Provance's normal approach at Morrow was a seven-week loop around the sun to kill velocity and then to spiral around to match Morrow's path. That wasn't possible now. Not only were there no engine controls, but their life support was dying. He had to inform the colony about the attack so they could pass the word to the next ship. The long-range data link was inoperable, but the ship still had short-range radio. He hoped its weak signal would reach the settlers. There was no other choice.

"There has been an alien attack at Jeaux," Silva said with one eye on the rapidly declining power level. "Warn Earth and take precautions." The transmit light flickered faintly as he keyed the message to repeat. *Was the warning clear? Would anyone hear it? Would they understand the danger?* Already the air grew stale. The lights dimmed. He glanced through the viewport and swore; three glistening prisms flanked *Provance*.

The aliens had followed them to Morrow.

BOOK ONE

Chapter One

Vicky Wallbarger hurried across Landing's compound. Jason Tsung had called her. Typically, she'd be annoyed at the interruption, but the urgency in his voice concerned her. He hadn't said what was wrong, just that he'd heard something weird. Unsettled, she shivered despite the warmth of the afternoon sun.

What the devil did "weird" mean? And why her? It was damn strange for Jason to disturb her when he knew she was getting ready for an excursion upriver.

"... lien...tack at Jeaux...[static]... Warn Err... [static] ...ecautions." Jason struggled to clarify the weak signal from the incoming Navy ship, but the message was garbled at best.

"Aliens?" Vicky's eyebrows lifted. "Did he really say 'aliens?' Adjust the filters; let's get some better definition."

Jason's adjustment made a slight improvement to understanding the first sentence: "...lien attack...Jeaux...." The name of the ships' previous stop was clear. Jeaux was a mature colony established dozens of years before. The Navy supply ships stopped there before winking to Morrow.

"I'll keep trying." Jason continued to fiddle with the settings. "Maybe we can pick out individual phonemes this time."

Vicky's breath caught as the signal cleared. The voice definitely said "an alien attack." Whether those aliens were native to Jeaux or somewhere else was unclear.

It made no sense. Jeaux had been thoroughly explored. There should be no unknown alien life forms anywhere on the planet, which meant the message had to be about other aliens. Vicky had trouble believing that. She found the idea of inimical aliens ridiculous. "Whoever made that broadcast must have been joking," she replied. "What's the data packet say?"

"That's what's so strange. There wasn't any," Jason replied. "Just this weak radio signal."

Vicky frowned. The arriving Navy ship should have sent a data packet with their identity, position, and course data the instant they emerged from seven-space, which was usually weeks before they settled into orbit. The fact that the message was transmitted over low-powered analog radio, without following proper protocol, disturbed her even more than the message itself.

"We got nothing since? I'd think they'd be more excited. Aliens! My God, that's got to be the most incredible news possible." Despite deep exploration of habitable zones around nearly three hundred stars in this arm of the galaxy no other sentient creatures had been discovered. There was life aplenty out there, but nothing they'd encountered possessed human-level intelligence. Even the bird-like Syphons of Ellipse 5, who created crude tools, held out only a modicum of hope, which was why settlement on that world had been forbidden so scientists could study the creatures' natural development in isolation.

"I'm still not clear on the other part of the message," Vicky continued. "Did he mean that the people on Jeaux attacked the aliens or vice versa? Could the Navy have screwed up and attacked the alien ships or was it the other way around? Probably the Navy going off half-cocked again..." She'd grown up hearing stories about the Colonial Wars and, like her forbearers, had a serious distrust of the military. "There are too damn many questions. Let's listen to that recording again."

"I don't like the way it cut off so suddenly," Jason said after another run-through. "That could indicate radio or power failure. What if the ship's transmitter is damaged? I really worry about why they didn't send us the standard data packet."

Vicky agreed. "We won't get any answers until they send us the packet. Maybe you should contact our other settlements and see if they picked anything up. Meanwhile, I brief the mayor."

Mayor Eve Gunning let everyone get settled before she rapped for attention.

"We just got a transmission from the arriving ship," she began and didn't have to explain further. *Provance* was the only scheduled supply ship. Morrow was too remote for more frequent runs.

"About time," Ken Gamble, the head of the farmers' association, shouted. "We'll need to get better seeds for next spring's planting. Too many failures in the last batch." Delivery of supplemental and experimental seeds that might help the colonies on Morrow survive was important. Adaptable foods tested on other worlds had already helped enrich and expand their diet.

"Medical machinery, too," Doc Molet said. "Dispensary's running a bit low on antibiotics and vaccines."

Eve interrupted. "Before anyone says anything else I need you to listen to the recording of the message."

Doc Molet rose to her feet. "A voice message? Was something wrong with the data channel?"

"I'll answer that later, but first, just listen." Eve nodded for Jason to play the static-filled message. He had to run it twice because the acoustics in the large room were so bad.

"*Aliens*, is that what he said?" The crowd muttered and fussed, their expressions incredulous. "Are you sure they weren't broadcasting some damn entertainment program?"

"There's no way we can tell," Eve said, raising her voice. "There has been no further contact, no more messages, and all attempts to contact them have failed. We did not receive their data packet either."

Someone shouted from the back, "He did say 'attack,' didn't he? Who attacked who—us or them, if there really is a *them*, that is."

"We can't be certain of what any of this means," Eve answered. "We don't know who shot first. We can't even be certain that *anyone* shot *anyone*—I mean any-*thing*," she amended, acknowledging that she believed she'd really heard '*aliens*.' "We need more information before we proceed."

The crowd grumbled and shifted in increasing agitation.

Annoyed, Vicky took a deep breath to calm herself before cutting in. "Aren't any of you listening, for God's sake? Jason, explain."

Jason rose, his voice shaking. "Er, the lack of a data stream might mean that the ship's main transmitters are inoperative. Beyond that, I have no idea what else might be wrong. We're going to have to wait until they send more information. Maybe when they reach orbit they can talk to us."

The senior scientist stood, not bothering to mask his contempt. "Your alien supposition is pure nonsense. Our explorers have never found any evidence of another intelligent race. The idea that our Navy supply ship would discover one, and immediately get into a fight is beyond my wildest imagination." He paused and glared at the others. "Surely there is a perfectly rational explanation for whatever we've misinterpreted. We should wait for more information and stay calm."

Greg Donovan, owner of the town's river barges, jumped up. "Damn it; what if you're wrong? We have to prepare to defend ourselves, just in case. It's clear that the message was a warning! Who knows what these aliens might do?" Panic crackled in his voice. "What's going to happen to us, to our families?"

In no mood for his hysterics, Vicky put her thumbs in her waistband and pinned Greg with a glance. Many of the councilmen recognized the non-nonsense stance and fell silent. "How do you propose we fight off these *aliens*, Greg? All we have are light weapons, handguns, shovels, and pitchforks to defend ourselves. How much good you think they're going to do? That is, if it comes down to a fight?"

"I still think we need to do something, Wallbarger," Greg grumbled. "We can't just sit on our asses as someone," he glared at the mayor, "is suggesting. Are you going to dither on this as well, Eve?"

"*Provance* isn't likely to make orbit for another couple of weeks, Greg," Eve advised. "What we need to do is keep an ear on the radio around the clock."

"It might be sooner than that," Jason volunteered. "The signal couldn't have been that strong if the ship was far away—it was on their orbit-to-ground frequency—that's low power," he explained to the puzzled faces turned toward him. "It had to be pretty close for us to get a decent signal. It could arrive any day now."

"Then we should watch the skies," someone suggested. "Anyone got a telescope?" That got a few laughs as the meeting broke up.

There had been no further word from the incoming Navy ship for more than two weeks and rumors about the message's contents had flown around faster than the approaching ship, gaining more interpretations with each retelling.

Everyone in town debated what should be done. At least half wanted to take their families into the mountains to hide from the approaching aliens. *That might not be a bad idea,* Vicky thought, but they still had time. As Eve had advised, better to wait until the ship arrived. Once they had all the facts they could plan. Right now there was too much interpretation and too little information.

In the meantime, Vicky had listened to the garbled message a dozen times without drawing any more sense out of it. Some of the other settlements radioed in with their opinions that whoever sent the message was simply panicked and blathering nonsense. "We'll get a perfectly sensible explanation when they arrive," they said.

One of the farmers took his family and struck out for the mountains.

"They stole one of my barges," Greg Donovan fumed. "Loaded it with everything they could carry. I'd say they were heading for Bamber's Reach."

Made sense to Vicky. Bamber's lay in a mountain valley to the west and could only be reached by river or a series of animal trails. Poling Greg's slender, heavy barges up the languid river was the easiest way to move people and cargo to and from Bamber's.

"Have Jason radio Bamber's to expect them around the tenth of Lan'down. It will take them that long at least to get there," Vicky advised Donovan. "They'll bring your barge back after *Provance* orbits," she assured him. She didn't add that they'd probably feel really foolish when this was over.

Tensions around town grew with each day that passed. Factional arguments escalated between those who believed and those who didn't. "Some people are taking the most dismal interpretation, others think it's a farce," Eve said as they went over the manifests for Vicky's supply trip up the river. "The scientists seem divided as well."

"Yeah, I heard that the alleged aliens are about to land, rape the women, eat the children, and ravish the land," Vicky responded.

"I'm surprised drinking all the whiskey isn't on the list." Eve laughed. "I think an insane crewman is the most reasonable explanation."

"Anybody supporting the sci-fi broadcast idea?" Vicky countered.

Eve chewed on that, obviously frustrated. "It's like arguing about religion with few facts and a shit-load of opinions. It could be either, none, or all of them. It's a puzzle that I don't have a clue about solving and it seems that everyone wants me to do something. We simply don't have enough information."

Vicky nodded. "I understand, but consider this. People tend to panic and do foolish things when it looks like nothing is being done. You might not have all the facts, but that doesn't mean there's *nothing* we can do."

Eve leaned forward. "I'm listening."

"I've been thinking about this. First, we need to let everyone know that you heard them. Then make a big show of setting up emergency measures. Remember the take precautions phrase in the message?"

"Do you really think we need to take this *that* seriously?" Eve answered. "I mean, the idea of invading aliens is so outrageous. You haven't really bought into this paranoia?"

"Look, Eve, making plans won't be a waste. You can always use the preparations for something else if this turns out to be nothing. Give people something to work on as a community so they don't go haring off half-cocked like those heading to Bamber's."

Eve considered what Vicky said. "What do you suggest?"

"For now, just make the announcement about the emergency. Now, can we get back to the manifests? I have to leave in a week."

It surprised Vicky how quickly Eve's *precaution* plan came together. The council members and concerned citizens came up with a list of basic supplies. Dried fish and fruit, spare farm tools, some cordage, fabric, and fishhooks were quickly bundled into caches and placed alongside the cargo meant for Bamber's. Every two days' distance she would stop and deposit one of the caches along the riverbank for use in case of emergency.

For this trip, she pulled her occasional helpers, Chuck and Tony, away from their work in the fields. Chuck was seventeen and serious, just starting to sprout a scraggly beard. Tony was two years younger and still beardless, but he matched Chuck in size and strength. Both boys knew how to push the barge along and, truth be told, appeared anxious to escape the arduous labor of spring planting.

She worked the barge's rudder as her two companions marched steadily along the barge's now-narrow walkways. There was hardly room along the sides to walk the poles. Until they unloaded the first two caches, the three of them would have to sleep atop the cargo.

The boys worked in a steady rhythm; push the pole and walk front to back, lift the pole and return to do the same. Slow but steady the barge moved up the shallow river as Vicky sang a cadence to keep them in synch.

Landing soon disappeared behind the river's gentle curve. By the end of the first day they were beyond all sign of civilization.

Two weeks later all that disturbed the tranquility of the river was the slow, steady rhythm of Chuck and Tony walking their poles. As they approached one of the last cache locations, the boys secured the barge and broke out their fishing poles, while Vicky headed off into the brush to find a good location to place the supplies. She found a game trail not far from the river bank.

Walking a short distance, she spotted an open space where they could place the cache. She preferred a rock outcropping or a cave but this location was dry, above the flood line, and easily accessible from either river or trail. Returning to the barge, she and the boys hauled the supplies to her chosen spot. Vicky attached a colored marker to the side of the cache to make it easier to spot.

Not that any of this is likely to be needed, she thought, *but they'll be easy to find when the panic dissipates.*

Two days after they placed the last cache, a huge ball of flame streaked overhead. Long after it disappeared from sight they heard a distant boom shattering the peace of the river.

"What the hell?" Chuck yelled.

Startled, Tony lost his pole.

All three of them searched the sky as if they would find the answer there.

"Sonic boom," Vicky explained as Chuck let the barge drift back to where Tony's pole stuck out of the water. "Grab it as we swing by," she ordered.

"What made that noise?" Chuck repeated as Tony leaned over to recapture his pole.

"I don't know," Vicky admitted. "It was too big to be a meteor. Besides, meteors don't flame like that, none that I've ever heard about, anyway. Maybe it was something from the ship." It was about the time they'd be sending down a lander, she estimated. Had something happened to send the craft flaming to ground? No, that wasn't likely; whatever it was had to be moving at transonic speeds to break the sound barrier.

Another horrid idea overcame her: The Navy ship was the only object that would have that much speed. Could the ship itself have hit the atmosphere instead of going into orbit? What if it had been damaged by the aliens? Were the settlement's nightmares about to become real?

Vicky found it hard to breath as she steered the barge to the bank. The boys looked too shook up to go on, and frankly so was she.

"We'll tie up here for the night." As the boys set up camp, Vicky powered up the radio. She needed to find out about that ball of fire.

"No idea," Jason responded. "Might learn more tonight after I talk to the other settlements. I'll let you know." He sounded like he still hoped to hear that the Navy ship had finally made orbit.

Vicky suspected he would be disappointed.

That evening the entire downriver sky lit up brighter than day.

Vicky braced for the sound of an explosion, but heard nothing. As the brightness faded and the night returned to normal she scrambled for the radio. Jason didn't answer. No one did, despite her repeated efforts to hail Landing. She told herself they were just sleeping. As she lay there waiting for the dawn, Vicky wrestled with her fears.

Before the sun rose the sky lit up again, this time in the direction of Bamber's Reach. Again, there was no explosion, just a gradual dimming of the light until it was washed out by the brightening dawn.

Fighting against panic, she keyed the radio. First Landing; then Bamber's. No reply.. After long minutes of nothing but static she shut it off. Numbly, she put the radio away.

"Aren't you going to keep trying?" Tony asked. "Find out what happened? What about my folks? I need to find out if they're all right!"

"Nobody's answering, Tony," Chuck added quietly. "They have more important things to do, I'd guess."

Chuck's attempt to keep his younger companion calm surprised Vicky. From his grim expression she knew he also suspected the worst.

"I'll try Jason again a little later," she said, striving to keep her voice calm, normal. "Right now, I think we'd better get away from the barge."

They unloaded everything, including the cargo for Bamber's. Vicky pulled out whatever would help them survive and carefully repacked the rest. "Might be I'm just an old worrier, but better safe, than not."

"Let's push the barge away. There's no sense giving *them* a hint as to where we are."

"Who do you mean by *them*?" Tony asked. He looked scared. Chuck was probably as shaken, but didn't show it. Good.

Vicky didn't answer. She divided the food and supplies into three compact bundles they could carry and still move quickly.

"Why are we doing this?" Tony asked.

Vicky cursed beneath her breath. He wasn't going to shut up until she said something.

"If it's aliens they might search the river for survivors," she answered.

Tony jerked and went pale. He asked no more questions as they set off toward the mountains.

By morning, Vicky was fairly certain that there was no pursuit. At least not yet. On the other hand, they had come so far from the river that she didn't know if anyone or anything had been searching or not.

Were they doing the right thing by running away? Or should they return to Landing and offer help? Abandoning the townsfolk bothered her, but she had to protect the boys. Going back was too risky. Considering the lack of communications so soon after those inexplicable flashes, she hoped she'd made the right choice.

The boys seemed to be holding up rather well, though she'd heard Tony crying softly in the night. Didn't blame him. She felt like bawling herself as she wondered what happened. Was it an attack? Had there been any survivors, if that's what it was? Those flashes had been awfully bright. The questions gnawed at her conscience until she reached a decision. The boys were safe for now, out here where no one could find them. Her responsibility now was to Landing, and any survivors who might need her help.

"I want you to keep moving toward Bamber's. Follow the river, but not too close, until you reach the mountains," she instructed as they ate a cold breakfast. "Take the radio. Maybe you can contact one of the families that left before..." She stopped. Maybe some of the families who fled along the river hadn't yet reached Bamber's.... Or maybe the boys would run into one of the colony's exploration teams. It was about time for some of them to return to Landing.

"When you get near the mountains, set up camp." She didn't add, "*Because Bamber's is probably gone.*" She hoped they wouldn't get that far before she caught up. Safer for them to be on the trail and moving. "I'll meet you there."

"What about you? Aren't you coming with us?" Tony's dismay was obvious.

"I've got to find out what happened to your mom," she said gently. "Keep heading toward Bamber's. I'll see what happened at Landing, then catch up with you."

Chuck stepped forward. "Look, if you need help..." he began, but she cut him off.

"Faster for me to travel light. You two get moving and stay away from any open spaces. We don't know what's happened so best to stay out of sight."

They hesitated. "Get moving!" she ordered and turned toward Landing without another word. *Stay safe,* she prayed for them.

Stay safe.

Vicky stood at the border of Ken Gamble's farmstead and stared down the slope. As she feared, something had happened, but the destruction she saw was beyond her wildest imagining. Landing had been completely destroyed. Neat wooden fences still divided the pastures and fields, but the dwellings, the huge shed that held the farm equipment, and the fuel storage were utterly destroyed. Only piles of rubble marked the cluster of wooden buildings, including the council hall where they'd tried to decipher the ambiguous message, which was no longer ambiguous to her. *Provance's* message had become brutally clear. The only thing standing was Greg's stone barn, wearing its collapsed roof like a shroud.

It didn't look like there had been an explosion; no evidence of fires, no craters pocking the landscape, and no sundered or torn fragments of equipment scattered about. It looked as if someone had simply collapsed all the wooden buildings.

At that point she realized what she was not seeing. Where were the bodies? Worse, why did she see no survivors? Had everyone been taken? She fought to suppress her rising terror: This was no time to lose control. It wasn't safe. Besides, she needed answers.

Vicky waited until nightfall before venturing into the destroyed town, wary that something might still be waiting and watching. She cautiously examined the debris for any indication of what had happened. Where was the farm equipment, the carts, the boats, the bins and cribs? Even the nails in the boards were gone! Gods, had everything made of metal been swept away?

Wait! Something glistened in the faint moonlight; a little gem. She picked it up and rubbed its surface. Smooth. The surface of a second gem had the same, somewhat greasy feel, as did the next until, by the time she'd examined a dozen, she had a pocketful. What could they be and what did they represent? There were too many questions, too much mystery about this for her liking.

A light rain began to fall. She had no desire to spend another night sleeping in the forest and Greg's ruined barn looked like it could still provide a bit of shelter. No fires, though. Nothing to betray her presence. No telling what might lurk nearby.

She found a dry spot in the corner under the barn's collapsed roof, spread her blanket, and tried to shake off the growing horror of what she had seen...and not seen. She desperately wanted to believe the absence of bodies meant survivors, but if they had fled, why hadn't they returned?

She didn't want to admit that they all might be gone, not yet. Better to think of everyone as alive and well, just elsewhere. Holding onto that faint hope helped keep her emotions in check. She feared that hope wouldn't last for long. Eventually she'd have to pay the toll of her loss.

In the morning she would follow the river trail toward Bamber's Reach. That is, if there still was a Bamber's Reach.

Either way, she had to catch up with her boys.

Chapter Two

CORPORAL LEO SWEENEY WAS PISSED. BIG TIME. HIS JAW CLENCHED AS HE caught his first glimpse of his new assignment: a decrepit, gods-be-damned, piece-of-crap Navy warship floating in orbit around Poonta Nega—a backwater colony in the freaking middle of nowhere.

All the battered ships he'd seen on the way to Navy Refit Station 678 had sustained considerable damage. Some showed gaping holes from the war or where they were being salvaged. The Refit Station 678, his destination was no different.

He hoped it could still hold an atmosphere.

Sweeney had been fuming about this twenty-four month assignment since he'd heard about it. ElRon! Had bashing an irritating asshole been so bad that he had to be punished? What did they expect him to do here? He was a Marine combat specialist for heaven's sake, not a damned deckhand!

He got his first hint of how miserable this assignment was going to be as he tried to squeeze his large frame through RS678's small airlock. "Report to the captain on B-6," the tiny midge of a sailor said as he scurried away.

Sweeney looked around for some indication of where BeeSix might be. Would it have hurt for the little midge to show him the way, or at least point him in the right direction? Sweeney searched through the narrow passage- and ladder-ways, dragging his kit behind. He barely fit through the small hatches. His head just cleared the overheads, except where the stupid conduits ran crosswise. There he hit his forehead. No wonder all the sailors were so short—the tall ones probably self-selected out.

He found an arrow pointing to B-deck and, with no help from any of the midges he encountered, found Captain Packard sitting at a fold-down desk. He snapped a sharp salute. "Marine Corporal Sweeney reporting for duty, sir."

Packard looked as if he'd tasted something bitter. "You must be our new fuck-up." He looked Sweeney up and down, head to boot, and sighed. "What the devil can you do besides take up valuable space and consume too much food?"

Sweeney wondered if he should snap another salute. "I'm a combat specialist, sir, Class Three Mobile Uniform Lifting Exoskeleton operator."

Packard sighed wearily. "Just what we need, another damned MULE driver. By the way, Corporal, we don't salute under cover." He pulled up a pad and stroked a few keys. "Space on board is at a premium so we stick to strict schedules. I expect you to follow orders and not make trouble. Miss your scheduled mealtime and you'll go hungry." He handed Sweeney a flimsy. "You can either do that, or step outside," he suggested, "and I can assure you that first step's a doozy." There was no hint that it was a joke.

"I understand, sir." Sweeney felt like telling the captain what he really thought about Navy rules and schedules and then thought better of it. To demonstrate his disregard for Packard's advice, he snapped yet another sharp salute. When his elbow slammed against the bulkhead, he winced.

Packard looked up and grinned. "Don't say I didn't warn you, Corporal. Now, go see Chief Rausch for your keys and mess schedule. He's down one and counter two."

Sweeney didn't understand. "Sir?"

Packard sighed again—he seemed to do that a lot—and said very slowly, "Take the first down ladder to the next deck, then go counterclockwise past the mess."

"I understand, sir!" Sweeney saluted automatically. His elbow struck a second time.

"You Rausch?" Sweeney asked a grim-faced chief knitting what looked like a curtain. Evidence of previous efforts festooned his tiny bay.

"Let me guess; you're my new MULE driver," the Chief answered, never bothering to look up as he looped and pulled, looped and pulled. "Your rack's down in G-4, near the cargo bay. Drop three, clock six, stow your gear, and report to your CO while I figure out what the hell to do with you." He looked up from his handiwork. "Nobody gets a free ride out here, Corporal—too much work to do." He shoved the two large needles through the ball of yarn and handed Sweeney a small chit. "This is your pass key: lets you get meals and gives you access to places you're allowed to visit. Lose the chit and you'll be locked out, starve, and probably get another year added to your tour." He extended a stylus. "Sign here."

"Come on, Chief," Sweeney began as he picked up the pad. "You wouldn't actually do those..."

"Damn straight I would," Chief Rausch grinned. "Look, we've got no tolerance for troublemakers, the careless, or the lazy. Now, get going. I've got important things to do." He picked up his work and continued looping and pulling.

The ladders to the lower deck were offset, often separated by too-small corridor hatches and accessed through even narrower portals. He knew the reason for setbacks on a warship; a drop of a single deck during maneuvers wouldn't be as bad as being thrown down five or six decks. The offsets might be a good safety feature if this decommissioned wreck were still a warship, instead of a floating barrack. As it was, they were a terrible pain in the ass.

The quarters on G-4 were a warren of compartments, each containing a rack and a fold-down seat. A small closet stood at the head of each rack. "Freaking spacious," he cursed. He could barely open his arms fully and would, he suspected, be unable to use the too-short rack without bending himself into a pretzel. "Why does the Navy have to make everything so damned small?" he muttered.

"Because that's the most efficient size," someone said from the corridor. "Little midges use less air, food, and can actually fit in these stupid racks."

Sweeney turned to see a woman wearing Marine green utilities. Her red hair was close-cropped on one side and long on the other—about a year out of style, he realized. She tapped the nametape on her otherwise unadorned chest. "Name's Yuang, Rita. And you are?"

Sweeney dropped his kit and extended his hand. "Sweeney, Leo. I'm a combat spec."

Rita raised an eyebrow. "Not much in the way of combat out here, that is, except for Acorn actions." She laughed but Sweeney didn't get the joke. "I've been hearing the Chief bitch about needing more bodies to lift bales and shift cargo for the past six months," Yuang went on.

"I'm a MULE op," Sweeney replied, realizing the reason for his reassignment.

Yuang grinned. "Chief's probably happy he's got someone besides Q Fortier. Now his midges won't have to break a sweat." She cocked her head as she examined him without embarrassment. "Won't get much use out of that physique. Other than manhandling cargo with our old MULE, the heaviest thing you'll lift on this station will be your spoon."

"Son of a bitch! I'm a combat spec, not a damn deckhand. I never should have..." Sweeney struck the bulkhead with his fist.

Rita didn't flinch. "Never should have what?"

Sweeney shifted his feet. "Everybody knew the guy was an asshole, but nobody had the balls to do anything. Served him right, which is probably why I didn't get sixteened."

Rita chuckled. "I've seen your records all the way back to Morrow. Troubles there? Fights?"

Sweeney was steamed that she had access to his records. What she couldn't know about was his trouble with that Wallbarger bitch who'd "suggested" that he ship out before she busted his ass. He might have tested her, but she was ten years older and a hell of a lot more experienced in handling unruly fifteen-year-old troublemakers.

Rita brought him back to reality. "You really must have impressed your commander to only bust you from Sergeant and get you sent to RS678. Being in the brig would have been easier, but it would have put a blot on your record. Trust me, this place is better."

Sweeney was puzzled. "You call this better?"

Rita smiled. "Sure. This is where the Navy sends otherwise valuable troublemakers; puts them out of the way long enough to cool off."

Sweeney was surprised to hear that the midges were in the same boat as him and then grinned at his inadvertent pun. "So everybody here is on somebody's crap list? Is that what you're saying?"

Rita laughed. "Yeah, so don't feel so damned special, Leo. All of us are pissed about it."

Sweeney raised an eyebrow. "You, too?"

"They said I kicked ass 'inappropriately' so they decided to send me here instead of doing the paperwork for an Article 16b(3). But that's all you're going to know. Not polite to ask anyone else. Could get you decked."

"You mentioned another name."

"I did." She held up her fingers. "There's four of us Marines so far—me, you, Q Fortier, and Elizabeth, although she goes by Acorn mostly—watch out for her; she's nuts." She grinned and, when Sweeney didn't respond, shrugged and continued. "Fortier and you will have to figure who gets to drive the station's MULE."

"There's a MULE on board?"

"Relic of the war, Rausch told me. Still serviceable, though."

"This Q Fortier guy; what did he...?"

"Like I said, we don't talk about that," Rita warned. "And don't ask. You're not the only hot-head."

Sweeney was sure she was joking, but best to wait and find out. Right now all he wanted to do was get some rest: he'd been awake for nearly twenty hours, most of that squeezed into confining spaces even smaller that this cramped compartment.

"Where do I find the fucking CO? I need to report in and get a rack assignment—I'm beat."

"You might as well take this one," Rita answered immediately. "Mine's just down the passageway," she pointed and winked, "within easy reach."

Sweeney wasn't sure how to take the wink: Was it an invitation or another joke? Best not to ask so soon.

Rita turned to go, paused, and said; "By the way; I'm your *fucking* CO."

She smiled.

Sweeney soon found out that Q Fortier was more than eager to share the decrepit MULE. It was an ancient model, three generations behind the ones Sweeney had operated. It dated from the Colonial War when the Navy used them to load dense ballistic rounds or assist where they needed great strength.

The old machine had lost most of its paint and had more dings than he could count. All of the pressure points were worn to shining knobs from hard use. Its actuators screeched protest with every move. A huge dent on the left arm restricted sideways movement to thirty degrees from center and, as he quickly discovered, the unit's counterbalance was so unreliable that Fortier said he was afraid to try lifting more than a ton for fear of breaking something: replacement parts were hard to come by for something this dated.

As far as Sweeney was concerned, the MULE was a just another part of his punishment.

It only took one six-hour session of operating the MULE for Sweeney to despise the grimy feel of the plastic straps that held the bruising sensors tight against his muscles, loathe the sour smell of the helmet that contained the heads-up displays, and hate the stiffness of the contraption's arms and legs with every aching muscle. He cursed at the noisy monster's continual squeaks and groans and swore at the pitifully underpowered circulator fan that failed to keep him cool and made sweat gather at his crotch and trickle down his legs. Worse, the damned engineers of this ancient piece-of-crap had overlooked the fact that an operator had to take an occasional piss, especially when they had to wear the MULE for hours on end.

Sweat wasn't the only thing that poured down his leg.

Navy Refit Station 678 was formerly the Navy destroyer *Protector*. It had been stripped of weapons, drives, and everything else not needed for life support. Even so, it was the most intact vessel in the salvaged fleet.

Constant improvement of *Protector*'s compartmentalized internal structure was Chief Rausch's preoccupation. Already, he had decided that taking out Anterior Hold C-2's bulkhead, which divided it from Hold C-1, would enlarge the space enough for a half-field football game.

Sweeney could think of no other reason for having so much open space on this wreck, not that he cared a whit. His job with the MULE was to move salvaged pieces and not to question Rausch's architectural fantasies.

"Move that piece over there," the Chief yelled as Sweeney strained to lift a heavy bulkhead section the welders had cut loose.

"Why the rush, Rausch?" Sweeney answered. "I don't see the point of getting this done any sooner." He hated the work, but then, if it weren't for the Chief's stupid plans he'd have nothing to do.

"Watch your tongue," the Chief warned. "Going to get you in deep crap, Marine." He didn't need to add "again."

Again! The fracas with the midges hadn't really been Sweeney's fault. If they had just stopped calling him HeeHaw all the time, stopped making jokes about the MULE operators being strong as an ox and half as smart, stopped hinting that Rita and Acorn were there to keep he and Fortier "satisfied." If they'd just done that, there wouldn't have been a problem. But the continual stream of insults about the Corps was more than any Marine could be expected to bear and he'd respectfully said so, strongly emphasizing his words by gently poking them.

The fact that he had been wearing the MULE at the time might have been the reason for their injuries, but he suspected the damage to their egos might have been the reason he and Rita had a rather serious chat with Captain Packard.

The result was that ever since most midges gave him a wide berth. Better that way.

"What did you say?" Sweeney replied to the Chief's question. "I couldn't hear you."

"Just do your job," the Chief groused.

"Yes, sir!" Sweeney watched the strain gauge as he lifted. This section massed near the safety limits of this MULE. He extended the counterweight to balance and took a careful, clanking step. The exoskeleton's right leg resisted a bit because of a sticky actuator in the hip joint so he had to put some extra muscle into it.

Working in a gravity field made him sweat. It seemed stupid for the engineers to maintain a one gee shipboard environment. Lower gravity would let him move heavy mass with greater ease. He'd complained about it twice to the ship's engineers without any result. Maybe, he mused, he could march the MULE to their space and...no...that was how he got into trouble the last time. Besides, he couldn't possibly get the huge MULE through the narrow passageways, much less up the stupid ladders.

Didn't stop him from imagining, though.

"Put it there," the Chief yelled and pointed, as if Sweeney hadn't heard his original instructions.

"Where else could I put it, for God's sake?" he yelled. "This wasn't what I signed up for, damn it!"

The newer MULEs were designed to carry huge equipment loads for a seven-man squad. A single MULE could carry the heavy rounds for the squad's M60 as well as fifty cases of ammo for a T8905k3.2 repeater. A MULE could handle much heavier loads, but too much mass limited its ability to perform rapid combat movements.

He recalled how learning to move the monstrous framework's arms, legs, and back had been hard, but he'd managed, if only because he loved being the biggest, baddest member of his company. Nobody messed with a MULE.

Although he'd thought that being selected to be a MULE operator was due to a natural aptitude, he later learned that he'd been selected solely on the basis of his strength.

He knew a lot of people thought a MULE was little more than a pack animal, but it was much more than that. MULEs were often outfitted with T8905k3.2 repeaters to supplement a squad's firepower. A MULE operator could even single-handedly operate the massively destructive M60, when necessary.

Visions of ripping Colonial armor to shreds, terrorizing rebellious settlers, and firing round after heavy round from an M60 had once fired Sweeney's imagination. At that time he'd never dreamed he'd wind up as a freaking cargo handler for a little dwarf bastard like Chief Rausch.

"I'm a Marine, damn it, not a deckhand!" he continued as he hefted the bulkhead. "I'm combat rated!" he screamed as he tossed the bulkhead section onto the scrap pile and watched the midges scatter.

He was pissed at the way everything was turning out. He'd probably never see any real action. The last engagement of the Colonial War had ended long before his enlistment. Only training simulations gave any hint of what real combat might be like. Of course, in a real engagement there would be bullets impacting his MULE instead of harmless red targeting dots.

He was pretty sure actual combat would be a lot more frightening.

Rita squeezed into the galley before the end of their scheduled mealtime. The mealtimes for the four of them were scheduled separately since there was no way even a midge could squeeze into the galley when they were there.

"About time you got here," Acorn grumbled as she shifted to make room for Rita. "What are you all excited about? Been playing grab ass with Packard?"

Rita sat down and caught her breath. "The resupply ship arrived with news about..." They waited for her to finish. Finally, she shouted. "Fuck all; they said there were aliens! Aliens have finally been discovered!"

"Aliens?" Sweeney repeated, as if saying it again would establish that he'd heard correctly. "And how is this news?" It seemed that alien life of one sort or another was discovered each week. "What makes this so special?"

Rita looked flushed. "They aren't bugs or some new type of plant, damn it. Finally, we've run into some star-traveling aliens." She hesitated and took a deep breath. "...but..."

Acorn caught it in one and threw down her spoon. "Crap. Somebody fucked it up, didn't they?"

Rita nodded. "Yeah, big time! Turns out these buggers are real bad-asses—attacked a colony, I'm told. Some place called Jeaux."

"Jeaux?" Sweeney asked as a thousand questions came to mind, the least of which was where the colony might be. "What happened? Who fired the first shot?"

Fortier chimed in. "Jesus H.—aliens! What did they look like?"

"They came in ships." Rita waved them to silence. "Navy has a few blurred images. Look like icebergs or something. Too indistinct to make out—maybe glass or crystal, which sounds stupid to me. Who'd fly a glass ship anyway?"

Sweeney couldn't care less about details. This sounded like an opportunity to see combat. "What are we supposed to do? Are they likely to attack us here?"

"I hope not," Fortier interrupted. "Can't imagine fighting aliens, much less in these cramped spaces. Our old MULE wouldn't be much help, that's for sure. No weapons."

"Like to see 'em try to mess with me," Acorn grunted as she played with her knife. "Show them a few tricks, I would."

"I doubt that," Rita smirked. "If any aliens came here there'd be no need to board; they'd just blow this wreck the hell away."

While Sweeney considered that horrid possibility, Acorn recovered her spoon and stirred the lumps around in the gravy. Fortier glowered.

"Packard tells me he's been ordered to get five of the mothballed ships operational," Rita added.

"Fat lot of luck with that," Acorn said. "This graveyard shit is way beyond being recovered." She tilted her head to the side. "Hey, what about this wreck—don't that make six ships?"

"Captain Packard didn't say 'six': five is all!"

Sweeney ignored the implications. He was still excited at the possibility that he might actually see action—and against aliens, too! What the hell was a combat spec for, if not to fight?

"Even if Packard manages to get five ships operational, how the hell is he going to staff them?" Acorn persisted.

"He can probably assemble enough crew to ferry the old buckets," Rita answered. "Not enough sailors to do more, unless Fleet sends help and," she finished, "maybe pulls us out of here."

Sweeney smiled: no more Chief Rausch bossing him around, no more hectoring midges, and he could finally stop having to squeeze his body through the tight spaces in this cramped station.

Better, he thought, *to be part of a real squad.*

Months went by, but reassignment orders never came. Instead the four Marines, along with most of the station's complement, were used to supplement the repurposed wrecking crews in getting the decrepit ships marginally operational.

During their breaks they complained about the cruelty of the universe, the fickleness of the Navy, officers in general, the unfairness of their lousy assignments, and why the hell headquarters hadn't sent them reassignment orders.

Sweeney stood at the cargo bay's port with Rita to watch the restored ships slowly depart until the glow of their engines became indistinguishable from the other stars.

"It's going to be an hour before they blink," Rita said. "I was told that if you look at just the right place the stars will shimmer when the drives activate."

"I hope they'll whoop some ass," Sweeney replied.

Rita shrugged. "I doubt those junkers are going to fight. More likely they'll support fleet ops."

Sweeney wondered if Rita, or anyone else on the station, knew more about the war than him. There was so much uncertainty and the infrequent updates seemed long on guess and short on facts.

Nobody seemed to know what these aliens were, what they were doing, or why they'd attacked. It didn't matter. Once the fleet hit them the war would be over. Maybe afterward there would be some answers.

He glanced at where he thought the ships might be and said a short prayer for the men on board.

Even if they were only midges.

Chapter Three

BEN GUNNING CHECKED THE SET OF *DAY'S END'S* SAILS AS HE TACKED across the wind. The boat turned sluggishly to windward, wallowed a bit in the waves, and then settled on its new course as the coarsely woven triangular sail switched sides.

Day's End was not pretty, being more of a raft than a proper boat. But she was seaworthy and could carry nearly four tons of cargo. Best of all, she made no demands on Landing's limited resources as she carried cargo along the coast.

It was unfortunate that the northerly wind had turned this morning and forced him to beat upwind and tack, a zigzag course that would cost him an extra day to reach Dockstal, where he could finally get a decent meal, a few drinks, and warm his chilled bones. At this deep southern latitude Morrow's sea was barely above freezing.

The evening wind chilled him despite mackinaw, sweater, and heavy pants. Even the small shelter amidships—the "captain's cabin," he'd often joked—offered minimal protection. It was barely wide enough to hold his sleeping bag and a spare sweater.

Morrow's lesser moon had not yet risen to dominate the night sky so he could watch the gradual appearance of the glorious stars in constellations so different from those of Earth. Hunter's, his guiding star, sparkled clear and crisp low on the horizon. He estimated his position based on Hunter's rise. Morrow was too raw and new to have satellites.

Ben knew that one of those twinkling stars might mark the incoming Navy ship making its scheduled stop. By his reckoning it was about time for *Provance*'s arrival, but her schedules were not precise. First she had to lose momentum after she emerged from her seven-space transit and then match Morrow's orbital speed to become a bright dot moving across the sky.

He spotted a few meteorite tracks and some moving dots that disappeared as soon as he glimpsed them. Staring up at the night sky for too long sometimes gave rise to hallucinations. If he wasn't careful he'd be seeing sea serpents, or worse.

He searched the southern sky for Hunter's Star. Hunter's should be just a few degrees above the horizon. Back at Landing, the star glowed nearly thirty degrees above the horizon at this time of night.

The angular difference would tell him if he was making slow, but steady progress. He might reach Dockstal in a matter of days, God willing and the winds right. With neither weather nor anything else of interest to keep him up, he secured the tiller and took to his sleeping bag.

Ben nervously watched the approaching inclement weather. *Day's End* was buoyant enough to shed water as fast as she took it on, but he didn't want the cargo to get drenched should the storm blow up high waves. As the weather gods turned unfriendly and heavy waves rocked the boat, he dropped the sail and lashed the booms. The last thing he needed was to be knocked overboard. Or worse, have his irreplaceable sails ripped to tatters.

He'd weathered storms earlier on the voyage, but with a full load of cargo as ballast his boat hadn't been tossed about. With only half the cargo left she was lighter. Her rudder groaned as he strained against the tiller to keep the boat headed into the wind.

Someday Morrow would have proper ships, fast enough to make this trip in a fraction of the time and in warm comfort, with hardly a thought to wind, weather, waves, or tide. Someday people would no longer be required to stand out in the rain on a wooden deck, with the bite of the wind in their face and the odor of the briny sea in their nose, as they watched the crashing waves against the boards.

But, damn it, today he was *cold!*

By night the wind died, leaving *Day's End* to wallow in the long waves. As soon as Hunter's appeared Ben started to calculate his position. He forgot his numbers when a flaming ball briefly rose just above the horizon in the northwest. He'd never seen a meteor that bright, much less flaming.

He was still estimating Hunter's angular height when an intense light suddenly illuminated the clouds to the south. It started as a dull glow, but quickly grew in blue-white intensity until it became bright enough to throw the shadow of the mast across the deck. Then, abruptly, it was no more.

It took long minutes for Ben to regain his night vision. Had something happened at Dockstal? The light had been in that direction. But what could it have been? There was nothing in Dockstal that could burn that bright. Hell, even if all the fuel they had manufactured exploded it wouldn't have made that big a flash. Besides, if it was an explosion, where was the shock wave? He should have heard *something.* Sound carried long distances over open water.

He fumbled through his pack and found the sealed pouch holding the radio. "Damn!" Somehow water had gotten into the pouch. Moisture and electronics seldom had pleasant encounters he recalled as he pulled the batteries and blew into the radio before replacing them. He thumbed the switch, relieved to see the red power indicator glow weakly.

"Dockstal, this is Ben Gunning on *Day's End*. Do you read me?"

There was no reply, nor to any of his next three attempts. Finally, there wasn't even a flicker from the power indicator.

The question about that blazing light stayed with him, niggling at his mind as *Day's End* ploughed onward.

At sunrise, Ben tried unsuccessfully to call Dockstal. According to his dead reckoning he should be close enough to see the oily black smoke of the settlement's distilleries.

He pulled out his worn notebook and checked his position. He'd been making a steady two knots since leaving Alder's Cove and had come at least five thousand kilometers from Landing. Everything said he should be able to see Dockstal by now.

He pushed the tiller's arm to starboard and let the wind carry the lateen sail across the deck with a *snap* as the fabric filled from the opposite side. Since *Day's End* was now heading directly toward shore Ben kept a careful eye on the waters ahead. Close to shore, he started tossing a line ahead every few minutes or so to let him know when the bottom started to rise so he could turn the boat seaward again.

The boat crept down the coast bit by bit, losing a little progress with each landward tack. Ben felt uneasy. There was still no sign of Dockstal. Finally, near noon, he recognized the stone promontory that marked the mouth of the little stream flowing into Dockstal's snug harbor.

Instead of a close-packed group of buildings, only native stone walls stood like broken teeth to show where Dockstal had been. Stunned, Ben lowered the stone anchor until *Day's End* jerked and began to lazily circle. There was only a mound of rubble near the loading dock. Further inland, where there had once been warehouses and homes, he spied more rubble. What the hell? What kind of explosion could have destroyed the buildings without leaving a massive crater?

Why wasn't Chang or Roy here to greet him? Where were the shopkeepers? He shivered when he realized there was no sign of bodies…alive or otherwise.

He paddled his kayak to shore and debarked to explore the remains of Dockstal. The dirt roads seemed untouched. So was the stone fireplace of the cookhouse/bar/store. Topak, the proprietor had been so proud of her fireplace. Now it was all that was left standing, its native stone unaffected by whatever had destroyed the rest of the structure.

He kept noticing small gem-like stones glittering in the sunlight. They were slightly smaller than the ball of his thumb, cloudy, and with a slick surface that felt greasy when he rubbed it, although nothing came off on his finger. It wasn't any mineral he recognized, which was not surprising given what little he knew of Morrow's geology. The smooth stones had a polished look. He dropped a few of them into his pocket and continued to search for some sign of flight, some indication of where escaping survivors might have run.

By dusk he had found no trace of the missing people.

He returned to his boat as the sun set, finding more of the strange stones along the way; too many to be someone's discards. By now he had half a dozen in his pocket, scant evidence of whatever had occurred here

Nervously, he glanced about. The long shadows cast by the ruins gave him chills. The rubble too closely resembled burial mounds.

Later, he sat on the deck, eating a meal of cold, hard biscuits and dried fish because he feared the brazier's light might draw the attention of whatever had caused this destruction. As he chewed the leathery fish, his eyes darted over the landscape, searching, ever wary for movement. As the last of the day's light disappeared he pulled a blanket around him and leaned back against the mast, still watching what remained of the silent, starlit ruins.

Ben woke with the first rays of sunshine. He felt cold and damp. A light dusting of frost covered his blanket and, on shore, the local avian creatures warbled from their roosts in preparation for the day's fishing. There were puffy clouds on the horizon, which could mean rain later in the day.

Nothing else had changed. The desolation was as it had been the day before, silent as to whatever had taken place. After relieving himself, he ate a sparse breakfast of dried fruit, washing it down with a little of his potable water, and set off in the kayak to explore the shallow stream. He needed to find something to explain what had happened.

He kept to the center of the waterway and stopped when his paddle started scraping the rocky bottom. He'd found nothing. He let the gentle flow of the stream carry him back, only occasionally adjusting his course to finally reach the harbor.

Other than the threatening rain clouds looming closer on the horizon, Dockstal's ruins remained as he'd left them. The wind was increasing in strength and blowing toward the advancing front. That, he knew from experience, presaged a hard blow. Time to move *Day's End*. The anchor wouldn't hold against a strong wind in open water. He estimated that he still had an hour or so before the storm arrived. Moving quickly, he raised the anchor and boom and let the wind take the sail. A quick twist of the tiller turned *Day's End* on a broad reach that drove her further into the estuary, where she'd be sheltered from the winds.

The front of the storm arrived just as he settled into the boat's tiny cabin. As raindrops pelted the deck he examined the handful of gems he'd found. Strange that someone would have collected these and stranger yet that they would have polished them. The colonists had little time for such frivolous pursuits. What could have been their motivation and, more puzzling, who among the small population of Dockstal would have had the time or resources to fashion them? Spare time was a precious commodity. He doubted anyone would use it to make jewelry.

Could the gems have occurred naturally, formed by some geological process? He recalled that Dockstal had a geologist. Perhaps she had found them, but where? This part of the landmass did not have the characteristic exposed uplift strata, old volcanoes, or deep caves where you would expect to find such things. Neither were there stony beaches where the washing waves could have polished them. Most of the shoreline nearby was compacted sand, likely from being an ancient seabed, with an occasional rocky upthrust, like the promontory near the harbor's entry.

The stones chimed like pieces of crystal when they hit each other. That characteristic possibly pointed to volcanism as a source, but the range of mountains where volcanoes might have been were hundreds of kilometers away, even if anyone had the time to spare or interest to get there. A flood might have carried them, although it was hard to imagine the sluggish stream ever having that much strength. Still, over geologic time...

Day's End rocked gently as the cold rain poured. The chill was a reminder that he needed to head home. He was only supposed to spend a few days here unloading supplies and picking up whatever Dockstal wanted transported...

Dockstal... Where were all the people? Was their absence temporary? Would they need the supplies he'd brought with him when they returned, if they ever did? He could not head home without unloading, not if there was even a possibility of returning survivors.

No, except for the rations he'd need for the return trip, he'd unload the cargo in the morning.

He settled in the cramped cabin for a night's sleep. There was nothing else he could do.

The storm passed, giving way to a crisp, clear dawn. A brisk southerly wind ruffled the treetops. Ben drifted back into the harbor, letting the outgoing tide dictate the boat's speed. He steered it to within a few meters of the bank, close enough to rig a boarding plank to horse the supplies ashore. Moving the cargo would be backbreaking work, but he had no other choice. He couldn't sail away without a thought for possible survivors.

Throughout the day, he wrestled the bales ashore and stacked them above the tide line. He then threw a tarpaulin over the pile, driving stakes along the edges to protect the supplies against the ravages of potential storms.

In late afternoon he anchored far from the shore, too exhausted to set sail, but leery of spending a night too close to whatever Dockstal had become.

Ben began the long sail north to warmer weather. With luck and the wind gods smiling, he'd make it to Alder's Cove within a week, refresh his supplies, and get his radio fixed, before setting out again.

The stones in his pocket rattled as he fingered them constantly. They had become his personal set of worry beads. Maybe someone at the Cove would know what they really were.

The fresh breeze moved *Day's End* quickly along, as if she sensed adventure and took on a spirited burst of speed in anticipation. Ben tossed the pit log overboard. He was making a decent two-and-a-half knots—which was not a bad turn of speed. The winds remained favorable, and the tides were in his favor. He expected to reach the Cove within a day. If he lost the wind it could take longer.

He wished again that he could radio somebody about Dockstal, but there was no sense agonizing over the dead batteries. One thing you learned on the sea was that you had to do the best you could with whatever the fates handed you. There was no one else to rely upon, not out on the sea, where there was only he and *Day's End*.

As if to disprove this he heard a distant whistling. Seconds later, a glistening, shining *thing* flashed in rainbow-colored hues as it passed overhead. Ben blinked. It hadn't looked like any craft he'd ever seen; no visible wings or drive and a body defined by sharply angled surfaces that looked like pieces of jewelry.

Had it been an illusion? He searched the sky and saw nothing now but the occasional cloud. No crystalline object, no rainbows; nothing out of the ordinary. Did the jewelry have any connection to the desolation? Or had it been a figment of his imagination?

He stuck his hand in his pocket to worry the stones. They'd grown unusually warm; yet another mystery to add to a list that seemed longer each day.

Flying jewelry was ridiculous.

If the damage at Dockstal had been a shock, discovering the ruins of Alder's Cove brought the horrid reality home. The complete destruction of everything that had been there a month earlier shook him to his core. He stared in disbelief as *Day's End* drifted closer, the details of the devastation becoming more apparent; drifts of wind-blown dirt and mounds of rubble. It was all too familiar.

Ben swung the tiller to turn the boat. He had no desire to examine the emptiness again or dwell on what might have happened. He *knew* that every trace of Alder's Cove had been erased.

As the Cove dwindled behind, he wished that the wind were as strong as his desire to return to Landing. He wondered if it had been spared.

Neither the wind nor the sea held an answer.

Chapter Four

ADMIRAL CUMMINS SAT STIFF AS A BOARD AT THE HEAD OF THE CONFERence table, his face a mask revealing no hint of emotion as the briefer droned on about the disturbing reports from the Talex mission.

Vice Admiral Jones braced himself. From Cummins' expressionless visage, he knew something bad was coming. He tried to steel himself. The sickening feeling in the pit of his stomach was worse than when they'd first heard about the fleet of aliens attacking Jeaux. One of the colony's survivors had managed to send a single description "...shards," before he fell silent. That word was the only description of the aliens they'd had, a description more apt than they had realized.

The briefer went over the details they'd learned about Jeaux. The unprovoked strike had been unbelievably fierce. The aliens had rammed the hulls of Navy warships, smashing themselves into fragments that left a cloud of glittering shards spinning into space, leaving no trace, no hint, of what had provoked them.

Even with the warnings, the losses at other colony worlds had been great, forcing the Navy to fall back as their ships engaged in a running battle with something nobody understood. The Navy moved defenses to these colonies and managed to engage the aliens. Every battle was fought hard and long, usually with massive losses on both sides. At best, the Navy's defensive forces only managed to achieve parity.

That all changed at Witca Station where heavily fortified military fleets had been forewarned about the Shards' attack patterns. Only the Shards that appeared had used new patterns, as if they were anticipating the fleet's reactions and countered them with ease. Witca Station had fallen with all hands lost. The Navy ships could no longer guarantee parity and began steadily losing.

No one could determine why an alien race would attack with such ferocity, why there hadn't been a single attempt at contact. And worse, strategists, and even the military elite, had failed at every attempt to understand the patterns of their attacks. Likewise, researchers were unable to deduce anything of the invaders' technology from the recovered fragments of the Shards' damaged ships. Every piece recovered appeared to be nothing but dirty glass. What sort of creatures were they fighting?

Shards... That one word, that one utterance from a lone observer on Jeaux, was all humanity had to go on.

Until now.

The young captain continued to drone in her monotone voice, like some news announcer. "As you know, Admiral Cummins, the wreckage from Shard ships contained no trace of aliens. There were only fragments of glass of various colors and shapes."

Jones fondled a smooth shard, one small piece of the millions they'd collected after the horrific engagement. This piece, which might have been a hull fragment, appeared to be nothing more than a solid piece of crystal with no apparent internal structure. Maybe this briefing would provide an answer.

"Yes," Cummins growled as he looked around. Not everyone in the room knew the latest discoveries about the attacks. "We've assumed that either the ships were highly automated, or the aliens destroyed themselves completely. Suicidal, that's what everyone says." He nodded at the captain. "Go on. Let's get this over with."

The captain paled and cleared her throat. Clearly this was not something she wanted to do. "Largely through a stroke of luck, our fleet isolated a lone Shard ship that, as usual, attacked on an evasion pattern that defied our best defensive efforts. We lost six ships before managing to prevent the alien from attempting a suicide run."

She flicked another image on the screens to show an intact alien ship. "Fleet Marines got inside immediately with high hopes of finding the crew." She choked.

"Continue," Cummins said softly. "Please, continue."

"Instead of aliens, they found four of what we later learned were Jeaux colonists." Gasps rose around the table. A few smiled.

"Wonderful," someone said moments before another image filled all the screens to depict what the Marine's head camera's had captured in gory, bloodless detail. The colonists were heads and bodies without arms, legs, and apparently most organs.

When the Secretary of Spatial Defense finally realized what was being shown, he threw up, right on the conference room's fancy rug. Two other staffers almost made it to the bathroom before doing the same.

The raggedly dissected settlers had been scattered around, their exposed brains linked together and to the remains of the alien ship with glassy fibers, while their much-reduced bodies were being supported by machinery salvaged from the wreckage of Navy ships. "There were a couple hundred strands of glass fiber running from the ship's walls into each skull, into each brain, and into each soul," the young briefer stumbled over her script.

"A little less emotion, Captain," Cummins growled.

She cleared her throat. "Clinical examination of the four revealed that each of the colonists was fully conscious and aware." She took a deep breath and continued. "The medics could find no sign that the aliens had dulled the senses of their victims. All four died during examination," she concluded.

"I'm sure the medics helped them along," Cummins said. "It was a mercy." He waved the captain aside and pointed to Mores, a young researcher, to take over.

Mores began without preamble or identifying himself. He did not shut off the display. "We theorize that the aliens must have linked these humans into their ships, probably as control mechanisms."

"How could the aliens do that so quickly?" Cummins asked. "It's only been what, a year since they hit Jeaux? What were they trying to achieve?"

Mores tapped one of the exposed brains with his pointer. "I suspect that they are doing this to make their ships 'think' like us."

"But how is that possible?" Jones asked, earning a frown from the Admiral. "The colonists weren't military. They wouldn't know anything about Naval strategy, or even understand our weapons…"

Mores smiled. "That is true, but I suspect it isn't the colonists' knowledge *per se* that the aliens used. My assumption is that they may be tapping into the fundamental mechanisms of human brains, using the mental processes that guide human thought to anticipate our probable actions.

"You see, General, It isn't what the colonists *know*; it's *how* our human brains *operate*. Like it or not, we are all hard-wired to think in a certain way. The aliens are obviously using that disposition against us. We are, essentially, fighting against our own minds."

"That's Admiral," Cummins corrected.

Mores ignored the remark and looked over the top of his glasses. "Didn't your reports say their ships reacted almost as if they could read our minds?"

Jones shrugged. "That business about the brains is just a theory, isn't it?"

"Yes," Doctor Mores agreed, "at least until I can get one of those colonists into the lab for a detailed examination. Once I see where and how those brains are connected to the fibers I can..."

"I said the medics terminated them," Admiral Cummins said quietly. "We already established there was no indication of drugs or anything else that might mediate the pain they had to endure. Since there was no chance of recovery, mercy was warranted."

Mores frowned. "That's unfortunate. It will make further analysis much more difficult." He seemed unfazed by the frowns this remark elicited.

"Thank you, Doctor," Cummins said frostily. "All right, everyone. We need to tell colonial services to begin evacuating everyone, except military forces, from the aliens' most likely targets. We can't allow any more people to become components of these damned alien ships. We have a war on our hands and either the Shards will be destroyed, or we will be. Already humanity has lost too much, too many for compromise. It is clear that there can be no middle ground.

"We must fight."

Chapter Five

IN THE AFTERNOON VICKY HEARD A FAINT WHISTLING SOUND AS SHE followed the river trail. Something glistening hovered overhead. She ducked under overhanging brush that provided less cover than she'd like, but she had few options. Were the aliens searching for survivors?

Why? Hadn't they already done all the damage they could? Then her thoughts went to Chuck and Tony. In hindsight, she regretted leaving them. Bile rose in her throat as she prayed they had not been discovered.

Part of her wanted to see what the object was doing, but her more prudent nature told her to remain safely hidden. She had no idea of the thing's detection capabilities. With that thing close by it would be dangerous to expose herself. She clasped her knees and huddled beneath the overhang, waiting for darkness to fall.

As she waited, she toyed with her pocketful of smooth gems and tried to figure out what part they played in the damage. There was no doubt that whatever the colonists had been warned about had destroyed Landing. But why had the invaders left these stones?

The gems themselves were warmer than she'd expect, as if they were slowly releasing stored heat. No, that couldn't be it. Given their size and weight they couldn't retain much energy. Was the warmth caused by a chemical process slowly consuming the stones? She couldn't tell.

Vicky stilled as the whistling began again, steadily increasing, drawing closer until she saw a prism slowly pass overhead illuminated by the fading sunlight. It was headed toward the mountains. Toward Bamber's Reach.

Toward her boys.

Fear of what she might discover drove Vicky along the trail. She ate dried food rather than waste time foraging. If she hurried, her chances were good for catching up to her boys. Boys of that age burned calories at a fierce rate so their provisions couldn't have lasted more than four or five days Foraging for food would slow their pace. She kept alert for any sign, afraid that she'd accidentally miss them.

Presuming that the prism thing hadn't already found them...

She shoved that fear aside and distracted herself with the questions she couldn't get out of her mind. None of this made sense. Why had Landing been destroyed? And were the colonists...living or dead? What had the Navy done to instigate such a brutal attack? Why hadn't they heard of the war before that ambiguous message? And why hadn't they heard of an alien contact?

Surely alien contact must have been going on for some time for conflicts to emerge. Enmity takes time to build and it's usually a painful step-by-step process before there's an outbreak of hostilities. Yet, wasn't the attack itself evidence of a war that must have blown up since *Provance's* last visit sixteen months before? No, that made even less sense. Things just don't happen that fast!

But even with the destruction, why were all the bodies missing? She still couldn't accept that everyone might be dead, although the thought of them in alien hands unsettled her even more.

A steady *thud-thud-thud* along the riverbank woke Vicky from a fitful sleep. The rhythm spoke of otherness, of alien presence. There was no way those footfalls were an animal. Not that noisy, steady pace.

She heard a branch break, followed by a sudden splash, as if whatever approached had fallen or stepped into the river. Something flashed brightly as a three-legged monster came into sight. The alien—it could be nothing else—was angular, as if made of panes of glass, and wider at its base, where three legs emerged. She saw no lenses or anything that might be sensors. She didn't know if it was a machine, vehicle, or suit.

What the hell does it matter? she chided herself. She was about to become alien sashimi. Vicky stifled a groan as her pants grew warm. Great time for her bladder to fail... Hell of an undignified way to die.

She held her breath as the thing drew closer. It came to an abrupt stop scarcely ten meters away and rotated. Turning away from her, or toward? Had it seen her? Should she run or cower? Any movement would reveal her presence. What should she do?

The monster moved away and continued to follow the river, parts of the bank collapsing whenever it moved too close. She waited until she could no longer hear its thudding footfalls before stirring. Why had the thing ignored her? It had to have known she was there, recognized that she wasn't some local bit of flora or fauna, yet it had still passed her by. Why?

The gems in her pocket burned hot—that must have been what she felt when she thought she'd pissed herself. Hot? What the devil did that have to do with the close encounter, if anything?

Damn, her list of questions just kept growing. And there was only one way she could get answers. Rising to her feet, she threw her blanket over her shoulder, lifted her pack, and followed the monster.

The thing's progress was relentless, never hastening, never slowing, and never deviating from its advance along the river. Vicky soon tired and fell behind. While she could easily move faster than the alien, she could not sustain its constant pace for more than a few hours. She hadn't the energy to continue and, exhausted, collapsed when darkness fell. She listened to the fading sounds of the monster's passage until they died away.

Wrapping herself tight against the evening's chill, she pulled the blanket over her ears, and leaned against the bole of a large bush. Her bundle lay beneath her knees where it would be safe. Anything trying to get to what little remained of her rations would have to deal with her, but she doubted she'd have the energy to fight off anything larger than a small cat, let alone a three-legged alien.

There was no trace of the alien's passage when she tried to pick up its trail in the morning. She had no idea if it had continued on its way, turned away from the river, or flew over the mountains. She caught herself. Did it matter where it went or was she allowing her curiosity of its purpose to prevent her from finding her boys? She could satisfy both impulses by following the river.

She found a barge tied to Bamber's rude pier, near the river's shallow headwaters. When she checked the trail from the pier she could easily separate recent tracks from older, more weathered ones. She saw no traces of the alien's footfalls, which gave her hope that Bamber's had been untouched.

As she climbed the winding ascent to the settlement she worried that the alien had taken a more direct route. The horrifying thought that the monster might have found the boys forced her along. She had to know if they were safe.

The vegetation grew sparser the higher she climbed. Her breath came easier as the trail leveled. She weaved her way among the scattered boulders—some the size of houses—which had tumbled from the steep sides of the pass, wary of every shadow that might be an alien.

The slightest sound made her flinch. Could that thing be lurking nearby? She grew more cautious, totally aware that there was no place to run, no place to hide should she encounter the monster. Nervous as hell, she finally topped the crest of the pass.

The lush fields surrounding Bamber's looked untouched, but a large prism lay tilted into the forest. It looked as if it had crashed. There were no signs of three-legged monsters, but that hardly made a difference. As with Landing, all evidence of human presence was gone, leaving only rubble remained where buildings had once stood.

Angry tears fell from Vicky's eyes as she searched in vain for any sign of movement, any indication of life, and saw none. She collapsed, all of her hopes shattered. Bamber's Reach was gone. Her worst nightmares come to fruition.

The next day she gathered her courage and descended to Bamber's once well-tended fields. The lack of recent attention to the crops grew obvious as she drew closer. The garden plots marking where the houses had once stood were choked with weeds, their vegetables unpicked, overripe, or rotting on the ground.

Almost without effort, she found more scattered gems among the rubble, though not as many as she'd found at Landing. She dropped a few more into her pocket for no reason other than curiosity and a measure of warm comfort.

Vicky picked ripe tomatoes, pulled carrots, and ate handfuls of sandy lettuce. Every dirt-encrusted bite tasted good after nothing but dried rations. She scanned the hillsides as she ate, looking for any sign that Tony and Chuck had reached this far. She hoped they'd been smart enough to evade that monster and find a secure place.

Her hopes rose when she discovered that someone had been harvesting vegetables before her, tending rows of tomatoes, squash, and potato vines. Most of the squash had become sagging, watery balloons. Some of the onions had been pulled up, and only green tomatoes were left on some plants. Had she found her boys, or some other survivor? Either way, excitement kindled in her breast.

"Hello!" she shouted and then winced. What if the monster heard her? As soon as she had the thought she realized how ridiculous it was: her presence was already quite obvious, standing in an open field among knee-high crops. Her cries were no more risky. "Hello!" she shouted again, hoping for a response.

"Hey!"

Vicky wept openly as Chuck and Tony raced down the hillside toward her. "Safe," she kept repeating as she ran to meet them. *My boys are safe!*

"Did you find Mom?" was Tony's first breathless question as he threw his arms around her. Chuck only offered a hand, but she could tell he was glad to see her.

Her joy at finding the boys dimmed. "I'm sorry. Landing looks just like this," Vicky replied. "Everything gone."

Tony looked closer to losing it than Chuck, whose expression had turned stoic. His lack of reaction said he'd already suspected the truth.

"It was those aliens everybody was talking about, wasn't it? We figured it out when we saw that thing crash." Chuck nodded toward the upended prism. "We've been afraid to get close to it."

"We'll get back at them," Vicky answered quickly. "As soon as the Navy gets here they'll take care of them." She hoped she spoke the truth. The Navy had to be pursuing the aliens if there was a war, wouldn't they? It made sense that they'd follow the action, and eventually check on the colony, if only to see which had been hit the worst. It was only a matter of time before they showed up. She had to believe that. She and the boys just had to wait it out.

Vicky changed the subject before the questions started. "Tell me how you made out. What did you eat? Did you get lost?" If she could just keep them talking maybe they wouldn't dwell on their losses.

If she could just keep them talking, maybe she wouldn't either.

That evening, over a small campfire beneath an overhang the boys had discovered high on the hillside, the questions began again.

"Why are these things lying around?" Tony asked as he dug a handful of gems from his pocket. "We found these all over the place." He rattled them. "What are they?"

Vicky produced her own handful. "At first I thought they might be somebody's jewelry, but that can't be true. There are too many and scattered so widely. Since you found more down there," she indicated where Bamber's had stood, "there must be some connection to the aliens."

"Why are you two talking about a bunch of damn stones?" Chuck spit. "Everything's gone. Everyone's *dead*. We're going to die out here and you're talking about these stupid rocks!" He threw his into the night and stomped away to curl up on his tattered blanket.

"I'd better turn in as well," Tony apologized with a concerned glance at his friend. "Don't worry about Chuck. He's just mad that there's nothing he can do."

Sleep didn't come easily as Vicky considered their situation. She understood that beneath Chuck's anger gnawed the same fear that was in her heart. In Tony's too, no doubt; he'd been crying softly earlier, muffling his sobbing with his blanket. The situation was tough for both the boys, but worse for her. She had to be the adult and keep them safe and under control. Their only chance for survival through the coming winter would depend on trusting each other, helping one another survive through the dark days that lay ahead, and, of course, staying away from the aliens. All on their own. Though, in her heart, she prayed they would find other survivors.

It felt strange to long for the company of others. Her solitary life on the river had been by choice. She'd always had an aversion to crowds, but now...now she was desperate to be surrounded by chattering, noisy, crowding, bothersome *people!*

"Maybe we should try to find anyone else who'd survived?" Tony suggested hopefully over breakfast. "I recall hearing about a base camp about a week north of here. Perhaps somebody's still there?"

Vicky heard the plea in his voice; both boys were eager to be away from Bamber's and its haunting rubble piles and weedy, rotting gardens. But searching for others was not their top priority. Their own survival was uppermost. Morrow's autumn came hard and winter fast. They needed better shelter than an overhang, and food, they most definitely needed to stockpile food.

"Before we do anything, I think we need to salvage as many supplies as we can from the caches."

Vicky could barely maintain the pace under the weight of the supplies they'd retrieved, but didn't dare complain. Tony and Chuck struggled equally hard beneath their own oversized loads. Even so, the two boys outpaced her with the energy of youth, while she plodded behind, ever the tail of the troop.

They'd stripped the closest cache of everything, even the packing material, and used the abandoned barge to transport it back to the pier. There was no way to know what might be useful, but the things in the caches were probably the only remaining human goods on the planet. Once they got these back to the overhang they could retrieve more from the distant caches, that is, until the autumn rains came and travel became difficult.

A whistling sound drew her from her plans. She shouted a warning as a prism flashed overhead, then dropped to make herself one with the ground. Was it a cousin of the one the boys saw crash? It disappeared toward Bamber's.

Where had Tony and Chuck gone? Had they hidden themselves? Crap! Did they know enough to hide themselves?

As if in answer to her unspoken question there was a bright flash followed by an agonizing scream. *No! No!* Vicky clambered to her feet, barely noticing the stones in her pocket again blazing. Heedless of danger, Vicky raced toward the cry as the prism sped away. She stumbled to a stop. Before her Tony huddled against a rock, a look of horror on his face. She saw no sign of Chuck, only the contents of his pack scattered on the ground.

"Where…" she started, but could not finish.

"It killed him," Tony cried. "It killed Chuck!"

Vicky gasped, struggling to breath. Chuck, gone? It was too abrupt, too radical. Without warning somebody she was responsible for was no more. Gone. "What did you see?" she demanded of the hysterical Tony. "What was that flash?"

Tony continued to sob uncontrollably. "It dropped something on him," he finally managed to croak out. "It flashed silver and he...*melted*."

Melted? "You're not making sense. People don't melt for God's sake!" She looked where Tony was staring. The burned husk of a body lay amidst a charred area. "What the hell happened?" she yelled as she shook Tony. "Are you sure of what you saw?"

"N...no, It happened so fast," he blurted. "The silver from the rainbow, I mean the flash! I was scared it was going to melt me too." Tony sounded young and lost and beyond frightened. When he pulled his knees to his chest Vicky saw the spreading dampness on his pants. She'd probably have wet herself if she'd been there.

"Why did they kill him and not me?" Tony cried softly. The anguish in his voice twisted her insides. She pulled herself back from the edge of her own panic and fought for balance. She had one boy left and damned if she wouldn't protect him with her last breath.

Vicky considered what Tony had said. Why Chuck, when the aliens ignored both of them? And why had her gems gotten so hot all of a sudden? Likely they would never know, but this wasn't the time or place to try and puzzle things out, not with the aliens active in the area. She looked around, but saw no sign of the monster.

"We've got to get back to the camp," she ordered. Tony wouldn't budge, still in shock over what he'd witnessed, no doubt. She hated to add to his fear, but she had to get him moving. "Now, Tony! We need to get out of here before it comes back. I'll come back later for Chuck's stuff."

Tony staggered up the hill like he was half asleep. When they reached the camp, he dumped his pack, collapsed beside it, and stared vacantly into space. Vicky recognized the early stages of survivor's guilt. No doubt she'd be fighting it herself as soon as the need for action subsided.

She tried not to stare at Chuck's empty blanket, tried not to think about his scraggly beard or the maturity he'd exhibited, and tried not to think about what remained of him near the river. For now, neither of them could afford to wallow in despair, not with prisms and monsters around.

Tony must have sensed her thoughts. "What's the point? Chuck's dead. Ma is dead. Everybody in the whole world is dead," he wailed, clearly on the thin edge of hysteria.

"*We're* still alive," she reminded him, "and we'll stay that way if I have anything to say about it." She stood and pulled him back to his feet. "There's still some daylight left. Let's dig some onions and gather something for dinner." Hopefully, the work would occupy them enough for the horror to fade.

Later, they could mourn all those who had passed, but for now, they had to work.

She tried to grasp for meaning as she stooped to pull the largest of the onions. She didn't know what bothered her most, Chuck's abrupt death or that she and Tony had been ignored by the aliens. Had the attack been arbitrary? A chance selection that meant either of them might be targeted next and with as little warning? Vicky shut that thought down. Believing that would drive her mad. Better to try to reason this out. What made Chuck a target? He'd been out in the open, but so had Tony. Try as she might she could think of nothing else that had set them apart.

The disappearance of the tools and cookware Chuck had been carrying was also puzzling. Why had the aliens taken only those items? She absently fingered her worry beads to help her think as she stood to stretch the kinks in her back. Why Chuck and not Tony? The question rattled around in her head as she continued gathering vegetables.

"The gems!" Her sudden cry made Tony jerk erect. "It has to be our gems. Don't you see? *That* must be why the aliens ignored us." She took Tony by the arms. "You were carrying them, weren't you?" It was as much a declaration as a question.

Tony nodded. "I like to play with them when I start to think about the people I never said good-bye to before...before..." He began to cry again.

Vicky ignored his grief. He'd have to deal with that himself. She recalled how the gems' warmth increased each time the prism or monster were near. Could there be some connection? Were the gems reacting to the aliens? Were the gems alive in some way?

No; that was a ridiculous idea: she was certain that the gems hadn't shown any signs of life. Had the heat been activated by proximity? Could she use that as a warning signal? Just how close would they have to be and, if she figured that out, would they give her sufficient warning? She didn't want to risk testing the idea.

"Gems," she whispered. "Who could have known?"

Chapter Six

EVERY SHIP HAD BEEN MUSTERED TO EVACUATE THE COLONIES ALONG THE projected line of alien attacks. Colonists were packed aboard ships not designed for passengers and whose life support could barely last long enough to reach a safer port.

"Incoming," Navigation reported when she spotted the line of glittering dots on the long-range.

"Prepare batteries," Hban cried. His ship was poorly armed with two mass drivers and a hell of a lot of shot. "Warn the freighters," he ordered as the ship sped to intercept the approaching aliens. His only chance to defend the fleeing ships was to draw the enemies' attention to him.

"No dispersal," Navigation reported calmly as she resolved the approaching dots into a tight cluster. They were two minutes away from contact.

"Fire two spreads," Hban ordered and felt the thump of the mass drivers loosing a deadly cloud of shot toward the oncoming ships. Given the kinetic energy of their two velocities any impact at all would be catastrophic.

"Fire a second burst," Hban ordered. The tight cluster suddenly became dozens of smaller ships. A few sparkled when they encountered shot, but most did not.

Then Hban's ship was among them, firing the mass drivers at the nearest targets. Most of the oncoming vessels moved and changed vectors incredibly fast, avoiding most of the rounds from his drivers.

The space around them glittered with a thousand points of light from the shattered glass ships. Suddenly his ship was alone with nothing to fire upon. Momentum had carried him well beyond the battle. Far to his stern he saw a corvette trying to harry the Shards. One freighter exploded as he spun the ship to take him back into the fray. Another turned into a debris field after it was rammed. The two remaining freighters blinked away, to safety, he hoped. But that left three freighters waiting to launch. There was no way their small fleet could defend them all.

As he was debating which should be saved, a brilliant star appeared on the surface where *City of Amok* had been parked.

"That looked like a core explosion," his First replied. 'The captain must have activated his drives and taken the entire city with him."

Hban gritted his teeth. That was their last resort measure to deny the Shardies access to more humans. It also meant that all hope had been lost and his role was to save himself and the corvette.

Sweeney felt discouraged. The only news in the two weeks since the last ship blinked away was boring recitations of how the outlying colonies were being ordered to evacuate and the closer ones were being fortified, but not a damn word about the role of the Marines.

Rita relayed the news about Blanco's fiasco soon after the departure of the last mothballed ship. "Scuttlebutt is that the Navy is losing most of the battles, but sometimes they come out best," she added

"Not exactly a victory for our side," Acorn replied. There was no joy in her words. The loss of even a single warship meant dozens of people had died.

"Doesn't anyone in command have the balls to send in troops to wipe the aliens out?" Sweeney complained. "When's the corps going to send for us?"

"Yeah," Fortier agreed. "When are they going to call us back? I want a chance to put a hurt on those bastards."

"HQ's freaking forgotten us," Acorn groused from across the mess, an arm's length away.

Rita agreed. "Possibly, but you got to remember why we trouble-makers were stuck in the Freezer. Might be we'll never get called back until the fucking war's over."

"Putting a massive force on the ground to hit the aliens along multiple fronts might confound their coordination," Colonel Thoss advised the Council.

Vice Admiral Jones moved his small shard of glass back and forth along the tabletop. He disliked Thoss' bravado. 'Shards,' that's what everyone called the aliens now—a reference to their glass-like nature. "Even augmented forces might not be effective," he said. "I understand that the alien ground forces made short work of your Marines."

"It might be our well-armed Marines are outmatched by those things, but I'm confident that heavy weapons can take care of the goddamn aliens. I say we deploy a battalion of our new MULEs. We've outfitted them with more effective weapons," Thoss replied. "You could drop them in one of the Navy's new stealth ships, which you said would be undetectable. Once on the ground they could hit the Shards before they realized we were there. Piece of cake."

"One ship?" Jones asked. "How many MULEs are we talking about, Colonel? The stealth ships are all Packets."

Thoss scowled. "A damn Packet's too small, sir. We'd need a force of two dozen MULEs, heavy weapons for each—say sixteen naught tens and four M180's, maybe a couple of M60's. That would be a cube of...."

"Sixteen cubic meters massing thirty metric tons," Jones' aide chirped in.

"That's impossible!" Jones said. "Our biggest landers can handle that mass but none of them have stealth technology. Landers are big targets. Hard to see one of them 'slipping by,' even if we could stealth them, which we cannot. We could lose it all to one shot, Sidney."

Thoss stiffened. He might be subordinate, but he had the full backing of the general staff. "Worth the risk, sir."

"That's your choice," Jones replied. "But if you lose them, what happens to your combat effectiveness? Two dozen of the new MULEs are three-quarters of the Marines' inventory. Do you want to risk them on some damn heroic action?"

Thoss bristled. "So we should just wait for the Shards to arrive at our doorstep? I don't like the idea of our Marines depending on your Navy to defeat them. Better to have Marines doing what they know best than sitting on their asses."

Jones picked up the glass shard and shook it at the colonel. "I also doubt the effectiveness of such an effort. But you are correct in saying that we have to take the fight to them. The Shardies need to learn that we are not going to let them drive us to extinction." He looked around the table. "We won't learn how to fight them unless we try." He rapped the tabletop with the glass fragment. "I'll approve the plans, Colonel, and may God protect your Marines."

Sweeney and Fortier had been working hard to get the antique MULE back into shape after the departure of the restored warships. The continuous pace had put more strain on each joint and actuator. In the end it took every bit of effort to have it lift just half a ton.

Fortier came into the section of the hold they'd claimed for their own to report on progress. "We've rebuilt the power assists on the

MULE's right leg, changed out the rotors on both articulators, and jury-rigged a cover plate from a scrap of hull." There was a measure of pride in his voice.

"It's all make-work," Acorn argued. "That old thing's too slow and cumbersome for anything now that the heavy work is over. Even if it had weapons, which it woefully does not, we'd have no use for it." The only weapons on board were Packard's ceremonial arms; a small sword and a brace of his precious compression pistols.

"Maybe we'll be reassigned now that they don't need us in the scrap yard," Rita mused. "Be nice to have a unit again. Maybe see some action."

Acorn grunted. "Careful 'bout that. Not many survivors, I'm told: aliens are deadly fast." That word had come down with the latest news about the war, along with the tragic loss of even more ships.

'Not many survivors,' was an understatement. Sweeney had heard that the Sixth Battalion, his old unit, had been practically eradicated; only a single, heavily compromised MULE managed to recover a few of her squad.

Sweeney wondered about that.

"Current rules of combat say it's better to burn the dead than let the aliens have the bodies, but nobody's explained the reason," Rita reported.

"Yeah," Sweeney replied. "Weird."

"The Willit skirmish showed that our heavy weapons were effective," Colonel Thoss argued. "We need to beef up our MULEs. The damned Shards are still overwhelming conventional forces."

"Resupply and distribution of heavy MULEs will take time, that is, if the Council can spare the expense." Sarcasm laced Admiral Cummin's voice. The Council's refusal to authorize additional warships and their threat to remove him should he disobey still hurt.

"Aren't there alternatives?" a representative prompted. "Can't you destroy them with air power? Bombs? Missiles?"

Vice Admiral Jones shook his head. "They've knocked out everything the Navy could put in the air and raining missiles destroys more than just the aliens, sir."

Thoss agreed. "Barring a tougher, better Marine, more MULEs and armored tanks might help, though."

"Tanks? The best we could do is commandeer local machinery. We can't afford to ship anything until we finish the evacuations."

"Do you realize how much mass you are talking about, Colonel?" one of the Navy staffers asked in a high-pitched voice. "We'd have to strip most weapons on our biggest transport's to reduce enough weight for a single tank."

Cummins frowned. "That would make our transports too vulnerable. No, Councilman, I don't believe tanks or repurposed machines are an option."

"There's your answer. Seems you need to train better Marines."

"We've used the toughest troops we had," came Thoss's bitter response. "And lost, damn it. Their too fast, too strong, and too heavily armored. Even weaponizing the MULEs doesn't do more than irritate them."

Doctor Mores, the new Science Advisor, had been following the exchange with interest. He spoke up. "Gentlemen, I think I need to tell you about a certain research project."

Everyone jerked to attention. "Use of the current MULE platforms is restricted by their gross controls. If we eliminate wiring, which is ten percent of the weight, and use more efficient servomechanisms, that shaves another few percentage points away. Incorporate cybernetic controls to handle routine functions such as running, lifting, and other predictable activities and you optimize the unit even more. These improvements will allow the operators to concentrate on the more important tactical tasks of targeting and firing."

"Firing? Aren't MULEs just transport logistical supports? Even when armed, they're not very effective," Jones replied.

Mores shook his head. "That was before the latest enhancements. Continuing to use these magnificent mechanisms as simple carriers has been a waste, sir."

Thoss leaned forward to press the point. "The new models are far more than beasts of burden, sir. Properly configured, the new MULEs will be a highly effective assault force on their own when they are outfitted with our most efficient weapons."

Jones raised an eyebrow. "They are outfitted with M60's?"

"Yes, and carry up to ten of its heaviest rounds as well."

The weeks dragged on when—just before Sweeney abandoned all hope—their orders arrived. Rita and Acorn were assigned to the Guard on the Hundred-Seventeenth fleet, while Fortier and Sweeney were part of a newly formed Seventy-Third Armored Company on Proximate, an established colony close to Earth.

"A ground assignment? What the hell does a colony world need with an armored Marine brigade?" Fortier wondered. "Are they going to have us driving freaking tanks?"

"More likely carrying them," Sweeney answered with a touch of malice. "Maybe they heard about how well you managed the MULE's drive units and figured you'd make a decent carrier."

"Carriers don't shoot aliens," Fortier grumbled.

Preparations were hurried, leaving them little time for long goodbyes, other than a few awkward hugs at the lock. Rita and Acorn were the first to go.

"Stay safe," Sweeney told Rita. "I'm going to miss you."

"Let's kick some ass," Acorn said and poked him.

The Admiral's staff meeting continued to be interminable and depressing as the briefers made their grim reports of battles lost and colonies evacuated. Cummins felt a century older than when he first heard about Jeaux. *I'm too old for this much pressure,* he thought and wondered how soon Jones would completely take over the reins.

More colonies had fallen to the Shards and the Navy had yet to win a significant victory. Even when they prevailed, there were great losses.

More colonies had fallen, and evacuations diverted much needed ships from defense. What's more, the recipient worlds were sorely strapped to provide for the influx of refugees.

"Our ground forces are proving ineffective, even when supplemented by the newer armored MULEs. Their improved agility is still not enough."

Cummins looked up. "Maybe you need some super Marines instead of machines."

"Curious that you should say that," Doctor Mores interrupted. "I believe that slow human reactions are at fault. We have been developing an autonomous model, the Mark 5 MULE which will prove more effective against the Shardies."

Jones laughed. "No fucking robot can be as effective, no matter how many smarts you pack into it."

There was a slight tightening around Mores' mouth. "I beg to differ, Admiral. We have run extensive simulations of the machine's speed, agility, and adaptability to almost any situation it may encounter on the battlefield. I assure you that the Mark 5 will hold its own."

Brigadier Thoss had also seen the simulations of the Mark 5's impressive speed and firepower. The current MULE-equipped Marines always came off second best. It was worth trying—anything was worth trying if it would help win the fight.

"There's still a small enclave of the Shardies on Willit," he said. "Too much trouble to scour now that we've neutralized their main force. Can we use some of your robots to supplement my ground forces?"

Mores rubbed his hands. "We are not at a stage where we can produce them quickly, General. However, I can provide the three prototypes. Would that do?"

"As a test, yes. I'm eager to see how these things perform under actual combat conditions."

The Seventy-Third Armored turned out to be a newly formed MULE company outfitted with the very latest models. As far as Sweeney was concerned, his retraining was less about learning how these advanced rigs operated and more on unlearning the bad habits he'd acquired in adapting to the quirks of the Freezer's old machine.

The new MULEs were a wonder. Instead of having to overcome considerable resistance to move the lifting arms the new model provided only enough resistance for feedback. He quickly learned about overcompensating for the rig's center of balance, so far forward of the backward-leaning old model. He loved how he didn't have to think in advance of every move he wanted to make. The machine's autonomous control almost acted as an extension of his mind.

Getting into these new machines was more like putting on a pressure suit than simply strapping himself into a framework. What he couldn't get used to were the sharp points that pressed against the key nerve axons. These were less comfortable than the older sensor straps. The points didn't bother him much, but afterward the pricks itched like mosquito bites.

Because of his experience and obvious skill Sweeney's rank was restored to Sergeant and he was assigned to head up TALON squad. Q Fortier was offered another squad that he promptly named HARRIER.

Only Sweeney got the joke.

Captain Chand Svare Ghei's briefings were revealing. "Previous engagements indicate that only massive force stands a chance against the Shards."

The screen displayed a fuzzy image of huge silver carriers surrounded by smaller things with three legs. Sweeney couldn't tell what sort of things the images represented.

Chand Svare Ghei continued: "The guerrilla tactics that we used to beat the ground forces in the Colonial Wars don't seem to work against these things. Nearly one hundred percent losses on Willit, and those were with our most experienced and well-armed forces."

"No surprise there," Fortier whispered. "All they had to fight during the Colonial uprising were poorly armed farmers."

"They were hardly farmers," Sweeney replied and drew a glare from Ghei. Sweeney grunted. The colonies had been more than farming backwaters. Some of the rebellious ones had produced their own spaceships.

The captain shuffled his notes. "We'll be joining the assault on Farside. That's the latest colony to fall to the Shardies' advance. We depart as soon as the Navy puts a fleet together."

The Marines groaned. Everyone knew it took the Navy forever to get organized.

This time they surprised everyone by mustering a massive collection of transports within six months. After that it was another month of waiting to load the Seventy-Third and its heavy equipment. Even after they blinked to Farside, Sweeney and the other Marines had to wait freaking forever.

Sweeney hated waiting.

"The fleet's initial attack on the aliens will cover our ground deployment," Chand Svare Ghei briefed them. "The plan is to knock out the alien ships in low orbit from a superior position and then strike ground concentrations. We'll follow once we get clearance," he continued.

One of the squad interrupted. "What about those big mothers, sir?" she asked. "I think we can handle the three-legged buggers, but not sure I want my MULE to go up against those big machines."

"Intelligence thinks the larger ones are transports, not fighting machines. Once we neutralize the tripods we'll make short work of them." A slight smile played beneath Ghei's mustache. "Should be fun."

It might well prove to be "fun" but that didn't dispel Sweeney's nervousness.

"Combat command and TALON will land at Delta sector," Chand Svare Ghei pointed on a map lacking much detail. "From there, TALON will work their way east to meet HARRIER." A second blip lit up.

"The main force will land here." Another arbitrary point lit to the west of TALON's landing spot. "We'll employ massive force to break the aliens into smaller units that we stand a chance of defeating."

"What if we don't win, sir? Is there a fallback strategy?"

Chand Svare Ghei remained silent for a long moment. "We have to win, Corporal. We have to fight as hard and as long as we can." He paused before saying in a quiet voice. "If we don't, then humanity is lost."

Farside had evacuated its few settlements and left only a couple of orbiting satellites behind. Recon had identified sixteen Shardie vessels in low orbit and three more in high. "Navy's still working on reducing the alien fleet to a safe number before we can be put on the surface," Sweeney's transport's pilot relayed.

Sweeney wished the damn Navy would get their part done so he could finally see some action. He'd been wearing his MULE for almost two hours. It was beginning to stink as his body heat released gases from the insulation. His butt was sore and the MULE's sharp sensors were starting to itch. These were all minor irritations, but they were the only things he could think about after he'd checked his sensor pack and verified the status of his actuators too many times. What he wouldn't give to stretch his arms, move his legs, or even take a crap. What was taking the Navy so damn long to…?

The Lander shuddered and, for an instant, Sweeney floated weightless before something forced him back hard and to the side. The Lander twisted and turned as it sped toward the surface. The aliens had proven deadly to airborne in past encounters, neutralizing remote drone operations, manned fighters, and even, Sweeney worried, Landers.

Every sickening shudder made his sphincter tingle at the thoughts that they'd been hit. Every shift and bump made Sweeney thankful he could relieve the pressure in his bladder, a feature of the new MULE he'd grown to love. What if the Lander turned into a flaming ball of plasma? Would he know it? Would it matter?

The Lander hit hard and bumped across the ground. In the few seconds it took for the ramp to drop Sweeney and the others had released their restraints and were moving out as gracefully as a herd of automated elephants.

Sweeney was off the ramp with the rest of TALON's troops before the Lander had come to a complete stop. A short distance away he saw Ghei's command cab roar from another Lander. It spurted ahead of the advancing wave of MULEs, almost too fast for TALON to keep up. In the distance, Sweeney saw a descending Lander become a beautiful red blossom. He hoped it hadn't been HARRIER.

"No imminent threats," Ghei reported as TALON's forces quickly fanned out on either side to provide cover.

After barely two kilometers of their advance, Ghei, with his more sophisticated sensors, detected the Shardies. "Four large vehicles moving your way," he reported. "One klick out, radial two six. I count a dozen three-legged mobile platforms accompanying."

Sweeney checked TALON's heavy weapons on that flank. "Harkins, use the em-eight-three-oh on the big guys," he ordered. "See how they like the taste!"

There were few things in the universe that could withstand the impulsive force of an M-830Kbar's rounds. It usually took three ordinary Marines—one of whom was a targeting spec—and a loader to operate. Harkins, TALON's heavy-weapons MULE, could do all that without help.

"Aye," Harkins replied. A few seconds faster than Sweeney expected, the sharp bark of the em-eight-three-oh echoed as a superdense round screamed at hypersonic speed toward the advancing transport. Trees and bushes below the round's path flattened or exploded from overpressure. The sound was still resonating as the round struck.

Sweeney hadn't waited to watch what happened but focused on the smaller aliens that had immediately turned toward the sound of the em-eight-three-oh, moving incredibly fast across the broken ground. "Peabody, Winston, see if you can neutralize them with your sixty's."

Before they could fire, his display showed an alien a hundred meters ahead. He brought his automated targeting systems on line and fired his chains. His MULE rocked back as the chain gun loosed multiple rounds at the onrushing alien. A few shots went astray, but worse, those that hit seemed to have little effect, other than making it wobble.

"Damn it! Where's the sixty?" Sweeney yelled. The alien was less than thirty meters away.

"Firing," Winston answered calmly from his immediate left. There was a *crump* and the advancing alien disappeared in a cloud of debris. "Take that, you bastard," she yelled and threw another round at four aliens closing on Harkins.

"I've got to stop the big one," Harkins barked.

Sweeney ran to help Peabody and Winston but his rig felt slow and cumbersome—adrenaline rush, he thought. He loosed his MULE's chain gun at an alien's skinny legs as he advanced. Even if just one explosive round in ten hit, it might cripple it.

Trails of golden tracer fire laced the battlefield. Sweeney heard another *crump* of the eight-oh. His display showed something shattering into glittering particles that sparkled and gleamed in the bright sunlight. It obscured whatever effect TALONs weapons were having. The three-legged aliens continued to advance on Harkins.

"Reloading," Harkins said calmly as the nearest alien disgorged a glowing silver river. There was a flash and the alien, Harkins, and his eight-oh disappeared in a glowing cloud.

Suddenly there were too many aliens coming in from every direction.

Winston was too close to use the sixty so Sweeney activated his chains, firing with little obvious effect.

The command override channel screamed. "HARRIER's been overrun and can't join up. TALON, pull back, pull back." Captain Ghei's voice sounded eerily calm in all the chaos.

Sweeney swore. This fight was turning into a freaking rout. "Concentrate firepower," he ordered as TALON began consolidating around him. Winston had already shifted her focus on the pair closing on the command cab, firing as she struggled to join Sweeney and the others. There was no time for her to take an aiming stance as she used the sixty. Each round fired rocked her back a pace. Sweeney hoped she had enough ammunition left.

"HARRIER's last report said they'd been attacked before the aliens could have heard the roar of our eight-oh," Ghei advised.

Did the fucking aliens have instant communications? Sweeney wondered. How had they managed to be so prepared at HARRIER's landing site?

Another of the large vehicles was advancing on the command cab, cutting Winston off.

Peabody, now on the flank, fired a burst from his sixty, shattering one of the aliens attacking Winston into fragments. One of the remaining aliens raced at Winston. "They're too freaking fast," she screamed. "Trying to..." A huge explosion from her position rocked Sweeney, nearly tipping him over.

"Winston!" Sweeney cried, even though he knew there would be no answer. The space where she had been was a smoking circle of destruction. But he couldn't linger on that as more aliens cut through the brush with apparent ease.

"Fall back to the Landers," the captain ordered. The remaining large alien vehicle continued to pursue his cab. *So much for the big jobs not being a threat,* Sweeney thought as he joined the remnants of TALON on his Lander's ramp.

"Keep coming, sir. We'll provide cover," he yelled as they all fired a continuous spray of harrying rounds to cover the command cab racing toward them.

It was obvious the cab wasn't going to make it.

"Get the hell out of here," Ghei ordered as his cab veered sharply left and away from the Lander. The huge alien swerved instantly to follow. "Go, go!"

Peabody brought his sixty up and fired. The shot bounced off the large transport with little effect.

Without warning, the Lander abruptly lifted, nearly pitching Sweeney from the ramp. "We can't abandon him, you asshole," Sweeney screamed at the pilot.

"Not about to die, either," the pilot answered.

"Freaking midges!" Sweeney swore as he emptied his entire load of ammunition in frustration. Their "surprise" attack had turned into a complete disaster, despite all of their supposedly superior heavy weapons.

As Winston had said, the aliens were too fast and too damned smart.

Only five of TALON returned to orbit, there to watch the Navy pummel the surface, hitting every identified alien emplacement. The night side view was punctuated by the occasional traces where a recon ship had made a sweep and identified more targets.

Sweeney marked his lost comrades with each explosion; Chand Svare Ghei, Harkins, Winston, Fortier, and all the grunts of HARRIER. He didn't know their names, but counted their number just the same. No matter how many explosions he added, the equation still wouldn't balance.

Finally, after the Navy reported that nothing remained of the alien presence but glittering glass shards, the Fleet's commander declared it a hard-won victory.

Sweeney felt otherwise.

Sweeney learned that the remains of the attacking force, including the few TALON survivors, were being rotated back to Proxima. Fleet was developing some new strategy and wanted help to analyze whatever had gone wrong.

Along the way, Sweeney realized that Chand Svare Ghei's sacrifice had changed the way he thought of officers. For the first time he realized that they were as flawed as he, and as brave. He no longer raged at their seemingly senseless orders and even began following the Navy's silly protocols. They were all on the same page now, all humans, anyway.

And that included the damn midges.

Chapter Seven

BEN'S HEART FELL AS *DAY'S END* DRIFTED INTO LANDING'S HARBOR. HIS terrified expectation had become cruel certainty. Not a single building remained erect amongst the rubble. It was just like Dockstal and the Cove. Everything…every*one* he'd loved was gone.

He wandered about shocked at the desolate emptiness where his friends had talked, argued, laughed, and cried, where kids had run about, and where men and women had worked to fashion a new life. Gods, what had happened to Eve, to Greg, to Cliff, and Asok, and Barberami, and...*and*...?

He knew he should feel sadness, horror, fear, or something appropriate to the enormity of his loss, but he felt only regret and emptiness. Eve, his poor Eve was gone! He remembered her birthday, their wedding, and the annual festivities marking Landing Day. There were a thousand memories, a dozen disappointments, and worst of all, the realization that he would never see any of them again. All were gone, as lost to him as distant Earth.

It was too much to absorb, too much to contemplate, too horrible to imagine. His legs folded as he slumped to the ground. His arms hung uselessly as his tears washed the afternoon away. He remained immobile until the shadows grew long and the wind drove grains of sand to sting his salt-dried cheeks. He told himself this had to be a nightmare. That he would wake, sweaty and breathless, still at sea. But he knew better. This devastation was neither dream nor delusion.

He returned to *Day's End.* As the stars appeared he nibbled on the last of the rations he'd been subsisting on since leaving Alder's Cove and wondered why he had been spared. Why hadn't *Day's End* been destroyed? Sleep came uneasy and, in the middle of the night, with Hunter's high overhead, he awoke to find himself crying inconsolably.

Dawn did nothing to ease his heartache.

The desolation gave him few clues. It seemed that the nails that held the buildings together had vanished. Despite his forebodings he continued to look for any evidence that indicated the possibility of survivors. Even a dead body would be a relief. As distasteful as that possibility seemed, at least it might provide some clue to whatever happened. But there was nothing, nothing, and nothing but rubble, and more rubble, scraps of fabric, and broken furniture. Stones like those he found at Dockstal littered the ground. Untended farm fields stood mute testimony to their owners' absence.

Rain clouds were gathering. Ben wanted to sleep dry for a night after so many damp weeks on the boat where dry was an abstract concept and damp was the best you could hope for. He debated if the remains of Greg's stone barn might serve. The dry shelter tempted him but, as night fell, he became increasingly fearful about remaining ashore. *Better to be away from the town,* he thought, as he boarded *Day's End* and sailed to a nearby cove where he'd not have to witness the destruction.

A light rain fell as he climbed into his sleeping bag with hopes that he would not be haunted by nightmares.

A whistling noise cut through the light fog as Ben was returning to Landing the next morning. The sound grew in intensity. A glistening thing hovered above Greg's ruined barn. It looked like the jewelry-looking thing he'd seen at sea. He lowered sail and let the boat drift. There was no way he'd enter the harbor, not with that thing there.

As the morning sun burned away the tendrils of fog, a glittering object dropped out of the prism. It moved to the ruined barn and disgorged something that sparkled brightly in the morning's light. Immediately the barn blazed in a coruscating fire, leaving behind only charred timbers tumbled into the stone foundation. As smoothly and silently as it had come, the strange object flew away.

Ben was glad he had not chosen to sleep in the barn.

He was horrified at whatever that prism and sparkling things were. Alien for sure. But where had it come from? Nobody had ever found evidence of another intelligence among the planets. No one had found alien cities, monuments, artifacts, or indecipherable texts. Nothing. Nada. Nil. It had seemed humanity was alone in the universe. Until now. Until bloody, damned, in-your-face NOW!

Where the fuck had they come from?

The prism whistled away toward the mountains as *Day's End* continued to drift. It was late afternoon before Ben finally mustered the courage to return. He shuddered as he stared at where the barn had been.

That night his nightmares were lit by rainbow-colored fires.

After convincing himself that the prism was not going to return, Ben resumed his search of Landing, but stayed alert. He found footprints in the mud along the river. They appeared to be heading in the same direction as the prism. What were the chances whoever left those prints had avoided notice and survived?

He had no choice but to find out.

Ben discovered scattered and burned supplies five days after securing *Day's End* and leaving Landing on foot. Was there anything left he could use? He found five packets of dried food, a hank of rope, and an emergency medical pack.

He hoped whoever he was following headed toward Bamber's. There was little or no chance of finding them otherwise. He clung to the hope someone else had survived.

A few days later he discovered a cache of supplies where the river bent. They looked as if they'd been placed deliberately next to the trail. Before he could investigate, he heard heavy footfalls approaching. Ben froze as a shining, angular thing stepped into view. It walked past him as if he wasn't there and approached the cache, destroying it with a spew of silver.

Shaken by the violence of the soundless explosion Ben fled. He dodged trees, jumped over boulders, and tripped on exposed roots, too frightened to worry at how much noise he was making. Behind him, something heavy thudded through the forest.

Ben continued running as fast as he could, but it wasn't fast enough. He heard the silver thing crashing through the trees behind him. Ben looked back and felt his bowels loosen. He stumbled to the ground, his teeth chattering uncontrollably as vomit filled his throat. The alien monster plodded closer. Ben was unable to draw a breath. His lungs were on fire, his legs burned, and sweat drenched him, steaming in the chill air. Blood dripped from his forehead. His hands were covered with scratches he hadn't felt. In sharp contrast, the approaching alien appeared unmarred.

Exhausted, Ben braced for the consuming fire.

But it did not come.

Ben opened his eyes to see the thing stop just ten meters away and then, inexplicably, retrace its steps.

Mercifully, he fainted.

Days later, Ben reached the trail to Bamber's Reach. It wound back and forth up the mountain to where the dense forest gave way to scrubby trees.

He followed the trail to the summit and stopped. Bamber's Reach was heartbreaking. Nothing but empty roads and overgrown fields surrounded it. There was nothing but rubble where people had lived, where they had slept in the safety of their beds.

Ben fell to his knees. Was no one left? Had everybody been killed? Landing, Dockstal, Alder's Cove, and now Bamber's: had the other towns scattered across Morrow, all of the other places where people had built a life been destroyed? Was he following the only other survivor? It was almost too much to accept, too horrible to bear. Were they alone?

Except for the prisms and the machines...

A sparkle caught his eye from a mass of downed trees. He looked closer and gasped as he grasped the shape of a large prism lying among a mass of downed trees. It looked just like the one that had briefly hovered over his boat. Was whatever had flown the thing down there?

The way it was canted told him the landing hadn't been deliberate. Did the crash kill whoever or whatever was inside?

Hours later, with no sign of activity, he decided that it must have crashed. And still he was uncertain; should he return to Landing or examine the strange ship and Bamber's before he left? He didn't really have the heart to search the ruined town. The emotional toll might be too great. No, he couldn't do it. Not now. Not yet.

This trip had been a mistake. Had the survivor he'd been following found safety at Bamber's, or been killed by another of those mysterious monsters? Perhaps he was better off not knowing which... No. Bamber's wasn't a cat in a box, its fate uncertain until it he observed it.

While he hoped there was someone here, he couldn't spare more time. He had to return to Day's End and sail north to warmer regions before winter.

Before he left he would take a look at the prism thing and walk through Bamber's, but not until morning. Night fell quickly here in the mountains and he wasn't about to risk taking the twisting trail in the dark. He made himself comfortable and settled for sleep under the cold stars.

Ben followed the trail by early morning's light. Bamber's fields were already fading to autumn's colors. He hoped he could find something to eat; maybe onions or potatoes in the weedy gardens. He would gather as much as he could to supplement the edible native vegetation and pile it on the barge. That would be the fastest way to get back to Landing.

He was most of the way to Bamber's ruins when he reached the tilted prism. It looked very much like the one that had consumed the barn. Had it had crashed or landed? The long gouge behind it and the angle it was leaning argued a crash, but what could have brought it down? The fiercest weapons on Morrow were a few rifles, hardly a match for something that size. He stayed alert as he entered the ruins. He didn't expect that he'd be lucky a second time if the machine showed up again.

He passed several weed-infested kitchen gardens but one appeared to have recently been tended. There were also no rotting vegetables on the ground. His spirits rose at these signs of a possible survivor. Was it the person he'd been following, or were their others that had been spared?

"Hey!" he shouted. "Hey! Anybody? I'm here! I'm here!" He heard no answering cry. Were they fearful or simply out of range?

"Hello!" he tried again with no reply.

Where would the survivor gone to ground? He continued searching, the renewed hope of finding someone else driving him on.

Ben's nose took him to the ripe refuse pit. The contents smelled fresh; a few days old he estimated. Nearby he found a reinforced cave; an easy walk on a cold morning, he imagined. Materials from Bamber's ruins made the cave more hospitable. There was even a rough door over the entrance. He found a few scraps of dried meat and fish alongside drying vegetables. There were also two food-stained trenchers, assorted ropes, and random scraps of clothing. This was more than the single survivor he'dd been following could have thrown together in a short time.

Despite a thorough search he could find no indication of where the occupants might have gone. Foraging for food, searching, or hunting were possibilities, but whichever it was they would surely return, if it only to collect their things. He had only to wait.

And a dry, cozy cave was far better than the damp ground.

Ben was returning from the pit when he saw two people crossing a distant field. He shouted and ran down the slope toward them. The smallest of the pair waved and shouted something, but Ben couldn't hear the words. It didn't matter. *Two* survivors, two other humans were alive. Tears streamed down his face.

They were a few hundred meters apart when he saw the silver thing speeding toward him. "No, no," he wailed. Not now! Not when he had found hope again.

He didn't know what to do. Would it ignore him again or bathe him in silver fire? Maybe he'd only been lucky before. He turned and ran, driven partly by self-preservation but also by the hope that he could at least lure the thing away from the others long enough for them to escape. He broke for the hillside, hoping at least that the scattered rocks would slow it. He could dodge around the larger boulders to keep it occupied while...

Instead of racing away, the pair ran toward him. Were they insane? They should have run and hidden, not dash across open ground. Didn't they know what the monster was capable of?

The woman shouted, "Come toward us!"

He ignored her and ran away but the pair continued to follow. Did they think numbers mattered in the face of what this thing could do? "Run away," he yelled desperately. "Hide!" His warning did no good. They had to be insane!

Ben skipped over boulders, dodged behind a barn-sized stele, and continued to keep away from his pursuer. It looked as if it couldn't maneuver well on the rocky hillside. That gave him a temporary advantage.

As if to put a lie to that, a loose rock sent him tumbling. He felt a sharp pain in his right wrist as he fell. His arm throbbed. Broken or sprained. Either way, his right arm was useless. He got his feet under him and kept moving.

"Run toward us, damn it!" the woman shouted. There was a man with her. Both of them had to be out of their minds, running into danger like this. He couldn't let them be killed. He ran toward the machine, hoping that would delay it enough for the others to escape. Otherwise, his fiery death would warn them. Either way he'd at least save two precious lives.

"Don't do it you bloody goddamn fool!" the woman shouted. He knew that voice—it was Vicky Wallbarger! How the devil had she survived? But it was too late to find out as he ran toward to his fate.

The machine stopped ten meters away from him, retreating when Ben continued toward it. He had been right; there was some sort of immunity about him. Now, if he could just keep his body between those two idiots and the machine long enough to let them get away maybe...

The thing stopped.

"My God! You know about it as well!" Vicky exclaimed. "I thought it was going to...Oh crap, it's good to see you again, Ben." She unexpectedly threw her arms around him, a display of affection that he would never have imagined possible, but the human embrace was more than welcome, as was that from the thin kid with her. When she stepped back Ben looked between her and the silver thing.

"Yeah," she grinned. "It's attracted to us, but when it gets close it seems to change its mind. Weird, isn't it?"

Ben examined Vicky's companion. One of the boys from Landing? Baker, was it? No…

"I'm Tony. Tony Donovan, Mister Gunning," the kid said.

"This is so strange. All of this," Ben was at a loss for words with so many conflicting emotions coursing through him. "How did you... What happened to...? Why are they...?"

Vicky laughed. "Yeah, we have the same questions and a lot more. Precious few answers, though." She began to move away. "Let's get to the cave where we can relax and talk about whatever happened."

Ben looked at their silver companion. "What about that thing?"

Vicky shrugged. "It will probably go away after a while. And no, I have no idea of why!"

"Did I tell you about the Navy's war?" Vicky asked as she fed the small fire. She had already told Ben what she'd learned since the *event*, as she termed it. Ben started when she described the Navy's strange warning message.

"War? Are you certain that's what was said? An interstellar war is so… so unbelievable."

"True, but now we know for certain what the Navy said and why these goddamned aliens are here. Whether they followed *Provance* or not, I can't say. Too much of a coincidence, for them to attack so soon after." She paused and stoked the fire. "The thing I'm most puzzled about is why they attacked Landing and Bamber's."

"It's not just those places," Ben answered slowly. "Alder's Cove and Dockstal are gone as well. That's where I got these." He pulled stones from his pocket as she silently absorbed his bitter news.

"Yeah, I think those are what keep us safe," Vicky answered in a gruff voice as she wiped her nose and showed him her own. "We figured it out after Chuck—he was the other boy with me and he..."

When she couldn't continue Ben realized that he shouldn't ask what had happened; an explanation would come in its own time. "Are you saying that's why it ignored me? Just because I had these rocks?"

Tony displayed his own half dozen. "We don't know how many it takes to protect us, but I don't want to experiment."

"We can assume that six is the minimum," Vicky added. "That's how many Tony had with him when Chuck got killed. Just the same, we carry as many as we can." She opened a wrap to display dozens more. "We plan to give them to anybody we find."

Ben wondered if the stones had protected him at sea, or was it being on the water? Why had the prism raced overhead without pause, instead of dropping silver fire on him?

"We have to find out if other sailors survived," he exclaimed. "If they were at sea maybe they were ignored as well." He quickly explained his ideas to a startled Vicky.

"But they'd be confronted when they came ashore, wouldn't they?" Vicky sounded doubtful.

"Only if they didn't collect some of these," he answered. "We can't be the only ones who discovered the trick."

"How do you propose to find them? Morrow's a damn big place."

Ben grinned. "Maybe, but sailors stick close to the coast. If I follow the trade routes I'll eventually run into them."

Vicky paled and turned mulish. "No way are we going to split up. We might be the only survivors. We have to stick together." She looked ready for a fight.

He wasn't about to dispute her; solitude was the last thing he wanted. "There's enough room on *Day's End* for you."

"I don't want to on a boat in the winter," she answered. "Why don't we hunker down here, and in the spring check the coastal settlements? Hey, maybe we could recover those supplies you left at Dockstal..."

"We need to fight," Tony said, his voice breaking on the last word. "I hate these bastards! They killed my folks."

Ben looked around the cave. "I appreciate the sentiment, kid, but there's not much we can do. Look around. We've got lots of rocks but what else?"

"We'll need to stay here for now," Vicky insisted. "Winter's coming."

Ben jiggled his stones. "I saw more of these back at Landing. Probably a lot more at the other places too. We should go after them." Vicky frowned. Before she could raise another objection, he continued. "Look, if these things do provide protection, we need to get as many as we can so the Navy can analyze them when they rescue us. Maybe they can turn them into weapons."

"You mean *if* we're right about the gems, *if* we can collect them, *if* the Navy ever returns, and *if* we can survive winter?" Vicky didn't seem convinced. "That's a mighty big string of ifs, sailor."

Ben grinned. "Pretty much, but what else do you suggest—that we sit on our asses until that silver thing decides to kill us?"

She didn't answer and, as her silence dragged on, Tony cleared his throat. "I'll go with you."

A moment later, Vicky reluctantly nodded. "But not until spring."

Ben agreed. They had a plan. They would survive. "We'll make the aliens pay," he promised Tony.

Some day.

BOOK TWO

Chapter Eight

A Navy analyst from Intelligence and Major Foster, the Seventy-Third's new CO grilled Sweeney for hours, trying to wring out every last description of the Shardies.

"They're fast." Sweeney told them what he could remember of his part of the brief battle. "Harkins was concentrating so hard on using the eight-oh he couldn't fight the mobiles that…" He searched for a word to describe that deadly silver fountain and finally gave up. "...that did whatever to him. After they overran the eight-oh they went after Winston. She was using her M60, but needed help. I used my M180's, not that it did much good." There was something else, but he couldn't remember at the moment; probably still a little combat fatigued. "I ran out of chain, and only had my repeaters left to protect the captain's cab. Emptied them on the way up, too. Didn't see if it did any damage."

The analyst activated a display. "We got some combat footage from the cab and helmets." Sweeney could hardly bear to watch as half-remembered images flashed on the screen.

Foster swore. "Damn, those things are even faster than I remember!" Sweeney realized the major must have seen combat.

"Yeah, and it looks like our augments are still too slow. There! It looks like the six-oh was effective," the intelligence analyst remarked, a moment before the figure holding the sixty and two aliens close by disappeared in an explosion. "I guess he didn't have enough rounds for the M60."

Sweeney choked. He had recognized Winston's bright red rig just before she was overrun. That's what he'd forgotten. He suddenly felt anger at the analyst and the stupidity of the rout. How had command believed they could fight these monsters? "Winston didn't run out of rounds. She blew herself up to take them out."

"Damn straight," Foster swore.

"Sorry," the analyst squeaked.

Other images from HARRIER's Lander showed Marines being swamped by an overwhelming Shardie response before they could get a hundred meters from the ramp.

"The *Shardies* couldn't have moved from their known locations to the drop points that quickly," Foster remarked, using the term that everyone had begun using.

"They had to be close to react that fast. How did they know where we'd land? What the devil are we fighting?" Sweeney asked.

The analyst shrugged. "That's what we're trying to find out," he hesitated. "Sergeant."

Sweeney watched Marines disappearing under the alien assault as HARRIER's Lander lifted off. One of the other cameras showed an alien dangling from the closing ramp for a second before a MULE flicked it off with a point-blank shot from their sixty.

"That was rather impulsive," the analyst remarked. "They could have let it hang on and brought it back for examination."

"You've got to be bat-shit crazy," Sweeney cried. "If that thing reached the ship we'd have lost everyone on board!"

Foster said nothing, but nodded approvingly.

Sweeney thought he'd never see Rita again but there she was, standing on the steps of the canteen, all bright and shiny with freaking flying eagles on each shoulder. "Congratulations on the promotion, Colonel," Sweeney said as he saluted.

Rita awkwardly returned the salute. "Good to see that you're still with us, Leo. What brings you back here?" Her eyes swept him from chin to toe. "You being deployed as well?"

"Still got all my parts, if that's what you're checking," Sweeney grinned, then realized how that sounded in light of Rita's obvious prostheses. "You're here for deployment? But what about…?"

She shrugged. "I'm still functional enough to command, Sergeant, even though I'm starting to look more like a robot with all these metal and plastic parts." She grinned and tapped her breasts. "The girls are probably bulletproof as well."

"Still looking damn fine, Colonel." He knew better than to ask where she'd taken on damage. Telling was up to her.

"I was helping clean up Bigass and stepped on some bad ordnance," she answered. "Next thing I knew I was being decanted out of a rescue bag in the ship's dispensary. Medic did what he could, but couldn't save a lot." She rolled up her right sleeve and tapped her forearm. "Smart-metal bones, they're the latest thing." She didn't mention the matte plas that had replaced her skin. "You could say I paid for my upcoming deployment in pieces."

Sweeney knew that refrain. He'd seen too many Marines come back with missing parts and more with less obvious damage. The fight against the aliens was brutal, unforgiving, where mere survival was an improbable victory. As she'd said, the recovered and repaired were becoming more machine than natural.

"We lost Acorn," she said quietly.

"And Fortier," he replied. "On Farside. I was there."

"So we're the last of the Freezer Four," she joked. "We can call this a reunion."

Sweeney changed the subject. "I'm getting fitted for the new MULEs. They want my experienced opinion on the improvements."

Rita scowled. "I heard about those—implants and brain probes. Not something for sissies."

"I don't think you could call Marines sissies," he answered, trying to keep it light. "But I didn't hear about the other things. Probes, you say?"

Rita smiled. "Yes, long, sharp needles that they drive into your skull." Sweeney blanched. "No anesthetic, I hear," she continued enthusiastically. "Supposed to toughen up the operator. They shave your beard as well, and swozzle your privates so you don't get distracted."

Now he knew she was joking. "Haven't had my balls swozzled for years, sir. Think they have a swozzler big enough?"

Rita raised an eyebrow. "I'd say those were medium, if I recall correctly, Sergeant." She reached out with her new arm and gently squeezed his in an expression of an intimacy they could no longer have. "You take care, Leo. Let's show those bastards what a pissed-off Marine can really do."

"I will, sir. It's really good to see you again." He tried not to notice the pronounced awkwardness of her movements as she walked away.

Sweeney was impressed by the new MULE. It was smaller than the standard model, although it still loomed over him. It looked deceptively simple and, as with all decent tech, could be repaired by any grunt's toolkit.

Weapon-attachment points were obvious. The huge, encompassing helmet seemed restrictive and he didn't see any sensors. He turned to the technician. "How the hell am I supposed to know what's going on?"

"Heads-up display," the technician explained. "Sensors are incorporated into the suit itself. Better protection."

"Won't the helmet restrict my vision?"

"Three-sixty panoramic with zoom," the tech replied. "Takes some getting used to, but you'll adapt; becomes second nature, I'm told. Makes your normal vision seem restricted afterward."

Sweeney learned the truth of that after a week of practice with a simulated MULE. In less time than expected he was easily moving the machine, firing simulated weapons, learning how to focus his sight on one area and zoom back out again, and enjoying the MULE's enhanced vision. He also embarrassed himself by switching to infrared for night vision instead of deploying the relief tube he'd intended.

Maintaining his sense of balance was difficult after the training sessions; he staggered about for an hour before he got used to the suit. The helmet kept him from scratching his head where the implant points itched. Rita had been wrong about them sticking long, sharp needles into his skull.

Most of them were relatively short.

Finally, after training, the engineers declared that he was ready. Suiting up was fast, but the total time to prepare hadn't changed: testing the probes still took time. Where before he had to adjust the restraints on his forearms and biceps, thighs and calves, slip his fingers into an awkward glove control, and keep track of a complex information panel, this MULE was simpler. All he had to do was wait for the needles to penetrate and, after that, a thought was sufficient for the MULE to act, or so the simulations had promised.

He hoped the actual rig performed the same way.

"Powering up," a voice announced as the heads-up flashed and gave him 360-degree vision. He moved his arm. There was no sense that he was wearing a MULE. It felt as comfortable as a dress uniform. He swung his arms about.

"Careful," the tech cautioned. "Take a couple of baby steps."

Baby steps? Why did he have to take baby steps? With these direct interfaces he no longer even felt like he was wearing a MULE. They were a single entity that responded to his every gesture. He felt like a fierce superman and jumped forward, turned, and squatted to test the limits of his mobility. He roared, leapt, and swung his arms with abandon, reveling in this feeling of awesome power. God, but this rig felt wonderful!

"Powering down," the tech croaked and the MULE became dead weight. Sweeney was pissed. He wanted to give this thing a real test, get out on the range with a full complement of weapons to see what havoc he could cause.

When they pulled his helmet off he saw techs racing about to repair the damage. Huge divots marked where his feet had struck, there were deep scrape marks along the walls, and, on the far side, were a huddle of very frightened engineers.

He waved at them. “Great job, guys. When can I take it out and see what it can really do?”

Sweeney was promoted to Chief Sergeant and sent to Research instead of combat. “You’re going to test our new toys,” a chirpy captain in a white coat assured him.

The toys were a trio of M-5 robotic MULEs. He thought the idea of a robot MULE was stupid, but he’d been told they’d performed well during simulated combat. “Field test,” they promised. He and his three obedient companions were to be tested on a partially recovered colony world with an eminently forgettable name.

All three M-5s were equipped with four of the new M920c2’s, which was a load even his own MULE couldn’t carry. He ordered them to check their weapons and noted their precisely coordinated movements. *Chief Rausch would have loved these obedient machines,* he thought. They could be the best damn close-order drill team in the Marines, bar none.

The ramp dropped as soon as the Lander hit the ground. Sweeney swung right as his three M-5s took flank positions.

“Impressive,” a Marine officer in full combat gear said. “These things keyed to you?”

“They respond to commands, sir,” Sweeney answered. “They aren’t remotes, if that’s what you mean.”

“Tried remotes. Didn’t work.” There was a deafening *WHUMP* in the distance. “That’s the artillery keeping the Shardies contained. They’ve spread out to make life difficult. Bastards move too fast, but a barrage keeps them moving instead of attacking.”

“Which means they’ll attack as soon as we stop lobbing shells at them?”

“That’s something we hope you and your robots can take care of, Sergeant. Don’t disappoint us.”

The battle was brief and decisive. Sweeney commanded from the rear, deploying the three M-5s at point and flanks. Their assignment was near the last known Shardie location.

They'd barely reached the edge of the forest when the first tripod raced directly at them. "Watch for a flank attack," Command warned just as three more tripods appeared on his left.

The M-5s didn't fire until the tripods were almost upon them and then, when they let loose, the roar of their nine-twenties turned the field aglitter with fragments of shattered glass.

The M-5 on the right flank went down in a torrent of silver. Sweeney swung his own M60 and fired. At this range he could hardly miss. Four more mobiles were advancing. His M-5s kept up their deadly fire, cutting the legs from under the tripods and pouring more rounds into them.

The M-5 on the left also came under intense attack. Sweeney activated his chains as more aliens swarmed out of the brush. Something struck his side just as he fired. The M-5 took out one attacker but failed to stop it. In an instant it too disappeared under a silver flood.

Sweeney retreated, continuously firing his sixty. Where the hell was the last M-5?

In answer to a prayer he hadn't thought to make, an artillery round exploded not twenty meters from him, then another, equally as accurate. The tripods dodged the rounds. They obviously spotted the incoming shells in time to move out of the way. That was an advantage for him since it delayed them enough for him to retreat.

When he reached the Marine base the observers had already retreated into the Lander. He fired a final round at the tripods before running up the Lander's ramp a fraction of a second before it lifted.

The M-5s had done no better than the MULEs.

Lieutenant General Thoss made no pretense of hiding his anger when Doctor Mores followed the others into the room. Thoss didn't wait for the admiral to speak before he lit into the doctor. "Your new MULEs aren't worth a bucket of warm piss and neither are those damned robots." He had gone over the grim combat assessments that very morning. "Damn it, your team needs to find some way to improve them and give them some chance of standing up to the Shards."

"As I've said repeatedly, General," Mores objected, "our MULEs' actions are as optimized as my engineers can possibly make them.

Unfortunately, there's a noticeable time delay between a sensor's detection and the MULE's reaction."

Thoss grunted. "I don't want to hear excuses. Look, we're sick of losing Marines because their equipment isn't working right. Tell your engineers to find a way to make the MULEs more responsive—brain shunts or something."

Mores tented his fingers. "Shunts *are* being used, General, but the brain only sends signals to the muscles at seven meters per second. Without the brain-to-muscle delay we could make the MULEs more effective."

"So we're fucking stuck?" Thoss cursed. "Are you saying our MULEs can't ever be fast enough to fight the damn things?" His frustration at the tide of the war was shared by everyone in the room and especially Jones, Admiral Cummins' replacement.

"Cranking out faster equipment won't win the war, not by itself," Jones said. "Council's gotten every industrialized asset working on ships, weapons, and support systems. This war's crippling the economies of twelve worlds, and even at that we haven't been able to slow the Shardie's advance."

"But we still need ground forces," Thoss shot back.

Mores stared directly at the general and spoke softly. "I forwarded a possible solution last week."

Vice Admiral Fritz scowled. "*Doctor* Mores, I hardly think this is an appropriate..."

Mores turned to address Jones. "We're on the losing side of a war, Admiral. We need to consider all of our options, regardless of how distasteful they may be to the general."

Jones glanced at Fritz. "I take it that whatever you want to say is less than welcome..."

"By a bunch of frightened moralists, Admiral," Mores replied. "We wouldn't need an operator if we eliminate the interfaces."

Jones raised an eyebrow. "But you already said our MULEs are too slow, despite the improvements. I don't see how removing anything will make them better."

"I'm not suggesting the operator wear a MULE like a suit," Mores continued. "We need to learn from our enemy and make the operator another machine component." He looked at the questioning faces around the table. "It's not that difficult," he quickly explained. "If we remove all the controls and use a lightweight life support system, we can build an integrated fighting machine." He flashed an image on the screen. It appeared to be a MULE, but streamlined; human heroic in scale.

Jones grunted. "Life support in something that size would hardly leave enough room for an operator."

Mores smiled. "Naturally, we would have to, uh, edit whoever is installed. We'd have to trim the body, reduce the brain, use a blood substitute with higher oxygenation capability, and replace the framework with more sturdy materials. Same with the muscles—a little modification of the connecting tissues..."

"It's an outrage!" Fritz stood. "You can't experiment on humans. It goes against your hypocritical oath!"

Mores smiled at the inadvertent mistake. "*Hippocratic* oath, you mean, Admiral. No, I am quite comfortable that the experiments we are running with seriously wounded warriors are within the bounds of informed consent. Our subjects have few options and have been quite willing to participate, despite the risks."

Jones was puzzled. "You indicated losses. Isn't it completely safe?"

"Science advances slowly and often at great cost," Mores answered. "Yes, there have been some unfortunate outcomes, but each failure moves us one step closer."

Fritz looked as if he would explode. "Giving hope to the wounded and using them as laboratory rats? That's more than '*unfortunate*' I'd say."

"We've had some successes: Patient one-fourteen bench-pressed a ton and a half before he was lost. Patient two-eleven could see far into the infrared spectrum and patient two-ninety-six exhibited full motor capability. All, every last one, seemed to accept their upgrades."

"Which proves what, that you can turn a Marine into fucking zombie?" Fritz leaned forward with clenched fists.

Mores stepped aback. "We haven't actually transferred an entire brain," he added softly. "Editing an entire cerebrum is too complex, so we are limited to transferring only the executive regions necessary for combat effectiveness. The subjects retain a few higher functions, but lose a few non-essential memories to allow the subject's gel brain to manage the operations that keep the MULE operational."

"You sound as if you want to remove the non-essential human elements of the people you experiment with," Fritz argued and turned to Jones. "As I said before, Admiral, this is a horrible idea. We should put a stop to it."

Mores interrupted. "Did I mention that they can move at ten times a human's normal speed?"

General Thoss grimaced. "I also believe that it's unpalatable, but horrid necessity forces our hand here, Admiral. Maybe a few thousand of these supermen are what we need."

Jones didn't agree. "Doctor Mores, thank you for your work thus far, but as my deputy said, this project strains ethical bounds. As of now, you are no longer needed. We'll send your personal things and final pay."

Mores looked stunned. "But, the technology is achievable, Admiral. We've shown that it does work. You can't throw all our research aside because of a few qualms."

Thoss spoke up. "Doctor, we've got a decent research facility that could use a scientist and..." He looked directly at Fritz. "If you are worried about security, we can keep out any unwelcome visitors."

Vice Admiral Fritz stood and glared. "Is that a threat, General?"

"Only if you want to see how secure my research facilities can be, Admiral." He turned back to Mores. "Let me know what resources you need to bring your techniques to production levels and I'll do everything I can to make it happen."

"You can't do that," Fritz turned to Jones. "Sir, medical ethics alone should forbid…"

When Jones remained silent Thoss realized the Admiral was cleverly distancing himself from responsibility. His hands would be clean and only Thoss would bear the blame for any failure.

Knowing that, Thoss looked directly at Fritz. "Don't you fucking tell me what I can or cannot do. We're in a losing war that threatens the fate of the human race. We need to do whatever it takes to fight these things and that includes putting your squeamish moral qualms aside."

He returned to the doctor. "I've got a hundred seriously wounded Marines who still want to fight, Doctor; men missing legs, arms, and most of their organs. I've got veterans on artificial lungs and perfusion machines. Hell, some of them are already mostly robotic…" He slapped Mores on the shoulder. "If you want volunteers, the Marines are where to find them."

He turned to his aide. "Charlie, I know you don't like the idea, but I think we'll need these if we're going to win the ground war. Work with the doctor here. Give him whatever he needs."

Mores smiled. "A few dozen wounded Marines would be a good start."

The abortive robot assignment behind him, Senior Chief Sergeant Sweeney found himself commanding TALON.

Five Landers under heavy cover from the orbiting ships deployed Sweeney's company a hundred kilometers from any known enemy emplacement. The plan was for squads to advance from multiple sides, forcing the Shardies to divide their forces or retreat into a siege formation.

Alternatively, if the Shardie forces spread out, another company could attack from the rear, squeezing the aliens in a fierce vise.

The entire battle plan faced a big risk, having so many Marines engaged at once. Command swore they stood at least a fifty-fifty chance of success given the number, speed, and combined strength of the new MULE companies.

Sweeney's squad was nearly wiped out immediately. Five effectives were lost within seconds and eight others went god-knows-where. Everybody scattered as an incredibly fast wave of aliens countered. They were targeting the slower, heavy MULE operators first.

"Spread and take cover," Sweeney ordered. He couldn't let his remaining squad bunch up as easy targets. Harassing the enemy was a proven guerrilla tactic for dealing with superior forces and, make no bones about it, these aliens were definitely a *superior* force.

Sweeney took position behind a large rock outcropping. He spotted a tripod vomiting silver crap into the bushes as someone's screams abruptly stopped. Little sparks appeared where the small arms fire struck it.

Without pause, the tripod ran toward the incoming fire. Sweeney hoped they'd pulled away. One never stayed when the enemy knew your location.

There was a sharp sound to his left. It was James, the sharpshooter, with his M80. "Thought I'd get a better shot from here," he said as he flipped the stand, braced the weapon, slammed a round into the chamber, and clicked the recoil brace into place in one continuous motion.

Sweeney saw a Shardie coming just as James fired directly into the tripod's center and rolled to his right, still holding the eighty. The round screamed for an instant before impacting.

Sweeney had veered left the instant James fired, his head coming up to see the tripod stagger backward, a gaping hole burned into it. It started to fall, but exploded before it hit the ground. Strange. The eighty didn't fire explosives. It depended on brute force and an expanding shower of fragments to do the damage. His link to command was down so he flagged the puzzling item for later analysis.

James had disappeared somewhere; probably hunting another target. Sweeney checked his heads-up to find somebody with an operational link so he could report the effectiveness of the eighties. There were five Marines about fifty meters to his left. One of them could help.

The five formed in a tight arc around a damaged MULE. It was Revek. Two grunts worked to get Revek's MULE back in operation. Another wrapped a tourniquet around the stump where Revek's leg had been.

"Who's got a command link?" Sweeney asked as he reached them.

"I do, Sarge," Revek responded; obviously shock had not yet set in. "Sorry about the MULE."

"Tell everyone the eighties are effective," Sweeney said. "Our chains only irritate them."

"I want my sixty back," Revek groaned and pointed where his weapon lay a few meters away.

"Just make the damn report," Sweeney cursed and moved toward the sixty. Revek's MULE was a mess, but he could still operate a weapon. A pair of aliens turned away from attacking the other MULEs and started toward them.

"Somebody use their damn sixty," Sweeney yelled as he fired his chains at the tripods' legs.

"Revek's is the only one left," a grunt shouted.

He heard a scream, saw a shimmer of silver, and, without thinking, picked up Revek's sixty.

Some silver shards must have splashed onto him, because his leg started to burn like hell. But he couldn't afford to check as the alien kept coming. He glimpsed a glistening silver stream erupting from the tripod.

"Not me, you son-of-a-bitch!" he screamed, feeling his rage take control as he swung the sixty and fired a round to obliterate the alien in a shower of glass. He saw more of the creatures rushing toward the other Marines. They seemed unimpaired by the continuous firing of the chains.

Sweeney's calf throbbed with intense, agonizing pain that prevented movement. He locked the MULE's leg and fired the sixty as fast as he could reload. He let his chains burp on full automatic, uncaring of the waste.

"Pull back! Pull back!" he ordered, forgetting that his link was out. There was no way he could move, not with his leg locked. The fire was crawling up to his hip. The sixty only had two rounds left.

"Sarge?" someone called. Sweeney didn't answer. Two aliens were practically on top of him. He fired.

The explosion flipped him into the air among a silver cloud of burning jewels. Even before he hit the ground, the heads-up display faded.

The pain in his leg disappeared into darkness.

Sweeney floated on a cloud where no feeling, no sense other than sight and sound penetrated. Was he dead? No, not likely, given how his head itched. He reached up to scratch but nothing touched his scalp. He tried to swing his legs to the side as he pressed back with his elbows to sit up, but didn't feel his body change position. "What the hell," he muttered, but couldn't hear his voice. What had happened?

"Ah, awake at last." A voice whispered. "I see the implants are doing well, Chief. No signs of infection so far. Oh, I see that you are trying to say something. You'll be able to do that when we get those parts of your brain wired up properly. So far we've had to concentrate on isolating you from your surgical pains."

Sweeney groaned.

"Yes, multiple surgeries. They removed your crushed calves in the field, and had to remove most of your thighs during transport because of infection. The arms, well, the only way they could remove you from the crushed remains of your MULE was to sacrifice those.

"Lucky for you, your head was preserved. You'll need that for your general prostheses. They're a civilian version of your MULE, but without weapons. It's the least we can do for what you've sacrificed."

Sweeney wondered about that. No arms or legs, and his nuts had probably been "swozzled" as well. He felt a pang of sorrow as he recalled his last meeting with Rita before she...whatever. She had been the last of the foursome from the Freezer, save him. Good men, all three of them. Good Marines.

And now, him.

Sweeney grew to hate the pathetic shell that contained his torso. There was no disguising what he'd become, no possibility that anyone would mistake him for a man. Thanks to the contraption he had mobility, but little else. He couldn't pet a dog, run up stairs, or hug someone. Hell, he couldn't even wipe himself—too delicate an action for his mechanical arms. Despite warnings, he'd tried, torn the tissue, and scraped his ass. Now he had to use a damned bidet and blot, blot, blot!

Seven months it had taken him to get to this point and he was certain that he would never get used to it.

"I understand that you have made remarkable progress," the too-young doctor said during Sweeney's monthly check-up.

"I'd like to see a few minor additions," Sweeney answered. "Arms and legs to start and then maybe you could strap on a few weapons?"

The doctor frowned. "Weapons? You've earned your rest, Chief. Let others do the fighting now."

Seven months of frustration brought his rage back; rage at the aliens, rage at the war, and rage at himself for becoming a dependent, crippled wreck. "I don't want to rest, damn it! I want to kick some ass. I want to have a sixty, with a pair of eight-ohs on my hips. I want to tear a leg off a damned alien tripod and use it to beat the crap out of whatever rides inside." He scowled. "I want to drive a MULE again, damn it!"

"Yes, I know. The therapist told me about your dangerous levels of frustration. She's afraid you might harm yourself."

"The damned fail-safes stop me," Sweeney replied. "But that won't stop me from trying."

The doctor looked thoughtful. "If you are serious I've heard about a project you might be interested in called Cyber something. There's a Doctor Mores who wants experienced, wounded ex-MULE operators that still want to fight."

Sweeney blinked. "Are you serious?" A faint hope that he might once again feel powerful and deadly flamed to life. "No shit?"

The doctor frowned. "I'm not comfortable with Mores' ethics, but the Council has given him permission to recruit volunteers. The price of winning the war, I suppose." The doctor sounded disappointed, but didn't explain why.

"Where do I sign up?" Sweeney said, without further thought.

The doctor hesitated. "I know little about Mores' plans except that your personal cost will be really high. You should reconsider before..."

"I didn't sign up to be useless," Sweeney shouted. "Put me in touch with this Mores character so I can get back into the war."

Chapter Nine

THE AUTUMN BREEZE HELD THE PROMISE OF WINTER'S BITE, BUT THE SUN still radiated some warmth. Vicky sat before their shelter with her eyes closed soaking in what warmth she could while her hands methodically wove rushes into new baskets. They were going to need many more to store enough food for both their journey to Landing and to hold them until they got settled.

"I hope we find survivors there," Ben said, as if he knew her thoughts. Not really, though. He'd been obsessing about survivors all winter. That and his blasted boat. She opened her eyes to stare at him. He sat where he could look over the river, but his gaze was far away, no doubt seeing his precious *Day's End* afloat on the sea in an endless search for others. In his lap lay a tangled mess of rushes that never would make a basket.

Vicky gritted her teeth and said nothing. They'd had this conversation for months and he didn't really expect her to reply. She had serious doubts anyone else had escaped the aliens, and what were the chances exploration parties or prospectors had also discovered the usefulness of the gems? Vicky had only seen them in Landing and Bamber's.

"Think Landing might have things we can use?" Ben suggested. "Might be worth a look..."

"Yeah, I think might have seen some crockery," Vicky replied. "Curious they would miss those. But we can worry about that in the spring. For now, we need to gather enough food and firewood to hold us for the winter, then if you want we can scour these ruins here for anything useful."

"Sure." Vicky thought Ben may have answered, but he'd sounded distracted, lost again in his thoughts about his damn boat. She got it. She felt the same about her barge on the river, but they didn't have the luxury of such daydreams anymore. Their own survival had to come first.

"Hey! Ben! Snap out of it," she growled, her patience at an end. "I could use some help making sure *we* survive! Do you know anything about making pots? I'm thinking the clay from the river might harden enough to hold water if we fire it."

When Ben looked confused, she added; "No? Then how about caulking the gaps between the boards, or weaving more baskets? Jump in whenever you think you can do something useful instead of daydreaming about your damn boat!"

Ben flinched. "We could experiment. I once watched Clarence Folger make pots. Clarence coated woven baskets with clay, as I recall, and fired his pots in a kiln. We can try that. It can't be that difficult. We don't have a kiln, but maybe a campfire would work."

"Great. You get on that."

Three weeks later, as the morning's chill painted the last unripe vegetables with frost, the three of them raced to harvest anything still sound enough to keep.

"Where are we going to store all this?" Ben asked.

Vicky lifted her head from where she'd been examining the beans. "Baskets and pots, where else?" The small cave's floor was already covered with what they'd gathered.

"The few pots we have are already filled," Ben answered. "And I doubt we have enough baskets."

"So you need to make more," Vicky answered. "But worry about that after we've saved what we can from the freeze."

The three of them worked quickly at their tasks, driven by the certainty that any misstep would be disastrous as a cold autumn wind blew summer's bountiful days away.

There was so much undone, so many things to do.

Ben blew on his raw, red hands as they worked to secure the cave against the coming winter weather. Vicky's looked white with cold, yet she persisted mixing straw into the clay. He scooped a handful of the wet clay mixture and slathered it into the cracks between the planks that covered their cave's entrance. "We need another couple of baskets of clay." That, and hours of agonizing pain before he'd finish patching the remaining gaps to make their shelter tight against the winter's wind.

He glanced overhead at the gathering clouds. "Looks like rain," he said.

"As long as it's just rain, I'm happy," Vicky said, her voice belying the statement. The chill winds and dark clouds that stole the sun's warmth hinted at an early snow. "This morning's damned frost killed everything left in the gardens. We still need more pots for storage."

"I'm doing the best I can," Ben snapped back. "And shelter is our priority."

"So we can starve in comfort, I suppose." Vicky turned back to mixing. "Running low on clay."

Ben watched Tony struggle up the scree leading to the cave. As always, the alien machine followed, but stopped at the edge of the loose rock. "Almost like a pet dog," Ben muttered.

"A dog that can kill, you mean," Vicky spit. "Monster reminds me of what it did to Chuck. I wish we could get rid of it."

"Maybe it will freeze when winter comes, or corrode from the rain."

"Or fall into the fucking river for all I care. I just want it *gone*."

Tony put the basket down and collapsed. "I don't know if I can make another trip. I'm beat." His tunic was drenched; partly from what he'd carried, but also from sweat. Carrying baskets of wet clay uphill to the ridge, and then over the treacherous scree was not easy and quickly sapped his young strength.

"We'll only need one more basketful," Vicky said as she began adding straw into the wet clay he'd brought.

Ben helped knead the straw, squeezing the clay to drive out excess water, and then slathering handfuls into the cracks.

"I'll fetch more," Tony said and picked up the basket.

"No!" Ben shot back. "You're already exhausted." They shouldn't be asking Tony to do any more. The boy had already done the hardest part by digging and hauling. He deserved a rest.

Rain began to fall. "Doesn't look like we can do much more today anyway," Vicky admitted. "Get this load on the cracks so we can get inside. My hands are too numb to mix anymore."

"I'll strike a fire so we can get warm," Tony said as he disappeared behind the barrier.

The rain increased and, with it, small pellets of hail. "At least it ain't snow," Vicky groused.

Winter had arrived.

A sudden and fierce snowstorm hit one month into winter, before they could complete their preparations. The daily temperatures quickly plunged below freezing and remained there for weeks.

The wind whistled through the cracks between the logs as snowflakes curled around the door, a scavenged sheet of packing material they were using to cover the entrance. "I told you that you needed to put more straw in the grout," Ben complained. "Most of the last batch has already flaked away."

"I might have if we had enough straw and the time," Vicky answered. "We should have started fixing the cave earlier."

"Instead of stocking the larder, digging the root crops, catching enough meat to sustain us, and…?" Ben answered.

Vicky sighed. "Yes, there was a lot to do, but..."

"I patched what I could," Ben snapped. "You'd be up to your ass in snow if I hadn't."

"Would you two please stop arguing," Tony pleaded. "We're snug enough for now, at least we have a fire going."

"Keeps us above freezing, anyway," Vicky replied.

When Ben squirmed for a moment Vicky thought he was going to say something sarcastic and braced for it. Between the weather and the close quarters, they had all been on edge. Instead he pulled two strings of clay beads from his blanket. "I made you each a present." He handed the longer string to Vicky. "It's a necklace," he declared as if that wasn't clearly evident.

"What? A string of clay beads?" Vicky answered. "Why did you waste time doing this when you should have been…?"

"There's one of your damned magic gems inside each clay bead," Ben said. "Now you don't have to carry them around in that pouch all the time."

Vicky didn't know what to say. It had been a long time since anyone had given her something so thoughtful. And to think Ben had made the effort despite all the sniping. She wasn't the romantic sort, but the gesture touched her.

"But why did you make Tony's so small?" she asked.

Ben grinned. "I figured a boy wouldn't want to wear a necklace."

Vicky tried not to laugh.

In the evenings, when darkness fell, they huddled in the cave and talked about their lives, ordinary, everyday things from before the disaster.

"There's nothing like feeling the wind in your face and seeing the distant unbroken horizon so full of promise," Ben said, his tone reverent. Tony hung on his words. "At night all you can see is the dark sea and the wonder of a clear sky full of stars."

"Sounds like sailing that boat of yours is a religious experience," Vicky declared.

"But don't you ever get lonely?" Tony mumbled wearily, making an obvious effort to keep his eyes open.

"Yes, sometimes I'll feel that way when I'm on the river," Vicky answered, thinking the question was directed at her.

"Not me," Ben protested. "When I have *Day's End* under me I'm never lonely. She's a living creature; at times docile and friendly, at others fractious, when the weather is bad. She has her own ways and if you know them she's the best companion you'll ever need."

"I wish I could sail her some day," Tony said.

Ben slapped him on the shoulder. "You will, and soon. In the spring I'll teach you all I know so you take *Day*'s tiller and man the sail."

"You'd better make good on that promise, if we survive until spring," Vicky whispered to Ben as they huddled for warmth. "The boy's lost too much to have another disappointment."

"As have we all," Ben replied softly.

"Were you serious? Don't you ever miss having someone with you, out there?" Vicky didn't give him a chance to answer. "How about now, I mean since the... well, since whatever happened?"

"That's a tough question," Ben answered. "I was never that friendly with anyone, except Eve, of course." He paused and took a deep breath. "The reason we separated was that I really did prefer the quiet of the sea. I was never a social person like Eve."

"Me neither," Vicky responded. "Better when I was on the river with only a couple of boys helping me. Not much to talk about with kids so I just ignored them, except to guide the barge. Didn't have any real friends at Landing or Bamber's."

"Didn't you have something going with Oscar Summerfield a few years ago?"

Vicky poked Ben. "Look, I had one night with that clumsy bastard. I got drunk and decided to see what all the fuss was about. Never had the urge before, and certainly didn't have it again after. Nasty experience as far as I'm concerned. Just as well; I've never been a beauty queen like Eve, so it's not like I'd been much in demand. "Besides, I could beat the shit out of most anyone that might have tried." She giggled, "And did on some."

Ben cleared his throat. "But...didn't you want to experiment?"

Vicky poked his ribs a second time. "Not really, I just...never had the particular urge. Maybe it's something genetic, or maybe I'm insane, but I prefer to keep to myself most of the time. Private, y'know."

Ben went so still Vicky thought he had fallen asleep, until he said, real quiet, "Well, if you ever change your mind…"

Well, hell. How was she supposed to respond to that?

"What? You give me fancy jewelry and now you expect me to put out? I've a good mind to slap you around," Vicky snarled. "Just go to sleep."

Things got real cold beneath their shared blankets.

A sound woke Vicky. At first she thought it was the hiss of wind-blown snow against the canvas covering the cave's entrance, not unexpected since a storm had been threatening all day. But as the sleep-drugged fog left her she realized the sound was much too near, scarcely a handbreadth away. It was Tony, his head wrapped deep within his blanket, sniffling softly.

She rolled and laid a comforting arm across him, not a difficult task since the three of them were huddled as tight as a pack of puppies.

"Don't worry; the Navy's coming," she whispered so as not to wake Ben. "It's just a matter of time."

"I know," Tony replied. "But I can't stop thinking about Chuck and how much better he would have been at this. Why did he have to die?" His voice broke on the last sentence.

"There were a lot of other people besides Chuck who deserved to survive, Tony. But fate chose us. We have to accept that and move on. Honor their memories by doing your very best to survive."

"But why me? It was so random, so…"

Vicky couldn't blame him. She struggled with the same questions herself, but if he didn't stop he'd get her going and neither of them would get their rest.

"Let it go, Tony. Asking that again and again won't help you and it sure as hell won't bring Chuck back. Now settle. We've got a lot to do tomorrow and need our rest." They both fell silent, but neither of them slept.

They had lost so much.

"We need real meat," Vicky declared from her place by the clay oven. It was little more than a hole in the wall so they wouldn't asphyxiate themselves. "These skinny fish won't sustain us for long."

"I could catch some of the squirrel things," Tony volunteered. "That is if I can find them."

"Most are hunkered down like us," Ben said. "I saw some tracks near the river. Let's set some snares and catch something with more meat than a squirrel."

"Best you both do it soon. I'm getting tired of fish and potatoes." She threw some more wood on the fire as Ben and Tony bundled up in all the spare clothing.

It took three more days before they caught anything in Ben's snares. Tony had continued to be unsuccessful at braining any squirrels, but swore his aim was improving.

"Looks something like a rabbit," Ben said as he butchered his catch. "Hope it tastes the same."

"It could taste like warmed-over shit for all I care. My mouth's been watering since you brought it in." She watched for moment before saying, "Careful skinning it. Might have some use for the hide."

"Two of them might be enough for your moccasins," Ben joked. "Tony and I will need at least six apiece."

"You catch that many and I'll make you a pair," Vicky promised with a grin.

"What's that?"

Tony's start of alarm roused Ben from a deep sleep. "Wassap?" he rasped as he sat up.

"I heard something sniffling around," Tony replied as he stepped toward the cave's entrance. He took a burning stick from the fire and fanned it into flame. "Sounded larger than a rat," Tony replied. "I'm going out to take a look."

"Think it's a cat?" Ben asked as he grabbed a large branch from the woodpile near the fire. The "cats" had been prowling around the campsite for the past few days and, from all indications, denning at night under the crashed alien ship. Tony had stumbled on their nest when collecting dry fallen branches. Their three-toed paw prints were all over the slope leading up to the cave. "Probably smell the fish guts," he guessed as Tony put one hand on the edge of the flap.

"Careful," Ben warned and raised his makeshift cudgel as Tony pulled the flap wide and thrust the burning torch through the opening.

There was nothing waiting outside. "Close the damn flap!" Vicky cried. "Isn't it cold enough in here already?"

There was no evidence of an animal's presence on the frozen ground within the lighted area of Tony's torch so he started down the slope toward the privy pit, wary for the slightest sound.

The cats weren't dangerous, but they could do damage with their sharp claws and dagger-like teeth. He'd seen one take a small brown creature on the run and rip it apart with two bites. They'd always kept their distance from the humans but now that their normal prey was scarce they might be after their fish and game.

Suddenly Tony lost his footing and fell on the torch.

"Are you all right?" Ben called as he hurried into the cold night. "I heard you yell and..." He cut off as he spied Tony sprawled on the ground.

"It hurts!" Tony yelled. "I burned my arm and..."

"We need to pack that in snow." Ben scooped up handfuls from a nearby bank and packed it around Tony's arm. "Can you stand? We need to get back to the cave."

Vicky was upset when she inspected his burns. "Not as bad as it could have been," she said, her tone gruff. "I don't see any big blisters so it didn't burn deep. I think we need to keep putting snow on it."

"When will it stop hurting, Ben?" Tony cried, tears rolling down his face.

"For at least a couple of days, son. Wish we had something for the pain but those days are long gone."

Vicky woke chilled. The fire in the clay oven had died down to embers. The short days had quickly lengthened as an early spring promised to chase winter's chill away. Their provisions had sustained them, though they were all tired of sour cabbage and wrinkled potatoes. She pushed aside the sheet that closed the entrance to their shelter. It was not yet warm enough to leave it open. She saw Tony making his careful way up the slope. Behind him, down in the valley, a green cast over the landscape showed where plants were coming to life in the sunlight.

The boy had recovered from his burns but bore ugly scars where the skin had improperly healed. They were trivial, but a stark reminder of how their lives had changed.

Vicky grinned widely as Tony came closer. He held a brace of furry animals with his good arm. "Found enough meat in Ben's traps for all of us. Good eating today. They're pretty scrawny, but better than potatoes."

Vicky's mouth watered at the thoughts of fresh meat. "How shall we cook them? Roasted slowly on the coals or on a skewer?"

"Skewer," Tony replied as he sat on one of their rough seats and grabbed a sharp stone. Vicky chuckled at his quick response. He sounded hungry and roasting would take longer.

"Skin them carefully so we can cure the hides. Ben's boots are worn so thin we could read a book through them…if we had a book, that is, or the time to read." As Tony began skinning the rats she asked, "Did *Dave* follow you this time?" Tony had named the murderous machine as if it were a pet. Vicky shuddered. She still considered the alien thing a monster, but giving it a name reduced the horror a bit.

"No, I think it went down to the river after Ben. He's still trying to catch that big fish he claims he saw." Tony said as he continued using the sharp edge of his stone knife to separate meat from skin and carefully skewering them afterward.

"So long as he brings back something fresh. I'm not choosey about its size," Vicky said as she added more sticks to the crackling fire. She needed to get it going enough to drive off the chill, but small enough that she could still cook Tony's small rats.

"Cooking! That's a laugh. More like sticking things on the hot coals or burning them on a spit. What I wouldn't give for a metal cooking pot, a frying pan, or even a decent knife. Plates would be welcomed too."

"You don't like the ones I made?" Tony had carved some bark trenchers.

"*Plates,* I said. We don't even have a damn pot for boiling water!"

Tony handed her the skewered rats. She thought each one might only be two or three bites. Not much, but a welcome supplement to their wrinkling potatoes. "I just wish the spring onions had sprouted so we could hide the meat's taste."

Ben arrived just as the fire was going well enough to start roasting the rats. "Get your big fish?" Tony asked.

Ben grinned and shrugged, but didn't look too disappointed. "Almost had a big one close enough to scoop it in the basket, but it got away." He handed his basket to Vicky, water dripping through the weave. There were four little fish inside.

"They're not much of a meal," Vicky remarked.

"Maybe we should dry them for our trip to Landing?" Ben answered, his tone a not-so-subtle reminder.

Vicky grimaced, but knew he was right. The time was fast approaching that they'd have to leave. They wouldn't have much time for foraging on the journey, even if they took advantage of Bamber's spring's bounty. "With luck there might be some rations still in the distant caches we haven't raided, that is if the damned aliens haven't destroyed them all."

"Sure, but those caches are weeks away. We need to carry enough to last us," Ben answered.

"That's a lot of food to carry."

"So what? You want to wait until the crops mature?" Ben asked. "The abandoned farms *might* produce a scattering of vegetables from the seeds of seasons past, but that's uncertain at best."

"We could wait for the tomatoes certainly and maybe onions, a little lettuce, and who knows what else?" Vicky pleaded.

"Those won't be ripe for months. Waiting that long wouldn't leave us much time to build a shelter and stock up for next winter at Landing." Ben replied. "We have to leave soon."

"I don't know, Ben. I've grown quite used to our cave, rough though it might be. Even the small comforts of worn blankets and clay pots makes leaving for unknown dangers frightening."

"Sure, but we have to plan for survival until the Navy comes."

She frowned. "*If* they come after all this time."

Ben ran a hand through his hair, swearing beneath his breath. "Why are you so stubborn? I don't want to be stuck here, freezing through another hard winter."

"What are we supposed to do? Take a vacation to someplace warm? No place like that around here!"

"We can go anywhere, with *Day's End*..."

Vicky didn't bother keeping her curse quiet. She was fed up with Ben's insistence about sailing his precious boat.

"Come on, Vicky, we can sail away. The further north we go the warmer it will be. The equator is only a few thousand kilometers away."

Further than that, Vicky thought but after a moment more said, "I can't argue it makes sense. Not like I want to weather another brutal winter weather in these mountains. But starting over...."

"We did okay here, we can do it again."

Vicky forced a smile. "I suppose we could forage along the river to extend what we can take," she added grudgingly. "It's just as likely we'll find something growing in the gardens at Landing. Enough to build up our larder for a trip north."

Ben grinned and looked like he would have hugged her, if he didn't know better. "We need to leave soon. *Day's End* may not have weathered the winter storms. She could need repairs before we can set to sea."

Vicky frowned but said nothing, wondering now if she should have given in at all.

"There's your little *pet*," Vicky pointed back at Dave as it followed them from the cave. "Guess it'll follow us down the river, as usual."

"It's kind of cute," Tony laughed. "Like a big puppy."

Vicky couldn't agree; not when she knew what the monsters had done. "I wish it would run down, lose power. I hate seeing it, reminding me of all we've lost, all the people, all of our…" She clenched her teeth and couldn't go on. Becoming maudlin about the attack helped no one.

"If we're doing this," she shouted, "Let's…get our shit together. Time we set off for Landing."

Tony and Ben made three trips to load the barge while Vicky packed everything they could carry. She felt a bit of panic as she looked around the cave at the rough furniture Tony had crafted, their empty shelves, and the fire pit. None of it was portable and would have to be left here. Deep inside something screamed at her not to leave behind these hard-won comforts, but there was no choice.

She turned her back on them and looked down the slope.

Ben and Tony were walking up toward her, the monster keeping a plodding pace behind. Was it her imagination or had *Dave* been moving slower than usual? Her men were a good twenty meters ahead of it by the time it stopped at the edge of the scree.

"What if we cross the ridge, and then come down by a different route?" Tony suggested. "Will it stay where it is or figure out we went another way?"

Ben grinned. "Think Dave's that dumb? It didn't have much trouble following us before."

"Worth a try. It seems a lot slower now," Vicky said to support Tony's idea. "Since we don't have much to carry going down the back slope shouldn't be a problem."

"Then we'd better get going, it's getting late." Ben picked up the largest remaining bundle and began climbing.

Once out of sight, they headed away from the cave. The route wasn't that steep, but pushing through the brush and trying not to lose their footing made for slow going. It was almost dark when they finally got to the barge.

"Do you see it?" Vicky panted, looking around for Tony's 'puppy'. She wasn't in as good shape as she'd imagined. *Must be all this indolent living,* she thought and grinned.

Ben glanced at her. "Something funny?"

"Just a thought," she replied without explaining. "Let's get this stuff aboard and push off before that monster shows up. I want to put as much distance as we can between us."

As the days passed they alternated duties. Whenever Vicky relieved Tony at the tiller, Ben took his turn at the pole. She noticed that it didn't take as much effort to push now that they had a decent amount of flowing water.

Ben sniffed the wind. "With a little sail we could probably move along faster."

Vicky sneered. "And where are you going to get the material for the sail? Use our clothes and blankets?" When Ben didn't reply she wondered if he was actually giving it serious consideration.

"Do you think there could be other survivors?" Vicky asked, changing to the subject.

"Probably," Ben answered. "Maybe at some of the prospecting sites. People out in the bush, away from the towns might have been missed. Hard to find people in all this wilderness."

"The aliens didn't have any problem finding us," Tony said, his tone sullen. "I mean, we weren't anywhere near Landing when they…"

Vicky cut him off. "That might have been accidental. It could have been heading for Bamber's and just stumbled on you two."

"They were scouring the riverbanks," Tony shouted. "It wasn't a damn accident."

"Hell, what about those in the mines? There were a couple outfits to the west as I recall," Ben interrupted. "Or maybe someone on a boat like me survived."

"Do you still think it was your dumb *boat* that protected you?" Vicky asked. "You had the gems with you."

Ben snorted. "Stones! I don't believe your magical stones have anything to do with our survival. Something else is at play."

Tony rattled his clay bracelet. "No, the gems really do protect us. That's why Dave wouldn't get close to us. The gems kept it away."

"I agree that's the way it *seems*, but on the face of it, that sounds ridiculous." Ben stumbled and nearly pitched overboard as his pole failed to find purchase. He recovered and probed to find the bottom with his pole.

"That's what Chuck said right before he threw his gems away…" Tony's jaw clenched as he left the rest of that point unspoken.

"I know this section," Vicky pointed out, trying to defuse the situation. "We're almost in the deeper channel now. We probably won't have to pole much more before we get to Landing."

Ben laid the pole aside and moved to the front of the raft. He sniffed. "Smell that? The breeze carries the scent of the sea. It won't be long before we reach the coast."

And his beloved Day's End, Vicky thought.

They poled into what remained of Landing's harbor as evening fell. Neither Tony nor Vicky said a word as they went ashore.

The town was as Ben remembered, although a bit more weathered from the winter's storms. The piles of rubble had subsided into low mounds and fresh weeds were springing up. The paths and roads were barely visible but he could still make out where the homes had stood. Where he had searched in vain for trace of anyone, victims or survivors. Where he'd last seen Eve…

They all remained silent as they looked out over what was left of Landing.

"Any particular place you want to bed down for the night?" Ben asked. "As for me, I'll stay on *Day's End."* The ungainly boat still rode at anchor just offshore where he'd tied it up seven months before.

Vicky put her hand on Ben's shoulder. "Mind if I join you? Be like sleeping in a graveyard, here."

"Me, too," Tony added as he gripped Ben's hand. Tears rolled down his cheeks.

Vicky's as well.

In the morning they walked the town, searching for anything left that they could use, checking the untended fields and gardens to see what had sprouted, and making plans for when they'd be heading north.

Day's End had weathered the winter well. The sails needed mending, many of the lines had dried to the point they'd fail in a heavy sea, and the lashings that held the logs tight had loosened a bit, but none of that would be hard for Ben to fix. Luckily, there was plenty of fresh vines and tree bark to make repairs.

"I cleared the weeds around the squash and whatever plants looked edible," Tony reported. "Maybe some tomato bushes or peppers will produce in a few weeks."

Vicky nodded. "Both would be welcome, but I'd rather we had some hardly vegetables we could store for the trip north; onions, potatoes, even some corn would be welcome."

"We should collect planks to build a temporary shelter," Ben suggested. "Keep off the rain, if nothing else. We have at least two months before the first winds of autumn. Time enough for the two of you to gather more food while I travel up the coast to look for any other survivors."

Vicky's head snapped up. "Excuse me?"

Ben looked at her. She'd gone white and her jaw seemed clenched. "I'll help you get settled first, then I'll head out. Makes more sense now, while you and Tony are preparing for our trip. I'll just go south along the coast for a couple of weeks, see if I can spot any sign of life. We can check the other places during our journey to the north."

"So...let me see if I got this right...You're going to leave *us* to do *all* the work while you sail off on your damned boat on the off chance you *might* find someone else?!" By the time Vicky was done she looked spitting mad. "What makes you think you'll find anyone? It's a foolish hope."

Ben held firm. "I have to try, Vicky. There could be people out there that need our help."

"What about the people *here* that need your help?"

"You did well for yourself before I showed up, you'll be fine for the few weeks until I'm back."

She glared at him. "I'm not going to change your mind, am I?"

Ben made every effort not to smile. "Nope, not a bit. Besides, I have to make certain *Day's End* is in shape for our longer voyage."

Clearly resigned, she nodded, but deep in her gaze he saw a flicker of fear. She evaded his touch as he reached out to her. As she moved past him she whispered, "I...*we* can't lose you, Ben. Not now."

Chapter Ten

I AWOKE TO DARKNESS, A BLOWTORCH BREATHING ON MY FACE AND ON MY *scalp a raging fire roared. Acid burned both eyes. Every tooth was a source of grinding misery that demanded a cry of rage. But I had no lips to form, no tongue to shape, no lungs to propel a scream. Neither could I flail an arm, lift fingers to face, or even twist a leg to display my agony.*

Was this hell and I one of the damned? There was no answer as the burning seared my tortured frame until, thankfully, darkness washed consciousness away.

A timeless interval later I awoke to a lesser agony. The burning sensations had ceased but intense pain still wracked my body.

Everywhere.

I feared I had become a nexus of suffering with no history or future. I could hear no sounds, smell no odors, feel neither warmth nor cold. Worse, I had no awareness of whether I stood or lay prone. That pain existed was all.

Only fitful sleep relieved the agony, but with the sleep came memories.

The squad of zombies—*cybermarines* they were called—were Command's newest weapon, something dreamed up by cyber-ghouls with ethic-otomies. Regardless of how many words and studies Command used to justify their actions, it still wasn't right to use dying Marines as machines instead of giving them a decent death, not right to turn them into fucking *zombies*!

Command had all the high-sounding justifications for the program—*getting a return from the money invested in training, allowing dying Marines a continuation of honorable service, providing new life to the nearly departed, etcetera, etcetera,* and *etcetera*. It's amazing the excuses leaders can use to rationalize their decisions. It was all about economics; a cybermarine was a lot cheaper than an automated tank and a lot more expendable.

The cybers didn't even look like Marines. From a distance, they were ideal—seven feet tall, broad of shoulder and thick of chest, with muscular arms and legs, but a glance at their faces was enough to make anyone puke.

They had no nose—just a couple of thumb-sized holes below the eyes. Yeah, *eyes*—six of them; a wide-set pair above the outside of the cheekbones, a tiny pair, quite close together where the bridge of the nose might have been, and another set, larger and circular, above them.

Their skulls were hairless from the brow to the nape of the neck. On either side, where you expect to find ears, were knobs of flesh on which they could hang six-lensed combat glasses to augment their already incredible vision.

Thank God, the combat helmets they wore obscured most of their features. They wore the visors down, most of the time, if only to spare everybody's sensitivities.

"The sailors do not like us, Captain," the squad leader said. It wore no rank. According to the tag its name was *Winslow, Harold.*

"You know that how?" I responded.

"When they saw us their faces became warmer than normal, indicating an adverse emotional reaction. We also noticed that they clench their fists and tense their muscular structure as if ready for either fight or flight." He tilted his head to the side. "By the way, sir, I note a sudden tension in your jaw. Your voice also expresses stress. Do you share their distaste, sir?"

"Great, just what I need—a walking lie detector."

"Simply infrared vision, sir. I also see into the ultraviolet spectrum and, before you ask, my binocular vision is far more acute than a normal human's."

"You are also faster than a fucking bullet and can leap tall buildings in a single bound, I suppose."

"Sir, I may have an enhanced body, but I doubt either of those apply." I couldn't tell if it was serious or not. Last thing I wanted was a smart-ass cyberzombie.

Then I remembered how most of Winslow, Harold's memories had been stripped away, along with a sense of humor. "Yes, it was a joke and I am quite well acquainted with your physical capabilities. I've read the specs. You will be an asset to our squad." I tried to put as much sincerity into my voice as I could, but I knew Winslow, Harold would know the truth.

"By your leave, sir. Where do we bunk?"

"I haven't made arrangements yet. Certainly you can't be bunked with the others. No way you'd fit into a standard Navy rack." I was actually wondering if I could put them in the cargo hold, out of sight. "I'll talk to the chief about it. In the meantime, why don't you wait in the mess?"

"What about our gear, sir? Each of us has two hundred kilos of food, five hundred kilos of weapons and ammunition, and one hundred kilograms of personal supplies."

Crap, each one of them came with more stuff than twenty men carried into deployment. "Food?"

"We require little. We carry special rations when we need to remain effective, sir."

Yes, and its weapons were probably heavier than anything even my beefiest Marine could carry. "See the quartermaster. He'll figure out where to store your kit."

"By your leave, sir." With that he spun on his heel and departed.

"You have a choice, Captain Savage," someone whispered softly from the depths of the conflagration that wracked my being. "We can save you as you are or..."

I knew the choice. It was standard option to the oath of office and drilled into us. "I don't know." I could not hear if the words had escaped my absent lips or not. The continuous pain told me that I had to be near death's door.

"It's life – of a sort," came the whispered promise. "We don't want to lose your knowledge and skills."

Which meant, I realized through agonizing waves of pain, that I could put an end to the suffering by simply saying I wanted to die.

Death wasn't appealing, but it was better than surviving as a pathetic remnant of my former self, horribly disfigured, covered with scars and missing eyes, ears, arms, and legs. They could probably restore some functions, but I'd sooner die than become some disgusting, crippled veteran.

I knew that the alternative to dying was to survive, albeit briefly, given the sorts of engagements where cybers were used. I remembered what Winslow, Harold had looked like and wondered if death might not be the better choice.

"We need your rage," the whisper continued.

The choice was less than living and more than dying. All they offered was a promise that I could continue to serve and, in serving, release my fury.

"Machines, that's all they are, damned machines," the quartermaster grumbled as the cybers formed up at the cargo bay's hatch.

"They're Marines, sailor," I barked in reply, a trifle loudly because Winslow, Harold had glanced my way. "I expect the cargo hold to be fixed up to accommodate them comfortably."

"Don't look like they need anything but a damn packing crate," he answered under his breath, just softly enough that I wasn't sure I heard correctly.

"Packing crates would be fine, sir," Winslow, Harold shouted from across the compartment and the quartermaster's ears turned bright red.

I thought the mess would be a problem. The regular Marines couldn't abide the cybers and the hostile sailors liked them even less. It was probably better that the cybers ate whatever suited their weird metabolism in the privacy of the cargo bay, among their own kind.

"By your leave, sir." I looked up to see Winslow, Harold's hulking presence at the door to the compartment I shared with the ship's engineer. Seeing its overwhelming form in such close quarters made Winslow appear all the more menacing.

"We were wondering when we would train with the rest of the troops."

"I don't think that would be a good idea," I replied. I'd kept my Marines separate mostly out of concern for their safety. With their power, the cybers could unintentionally harm someone, not that there weren't a few hotheads who might test them. Best, I thought, to keep training exercises separate. That wouldn't make a difference in combat, seeing as how the cybers would operate as an autonomous element of the force and not part of a standard squad.

No burning or agonizing pain touched me on my next awakening as I blissfully floated on a sea of darkness. The absence of pain was sufficient and that was comfort enough.

Without warning, I became aware of my body. Sounds assaulted my ears, far too loud to interpret. Bright, formless light blinded me. My entire body tingled with a thousand tiny bites, each demanding my attention. I flexed an arm to scratch the bothersome itch at my hip and somebody screamed: "Holy shit, watch out for the..."

Darkness ensued.

I could make no sense of the vague shadowy forms that swam before my eyes. Caricatures they were, rude representations of the human form, huge and threatening. I could make out no details save that one was somewhat larger than the rest – closer, I wondered and tried to blink away the fogginess. That's when I realized I had no eyelids, nor even the sensation of them.

Sound assailed my ears. An intermittent, dull, and loud rattle that echoed in my skull like a dentist's burr drill. On and on it went, repeating endlessly. No, I noted that it was slightly different each time, varying in volume and intensity.

I felt something brush my cheek; a woman's caress, judging by the silky smoothness of it. I recalled how my mother's hand had stroked me like that so many years ago as she sent me off to school. Where was she now? "Mother," I tried to cry, but still had no voice or breath; no way to speak.

Mother was gone now, I recalled. Lost like father and brother over the years and billions of miles, so far away that the news of her passing had not reached me until long after her services. She was my last and only remaining family connection.

I recalled the farm, my prize calf, and the family of silly cats in the barns who thought they owned the cattle. I remembered my many dogs, short-lived all, and the kitchen garden I'd planted with its even shorter-lived crops.

Gone now, all gone.

The sound gradually became a harsh voice that formed words. "David? Ah, good. We got a reaction that time. Set the [something, mumble, mumble] down."

Cairo, Bulgaria, and *Cuba* happened upon the Shardie vessels off Farthing. The automatics from our ships fired before anyone had recovered from the quantum probability drive's blink syndrome.

There had been four alien ships; small ones or we wouldn't have survived. The first two were atomized when our ballistic rounds struck, shattering them into a million glass fragments. The third Shardie craft dodged one round successfully but moved directly into the path of a second salvo.

A surviving Shardie accelerated away from the scattered fragments of its companions. The failure of it to immediately attack was so unexpected that all ships lost precious milliseconds as each vessel's autonomous battle controls spun the main drives, then kicked in to pursue the escaping craft.

The Shardie was boosting eight gees, a lot faster than *Cairo* could match. There was no chance of catching up if it continued its straight-line flight. Unlike the Shardies, frail humans couldn't survive sustained high acceleration.

Cairo fired high-velocity ballistic rounds continuously. The Shardie ship dodged as if it knew where she would place them. It didn't matter if *Cairo* hit it or not. Every evasive movement the Shardie made took time away from escape. That gave the squadron a chance to keep up.

In five minutes we had two ships within fifty klicks and still the Shardie hadn't fired back or turned to drive full speed into one of our ships. That was a common tactic, using their ships as ballistic missiles.

But this one hadn't, which was strange. *What is different about this ship?* I wondered as we closed on the target. By the standards of all previous encounters our squadron should have come out of the engagement down one ship at best.

The escaping Shard's actions were so far from the norms of behavior that I momentarily wondered if we were dealing with the same aliens. No, that couldn't be true. The identifying characteristics were within 99.9999% of the Shardie profile. There was no mistake.

Maybe it was carrying something so valuable that escape was preferable? If so, we were within moments of overtaking a functional alien ship and, hopefully, whatever it held. For the first time we might be able to communicate. Implicit was the hope that communications might lead to a way of averting the path of war away from total annihilation. Anything would be an improvement.

Most people wanted complete obliteration of the Shardies; genocide and retribution.

"Armed and ready," Guns reported automatically when *Cairo* was within twenty klicks, a range where a miss was improbable and a kill a certainty.

"Stand down. Go manual," the captain ordered. "I don't want some automatic defense logic to screw up our chances of capturing this ship. Chief, use the small gun to disable its drives if we can't overtake."

Guns looked at him and hesitated. "Where you want me to aim, Cap'n? I don't know where their frigging drives might be."

"Hit them in the ass then!" the captain ordered

"Closing at two kilometers per second," Navigation reported. "Range five kilometers. Contact in ninety seconds."

Guns fired at the Shardie stern, with little effect. *Bulgaria* tried to seize it, but her magnetic grapples failed to engage.

"Pull ahead," the captain ordered. "If ordnance didn't work, maybe baking it with our main engines will. *Cairo, Bulgaria,* and *Cuba:* box her in and bracket the bastard. Lock it to a single heading."

Cairo spun clockwise and reached the ship while *Bulgaria* and *Cuba* executed similar maneuvers. Savage admired the beauty as the three massive ships moved like ballet dancers. Command would probably have flayed the captain's hide for ordering such a move in such close quarters. But not now. Not with this opportunity.

The Shardie ship tried to turn as the *Bulgaria* came abreast but was blocked by *Cuba*. A second evasive move was blocked by *Cairo*.

"Wheels, give us a boost. I want to place our engines directly ahead of it." Thus far the alien had maintained a steady velocity.

"Engines, retro fire at one quarter full and slowly bring our speed down." The forward steering engines fired intermittently, each blast decreasing our velocity by fifty kilometers per second as the crew balanced the forward braking against the thrust of the mains.

A plume of burning violet plasma reached a quarter kilometer behind us, its white-hot tip closing on the Shardie. It had to shut down or be melted into submission.

The tip of flame touched the bow of the alien ship. "She's slowed," *Cairo* reported. "Adjusting to maintain position." *Bulgaria* and *Cuba* moved accordingly.

"Close the bracket," the captain ordered. "Tight as you can."

"I can push it against *Cuba*," *Bulgaria* reported.

"No. We don't know what tricks this bastard might have. Engines, cut our plume slowly as we close. I want to put our mains tight against the bow of that thing. One hint of trouble and I want to immediately incinerate it."

A second later the call for all hands to secure themselves rang through the ship. If the mains fired on full the ship would pull seven gees.

"Get your Marines ready to board," the captain instructed.

I could sense something exercising my body when I emerged from the dream state. I could see mountains in the distance and, before them, a broad lake. The water rippled slowly, as if a slight breeze played across its surface. Somewhere a bird sang a cheery song. There should have been pine scent or the earthy smell of loam, but I detected none of that. There was no smell whatsoever.

Another glance at the lake and a memory came flooding back. This was the lake where we vacationed. But was this just a memory or was it an actual scene? I flicked eyes left and right, taking in the three-dimensional reality of the sight. No, this was no memory. Somehow I had been transported several million miles to Earth and brought to this lovely spot.

But then I recalled that the lake had been drained before I was commissioned and the mountains leveled for ore. Unless I had been taken back in time this scene couldn't be real, despite the evidence of my senses.

I felt my legs bending and my arms twisting, but when I tried to resist I realized I still had no control, no volition. It was as if my limbs had minds of their own. Still, the movement felt good after so long, the muscles moving with strength and purpose.

Whatever was causing this stayed out of sight, beyond every perception but the sense of movement – kinesthetic; I think it's called. I tried to move my head to see my feet but it felt as if my neck was made of stone. Neither did I catch a glimpse of forearms or hands even though my senses said they should be in plain sight.

So many mysteries and so little knowledge. I tried to recall how I had come to this, tried to remember anything more recent than my boyhood memories.

And failed.

My Marines and three cybers jumped through the hatch to the surface of the Shardie ship. I hoped they could get inside. Killing might be necessary, but maybe it wouldn't come to that. I made sure that Corporal Henderson wasn't among the four. He'd lost his family to the Shardies and might not be shy about using his weapon.

"No apparent hatches," the squad leader reported. "Little holes everywhere, about a hands-breadth wide. Infrared shows something really hot amidships. Might be the engine." There was a long pause. "Downloading images now."

"See what your engineers can make of those pictures," the captain instructed. "Let's see if we can chip off some samples."

The squad rigged netting to give the departing engineers a way to secure themselves. The cybers still searched for a hatch.

We watched the tactical feeds streaming back. "Make sure to get a sample of that thing," the captain said. "If I have to fire the mains and melt the son-of-a-bitch we'll need something for the scientists to analyze."

I knew he wouldn't hesitate if the alien ship tried to escape. "All ships, link your mains to mine," he ordered. "If I have to blow this guy I want to be sure you are with me and not part of the melt." That got a few chuckles.

Nobody mentioned my Marines.

"Count backward from ten," the voice asked as I groggily awakened. Must not have kept the covers on, was my first thought. I felt cold, but wasn't shivering. Must be autumn if the nights were so cool. "T. te...Ten," I tried to say but couldn't feel my mouth forming the words.

"I need you to say it out loud," the voice prompted as I struggled to make sense of what he said. Hadn't he heard me?

I took a deep breath and struggled to form the words, but still couldn't feel tongue or lips. "Ten!" Something screeched behind me. "Nine." Lower this time. "Eight." A normal voice I thought.

"Excellent."

There were some mechanical sounds. Something touched my face, a feather of sensation, quickly gone. There was a flash and then I could see! It took a moment to adjust before I noticed that the lights were too bright and the colors garish. I tried, but couldn't squint. "Hurts," I said and the lights immediately dimmed. There seemed to be a doctor looking into my eyes, a doctor with a bright red face and hands, as if he were wearing florescent paint. I noticed that his gown was pale violet instead of the traditional white. When he smiled his teeth glowed.

"Funny colors," I said, and heard my voice coming from somewhere behind me.

"We'll fix that in a few days, but for now we're going to reconnect you. Don't try to move until I tell you."

Stupid thing to say, besides, my cheek itched where the feather had touched. I lifted my hand to scratch and heard whirling sounds as something moved. It sounded mechanical and heavy. Somebody screamed.

It was me.

"I've got her tight as a tick," the quartermaster reported, meaning that the Shardie ship had been trussed tightly and blanketed by every bit of our electronic suppression gear. "Charges armed and ready." If need be, the captain could instantly sever the cables between the Shardie and our ships.

The engineers moved equipment across the gap as they went about their work. Small sparks of their cutting torches sparked against the starry background. Their drills and saws had failed them.

"Some sort of ceramic, it looks like," the engineering chief in the bright red suit reported. The cybers' were dull black. The engineers in their glaring white suits set up a large tripod connected by thick cables. "Never seen anything like this hull material, but there ain't nothing can stand up to a laser torch. We'll have that sample for you soon."

The captured ship hadn't moved. There was no sign that it was anything but an inert hunk of glass with something hot in the middle.

The engineers got the laser working. A pale blue beam grew to white brilliance beneath the tripod. "Looks like she's cutting through," the chief said seconds before a gout of flame shot up to consume the red and white suits in a rapidly expanding circle. The Shardie began to. . .

"What the…" was all the captain had time to say before the Shardie became a miniature nova.

Alarm bells clamored. Whistling air screamed where the hull was torn, pressure changed as blast doors slammed shut. The command board was a sea of warning crimson. The heavy, twisted hatch blocked bridge access.

The pain was immense, almost more than I could bear. Each breath was an agony of scorching air, each exhalation rasping torture. I kept hoping it would subside, but the horror of each breath added to the previous, growing ever more intense as the moments passed.

I looked across the slick deck, past assorted arms and legs, one wearing my boot. "Captain, Captain," screamed Guns as he clutched the captain's body. "Oh God, we've got to save him." That wasn't possible since his head had been thrown across the room.

"He's dead," I said calmly. I couldn't feel my leg. One arm was on fire. My gut felt cold and empty. My pants felt full, warm, and smelled like shit.

A pair of hands ripped the twisted hatch aside. Winslow, Harold stepped onto the bridge. "Lieutenant?"

"Here," I groaned.

"You are seriously injured, sir," he said as he lifted me effortlessly and carried me through the hatch. I screamed from the pain as bone grated on bone. Guns staggered behind us, carrying his right arm with what remained of his left hand.

Winslow continued to carry me. "Our men?" I whispered, meaning the ones outside.

"All gone," he replied and I hoped he meant the same.

"Help Guns," I ordered.

"He is bleeding profusely from multiple trauma and will likely die within minutes," Winslow replied. "I believe that you can survive."

Two Navy ratings stumbled into the corridor. "Decks Four and Five gone," the one with a bloody leg yelled. "Access from this deck's cut off by the fire."

I noticed severe burns on the left side of the other rating's face when he glanced my way. "Jesus, how can he still be alive?" he cried.

"Help me get him into the escape pod," Winslow ordered, his voice crackling in command mode. "You, put a tourniquet on his leg. There's a medical pack on board."

"What about me?" the other rating asked with a catch in his voice and a glance at Guns' bloody body on the deck.

"We do what we can to save the ship and crew," Winslow replied as he slammed the hatch shut. A few seconds later the force of the pod's ejection sequence blew it free and sent me into unconsciousness.

I awoke so free from pain that I wondered if I had made the wrong choice and was in heaven. Then I realized that I was breathing, there were things happening in my body, and smells assailed my nostrils. "I was saved?"

"You were close to death, Lieutenant Savage," a distant voice replied. "We saved what we could." He went on to describe extensive body modifications and I recalled Winslow, Harold's six eyes—and all of the other things that separated a cyber from ordinary humans.

"What else did you do?" I said. I never felt more alive and vigorous. This might not be bad at all.

The voice didn't respond immediately and when it did it was a different voice—probably a psychologist. "We had to choose what parts of your memories to retain," the new voice said softly. "Lieutenant Savage, your new brain is artificial, a silicon and gel mixture that gives you consciousness, volition, and memories but doesn't have the capacity of... Look, there wasn't enough for most of your past so we had to choose what would be most important to you. We preserved education, training, and recent war experiences. They use most of your brain, leaving room only for a few boyhood memories."

No, that can't be true, I thought, the memories of my prize calf, the lake, and mother clear in my mind. Try as I might, there was nothing else I could recall with such clarity. There were fragments, just flashes of scenes without context, and faces without names. On the other hand, every memory of my twelve years in the Corps, of training and skills were clear as if they had happened seconds before. Most of what had made me unique was gone forever, along with emotions, faith, and the important things that had formed my personality. "Did I have any family beside my mother?"

"Sorry," the voice added. It didn't sound terribly apologetic.

"You have a choice, Lieutenant Savage," someone had whispered softly weeks before. "Do you want to get back at those who did this?" they'd asked.

Now I realized there was some way I could still contribute. "Yes," I'd whispered. It would be a way to pay back those bastards for what they'd done to my squad.

But most of all, it was a way of honoring Winslow, Harold for his sacrifice.

Chapter Eleven

Summer at Landing was a welcome relief after the harsh winter they'd endured at Bamber's. The abandoned orchards looked to produce a bounty of fruit, and fresh shoots were appearing among the stubble of the fields. They slept in blankets beneath the stars until they had the time to throw together a shelter to protect them from the wind and rain. Husbanding the gardens to ensure they'd grow enough food to survive another winter consumed most of the daylight hours and left them exhausted.

Ben was drying himself on the beach after his evening's swim. The sun's fading rays felt so good on his body, now recovering from winter's privation. Thanks to the plentiful food, his pants no longer needed to be cinched so tight.

Vicky collapsed beside him, dripping wet, her smile bright and easy. "Things are really going well, aren't they?" she said.

Ben nodded agreement and watched as Tony splashed away the grime from his day's work in the garden. "Yes, the gardens are coming back. Once we get a decent shelter finished we'll be ready for whatever next winter throws at us."

When Vicky said nothing, he continued. "Well, now that we've got a shelter and have the crops underway, it's time I head out to look for other survivors. They've got to be out there. We can't be the only lucky ones."

Vicky's smile disappeared and her eyes lost their sparkle. "I wouldn't exactly call this lucky." She fell silent a moment, her easy manner growing sullen. "I was wondering how long you were going to hang around. Kind of hoped you'd decided not to go." She gave a bitter laugh. "But this isn't really about finding other survivors, is it? It's about being on that damned boat of yours..."

Ben couldn't honestly tell her no.

Ben hadn't planned to search for more than a few weeks, but when he discovered that Wincker was as ruined as Landing he had to keep going, clinging to the hope there really was someone else out there. He ventured further south to Terrahaut where a fire had swept the entire coastline leaving nothing but rubble and scorched trees. Even if there had been survivors, they would have abandoned this desolate place.

Jelico was the last stop before the five-day sail back to Landing. He'd been so disturbed at the sight of the ruins at Wincker and Terrahaut that he'd didn't know if he had the courage to see another ruined settlement. Maybe Vicky had been right and the expectation of more survivors was a foolish hope. But he wasn't ready to give up; not yet.

He turned *Day's End* toward Jelico's harbor.

The coastline wasn't promising. Ben saw no signs of life as he approached where the harbor might have been, but decided to swing by for a closer look. There was no sense dropping anchor to examine another deserted village…except…was that something moving along the shore? Animal…or human? He was too far away to make out what it might be. Man-sized for sure, and that was enough to rekindle his waning hope.

As Day's End drew closer to the shore the dark mass resolved into a small figure that quickly disappeared into the tree line. Ben gave a whoop of joy. Definitely human!

Then a larger figure returned to the shore with the first one and waved furiously. Ben smiled and laughed as he guided *Day's End* into the shallows. Not one person, but two! Finally, after all this time, he'd found survivors! He dropped the anchor rock and leaped into the water to embrace the pair, all three of them crying and shouting for joy. Tears ran down the man's heavily tanned face.

"How many…?" the man asked. "Oh God, I never expected to find… How did you…Where?" The questions poured out fractured and fast, as if the stranger was as overwhelmed as he was curious. He didn't give Ben a chance to answer.

None of that matters, Ben thought with a crazy grin on his face. *I've found survivors, at long last!*

"We've been barely surviving on the remains of the gardens and squirrels," the man, Joseph explained. "The squirrels live in the trees. Hard as a bitch to spear…"

Ben could imagine. The pair were scarcely more than skeletons. He waded back to the boat and retrieved a string of fish and some of his dried fruit to share with them.

Joseph and the youngster didn't immediately fall upon the food as Ben expected. As the excitement died down, Joseph stepped back, his expression wary. "Why didn't you ask about what happened to Jelico?" he demanded as he drew the youngster behind him.

Ben was alarmed by the sudden change. "I didn't need to, it's been the same everywhere I've sailed. You two are the only survivors I've found along this coast."

"No one else?" Joseph's voice broke and horror filled his gaze. "What happened?"

Ben spit. "Aliens. Destroyed nearly every damn thing."

There was a taut silence and Ben could see Joseph's struggle to trust. After a moment the man reached out and took the offered food.

"Aliens?" Joseph sounded skeptical as he produced a folding knife and cut the fish into chunks that were quickly added to a pot of boiling vegetables beside their crude shelter.

"Yes, I've seen…" Ben started before curiosity got the better of him. "How is it you still have metal tools? I thought the aliens took every bit of refined metal. They even took the damned nails."

"That's hard to believe."

Ben nodded. "I know, but I saw one of their ships, and there's this glass machine that…never mind. I'll tell you about that later. First I need to show you this." He reached up to the small pouch suspended around his neck. "These are our good luck charms. Vicky believes they protect us from the aliens. Maybe they do, maybe they don't. I don't hold much store by it."

"Vicky?"

"Oh, she's another survivor, then there's Vicky's boy, Tony, although he really isn't, but you'll learn that when I take you to Landing."

"Are there more survivors? How many?"

"Just three of us: Vicky, Tony, and me." He brightened. "But now we have you and your boy!"

"Girl," Joseph answered. "Her name's Catherine, but she prefers Kat."

After Kat went to sleep for the night, Joseph explained how they'd survived. "We'd gone camping at the copper mines because my…my wife, Pre, thought the exposed layers were so beautiful. She's…*was*…a geologist." He choked. "Sorry."

Ben looked down out of respect. "Yeah, I lost a wife, too," he poked the embers with a stick. "Ex-wife, but that's another story." He picked up Joseph's knife and tested its edge. "Your metal tools will be really useful. Tony figured out how to flake volcanic glass with rocks to get an edge, but a metal knife is better. We'll need to take really good care of them."

As the embers died they spoke in low tones, Joseph told how they'd managed to survive the starving winter weeks, Ben shared stories of their time at Bamber's. Neither spoke of the time before, but they stayed there long into the night talking, as if hungry for another person's voice.

The next morning, as they were loading Joseph and Kat's things onto *Day's End*, Ben noticed how the man favored his leg.

"Broke it climbing a tree," Joseph explained. "Kat and I splinted it, but the bones didn't knit properly. Aches like hell in cold weather." He shrugged as if it was a minor thing.

"I wish there was something I could do, but all I can offer is sympathy," Ben replied.

"At least I survived," Joseph reflected. "At least I survived."

Ben wasn't sure that was a blessing.

Vicky noticed a dark spot on the horizon. She told herself not to hope. Too many times already she'd convinced herself the tide brought Ben home. She moved to the edge of the dock, where she wrapped her arms tight around herself and waited, straining to see better. As the spot became a smudge and the smudge a boat she began to tremble, feeling like a fool as her hope grew. *Was it him, or someone else?* It would be ironic to be found by survivors when that is what Ben went in search of.

Damn her eyes, she couldn't see if it was *Day's End*. She shouted for Tony. He would be able to see, surely. She needed it to be Ben. To know that he had not been lost, not fallen prey to aliens, not drowned, or any of the other calamities that had filled her sleepless nights. Ben had been, *was* her anchor, her single point of connection with all that they had lost. They both needed Ben's comfortable presence.

Tony came running up, his breath harsh and his expression panicked. Vicky couldn't speak. She pointed out toward the horizon.

The boy laughed and grabbed her in a hug. "It's him! It's him!"

Vicky smiled, but smacked him lightly away when Tony tried to dance her around the dock.

"Enough, settle," she told him. "There are things to be done."

They reluctantly returned to their chores. It would be hours before *Day's End* reached shore and they needed to prepare for the next journey. The growing season was coming to a close. The sea birds had begun to wing their way north toward their winter feeding grounds.

They would soon have to follow, hopefully before the cold southern winds blew.

Ben's boat was only a kilometer from shore when Tony stopped working and grabbed her arm. He gave it a little shake before letting go then pointed toward the water. "Do you see, Vicky?"

She tried, but her eyes just weren't up to distances anymore. "What?"

He grinned like crazy until she feared he'd start dancing around again.

"I think there's somebody with him!" he shouted as he headed for the dock.

"Oh my god!" she said on a breath as she dropped the fish net she was weaving and raced to join him. As the ship drew closer there appeared to be two blobs on the deck and, amazingly, a smaller one beside them. "Are you sure they're people?"

"Yes, two of them!"

Despite all her doubts, it looked as if Ben had actually found more survivors. *That insufferable man will never let me forget he was right.* But damn, he'd actually located more people! Tears welled in her eyes as the boat came closer and the figures resolved into Ben, a man, and a smaller figure.

She waded into the water with Tony as soon as the boat reached the shallows. Ben leaped off the deck and handed Tony the line to secure the boat to an anchor rock before he gave Vicky a quick hug.

"These two are Joseph and Kat," Ben said enthusiastically with a wave at his companions. "Found them up at Jelico, barely hanging on."

Vicky looked at the two thin figures staring dumbfounded at her, Tony, and their rough encampment. "We must be quite a sight, eh?" she said with a laugh. "Well, don't just stand there! Come on, jump down and join us." She hardly noticed the tears rolling down her face. "Welcome, welcome, welcome!" She was going to say more when she noticed Tony's expression as he stared open-mouthed at the young girl climb from the boat.

This was going to be interesting.

Vicky cornered Ben when they were alone. "You said a couple of god-damned weeks!" She scowled deeply and resisted the urge to punch him. "Damn it, Ben Gunning, didn't you give a single thought about how we would feel when you didn't show up when you said you would?"

"I'm sorry I worried you, but the winds weren't with us."

Vicky crossed her arms. "How far did you go? All the way to Wincker? Further, I'll wager."

"I had to know, Vicky." Ben gestured where Tony proudly showed Joseph and Kat around the camp. "I couldn't ignore the possibility that someone else might be as desperate as us to know that others had survived."

"I know...I know..." Vicky couldn't stay mad now that she said her piece, not when she was so happy to have him back. She briefly hugged him then stepped away.

"Now, come along. Let me show you what we've done." She glared at him. "Without your help, thank you very much."

Ben winced.

That night they had a welcoming feast. Mostly fish and fresh vegetables. Tony also boiled a small fat animal that might have been a rat in a clay pot. Vicky made sure that the newcomers got most of the meat and the broth. The two looked so thin that she wondered how much longer they would have survived had Ben not happened along.

The girl insisted she was fourteen but looked older in her tattered clothes. "Have to get you dressed into something more substantial," Vicky said. *And covering*, she thought.

"We've still got our camping clothes," Joseph replied. "Not much, but they're pretty rugged." He opened their packs and drew out their clothes and possessions.

"That's mine," the girl insisted defiantly as he pulled out a coat.

"Of course it is but you won't mind if I take a look, will you?" Vicky replied. "It's important to know what resources we have." Most of her own clothing was near useless from continuous wear. Luckily, she and Ben were close enough in size that they could exchange.

Tony had worn out his pants and shirts long ago, not that he could barely squeeze into them any longer, he'd shot up so fast recently. Ben's pants were still too big for him so, as a result, he wore whatever was handy.

Vicky estimated Joseph's size and wondered if any of the man's clothing would fit Tony. A pair of pants might stop him from acting so shy and embarrassed around the newcomers. Shame was a silly thing, given their present circumstances.

Most surprising of all was the clothing Joseph's late wife had left at their campsite. "Don't know why we've hung on to it," Joseph said as he lifted each piece from his pack.

Vicky eyed the hiking slacks. They were too narrow in the hips for her, but they should do for Kat once she grew more. "What else do you have?"

The blouse Joseph next pulled from the pack was a silken dream in her hands. It was not the sort of thing she'd ever consider owning simply because of its impracticality. Yet, holding it, feeling its smooth texture in her work-roughened hands, made her feel as if she held a piece of something she'd imagined to be lost forever

"I was going to give it to my wife as a birthday present…" Joseph wiped a tear away before he could continue. "I was hoping that maybe Kat could wear them some day. They're still too big for her."

Vicky stroked the blouse before carefully handing it back. "Not very practical, is it?"

Joseph nodded as he carefully repacked it. "No, but that was the point."

In the months since their arrival Joseph and Catherine—*Kat*, damn it!—had put on a little more weight. They quickly became productive members of the family. It was nice to see faces other than Ben and Tony's after more than a year. Five was a better number for a family and Vicky hoped that there would be many more in the future: you couldn't have a community with so few.

Like all the youngsters she had known, it seemed that Tony and Kat consumed more than the rest of them combined. Tony's growth spurt had continued and he starting to regain the muscular frame he'd had on that fateful day they had set out for Bamber's. Somehow unnoticed he had added ten centimeters to his height and was now taller than her. Kat hadn't grown any taller, but she'd filled out more than Vicky cared to think.

As they settled into the new routine they distribute the chores, Kat helped Tony with the garden, while Joseph helped Ben expand the rude shelter they had erected with materials from Landing's ruins. It wasn't much but it protected them from the rain and wind, which was all they needed for the short time they'd be here. Vicky, Ben, and Tony had already agreed that they needed to find a warmer camp to escape another harsh winter.

"But shouldn't somebody stay at Landing?" Joseph protested. "It's the logical place for rescuers to find us."

"Find our cold, dead bones, you mean," Vicky shot back. "I want to lay in the sun, not shiver my ass off. Look, we can leave some sign about where we're going should anybody show up." Her tone reflected her lack of confidence in that possibility.

"We could spend the winter near Tower Bridge, about a month's sail from here," Ben suggested. "The weather will be milder and it's far enough inland that we won't be bothered by the coastal storms..."

Vicky smiled. "Sounds like a plan." The others agreed.

Even Joseph.

The things that had to be accomplished before they could leave seemed endless. Not only was *Day's End* being expanded to accommodate them all, but they'd need to gather or raise enough food both to last the journey and to give them a stake until they became self-sufficient at their new location.

Kat worked with Tony on the garden expansion; clearing weeds from around the emerging crops. He'd explained there was still a couple more months before they needed to harvest. He'd planted some squash seeds he'd found in the ruined storehouse and thought they might sprout in the time remaining.

Kat clearly didn't have much experience with gardening. She tried, but sat there staring back and forth from plant to plant with a look of confusion. Vicky watched as she bit her lip and tentatively reached out to pull clumps of green from the ground. She'd only yanked a few when Tony shouted at her.

"What are you doing? Those aren't weeds. Can't you see my plants?"

"I'm sorry," Kat wailed.

"Over there," Tony pointed. "That's the area I need cleared."

"You don't have to yell," Kat replied as she threw down the plants. "I'm doing my best. Why don't you pull the weeds if you know so much?"

"Because *I* know what I'm doing and *you* obviously don't," Tony replied.

Vicky frowned at their behavior. Their survival depended on everyone working and getting along together.

Joseph intervened at that point, sending Kat to gather firewood while he took on her job of clearing weeds.

That put a temporary stop to the bickering, but wouldn't solve the problem. Vicky couldn't tell if Kat resented being told what to do in general, or just by Tony. Either way, she was becoming more assertive as her health improved. Joseph had mentioned how difficult the girl had been before the disaster, something Vicky hadn't noticed until recently.

The tension it put on all of them didn't bode well for the upcoming journey.

"We'll need to leave," Ben announced when a fresh breeze blew out of the southwest. "Weather's starting to cool."

Vicky frowned. "Why so soon? There's still another month. We can harvest more crops and dry more fish in that time."

"*Day's End*'s always been slow and with the added weight she'll be slower yet. It's a long way to Tower Bridge. Going to take at least four or five weeks even if the wind and currents favor us."

Vicky didn't look happy, but she couldn't argue.

As the garden began to mature, preparations for the trip occupied all of their waking hours. If nothing else, it stopped the bickering between the youngsters.

"I was thinking," Ben said over a dinner featuring the big silver fish Joseph had caught and baked. "*Day* would move faster if I could add more sail. We could sew some of the roofing material we brought from Dockstal to her sail." The cloth had been among the supplies he'd originally left there in the vain hope they would help any survivors.

"How would you do that?" Vicky asked. "We don't have anything to cut it with except Joseph's camp knife and even if we could do that how would we sew it?"

"My mother taught me to sew," Kat volunteered. "I could do it, that is, if I had a machine."

"That's dumb," Tony scoffed. "Where would you get the power, even if you did have your stupid machine? It's gone, just like the rest of the equipment, houses, and everybody we ever knew or loved!" He was already running away even as Kat's tears began to flow.

Ben started to follow, but Vicky stopped him. "Let him work it out on his own," she advised. "He just needs to calm down for a while."

Joseph put his arm around his sobbing daughter and held her tight.

When Tony returned Vicky could tell that he'd been crying and tried to recall what might have set him off. He hadn't gotten that upset since they'd lost Chuck.

Tony and Kat had been pointedly ignoring each other for days after Tony's blow-up, hardly speaking even when they were working side by side cleaning the fish or taking their turn at cooking.

Vicky knew they would have to resolve their differences before the family sailed. Crowded together on the boat, where there would be no escape, any bad feelings could easily escalate beyond control. She wondered if Joseph could help. He had been warming to her as the summer progressed and, at times, she wondered if he had more than conversation on his mind, her being the only remaining woman on the planet. Best not to think much about *that*. Ben's infrequent attempts at intimacy were already more than she was comfortable with.

She did sympathize with Joseph's loss of his wife. She'd been a geologist he said, although maybe it should have been *Morrologist* or something like that since this certainly wasn't Earth.

Not by a damn shot!

Ben didn't seem upset by Joseph's giving her so much attention. Or maybe he realized, as she had, that there were no sparks. She was somewhat attached to Ben, although he didn't seem anything more than just fond of her, except on those rare occasions when they both felt the need for mutual comfort.

Still, she wished he'd be a little jealous.

Vicky inventoried their food, trying to determine how much more they could collect before they sailed. Things would certainly be more complicated with five people on board the boat. They still didn't have enough fish, but with more helpers surely they could catch more of the tasty blue ones to dry. They'd also need additional pots and baskets for the root vegetables!

Sleeping arrangements on the boat would be crowded and they didn't have enough mats for everyone. Maybe she could set Kat to weaving another pair for her and her father; give her something to do besides arguing with Tony. Things were getting better among the adults, but there were still way more teenage spats than there should be. She hoped that, by the time *Day's End* was fully loaded for the trip, the youngsters would find a balance, or it was going to be a long voyage.

Ben was testing the sail on *Day's End* when Vicky reached him. "I hope you aren't getting ready to sail somewhere. We have to leave soon and I don't want to be stuck here for the winter."

Ben tightened one of the stays on *Day's End*'s mast. "You're right, of course. But maybe we can leave early to check a few places not far off our route? That wouldn't cost us too much time."

Vicky considered the compromise. "As long as you don't abandon us for some wild-assed side trip. We need you, Ben. We need your boat and your skills, damn it!"

Ben grinned. "Why, Vicky, I thought you only wanted my body."

Vicky rolled her eyes. She'd never felt anything but friendly toward Ben, nor had he ever acted other than as a companion and occasional way of gaining some release. Their hard life had pretty much extinguished whatever flames of youth they'd had, not that she'd ever had many to begin with. Besides, the daily needs of living usually kept them too exhausted for even that desperate grasp at humanity. What infrequent sex they'd had was more for Ben's comfort than her needs.

Vicky jerked abruptly and looked back toward the kids. Could Kat...and Tony... No, surely not. They weren't old enough, were they? She would have to talk to the kids about that later.

Unless it was already too late.

The voyage north was uneventful thanks to a strong southwesterly breeze. And once they arrived, setting up camp and restoring their food reserves kept everyone busy.

As they settled into life in at Tower Bridge, the relationship between the youngsters grew less fractious. Vicky had caught Tony and Kat alone together too often not to expect they were moving beyond friendship. She knew it was ridiculous to worry about, Kat being too young. The reality of their situation was that the two youngsters had only each other. It wouldn't take long for nature to assert itself.

"Have you said anything to Kat about their relationship?" Vicky asked as she and Joseph watched Tony and Kat help Ben work on the boat.

"What relationship?" he blustered.

Vicky fixed him with a hard gaze. "The one that has been forming right before all our eyes, if you'd been paying attention."

"What do you mean? Kat's a sensible girl, a good girl. Her mother and I raised her better than to do anything foolish."

"I hope you're right. But just in case I'll ask Ben to talk to Tony about being careful."

Joseph scowled at her. "I hardly think that's necessary! Kat is still too young. Besides they bicker more like brother and sister."

"Don't be a fool, Joseph. Kat's old enough to be curious, damn it. And kids are prone to doing stupid things. I have no doubts that she and Tony will succumb to their hormones sooner than we'd like, if they haven't already."

"But..." Joseph began.

"Nothing we can do about it," Vicky sighed. "We'll just have to hope they'll be careful."

Ben insisted that it was time they started getting ready for the return to Landing but Vicky objected. "Why return to Landing? I want to stay here, where it's warm and sunny."

"And where the damn bugs are too hungry!" Joseph said as he slapped at something on his arm.

"Winter's coming to a close and it'll get pretty hot at this latitude," Ben warned.

"Why Landing?" Vicky demanded. "There's plenty of nearer places that are cooler." *Besides,* she thought, *then I wouldn't have to endure another long voyage on that stupid raft.*

"We've already established it as a base camp," Ben replied. "Also, it's the logical place for the Navy to look, that is, if they ever come. Besides," he added with a grin. "I need to build a second boat for us and for that I need the seasoned hardwood from Landing's wood lot."

Tony wholeheartedly supported Ben's idea, as did Kat. Vicky knew Joseph would agree with her, but they were outnumbered and she'd learned that without compromise they'd not survive.

"We need to get started now so we can get there in time for our spring planting," Ben announced.

"I agree," Vicky responded. "Like it or not we'll have to tend the gardens if we want to eat. I for one, don't want to forage any longer. Gardens won't survive without care."

"Then let's get busy," Joseph said, adding his voice to the discussion.

Within a month of their return to Landing Ben started on the hull of a longer, narrower, and sleeker boat. "Different sail design from *Day's End*," he said. "It'll have outriggers to provide stability. The longer hull will let it move faster, but a lanteen rig will make her more difficult to maneuver."

"But we barely know how to sail this one," Joseph complained.

"Don't worry. I'm going to make certain that everyone, even you, will know how to handle her."

In the weeks that followed, Ben and Tony hauled the timbers they needed to the shoreline and put Joseph to work trimming them with his camp tools and gouging hollows with carefully tended fires that ate into the tree's core.

The new boat, *Summer's Breeze*, took form slowly. Ben intended for it to be longer than *Day's End*, but with spars at the bow and stern to hold outrigger logs on either side. "Gives her greater speed and stability," Ben explained about the design. The sail, fashioned from the recovered supplies, was somewhat larger than the one on *Day's End*, an increase of nearly twenty percent, but rigged on a long pole suspended from a stubby mast. "She can't tack as well as *Day's*, but she'll be easy to handle in a following breeze," he explained.

Vicky heard the unspoken message. "You mean if we have to sail *Day's* without you."

Ben hesitated. "No; not at all. I just figured we could carry more with two boats. Be more comfortable, you know."

Vicky punched his arm. "You expect me to believe that?"

Later she posed another question. "Are we going continue coming back to Landing once the second boat is finished, Ben? Personally, I'd prefer living somewhere temperate, maybe somewhere between Tower Bridge and here."

"But why would the Navy look anywhere else, Vicky?" Tony asked. "We already agreed that Landing was a logical place to look for any remaining survivors—and I mean *us*."

"I don't want to freeze my butt off each winter," Joseph argued. "I say we go north with the warm weather. We can always leave a sign at Landing."

"As if our camp isn't sign enough," Ben argued. "Who else wants to change our summer camp site?"

Neither Joseph nor Kat said anything, but Vicky could tell by their expressions that she'd have to accept another migration to the north when the fall winds began to blow.

As they were preparing for the trip, Kat casually mentioned that she had missed her period.

"Happens," Vicky replied with a laugh. "My own periods were pretty irregular when I was your age."

"But mine never have been," Kat protested.

"Probably something you ate, or an early sign of some sickness, like that cold you had a month ago. I wouldn't worry just yet."

She kept her own concerns to herself and hoped what she'd told Kat was the truth.

Chapter Twelve

SWEENEY DIDN'T FEEL LIKE HIMSELF. IN FACT, HE FELT NOTHING AT ALL. He felt, well, *weird!* Wait, hadn't he felt this before? Slowly, bits of memories shifted into place. He recalled somebody saying they'd make him a badass Marine. Had they done that? He was too groggy to recall.

Slowly sight returned. Everything was sharp and strangely tinged. Sound was muffled. His muscles felt tight. He flexed an arm.

"Careful there, Sergeant," someone warned. "Those are stronger than you think."

Sweeney looked down. He wore an armored suit similar to his MULE, but lighter. He flexed his arm again and marveled at its response.

Wait a minute. Hadn't his arms been shot off? Legs, too? "What the fuck?"

"You agreed to become a cyber," the voice continued. "But probably forgot that, along with some other memories. No matter: Once we get your new body checked out you can return to the war."

New *body*? Oh yeah, now he recalled Mores saying something about that. Did a decent job from what he could feel: Natural.

"I'm going to run some tests, ask a few questions, and then we can move on to training," the voice continued.

"When can I get out of this suit?" Sweeney asked. "It feels kinda tight."

The voice was silent for a long time. "Sergeant," it said at last. "There's another thing you might have forgotten."

"Yeah? What's that?"

"You've been in and out of surgery for six months. We had to remove part of your brain, and… do other things. You are neither in a suit nor wearing a new type of MULE. Sergeant Sweeney, you are now a Cybermarine. That is your new body."

Sweeney found that he could only remember a few things about his boyhood on Morrow; a dog he took when he went fishing with his dad, holiday dinners filled with faces but no names, and a nasty woman, Vicky something or other.

His memories of being a Marine were more complete, although lacking in details. There seemed to be no memories prior to becoming a MULE operator. It didn't matter. He was pretty certain that most of his earlier life had been less than memorable; why else would he become a grunt? The one thing he did remember clearly was his absolute hatred of the Shardies.

He couldn't recall how his old body felt but he didn't particularly missed it. In this one, he could see perfectly, even in low light and almost complete darkness. His hearing was acute enough to hear a cat's footfall a quarter klick away. He couldn't smell anything, but his other senses more than compensated.

He loved the feeling of power, the sheer shot of pleasure it gave him to race across the landscape, handle the huge weights of M-60 and AN-80's far easier than a squad of ordinary Marines. The dexterity in his new hands was amazing. He could field strip and reassemble any weapon they placed in his grip, which was delicate enough to hold an egg without crushing it. He knew his new body was a vast improvement over what he had been, even when he was operating a super MULE. He felt like a god; invincible and mighty.

That was before he realized what they had done to him. Mighty he might have become, but the machine that was him was ugly as refined sin. Christ, the face alone would give his mother, if she were still alive, nightmares. But then, he didn't have to look at it, did he?

Sweeney preened. This new version of him was the biggest, baddest Marine he'd ever seen. "Let anybody try to mess with me now," he boasted. "I'll show them what a Cybermarine can do!"

Sweeney looked around as he led his squad. Their company was one of many scouring for any residual Shardie activity. Although the place seemed to have been abandoned, the entire first wave had been wiped out within moments of setting down.

Four bombardments and forays later the Corps began locating the hidden pockets of tripods and calling down the wrath of hell. In other words; Cybermarines. No unenhanced Marine wanted to test their limitations by direct confrontation with the Shardies. The things seemed as brutally effective as ever.

Rofulous Four was the same as the other colonies; collapsed structures, piles of sand and wood everywhere, and not a single living soul. He had been somewhat disappointed that they'd run into no aliens either. Sweeney knew he was now, unlike the MULE he'd worn in his last encounter, faster, stronger, and more capable of doing considerable damage to any enemy he encountered. Better, his enhanced senses put him on equal footing with the damned things. This time he would push that silver shit back down their throats.

But first he had to find one.

He noticed the buildings' residual heat signature was just a fraction of a degree above ambient. Was that significant? Did it mean the aliens were near? He passed the data along to the officer from MI while he scanned the surrounding forest.

"Chief, take point and perimeter with your squad," the captain ordered.

Sweeney's squad quickly sorted out assignments and areas without his guidance. It was always better to spread their forces whenever entering new territory. *Good men, or what used to be men,* he mused, *but better now they'd been enhanced.*

"Move ahead a klick," the captain ordered. They were nearly three kilometers from the recovery ship now, a shade too far to retreat should any problems occur.

Sweeney's heads-up showed the bright dots of the squad approaching his position. The blue ones were combat Marines, the green were his squad, and the red dots, the cumbersome MULEs. Two of the blue dots remained at the ruins.

"Let's search the next sector," the captain ordered. Immediately, Sweeney's display dots dispersed into a rainbow arc. Each segment contained a cyber, a MULE, and a pair of specialists. Closest to him was the bright golden dot that was the captain.

The company spiraled outward for a distance of a thousand meters without finding any sign of aliens. That could be good or bad. The captain's basic tactic was to bend his arc inward as they progressed, much like using a seine to gather the fish of Sweeney's childhood. "Huh, where did that memory come from?" he wondered.

"Let's move," the captain ordered as his fishermen swept for deadly fish.

The center of the company's search arc had advanced half a kilometer with another half to go to reach the edge of their quadrant. Arc ends were less than two hundred meters apart. There had been no sign of aliens since they left the ruins.

"Shards!" someone yelled. Fire opened. An eruption of shining forms rushed through the trees. There was a hissing noise as specialists unleashed their electronic weapons. They could barely be heard beneath the thundering roar of the intense firepower.

Sweeney fought to reorganize and protect the captain. He called for targeting to saturate the area.

"To me," the captain ordered. "Comms, get the data back to command—now!"

One of the tripods ran directly at Sweeney, probably after the captain, he thought as he fired a full clip from his repeater into the alien machine. It had little effect. He shifted and blocked the attacker with his arms.

It was like trying to wrestle with a stone statue. Sweeney kicked at the legs, pulled on its chest, and finally fell to embrace the legs and trip it. All the time, the captain and the others were firing, firing, firing at the thing he held so tightly. He could barely feel the impacts as the rounds shredded his uniform and penetrated his body.

The last thing he saw was a silver waterfall.

Chapter Thirteen

BEN STEPPED OUTSIDE INTO THE PREDAWN DIM AND SHIVERED IN THE early autumn chill. Vicky had taken his blanket during the night and had wrapped herself into a ball.. Somewhere a squirrel chattered a challenge. A light mist cover seeped through the forest around Landing, hiding the ruins of Greg's barn.

The sudden cold snap was unexpected. Yesterday had been balmy, cool, but not unusually so at this time of year. Typically the change from summer's warmth to winter's wrath was a process of progressively cooler nights and days.

He didn't know if the cold wind presaged an early winter or was simply a freakish blast. They were still weeks away from leaving. The gardens needed harvesting and Vicky hadn't finished stocking the larder.

Tony emerged from the rude shelter they'd built. It was sufficient shelter for summer but hardly sturdy enough for winter weather. "Feels cold enough to snow," he complained and shivered. "Didn't expect this."

"Kat all right?" Ben asked. She'd been restless for days, unable to find a comfortable position to sit, lie, or even stand. The pregnancy was hard on her and there were no modern comforts to alleviate her suffering.

"Tossed and turned all night," Tony replied. "I hope nothing's wrong."

Ben bit his tongue. Despite all the warnings the three adults had provided, Kat nevertheless managed to get pregnant. Or maybe it was Tony's fault, forgetting to remember Ben's warnings in the heat of the moment, so to speak. Regardless of who was to blame it was reckless to allow it to happen given their circumstances, and to make matters worse Kat and Tony hadn't mentioned it until well into the pregnancy.

"I think she'll be fine," Ben tried to reassure Tony. "Women have been having babies since the beginning of time and most of that in conditions similar to ours."

"She threw up yesterday," Tony said. "While she was skinning the blues."

"Maybe their smell," Ben guessed.

Kat had become averse to some food, while ravenous for others. Joseph said her mother had been the same way when she was carrying so it probably meant little.

The lack of medical help extended beyond Kat's problems. They'd had to deal with no end of fevers, rashes, and innumerable scrapes and bruises over the past few years. Vicky had discovered some leaves that helped reduce pain when chewed, but whether there was any actual alleviation was doubtful. Ben suspected their value was mental trickery since the leaves didn't affect him at all.

"Looks like it's going to be a cloudy day," Tony said with a glance to the east.

"Good fishing then," Ben replied. The fish always seemed more plentiful on cloudy days, something to do with the light.

There was a sudden cry from inside the shelter. "Come quick," Vicky shouted a moment later. "It's Kat. I need help!"

Ben and Tony charged inside. Kat was spitting up onto the bedding. Her face was grey. Sweat poured off of her as she shivered. "It hurts," she said holding her stomach and rocking back and forth. "It hurts so much." She gagged again but nothing came up.

"Was it the fish?" Ben asked without thinking and got a glare from Vicky as she mopped Kat's brow. Tony put his arms around Kat and made comforting sounds.

"Ben, get a fire going," Vicky ordered. "Make some hot tea. She needs to get something in her stomach."

Ben ran into Joseph as he left the shelter. "What's the matter?"

"It's Kat," Ben answered hurriedly. "She's having some problems."

There was a scream from within the shelter.

"Get some goddamned water," Vicky yelled. "Tony, keep working on that fire." The screaming continued as Kat thrashed, pounding the blanket with balled fists.

Suddenly she stopped and groaned. "It's coming, it's coming!"

Vicky raised the blanket and saw Kat's dilation. "Tony, I'll need the knife. Make sure it's sharp and clean." She'd never cut a birth cord before, but how hard could it be?

There was something wrong with the baby's head as it emerged. "Should it be blue like that?" an obviously panicked Tony asked.

When more of the child emerged Vicky saw the cord wrapped around its throat. "I don't think that's supposed to..." Whatever she was about to say stopped as the baby slid smoothly into her waiting hands. She unwrapped the cord and tried to get the baby to breathe.

"Is it all right?" a weary Kat whispered. "Tell me it's all right."

But Vicky could not.

They'd buried the baby's body in Kat's favorite glen, where she'd sometimes sat and watched the setting sun. Tony held the tiny bundle, wrapped in Pre's silk blouse, as Joseph and Ben finished digging a small grave.

"Someone should say something," Vicky whispered.

Ben wondered if everyone's heart was as heavy as his. The baby would have been a terrible burden, drain too much of their energy, and probably ruin their lives. But… damn!

Joseph must have been as affected although he just nodded, his cheeks glossy with tears. Those might have been for his daughter's pain and probably for the grandchild he'd never have.. He fliched when Vicky awkwardly patted his shoulder.

Ben struggled to think of something appropriate, cleared his throat and said, "Rest in peace little one? Sorry you never stood a chance to be born? Sorry you never had a chance of knowing Tony and Kat…Sorry we couldn't do more for your mother, but maybe it's better this way; not much of a future anymore…"

"That's pretty damn cruel," Tony cried with tears streaming down his cheeks.

"But true," Vicky added. Ben thought she was about to launch into another lecture on the foolishness of childbearing and shook his head. "Not now, Vicky. Not now."

Ben had no doubt winter was approaching, despite the temperate weather. The nightly temperature had continued to drop and the winds had grown brutal. The others bore the chill in stoic silence, but Kat constantly complained of being cold, no matter how many layers of clothes she wore or the number of blankets piled on her. The constant reminder of winter's approach only increased his tension. They should have set sail by now.

"I don't think warm weather's coming back," he said. The cold wind had been picking up since morning and whistling through the many gaps in the shelter's walls. "We need to leave soon."

Joseph shook his head. "Not until Kat improves. She's still too weak." Clearly feeling he needed an ally, he turned to Vicky. "Don't you agree? Kat needs to get her strength back."

"We *need* to leave. We're nearly a month late and this," Ben waved his arm, "won't get any better. How cold do you think she'll be if we get trapped here by the winter storms? We have to leave as soon as this one passes."

"We shouldn't take the risk," Joseph insisted. "Kat can't take the cold and wet in her condition. I'm sure Tony will back me up on this."

"I do," Tony said. "Joseph's right: Kat's too delicate. Even bundled up she can't get warm. What's she going to do on an open boat where we can't even have a fire?"

A sudden gust of wind drove sand and grit against the walls of the shelter. Chill drops of rain followed. Ben ground his teeth in frustration. "That's going to be snow and ice if we wait any longer," he shouted.

"We wait," Tony insisted. "Please, just another few days."

Joseph started to add more wood to the fire.

"Be careful," Vicky objected.

"But Kat needs the warmth."

"I know she does, but it's dangerous to let the fire get too big in this small space."

.Joseph grumbled and put the firewood back on the pile.

That night the full fury of the autumn storm struck, driving heavy rains against the shelter's wooden sides. Kat shivered as Tony held her tight for warmth. Despite Vicky's warnings, Joseph put more wood on the fire, earning a frown from Tony, but no objection. A gust of wind briefly fanned the flames and threw dancing shadows.

Ben settled down beside Vicky and whispered, "We really need to leave. I don't like the signs. You know how bad the sea gets this time of year. We'll be warmer further north of here."

"It'll take too many weeks to find warmer weather," Vicky replied quietly. "That's at least a half month of cold camps and open seas. I'm not sure Kat could take it."

Ben frowned. "And the later we wait the worse it will be. Maybe Joseph and you should go ahead on *Summer's Breeze*? Tony, Kat, and I can follow on *Day's End* when Kat's stronger."

"I don't think it's a good idea to separate," Vicky protested. "We have to stay together so we can help each other."

"In a few days, then," Ben insisted.

Kat's scream woke Ben to the smell of smoke and the glare of flames. Tony was beating at Kat's flaming blanket. Embers flew everywhere, driven by the wind whipping through the shelter's open flap. Kat struggled to free herself as another ember ignited Joseph's abandoned blanket. Ben looked about. Where was Joseph?

Tongues of fire began to climb the walls. "Get everything out of here," Ben shouted, gathering up as much of their sleeping material as he could and tossing it outside. Vicky started throwing clothing and baskets toward the exit, while Tony continued fighting the fire.

Kat huddled just inside the opening, as if unwilling to face the storm despite the fierce fire.

The wind-driven flames burned through the roof and turned the shelter into a raging furnace. Tony abandoned his efforts and carried Kat into the heavy rain. Vicky followed with an armload of clothing.

Ben hesitated, still looking for Joseph, as he gathered whatever he could reach before the fire's intensity became unbearable. He struggled to breathe in the enveloping smoke as he tried to escape and fell forward.

The roof began to collapse as vines holding the trusses in place burned through. One of the trusses fell, setting Ben's shirt afire. He couldn't feel his left hand and he didn't have enough strength to pull his arm away from the burning truss. I'm going to die here, he thought a moment before someone pulled him into the blessedly cold rain.

In the sodden morning Vicky fed Ben some of her weeds to alleviate his pain. Feeling had gradually returned to his badly burned arm, but not the strength. "Give it time, that will come back as you recover," she promised.

Ben felt light-headed, as if the ground beneath him were unstable. "We're on *Day's End*?" he croaked.

"Only place I could keep you dry and dress your burns," she answered and patted his good shoulder.

"Joseph?" he croaked.

"He swears he closed the flap when he went to the latrine, but I think he still feels responsible."

"Kat?"

"Tony has her in the cabin." Ben knew there would be no warmth there, only shelter from the driving rain.

"Good thing you got the boats partially loaded or we would have lost everything. Bad enough we lost what we did, but we can replace things later."

He grasped at that. "So we're leaving?"

"What choice do we have?" Vicky placed another wad of weed in his mouth. "Chew this and sleep. Joseph, Tony, and I have a lot of work to do to get these boats moving."

Chapter Fourteen

WE'RE UNDER ATTACK," THE CAPTAIN CALLED OUT. "HARKINS, GET your ass back to recovery!"

Private Thaddeus Soffut tried not to drop the sample bag during their panicked headlong retreat. "Careful there," Lieutenant Harkins barked as they broke through some dense growth.

Earlier in the day, Harkins had found dozens of smooth crystalline pebbles in the remains of six stone foundations. The ruins were like others they'd encountered: nothing but rubble and lumber. Every trace of metal was gone—nails, screws, brackets, and buckets, farm implements and tools, cook pots and frying pans. Their theft of metal was catholic in scope. It mattered little if it had been copper or iron, aluminum or titanium. Every trace was missing.

The captain had ordered the lieutenant to examine the ruins while everyone else checked the perimeter. Lieutenant Harkins was one of the intelligence-gathering agents trying to learn everything they could about the aliens. Everybody tolerated Harkins, who wasn't a *real* Marine. Hell, he didn't even carry a rifle, just a ton of cameras, recorders, and comm gear.

"The screw-up will make sure you don't do something stupid," the captain said when he told Soffut to stay. "And if you don't know what stupid is, then ask Corporal Soffut. He's been busted to corporal three times."

"I deserve to be fighting those fucking, silver-shit-spewing aliens!" Soffut swore as he staggered behind the lieutenant, who seemed pretty fit for a desk jockey. "I shouldn't be running away like a freaking coward!"

"Keep up!" the lieutenant shouted. "And don't drop the bag." Soffut clutched the pouch. It made a sound like broken glass every time his right foot hit the ground. Well...not *exactly* like broken glass—more musical, definitely glass-like.

Were the Shardies really chasing them? The sounds of battle had faded. The link to the captain was silent. All he could hear was his own heaving breath and Harkin's pounding feet.

When they first saw the pebbles they'd both noticed how the sunlight seemed to fill them with coruscating rainbows, giving them the appearance of sparkling jewels. He reached down to pick one up.

"Careful there, corporal," Harkins warned. "These things could be a Shardie trap." The lieutenant was right to be worried about a possible trap. One squad of the ill-fated sixty-fourth had been examining one of the supposedly inactive alien tripods when it suddenly came to life and shit silver all over them. Two other tripods that had hidden nearby took out the rest of the squad. Luckily, their combat imagers had been running to record the encounter, that is, until the silver erupted. Nobody survived.

"Aw crap, Lieutenant. I hardly think a bunch of pretty little rocks are any kind of threat." Instead of one, he picked up a handful and shook them in his glove. "They're just pretty rocks."

Harkins was still wary. He wouldn't get within two meters of the pebbles. "Yeah…Shardie rocks! Command says they might be important and wants them for analysis, but I'm not letting my guard down."

Soffut dumped some trash out of his ammo can and unfolded his trenching tool, ready to scoop the pebbles in, when Harkins stopped him. "I don't think you should use the shovel or can. There's got to be a reason there's no metal left and maybe these pebbles have something to do with it."

Soffut sighed, shook out a plastic ration pack and began picking up pebbles, one after another. "Jesus, this is going to take all day," he complained after he'd collected a dozen.

That's when he heard the captain's warning and the weapons started hammering.

Harkins had started toward the ship as soon they had heard the warning. "Move! And don't drop those samples, Soffut," he yelled.

Soffut glimpsed bright flashes and, moments later, heard the impact of exploding ordnance amid the ratcheting roar of heavy M160 repeaters in the distance. It irked him that he'd been stuck with the lieutenant from Intelligence instead of being on the front line. He should be in combat, not helping Harkins gather more of those damn glistening pebbles from the ruins. The sound meant the aliens were only seconds behind. There was no time to secure the bag, so he clutched it and ran.

"Split up," Harkins shouted and took off on an angle to the right, his equipment looking awkward as it swayed on his back as bad as a full combat pack. Soffut wondered why the guy didn't ditch it so he could run faster.

With that idea, he released his own twenty-kilo pack and continued racing toward the recovery ship.

The crashing sounds increased, drawing closer as he crested a rise. Off to his right he heard a scream and saw a bright flash of light. Harkins? Hard to tell. Soffut had his own worries.

An immense tripod appeared just ten meters behind him and the ship was still too far. His foot hit a root. He pitched forward and slammed the ground hard. Pain lanced up his left side. He braced himself for the Shardie's attack.

But nothing happened.

He looked up. The tripod had stopped moving. Soffut slowly rose. It still didn't move. He stood. "You are one ugly mother," he whispered. No reaction. Had the tripod run out of gas? He stepped forward. It retreated. Stranger yet.

Suddenly, the thing turned and headed back the way it had come. In the distance, Soffut glimpsed more advancing tripods. He turned and raced for the ship, the bag of stones still gripped tight in his hand.

He hoped they had the ship on hot standby.

Six months later Soffut's pebbles arrived in Leonard Lansington's laboratory after passing through a chain of intermediate labs, all of which had puzzled over the pretty rocks before passing them upstairs.

The report that accompanied the collection was a fanciful tale of how a lowly Marine private had singlehandedly driven off a Shardie attacker in order to deliver the pebbles. Since there were no other survivors of the attack, his was the only account they had. Many were skeptical, owing to Soffut's successive demotions for drunkenness, laziness, and general inability to follow orders.

Not exactly your ideal Marine to be sure.

But the description of the metal-free ruins matched other reports. Lansington wondered if, as early accounts had suggested, the pebbles were a byproduct of whatever weapon laid waste to the colonies? He had no idea of what that weapon might be, nor had anyone else guessed. There were mysteries upon mysteries here, it seemed, and none of them offered insight on the Shardies.

The samples appeared to be nothing more than inert pieces of crystal somehow worn to smoothness. All were oval in cross section, flatter on top and bottom. Their longitudinal and latitudinal axes differed by no more than a margin of plus or minus fifteen percent. All were as smooth as polished river rocks, but water wear and other mechanical grinding mechanisms were not possible. They reportedly had been found in ruined structures at every colony that had been examined, across various planets. Given that, it was unlikely they were naturally occurring.

Leonard considered his small sample. Hardly more than a handful remained of the original number after passing through so many hands. They varied in size, but the dimensional differences between them were so slight that only precise measurements had revealed the differences; less than a millimeter along the longer axis.

X-ray bombardment showed that they contained planar cracks that propagated for nanometers and stopped at the fractured face of another plane. It was those fractures that gave rise to their rainbow appearance. No two that he'd imaged seemed to be structured precisely alike, but all followed a similar morphology.

The samples neither exhibited piezo crystal-like characteristics nor were they affected by mechanical shocks, pressure, heat, or cold. His search for a resonant frequency surprisingly shattered one into a shower of dust. Pursuing that feature, further tests revealed that the resonant frequency was between thirty and forty megahertz. That seemed a useless bit of data, but he noted it anyway.

Spectrographic analysis of the dust showed that the pebble had been composed mostly of silicon, but also contained trace amounts of iron, ytterbium, rhodium, and platinum.

One day was all the time he could devote to this puzzle as higher priority analytical requests rolled in. Lansington wrote that he would be interested in obtaining more samples, put the few remaining pebbles back into storage as one more unresolved mystery, and went on to more interesting work pertinent to the war effort.

Chapter Fifteen

THE ASSEMBLY ROOM WAS COLD AND STERILE. AT THE FAR END STOOD A cybermarine. It was slightly inclined and connected by thousands of wires to an armature covered with mechanical arms, legs, and even a head with a half dozen lenses.

The cyber's brains had been dissected, diced, and turned into code for the gel "brains" of another cyber in an adjacent room. That was something Admiral Jones had viewed once and had no desire to repeat the experience.

"It's not activated yet," Doctor Mores said when he noticed Major General Thoss staring at the armature. "Those are just remote units. We'll use them to familiarize the inductee with his new augmentations. It is only after he learns how to use his new motor skills that we enable the equivalent parts of his new body."

Thoss had seen other cybers being activated. He watched partially as expiation for his guilt in approving the conversions and partly to give each new cybermarine a morale boost. He wanted each volunteer to know that they had earned the respect of the highest level of command.

That was his primary motivation, but it was also bloody neat to see a converted Marine realize the awesome capabilities and power of their new body.

A cybermarine's awakening was like witnessing a birth.

General Thoss had been brooding over the latest reports. He'd quickly learned that, after every promotion, choices became more difficult, and not only because of working over a broader canvas. The difference between the decisions he'd learned to make when he was a colonel and the ones he faced now were qualitatively different. Now he had to deal with issues of economics, logistics, politics, and of why the hell it took so damn long to get something done once a decision had been made.

He breezed through the reports, reading the summaries and ignoring the dense references and attachments. *My staff can sort through this stuff,* he thought idly, before realizing that they already had: These were the issues they thought important enough to require his attention.

He flagged a few items for later discussion, signed a half-dozen others, and sent the rest of them to be handled by Brigadier Gould. That's what a deputy was for, wasn't it?

The reports had been grim, filled with news of insufficient civilian evacuations and Capitol ships lost in the brutal battle at Ginck's Follt. Worse, none of the damned alien bastards had been captured.

As usual.

He ran his hand through his thinning hair: Capturing one of the Shardie ships had become the Navy's primary objective. But every failed attempt had cost ships and lives. The Shardies were implacable and simply surviving an encounter was considered a success.

The Shardie ships were unbelievably maneuverable, accelerating at rates far in excess of any Naval vessel. Capturing an intact ship might reveal its secrets and allow Earth's forces to gain some sort of parity. But there had been only one disabled ship and that without intact drives. Every other damaged Shardie ship made a suicide run, turning them into scattered bits of crystal and…other things.

Thoss felt a shiver of revulsion at the images of people woven bloodily into the guts of the Shardie ship. Since that discovery, the overriding policy had been to deny the enemy any victims through evacuation and other means.

There were too few Navy ships and too few Marines. Ground-based defenses wouldn't help. Most were little more than police forces. Even a full regiment of Marines would be as useful as a toilet paper umbrella in a rainstorm.

He hoped for better news at every dismal briefing, but the facts stayed distressingly the same. If they couldn't stop the Shardies' implacable advance, it was clear that the human race would end.

Things were no better on the diplomatic side: You can't negotiate when the enemy failed to communicate, failed to express intentions or purpose, and attacked with insane ferocity. Was it hatred? If they shared that sort of unbridled emotion, then humanity might find an opening to understanding. But they had given no sign. Attack, attack, attack seemed to be their entire repertoire.

And the humans were losing the war.

"Status update in five minutes, sir," his aide swept everything clear except the précis of the proposal from the conversion team, allowing him a glimpse of what would be discussed so he would not look uninformed.

That had been a problem with every advance, he never had enough time to grasp the whole of anything. Days were filled with brief, but imperfect summaries of serious matters that required command decisions. Were it not for the analysts' summarizing complex issues, he'd not be able to function. As it was, he was forced to rely on possibly hidden biases and perceptions that made them appear proper, logical, and necessary. And sometimes, misleading.

He sighed. What he wouldn't give to delve deeply into an issue and develop his own conclusions. He knew he'd never get that opportunity and, even if he did, he would probably lack the knowledge needed for a proper analysis. He was damned if he did and damned if he didn't. That was the curse of command.

He entered the briefing room.

"We're resurrecting a copy of Captain David Savage," Mores stood beside the cyber's inert body. "This is our latest body design; lighter but more rugged." He nodded to where technicians fiddled with the armature. "To Savage, it will seem as if he just came out of surgery, awakening for the *first* time. He will not be aware of his earlier…um... resurrection."

Thoss read the briefing sheet. *Savage had become a cyber in 2932, self-destructed in 2935, and was awarded a posthumous promotion that same year.* He hoped that someone on the command staff had attended Savage's funeral. It would have been the least they could have done as they buried his true remains. "Will he be able to speak?"

Mores nodded. "We've trained him to operate his vocal cords, although they really aren't..."

"Spare me the technical details. All I want to know is if he can answer questions."

"Yes, but it will be a synthesized voice and not his..."

Colonel Mills tapped her foot impatiently. "Let's see it then. We only have ten more minutes."

"I didn't realize we were so time constrained," Doctor Mores complained. "We need to run a few more checks before…"

"Checks you should have done before the general got here, Doctor," Mills cut in. "Turn the damn thing on, for God's sake." A moment later she blushed through her scars and mumbled. "I didn't mean that, sir. Honest to God, I didn't think..."

"I understand," Thoss answered. He was a bit surprised at seeing Mills reveal a spark of humanity, but knew why she'd slipped. It was not easy to think of a cyber as anything but a "thing."

That it was also a living human being could too easily be ignored.

"Sir." A young analyst was standing beside Doctor Hector Mores, his R&D chief, when Thoss entered the briefing room. She was of medium height, broad of shoulder, and had a rather nice ass, he mused as she took her seat.

Thoss sat. "Please begin."

The woman cleared her throat. "I won't try to soft pedal this, sir, but we've determined that the Shardies have been generating captives."

Brigadier Gould looked surprised. Obviously he had not read the file. "How the hell can they be *generating* humans?"

"Probably the old-fashioned way," his aide, Colonel Mills guessed.

The woman nodded. "It's their brains they want, sir, not knowledge or experiences. A young child's brain is probably best."

"That's disgusting." Gould's distaste was evident. "Breeding humans like animals? Has this been confirmed?"

Mores handed him a folder marked TOP SECRET in fiery red block letters. "This contains the analysis of the human fragments found in the wreckage at the End Point battle." As Gould hurriedly scanned the contents, Mores continued, "Analysis indicates that the fragments belonged to individuals who were not captured at Jeaux."

"Are our databases that detailed, Doctor?" Gould demanded. "Couldn't the fragments have come from other captives? If the samples were degraded by exposure to vacuum they could provide false indicators."

Thoss said nothing, allowing his deputy to be the foil for the moment. He was certain that someone as careful as Mores wouldn't bring this to their attention without verifying the facts two, three, or more times.

"They only used *fresh* samples, sir," the woman answered grimly. "Developing information is not pretty. Yes, we're positive, sir. The immaturity of the chunks," she blushed. "Excuse me, sir. I meant tissue, not... well, not what I said."

"I understand," Thoss answered. "We all get inured to reality after a while. Please continue."

She recovered her composure. "The recovered samples indicate that their owners had been born after the invasions started. They had strong matches to DNA of the original Jeaux colonists. The range of ages, based on their telomere lengths, ranged from three to five years. We conclude that the breeding program started soon after the Shardies obtained their first captives."

"It's horrifying!" Gould slapped the folder closed. "Living, breathing children are more than components. Breeding people is sinful."

Mores nodded. "I don't disagree that it's sinful, sir, but you've got to admit it's a pretty smart use of scarce resources."

Gould glared, clearly on the edge of anger. "I can't believe you approve, Doctor."

Mores didn't flinch. "No, I was merely commenting on the Shard's efficiency. When you're in a war you use everything you have to win and it looks like that's what they've done."

Gould wasn't buying it. "Your attitude makes me want to puke. I expected more of you."

The doctor smiled, but there was no humor in it. "I'm being realistic, sir. It is what it is."

Thoss spoke up before the argument escalated any further. "What's the proposal, Colonel?"

"As you've observed at the last weekly update, General," his aide began. "Our volunteer conversion rate has continued to fall." An incomprehensible graph blossomed. "The majority of our wounded Marines are choosing radical rehabilitation instead of becoming cybermarines."

"Probably because of advances in medicine," Thoss mused. "I don't blame them."

"There's still about thirty percent of eligible wounded who chose to die rather than live, even with advanced prosthetics," Mills continued. "Given the nature of their injuries, I'm not surprised. The amount of prosthetics these few need would make them more machine than human."

Colonel Mills caught his attention. "General, unless we do something we are going to be in real trouble. Our attrition rate exceeds production and our cyber forces are seriously close to being understaffed."

As if he didn't already know that. Referring to the steady numbers of suicide missions they'd sent Marines on as the "attrition rate" demeaned the substance of what happened. Marines, men and women, were dying in increasing numbers.

Thoss looked at Mills's vacuum-scarred face and noted the barely noticeable strain of her facial muscles, the tenseness of her body, and the white of her fingers grasping the edge of the table. Clearly there was more to this briefing than a dry recounting of statistics. "Just how serious has it become?"

"We've only produced half the number as last year," Doctor Mores answered. "One-fifty, and the trend continues downward."

"We expended two hundred cybers in the same time period last year," Mills added.

"Killed, you mean," Gould barked. "Those were Marines! They made the ultimate sacrifices, and did so after already having proven themselves, so let's not use bullshit words like 'cybers' and 'expended.'"

"I agree," Thoss said. "We all can get rather removed from reality when we deal with statistics. Please show a bit more respect."

"I've been in battles, sir," Mills replied calmly. "I've worked with augmented Marines more than a few times." She looked directly at Gould. "Don't presume that I don't understand the sacrifices and difficult choices they made when they became cybers. It's just that I find abstraction easier to deal with when hard choices are necessary."

"Choices, Colonel? " Gould responded. "I assume that you have a reason for bringing up our declining strength?"

Thoss knew she was merely bringing the matter to their attention with that nice ass of hers and... He mentally kicked himself for even thinking that way. She was an officer under his command and any relationship, no matter how innocent, was improper. Why he should keep thinking about her when there were a lot more cute young women around mystified him. She was well beyond the cute stage, but damn; she did have a nice bottom.

Another graph, equally as dense and incomprehensible appeared.

"You have to understand exactly what we need," Mores began. "The cyber has to retain enough mental capability to function, enough intelligence to understand the mission, and a dedicated sense of purpose."

"We know all of that," Gould said. "So what?"

The doctor coughed apologetically. "That's what everybody's been told and, as far as it goes, is perfectly correct. What is not widely publicized is that we don't transfer all of a Marine's memories. The gel brains only have so much capacity and we have to include only practical elements."

"But the rest of them isn't," Gould added.

"It's made clear to those who volunteer," the young woman apologized.

"Each cybermarine is a man that's died," Gould said.

"Yes, we only use one Marine per cyber," Mores added. "It is an *artificial* restriction. Without that restriction I could produce many cybers from a single volunteer."

Gould grimaced. "Just run off a few more copies; right?"

"It is possible," Mores confirmed.

"You can't be seriously considering making copies!" Gould came to his feet. "Your idea is disgraceful; an obscenity as horrifying as those poor souls linked to the Shardie ships. We'd be just like the fucking aliens."

"We've preserved partial scans of over two thousand volunteers," the young woman said softly. "It would be a dishonor to destroy them."

"Also wasteful of resources," Doctor Mores added dryly. "By using our inventory we could cut the cost of the hideously expensive conversion program in half."

Brigadier Gould shook his head. "More bullshit. I think it's horrid. How would you feel about being stamped out like license plates, for God's sake?"

Mores didn't flinch. "As far as each resurrected individual is concerned they'd be unique, with no awareness that other copies had preceded them. They wouldn't feel as if they had been used, other than as they volunteered to be."

Mills spoke, "General, look on this as a way our brave Marines can continue to serve, giving them the opportunity to continue the battle, to honor their commitment to the Corps."

Gould bristled. "That's a nice sentiment, Colonel, but would making copies be right? If each copy is a fully realized individual, then sending them to another death would be no more morally defensible than with any other human."

"It would be far more efficient," Mores replied. "I can produce ten augmented Marines in the time it now takes to convert one. Further, without the extensive surgery, recovery, costs of transport, and maintenance costs that keeps the wounded alive long enough to process, we'd double our production without an attendant increase in cost. It would also relieve the pressure on our inflow stream."

Gould stormed from the room.

"The captain is ready, sir," Mores interrupted Thoss' reflections. "You can talk to him now." Despite Mores' supposed objectivity it was obvious that he didn't think of the cyber as an object.

"Yes, I'd like to talk to 'him'." He stepped closer to the microphone. "Captain Savage? This is General Thoss. How do you feel?"

"Fine, sir. Ready to do my duty, sir!" The response was crisp, his eagerness to serve obvious by inflection and emphasis. "Er, did you get promoted, sir?" Mores jerked.

Thoss had forgotten that he'd only been a Colonel when Savage had first been converted. "Yes, recently," he replied and saw Mores's relief. "Do you remember who you are?" He'd almost said "what." Have to be careful about that.

"Captain David Savage, sir. Serial number 030586734..."

Thoss didn't let him finish. "I meant, do you remember how you got here?"

There was a pause before Savage answered. "I was almost dead when they offered me a chance to serve, sir. I was so pissed—excuse me, sir—so angry that I wanted to get back at the bastards that...sorry, sir...at the aliens we were fighting."

Gould slapped the table. "Our volunteers' remains are not objects. If we use them this way we lose whatever moral superiority we have over the enemy."

"And where has ethics gotten us so far?" Thoss shot back. Gould was becoming tiresome. Admittedly, he'd felt the same when the idea had first been broached. But Mores and Mills were right. They'd made a promise to each volunteer, a bond that had not yet been broken. It was a bond of honor, of remaining true to the oath that they took when they chose to serve.

Mills defended the proposal. "If we do as Doctor Mores suggests we'd have battalions of cybers. Hell, we could send an entire regiment if we chose." She had obviously thought deeply about the proposal's implications. "Sir."

Mores stuttered with excitement. "We don't have to limit ourselves to cybers. A human configuration is highly inefficient. We could as easily install them in rugged machines—tanks, ships or..." his voice tapered off as he realized the line he'd crossed.

"Yes," Gould said bitterly. "Put them in ships. Just like the fucking Shardies."

Mores defended himself. "But these are volunteers, not unwilling captives or innocents bred for the purpose. That's a moral difference, General. It's no different from giving a Marine a bigger weapon or driving an assault vehicle. It would enormously expand our combat capabilities."

"But still..." Gould was unrelenting. "We can't permit this abomination. There's an ethical principle involved!"

Mores smiled. "Yes, sir, I agree that we can stand on our principles. We can also ask the Shardies to chisel that on our tombstones."

Gould looked as if he were about to explode.

Mores addressed Thoss. "Sir, General, you need to approve this program. We've spent the majority of our wealth on evacuations and recoveries because we haven't enough defensive ground forces." He looked at Gould. "Sir, this isn't a matter of ethics or economics; it's about survival. We desperately need these copies."

Thoss could not deny the appeal of having a large army of supermen at his disposal. Instead of parsing cybers out piecemeal, they could load entire transports to mount massive assaults that they hadn't had either the power or opportunity to pursue.

"I agree," he said before Gould could argue any further. "The brutal truth is that we are losing the war. We have to do something, however distasteful it might be."

As his words died away Thoss wished this decision had landed on someone else's watch, someone with more balls, someone with less consideration of the long-term effects.

Someone without principles.

Thoss knew it mattered little that the only reason for the original conversions was to give seriously wounded Marines another chance to serve, just as David Savage had so strongly stated.

The captain's answers proved he was still filled with fighting fury and dedicated to his role, despite the fact that he was unknowingly a copy of the other Savages who had already died.

But Mores' proposal could change that. He imagined that he would still feel somewhat guilty about each suicide assignment, but that guilt would be mitigated by the knowledge that that same Marine could be resurrected to fight another day as if it were for the first time. If this program went forward he'd no longer be sending men to a final death but giving them the opportunity to fight again and again, and yet again in iterations beyond imagining.

The concept was both exciting and horrifying. Pursuing this program might help win the war, but at what cost? What were the long-term implications of this technology?

He turned to Gould. "Charlie, you called these additional conversions sinful. When did you get religion?"

Gould turned away. "It wasn't a religious objection. It's about ethics, a matter of respecting human beings as individuals instead of pieces on a chessboard."

"Nonsense. We think of all our Marines the same way when we plan missions. They're *all* just pieces on a game board at our level, not individuals. These duplicates wouldn't be individuals at all, they'd just be copies of men who volunteered to serve honorably and to the extent of their capabilities, capabilities, I should remind you, that are well beyond those of any ordinary Marine."

"They might be copies, but as far as each Marine is concerned, they are the original, with all the hopes and dreams of their precursors." He leaned forward, intent on pressing his point. "I know they all say that they'd fight for life just like every other cyber and die knowing that they'd given their best. Those copies are damn well human where it matters. But we need to honor our social contract, not treat Marines like disposables."

Gould's appeal was irrelevant, not when it was a matter of how they could survive in the face of an overwhelming force. "I agree with much of what you say, but there are more important issues: our declining strength, the lack of any progress on the political side, the Navy's reduced capability. We've got our backs to the wall, Charlie."

"We need to put a stop this," Gould insisted. "Tell Mores that we'll have no part of this."

Thoss understood Gould's objections, but he had to do what was best. Sharp and capable as he was, Brigadier Gould was still his subordinate. "That decision is mine, Charlie. That decision is mine."

"And why did you choose to become a cybermarine?" Thoss continued his questioning. "You were given other options."

There was no hesitation. "You mean death or life as a cripple, sir?" Savage snapped back. "Not a great choice, but even so I'd rather be helping win the war than sitting on the sidelines waiting for the Shards. No, sir, there wasn't any other choice, as far as I'm concerned. Serving as a cybermarine gives me purpose."

"That's very noble, Captain, but what about enjoying life; fishing, hunting, playing ball with your kids..." Thoss stopped. There was no chance a cyber such as Savage would ever have had kids. "...or enjoying a fine meal?" he finished with nary a pause and realized how stupid those last words sounded.

"Those things are for civilians, sir. I've been given this new life and I'm damn well going to use it to kill as many of the Shards as I can. I'm a cybermarine, sir. I'll do my duty."

Mills motioned. It was time to leave. "Thank you, Captain Savage. You've answered my question."

Savage's answers had shown Thoss that Mills had been right. The proposal meant more than making copies. It would allow the preservation of that sense of honor, that sense of mission, that desire to serve to continue beyond death that was at the core of every volunteer. Each copy would be a resurrection of all that was noble and good. It would let each Marine continue to be true to their oath. Those who made the hard choice to become cybers were those whose sense of purpose and dedication exceeded all others.

Copies they might become, but they were more than human in all that mattered.

"I'm going to officially confirm my approval, Charlie," Thoss said to the appalled Gould. "Repugnant and sinful it might be, but by damn it's the right thing to do." He had, like Savage, made the hard choice. "It's a matter of survival."

"But at the cost of our souls, sir," Gould replied angrily. "At the cost of our souls."

Chapter Sixteen

SUMMER WAS FADING AS THEY PREPARED YET AGAIN FOR ANOTHER OF their annual voyages to Tower Bridge. Vicky was helping Ben as he maintained *Day's End*, when he started going on about searching for survivors again.

She cut him off, having long ago lost patience. "It's ridiculous to think that anybody else could have survived after—what has it been? Ten, no, *eleven* years?—let alone that you'll be able to find them."

"But we've managed to survive," Ben shot back. "Who's to say others haven't? I'm not giving up. There were settlements north of the equator."

It was a familiar argument, rehashed every damn time he wanted to take to sea. Even when he went fishing Vicky had to insist that he take Joseph or Tony along "for safety's sake," just to make sure he came back. As if Ben hadn't managed quite well alone in all of his years on the water.

"I prefer, have *always* preferred the solitude of sailing. There's a pleasure drawn from the long stretches of absolute silence on the peaceful sea, feeling the gentle rocking of the deck, watching the clean breeze belly the sail, and watching the magnificent span of sky at night when every star in the universe seemed to dot the heavens." That was probably the most profound statement he'd ever made, and one repeated every time he wanted to go to sea.

"It's futile to search after this long," Vicky argued. "Too much time has gone by."

"But damn it," he replied, as usual, "there's always a chance! What about my discovery of Joseph and Kat? Eh?"

"The only way anyone could have survived this long is as part of a team. There's too many factors weighing against a lone survivor."

"But maybe there may be other groups."

Vicky shook her head. "You're getting too damned old to go haring off. "Look at you, almost fifty by my reckoning. You aren't a young buck anymore, Ben, and this hard life is taking a toll on both of us."

"I feel damn good about my ability to handle *Day's End*. We've survived storms, being becalmed for weeks, and even managed to come back when blown into unknown waters. We've always survived. Even the damn aliens couldn't stop us, for God's sake!"

Vicky spit. "What if your luck runs out and you can't make it back? Where does that leave us?"

Ben continued pounding vines between *Day's* logs. The wrappings would swell when wet and keep him dry. "You're right, but I'm not planning on letting that happen. Besides," he laughed as he forced more vines between the decking planks, "I'm still too young to die."

"Like all the rest of Morrow was? Like Kat's unborn baby was?"

Ben wouldn't meet her gaze.

Vicky remained stone-faced. "You're a damned fool." She sighed. "There's another reason I don't want to lose you," she added quietly. "I think Catherine's pregnant again."

"Damn!" Ben slammed down the wooden hammer. "How the hell could they be so stupid?"

"It's not like this was planned, Ben, not that that matters. With Kat taking care of the baby we'll need your help. Joseph, Tony, and I can't do this all by ourselves."

Rolling thunder woke Ben as lightning flashed on the horizon. Driving winds blew hard from the southwest, arriving at night without warning. Though they'd gotten better at building sound structures over the years, nothing they could manage was up to resisting gale-force winds. It shook and rattled around them, ready to give way at any moment as the wind tore it.

Ben left Tony to help the others secure their things as he headed to secure *Day's End* and *Summer's Breeze*. If they lost those… He didn't want to finish that thought as he added more lines to hold the boats fast. He left the lines slack enough to let them ride free and taut enough that they wouldn't be dashed against each other.

He debated cutting the boats loose to ride out the storm on open water, but that might be more dangerous. They could lose their supplies or the vessels might be swept far away by the winds and currents. *No, better not to risk it,* he thought, and spent another hour in the pounding rain adding even more line and praying they'd hold.

As the night went on the wind howled through the trees and whipped debris across the clearing. The boards from their shelter loosened with each assault, some nearly ripped away, allowing rain and wind to reach them. A particularly violent gust swept the door off its hinge.

"We can't stay here," Vicky shouted. "We've got to find better shelter!"

Ben agreed. "We should get out of here before the storm gets worse." He tried to sound calm. "Let's head to the remains of the pub. Maybe we can find shelter there."

The pub, like every other structure in the colony, had been destroyed during the disaster, but the stone foundation, remained. Its cellar had been dug to store the winter's ice and preserve food that would otherwise rot. Surely the shallow ditch would provide a measure of protection against the storm.

"Let's go," Ben shouted. The wind tore at them as they left the disintegrating shelter, threatening to tear away anything not firmly anchored. Tony clutched Kat to his side. Ben threw a hank of line over his shoulder for the others to hold on to and led the way, Joseph and Vicky stayed close behind.

Ben staggered as a strong blast of wind struck when he stepped from the lee of the shelter. He nearly lost his footing. Vicky, close behind him, seemed to fare better, moving in a crouch to keep her center of gravity low and her profile minimized. Tony and Kat struggled keep their footing while Joseph slipped and fell twice in the slick, sticky mud.

Despite the wind, they finally reached the cellar. Ben tumbled over the edge and slid into the darkness, only to get caught up in the branches of a downed tree. Before he could call out a warning a heavy body came crashing into him and, a second later, more piled on top.

They'd fallen into in a foot of water. Broken branches poked them from every side. The howl of the wind was dampened enough that Ben could hear Kat crying somewhere in the dark. He worried that she or the baby she carried had been injured the fall.

"Is everyone okay?" Ben called out.

"I'm fine," Tony replied. Vicky and Joseph answered the same.

"See if you can find someplace dry," Ben said as he freed himself from Vicky's legs and crawled toward the sound of Kat's whimpers, pushing brush and tree limbs aside, going over where he couldn't move them, and under others. The storm must have blown the entire crown of a tree into the pit. And not some dead tree either, which explained the suppleness of the limbs.

The corner provided shelter from the wind, but left them at the mercy of the incessant rain. Ben and Joseph sat in cold water up to their waists, giving Vicky, Tony, and Kat the drier spots.

Ben prayed that both boats would weather the storm. He prayed they would *all* weather the storm.

The destructive gale had ripped the gardens apart, scattered everything loose, and destroyed most of their camp. They collected their soaked bedrolls and scattered clothing. The losses were less than expected, but each blow to their resources hurt.

"We might as well head to Tower Bridge early," Ben suggested over their evening meal. "No reason to wait for the autumn winds. I say we gather what we can and load *Day's End*."

"Load both boats," Tony insisted. "We don't want to risk losing everything."

"Tony's right," Vicky declared. "Even though we took that risk earlier there's no reason to keep doing it. Besides, the extra boat will give us enough room to stretch out and sleep."

Joseph and Kat agreed.

"Leaving early will give us time to check the islands in Gorgon Bay to see if we can find anything salvageable," Ben said. "It will only delay us a few days," he assured Vicky. "If there's nothing useful, we can continue north."

"Once we get there though..." Vicky said softly.

Ben shuffled his feet and looked down where once he'd worn boots but now wore only the bark sandals Tony had crafted. "After we're settled in I might check out a few places on the other side of the equator," he added softly.

"That's a long trip," Vicky answered. "You'd be sailing on open seas for weeks. Damn it, Ben, you know you can't take that risk. We *all* depend on you." Her emphasis told him that Kat's baby was on her mind.

"More likely, you mean you'd miss my boat," Ben replied, deliberately misunderstanding her. "Come on, Vicky. We're never going to be rescued. Hell, for all we know the entire human race might have been wiped out by those aliens."

"Don't say that!" Vicky screamed. "Don't you *ever* say that. We're going to be rescued. We have to believe that, else why have we struggled so hard?"

Ben shrugged. "All right, maybe it's just that the Navy's so involved fighting aliens they can't afford the time to rescue us. For that matter, they might have already marked Morrow off the list as a lost cause. Face it, Vicky, I'm going to die here and whether I do it now or some distant day when I'm too old to hold the tiller doesn't make a bit of difference. If I lose my life on the boat trying to find more people I will figure it a good death. Sitting on my ass waiting for rescue is not the way I want to go."

"*You* matter to me," she argued. "And to Tony, and Joseph, and Kat! It's important that we stay together."

"At least until we get to our winter camp." Ben left it at that. He knew the argument would only continue, as it had for years.

The fishing settlements in Gordon Bay proved empty of anything useful. Vicky was disappointed that not even a jar or pot could be found.

There was little change to note as they approached Tower Bridge. A tree had fallen across the clearing and their salvaged barge was gone, leaving only a few frayed dock lines where it had been secured. It was not a great loss. Otherwise everything was much the same.

They pulled *Day's End* and *Summer's Breeze* to shore just in time for the spring rains and, in the days between showers, managed to get their crops planted in the sandy soil.

While the three men worked on shoring up the shelter, Vicky helped Kat weave fresh vines into useful baskets. Their crude furniture, a table and three chairs that Tony made, were intact. Tony swore he'd make a cradle for the baby once things settled down into a routine.

Vicky could tell that Ben was still thinking about exploring north of the equator. He'd become increasingly restless over the weeks after arrival and kept puttering with *Day's End*, which meant he was eager to be off and away.

She finally confronted him. "You're leaving us, aren't you? That was your plan all along... All you want to do is sail on your precious boat and the hell with the rest of us. How can you be so selfish, Ben?"

"Selfish? All I want to do is make certain that there are no more people out there. I want to add them to Joseph, Kat, Tony, and you. I want to enlarge our family."

Vicky frowned. "Have you forgotten that Tony and Kat are already working on that?"

But her attempts to change Ben's mind did no good. He sailed away on the morning tide, leaving them *Summer's Breeze*. Vicky watched with a heavy heart until he disappeared into the mist and prayed for his safe return.

She hoped they'd not have to sail south alone.

It had been three weeks since Ben left the others at the Tower Bridge camp. The sea stretched endlessly in all directions.

Day's End turned slowly, bringing her bow to the wind. Ben adjusted sail and tiller to keep her on a course. Hunter's Star wouldn't rise until dark. Its angle above the southern horizon would measure his progress toward the equator. Dead reckoning was his only method of navigating once they were away from land. All he had to guide him was Hunter's at night and the angle of the sun in the morning, neither of which was as precise as a positioning satellite. *Huh, might as well wish for a three-mast clipper and a hearty crew,* he thought…

Day's End was a good boat. She'd carried their seasonal migration for years and was good for several more. He probably should have taken *Summer's Breeze,* the sleeker catamaran for this trip, but he chose *Day's* instead. *Summer* would have made better headway in the light breezes but *Day's* was more suited to the sudden storms.

Ben couldn't think of anything better than a stout boat under his butt, a steady sea breeze, and hope of finding survivors on the northern shores. It was good to be one with the boat, sailing across a sea that seemed to stretch forever.

The threatening gray clouds appeared suddenly, cresting the western horizon like a black invader. The menacing summer storm looked to be thirty kilometers away at most and too wide to avoid. Weather racing across the sea had nothing to impede its progress or curb its growth. Ben turned *Day's* toward the edge where the winds would hopefully be weaker.

Too short a time later he realized that the storm was larger than he thought and approaching too fast. He'd never reach the edge. The churning dark clouds obscured the entire western horizon. The strong wind suddenly shifted, promising fierce rain and battering waves. He debated lowering the sail to ride it out, but thought it better to let the heavy winds drive him. It would be miserably wet and uncomfortable, but better than being battered, tossed this way and that, and rain drenched.

He put *Day's* stern to the storm and let the sail fill. The heavy wind might push him farther to the east, but he could turn back later. These thunderstorms never lasted long, even ones this large.

By late afternoon the darkest clouds were on his stern. With the sail catching the full force of the wind *Day's* drove powerfully forward, pushing through wind-churned waves. Foam blew off the wave tops. Had *Day's* been lighter she would have taken the waves, skipping from crest to crest, but she was a heavy, lumbering cargo boat. The bow was driven into the wave backs whenever her stern lifted.

The forces of wind and water were so strong that it was all Ben could do to hang on to the tiller with one arm and brace the boom with the other. *Day's* tried to turn to relieve the pressure on her sail, but Ben fought to maintain her heading. The boat topped one huge wave and plunged into the back of another. Water swept across the deck, carrying away the blanket he'd forgotten to secure. He heard the clatter of his water pots as they struck against each other and hoped none had cracked.

As they crested another wave the wind suddenly shifted. Before Ben could react, the boom swung across the deck and snapped the upper arm hard against the lifting eye, breaking the boom. *Day's End* swiveled as the sail ripped. Water washed across the deck, a swirling, grasping torrent that swept everything loose before it. Ben held tight onto the whipping tiller with both arms to keep from being swept away.

He prayed that the wind would soon ease.

The bright morning light reflected on a calm and placid sea. No ripple creased the mirror-like surface. There was not a cloud to be seen. Not a breeze stirred. Ben groaned at the destruction the storm's passing had caused.

All but two of the water jugs had cracked—a week's water lost. The food wrappings were sodden. He'd have to dry everything in the sun before they spoiled. Half of his fishing tackle was lost, but he still had line and a bone hook. The two spare hanks of rope were gone, as was half his cabin. The sail hung in forlorn tatters from the shattered boom. There was barely enough fabric left to rig a small sail, if he had some way to knit the tatters together and could rig a useful boom.

He slumped against the base of the mast. Without a sail *Day's End* was at the mercy of winds and water, unknown kilometers from land. He tried to remember his last position when the storm hit. Had he been halfway to the equator? Perhaps Hunter's nightly rise would give him some indication of where he was even though knowing that might not help.

What else could he do?

Even this close to the equator the nights were cool, but not so cold that Ben needed his single remaining blanket. Could he rig that as a sail? He would still have to figure out a way of attaching it to the broken boom, but it would give him options. Even with that jury rig and a slight breeze, the best he could hope for was to run ahead of the wind on a broad reach.

He tore some lengths of line hanging from the broken boom and cut them with the copper knife Joseph had forged. When he had enough line, he threaded it through a block and tied the blanket to the boom.

Now, all he needed was a breeze.

Vicky tried not to dwell on Ben's absence. She sat outside the shelter weaving yet more baskets, her eyes on her hands and studiously not out at sea. Her thoughts wandered as they would with nothing to anchor them. She never realized how much she'd miss Ben, or how much she'd envy him. How simple life had been on her barge, with no one to deal with, except maybe her boys...

"Hey…come on…"

She jumped, looking up to find Tony standing over her. He took her hand before she could pull it back, gently setting aside the half-finished basket. "Come on," he repeated as he tugged her to her feet and toward the beach, where she saw Joseph building a bonfire as Kat piled dry wood beside it.

Vicky shook her head and tried to pull away from Tony's grasp. "No time for that nonsense," she grumbled. "We have too much to do and…"

Tony grinned and refused to let her loose. "Just a little while. You work too much…we all work too much. What's the point of surviving if that's all we do?"

Now if that wasn't a truer statement. *So easy to forget to enjoy life when you're fighting to survive,* she thought. Kind of like Ben's need to sail off on his boat…With a frown, she shut down that thought.

"Okay, fine. Quit pulling."

Laughter rang through the twilight as the bonfire finally roared to life, giving welcome warmth as they sprawled on the upwind side.

Vicky flopped beside Joseph and folded her arms around herself as Tony moved to Kat's side.

For a while they simply enjoyed the fire's warmth and listened to the gentle splash of the sea. Gradually, Joseph began humming a familiar tune from the time before their world changed. As he continued, most likely because he'd forgotten the words, Tony tapped accompaniment on his leg. Kat began singing indistinct words as he patted gently on her domed belly.

Something loosened in Vicky. She felt the relaxation of tension she hadn't been conscious of and for a little while forgot the reality of their life. She surrendered herself to the peaceful companionship and hummed along, forcing back the closing night.

She couldn't help thinking Ben would have liked this.

There was little relief over the days following the storm. Ben managed to hook a few small fish to supplement his dwindling food supplies, most of which had been eaten. Pretty soon he'd be surviving on fish alone, assuming he didn't die of thirst first.

A brief rain had fallen the night before, caught by the tattered remnants of the sail he'd rigged to divert the trickle of water into the unbroken pots, but that gave him less than a week's worth of water, if he used it sparingly.

He scanned the horizon for any sign of a storm that might bring more rain or, better still, a strong breeze. He hoped *Day's* was not circling but there was no way to tell. There were few guideposts on the open sea.

This morning the sun had risen over the bow instead of to starboard. Did that mean that the currents were taking him east or that the boat had simply turned during the night? It was an interesting question, but hardly useful.

As he baked in the sun he thought about all the things he could have done and those that he hadn't. Uppermost was the irony that his love of the sea would soon bring his death. Such dismal thoughts were not productive, but unavoidable given his situation.

To distract himself, he sang songs from his youth, those he'd heard at Dockstal, or something that Eve had softly hummed in her restless moments after sex, but before sleep. They saddened him more often than not.

And at night he had dreadful dreams.

There wasn't a cloud to be seen. No possibility of wind or rain. Worse, he found that something had viciously ripped his remaining fishhook from the shredded end of his line. It was a disaster. At this point he needed the moisture from the fish, more than the protein, to sustain him. Without a hook he could only try snatching at small fish feeding on the boat's bottom growth, but they proved too elusive. He'd attempted using a whittled hook but without a small fish for bait it was of no use. He could get by for maybe a month without food, but without water he'd not last a week.

He should have listened to Vicky, but it was too late for that sort of regret. The only thing that pissed him off was knowing that Vicky would say; "Damn that Ben Gunning. I told him he shouldn't go."

He'd have liked to hear her say that.

More days passed without rain. Ben looked for clouds that might promise relief, but saw none. Even looking west, where the weather came from, didn't show a hint of inclement weather.

Water was now a serious problem. His supply was down to two porous pots. The faint breeze, as always too little to flutter his makeshift sail, sucked moisture from them.

He'd eaten the last of his food—a shriveled plum and a dried apple—three days before, so there was no need to rehydrate anything but himself.

He hadn't glimpsed any fish near the boat for days. Earlier they'd clustered in the boat's shade and nibbled on the growth. Now, even those were gone.

He decided to take another nap. Sleeping seemed his primary occupation. His waking time consisted of praying for rain and taking tiny sips of water. He knew it was foolish to ration, depriving his body of water, but thoughts of drinking that last drop terrified him. Without water he'd die within three days, maybe less, given his condition.

He'd been rinsing his dry mouth with seawater. Swallowing too much would rupture his stomach's lining and kill him. That was a laugh; thirst would finish him long before that could happen.

Nevertheless, he tried not to swallow.

The hot sun beat on Ben's face, waking him from a delirious montage of faces and places, aliens, kids, Navy rescuers, Vicky's calming voice, Tony's garden, Joseph's complaining about his damned bladder, and dear Kat, shattered by misery, all growing old, abandoned and forgotten.

Had it all been a delirious dream or had parts of it been real memories? He recalled hearing Dave chasing the boat, its three legs churning the water, but never reaching, held back by his necklace of silly magic beads that Vicky made him wear. Could those imagined sounds have been a fish splashing nearby? Had something finally bitten on his lure?

He crawled from the cabin, too weak to stand, pausing as usual to look at the sky. There were no clouds. No rain. No water.

And neither Dave nor splashing fish.

He snapped awake. It was dark. Had a day passed or had that been another dream? It was increasingly hard to tell which were dreams, memories, and reality. Was he still drifting becalmed or on their annual migration? "Vicky?" he called out.

There was no answer but the sigh of a weak breeze fluttering the sail.

Ben jerked awake. Above him the stars dotted the night sky. Where were Vicky and Kat? Tony and Joseph? Had they been another dream?

He slept.

When he woke he was holding the tiller. His dreams must have confused him, but his mind was clear again and he was on *Day's End*. He glimpsed Tony single-handing *Summer's Breeze* a dozen meters to port and waved. Were they on their migration north, or was he dreaming about a different voyage?

How long had they been sailing and why was he so terribly weak and thirsty?

Oh yes; the storm. How long had it been? Days, weeks, months? It seemed more like years, and an eternity since he'd licked that last bit of morning moisture off the deck to wet his cracked lips. There were no ways of marking time on the open sea save the rising and falling of the sun, the glittering uncaring stars at night, and the whispers of the dead drifting around this dying world.

He felt too weak to stand. He looked beyond the bow. His heart fluttered as he spied a smudge on the horizon. He was certain that it was a shoreline. Somehow, after all this time and seemingly little movement the sea had delivered him to safety.

The excitement of being so near to rescue gave him enough strength to pull himself erect and lean against the mast as his beloved *Day's End* carried him shoreward. Above him her makeshift sail billowed, filled by the strong following wind. Her lines creaked with strain as she leaped over the waves, plunging forward like an eager lover returning to her home port.

People were standing on the shore, waving and shouting. Familiar voices cried encouragement as *Day's End* approached. He was close enough to recognize their smiling faces and, among them, standing beautifully tall and radiant with her arms spread wide, was Eve, welcoming him to his final port.

BOOK THREE

Chapter Seventeen

OUR BOAT FLOATED SILENT AS OWLS' WINGS AND SETTLED SOFTLY AS AN autumn snowflake. There was no doubt that the enemy had spotted us—the stealth could only minimize signs of our presence. We'd done everything we could to reduce detectability: hardened plastics, ceramics, charged ice, and hardly any metal. All that did was create doubt, and, possibly, delay. Or so we hoped.

We tumbled quickly from the boat as landing automatically grounded the ship charge, without which the boat's ice frame would quickly melt. In a matter of minutes, the only remaining trace of our ship would be a puddle of impure water and the gossamer-thin spider-web of the stealth shield—and that would dissipate at the first hint of a breeze.

We deployed in pincer and arrowhead formation, sending two troops to the north to parallel our advance, two likewise to the south, and two to the point. Hunter and I followed in column.

We moved quickly, carefully, ever wary. That the Shardies would eventually find us was not in doubt, neither was the certainty of our death when they did so. They did not use humans well; however, I doubted they'd find much use for us.

Tactical estimates gave us an hour to save the recalcitrant settlers' souls. They were some sort of colony—religious or otherwise, it made no difference—only that they had foolishly chosen to remain when everyone else fled.

There was a slight probability we'd have less than an hour and an even smaller possibility of having more, so we moved quickly. I'd estimated twenty minutes to reach their position and ten to twenty to ensure we'd located everyone. That left us five minutes for action and ten as margin for contingencies.

I knew we'd fail if we used more than fifty-five minutes.

The trip to the site of the single communications burst was uneventful. We didn't expect to encounter resistance. The Shardies didn't settle on the planets they took from us. No, they just wiped them clean of humanity and then moved on. There could, however, be Shardie searchers trying to find the remaining fresh meat or, what was worse, breeding stock. Command had determined long ago that the Shardies were obviously using human brains to "think" like us and ordered everyone, except combat types like us, from the most likely targets. Humanity couldn't allow any more people to become components for the Shardie offense.

But civilians never listen. Farmers were the worst, hanging onto their little plots and crops until somebody dragged them away, kicking and screaming at the injustice of it all. That's why we were here. Forty settlers had stupidly refused to be evacuated from New Mars. Forty we didn't know about until we got that one brief burst.

My mission was to make certain that they didn't become forty armless, legless, gutless, screamless weapon components.

With a little luck, we had a slight advantage by knowing the group's location. Without luck, we'd find that the Shardies had beaten us to them.

The location was a hill, close by a half-destroyed farming complex whose tower leaned precariously toward the north. We hoped to find whoever made the call nearby. First place to check were the buildings, or what remained of them.

A sweep of the barn was negative, as were the remains of the silo, and the outbuildings. The house was a different matter. There were opened jars on the counter, preserves mostly. Outside we found footprints—a child's perhaps, or a small woman's. The tracks led up the hill and into the woods.

I sent the outriders wide to cover while Hunter followed the tracks. Could be a trap, so I waited, senses alert for any indication of a problem.

The crack of a twig brought me to my feet. It was Hunter and a little girl. "Cave up there, Captain," Hunter said, head nodding the direction. "Three dead men—three, four days gone." That tied with the time we'd received the burst.

The girl was a tiny thing—about nine or ten, I'd say—bright eyes and scraggly red hair. Good teeth. Looked scared as hell. I could understand that—Hunter wasn't gentle as she dumped the girl at my feet.

I stooped to bring my head to her level. "What's your name?"

"You them aliens?" she asked all wide-eyed. "How come you talk like us?"

"We're combat soldiers," I answered. "We're human, just like you, sweetheart. Now, come on; what's your name?"

"Becky," she finally spit out. "How come you're still here? Paw said everybody left."

"We came back to take care you and the others," I answered truthfully. "We can't afford to let you fall into enemy hands."

"Paw and the Paston boys thought you'd come," she said.

"How did the others die?"

Becky seemed fascinated by my sidearm. "They shot them after they took the mayday thing. I hid in the back where they couldn't find me. Are you going to punish them for doing that?"

That got my attention. Takes a real idiot to shoot the people demonstrating good sense. I began to doubt that the Shardies would've gotten much use out of whatever mush these jerks used for brains. "Right, sweetheart, we'll punish them, but first you have to tell us where they are."

"Did you bring a ship to take us away?" Becky asked as she fingered the butt of my AC-43. "That was why Paw grabbed the mayday—to get us a rescue ship."

"We came to make sure the enemy doesn't get you," I answered honestly. "Listen, we don't have much time. Can you take us to where the others are hiding?"

"I think they're still over at the Truett place," she said, pointing to the east.

I nodded to Hunter, who was already directing the scouts eastward. I picked up Becky and moved out. Hunter covered my rear. "Can you tell us how to get there?"

"You mean to the Truett's' place?" Becky asked. "Sure. There's a big field there. That where the rescue ship's going to land?"

"Why do you act so funny?" Becky asked as we jogged along. Her question was expected. Few civilians ever saw combat troops like us. Luckily, most of modifications I had undergone were hidden, by my combat gear. The dark hid the rest. Cybernetic heart-lung pump with reserve oxygen so I could operate in any atmosphere or even underwater; augmented muscles on legs and arms that bulked me up like a cartoon giant on steroids; amped vision that ran from the near infrared up toward the UV range—I could even switch to black-and-white for better night vision—and smart-metal skeleton structures to provide a good base for my massive muscles. Flesh had been stripped from anything exposed and replaced with impervious plas. My hands were electro-mechanical marvels capable of ripping weapons-grade plating off a spaceship, and sensitive enough to lift a tiny girl without harm.

Then there was my glucose pump, a nasty, but useful technology we'd copied from the captured Shardie ship. Even my brain had been altered—substituting silicon and gel for the mass of pink jelly I was born with. Definitely not something you'd want your daughter to date. I'm glad it was dark. In daylight, my six eyes alone would probably scare the bejesus out of her.

"We're modified so we can fight the bastards," I answered, barely suppressing my rage. Revenge for my unremembered relatives was my overt reason. Curiosity about the Shardies, and getting a piece of them, was secondary. I saw no sense going into the gory details or the agonizing processes involved with a little girl who wouldn't understand. "Tell me about the rest of your group. Are they all right?"

"Mr. Robbarts is still the boss. He's the one that shot Paw, I think. And there's Jake and Sally and little Billy. Billy's my friend. Jake's got a bad leg.

"Then there's all the Thomas women. They have big wagon, or they did before the men came and burned it." She started crying.

I was certain she was talking about the roaming gangs. Lots of people didn't want to leave anything the Shardies might be able to use. Senseless; Shardies couldn't care less, but most civilians thought it was best to destroy what you left behind, and had taken their anger out on things they could reach.

"Mr. Robbarts said we didn't have to worry because we weren't soldiers. He said we'd have the whole world to ourselves. But after everybody left, Paw got really afraid of what might happen."

Robbarts must be the leader of this group. "Robbarts was wrong, Becky. You all should have left," I said. "Didn't they tell you that it wouldn't matter if you were a soldier or not? Being human is all that matters."

"Mr. Robbarts got real mad when Paw argued with him and said he wanted to use the mayday thing. Then Paw and the boys and me ran away with it. You got to go along this stream for a bit now," she directed.

That explained the burst message that told us there were people left behind. They must have used one of the emergency broadcast units the evacuation team had scattered across New Mars in the last days, just in case. "What happened then?" I asked as I followed her pointing finger down the stream. The scouts picked up my changed direction and reacted.

"They told Paw to come out to talk," Becky continued, chatting away. "Paw told me to hide. Then I heard them arguing and shouting and I got really afraid. Then there was some shots and I heard the men searching. Mr. Robbarts was cussing a lot and calling me all sorts of names, but I stayed where I was. I was scared."

"What did you do then?" I stepped around a huge boulder and wondered if it would be easier, and faster, to wade in the stream instead of through the woods on either side. Hunter was close by my side now in this narrow section.

"After it got quiet, I snuck out and found Paw and the boys laying on the ground. Paw was bleeding bad. I tried to stop it, but it wouldn't stop. Then he went to sleep and didn't move for a long time. I got hungry waiting for the rescue ship Paw said would come." That explained the jelly and jam jars. "Are you going to bury Paw and the boys?"

"Burial wastes time—something we can't afford," Hunter said sharply. Down, she signaled as a shot ricocheted off my chest armor.

I dropped immediately, instinctively tucking Becky underneath to protect her. Hunter slipped to the side and disappeared. I switched to infrared and made out fuzzy heat forms in the brush a dozen meters ahead. The muzzle of a rifle glowed heat-bright from the shot the shooter had taken. None of the forms moved.

I waited. Silent. Becky groaned and wiggled feebly. "It really hurts," she said. Her voice was muffled.

"Shh," I whispered, waiting for Hunter to get into position.

"Let her up," a man's voice barked from behind me. "Move easy now. I got you covered."

I pushed up, allowing Becky to crawl out before I came to my feet. The man took a step back. "Huh, you sure are a big one." He peered closer. "Ugly, too."

"He's come to rescue us, Mister Robbarts." Becky said. "He's got another soldier with him." Becky's voice sounded strained. I glanced at her and saw the blood. Damn, the ricochet had hit her.

I noticed the heat signatures of two more men in the brush, one behind Robbarts and another somewhat further back. That made six in all. I had no doubt all were armed and ready to shoot.

"You shot Becky," I said calmly. "She needs help."

"The hell with her," Robbarts said nastily. "Her damn family's been nothing but trouble. Killed one of my boys, they did. Let the little bitch bleed."

"They're going to take us away in a ship," Becky said in a rush. "That's why we're going to the Truetts' place. The field's a place they can land."

Robbarts didn't answer her directly. "That true, soldier? You got a ship?"

I really didn't like this man. "Nobody, nothing, could find a trace of the boat we came in. Becky's the one who said there'd be a rescue ship."

"Ain't no damn ship taking me or my people off our land," Robbarts spit, ignoring what I had said. "We're going to hold on to this place come whatever. This'll be a damn nice place for me and mine after the war moves on."

Did he really believe that? "The Shardies are going to comb this planet and glean whatever human stock they can find. Do you know what they do to the people they capture?"

Robbarts sneered. "I seen the news about what they did to them poor sailors. But we're civilians, not some combat-trained space jockeys. They won't bother us. We don't know military stuff."

I couldn't believe Robbarts's ignorance. "The aliens don't care what you know. It's the human thought processes, the way our minds form associations, our ability to recognize patterns—*that's* what they use. They don't give a damn if a brain comes from a soldier, a navigator, or even some dumb-assed farmer!" As soon as the angry words popped out of my mouth I regretted them.

"Well, I might be a dumb-assed farmer, soldier boy," Robbarts drawled, "but it's you who's at the wrong end of this here gun."

"Not exactly," I said as I watched Hunter silently taking out the two forms behind Robbarts. That action told me the other three had already been neutralized. Hunter is good at what she does—thorough.

"You really shouldn't have said that about Becky," I said calmly. Robbarts' normal human reaction time was no match for my enhanced speed. As I quickly swiped the knife-edge of my forearm sleeve across his throat, a wet, red grin grew beneath his chin.

Severing the carotid arteries released the pressure and drained blood from the brain. It caused death in seconds, while slashing his larynx prevented any outcry. Robbarts stood quietly erect for a moment until his body got the message that blood was no longer flowing to the head and no more signals were coming from the dying brain. Then he toppled over.

I scooped up Becky and continued. Hunter would destroy Robbarts' head, just as she had the others, and catch up. I hoped the rest of Robbarts' flock wouldn't waste more of what little time we had left.

While I jogged along, I checked to see where Becky had been hit. It wasn't fatal, so I put a compress over the wound to staunch the bleeding. It would do well enough until we found the others.

"Where now?" I asked.

Becky stopped sobbing for a moment. "There's a pond down there. It's up the hill from there. There's a hiding hole near the barn."

So that's how they managed to evade the evacuation search teams—by hiding in a bunker. Hunter had caught up by then and I briefed her. She directed the scouts to converge on the spot. "What if it's sealed?" she asked.

"You know what to do," I answered and she smiled. That was the difference between us—she enjoyed this, enjoyed the danger, enjoyed the blood. When we got within sight of the entrance to the bunker I put Becky down. "You have to call them out," I said. "Can you do that?"

"They'll shoot me like they did Paw," Becky protested. "I hurt real bad, mister. Can't you do something?" She was crying.

"Listen, Becky, it's really important that we get to those people quickly. I tell you what; if they shoot at you I'll punish them like I did Mr. Robbarts, all right?"

She nodded, but reluctantly.

"Becky, just walk over there and yell. Tell them you're hurt and need help. I don't think they'll shoot a little girl."

"Aren't you coming with me?" she said.

I shook my head. "No, they might be afraid if they saw me. You can tell them who we are if you want and then I'll show myself." I wiped her nose and pushed her behind to get her moving.

Becky hesitated and then slowly hobbled across the field. "Help! I been shot!" she screamed.

A black hole appeared in the ground by the barn and a man climbed out. "Becky?" he called out. "Robbarts said you were dead." I noticed he'd left the hatch open. Good.

"He just shot me, like he did Paw and the Pastons," she answered.

"We heard a shot, but didn't know it was you," the man said as he approached and knelt before Becky. "Damn, that looks bad. How did you manage to get here—and where are Robbarts and his men?" He was looking around nervously.

"The rescue soldiers took care of him," Becky answered innocently.

"Soldiers!" That didn't sound like a curse. More like a man with hope in his voice. I stepped forward.

"Captain Savage; forty-fifth combat arm," I said. "We came to save your souls." I could see by his frightened reaction that he wasn't going to be a problem.

"He's got a ship to take us all away, Mr. Truett, just like Paw said," Becky said. "They'll have a doctor to fix me up and we'll all be safe."

Truett stepped closer. "I heard things." I could hear the fear in his voice.

"We can't be used by the Shardies," I said calmly. "Can't survive more than a few minutes without our combat rations." I figured he knew about the measured doses of anticoagulants fed into my bloodstream. When those stopped, my brain would suffuse with thick blood, hemorrhaging and destroying the remaining organic brain cells. "We're running out of time here."

"How long?" he said, showing more understanding than I expected from a dumb-assed farmer who hadn't had the good sense to save himself and his family when he could.

"I've only got about another forty minutes," I answered.

Truett turned his head and whistled. "Suicide trooper." He blinked, but that didn't stop a tear from running down his cheek. He understood. Without another word he led the way toward the black hole. "They're all inside," he remarked quietly. "There are thirty of us. Mostly women. Some are just kids," he added sadly. "I was hoping..." He stopped, looked at Becky, and sighed. "Never mind."

Thirty in the bunker. That meant that all forty were accounted for, counting the three men of Becky's family, the six Hunter had taken out, Becky, and Truett. Good. "We'll take care of them quickly," I said and he nodded. Quiet. Yeah, I guess he did know "things."

Hunter and the scouts had already converged on the hole and were dropping through, one after another. I had no doubt of their effectiveness.

"What's it like for you?" Truett asked. He was holding Becky tightly in his arms.

"Being here, or being a cyber?" I answered.

"Both. I can't see how you can be so cold and distant. Hell, man, can't you at least show some emotion? Or are you mostly machine now?" His voice was a mixture of anger and fear.

"I grew up on a farm," I said slowly, trying to dredge up memories of a happier past on a planet now lost beyond redemption. "I still remember the smell of autumn, the feeling of mud between my toes, and how it felt to kill my prize calf when it was time. This mission's no different. I do what I have to do because there are worse things for a human being than dying."

"I saw the news tapes," he said. "Ugly. Horrible. But what about your own hide? Don't you have any sense of self-preservation?"

"When you've been taken care of, we'll go after the Shardies," I bit out. "Our secondary mission is to gather whatever data we can and squirt a message to the fleet. After that, well, there's four, five thousand tons of explosive force in our packs." I patted the small canister strapped to my back. "I figure a dead-man switch will take care of them if we get close."

Truett smiled. "Brave, but it was a foolish waste of resources to come back for us. We made our own mess—stupid as it was to believe Robbarts—and we deserve to lie in it."

I checked the time. We only had a few minutes of good time left. Hunter was taking far too long.

"I'm sorry," I said quickly. "You don't have any time left."

Truett grabbed my hand and squeezed. "I just want you to know..." he began and then choked off whatever he was going to say. Instead he slapped my shoulder. "Yeah." I could tell he was trying hard not to cry, but his voice cracked at the end. "Well," he said to Becky. "Looks like we've got a ship to catch," he said cheerily.

Hunter popped out of the hole and came toward me at a run. "We're done," she said quickly. Moments later, the ground surged upward with a roar as smoke and flame shot from the burrow's entrance. If that didn't get the Shardies' attention, nothing would.

"Becky," I said, and gently took her from Truett's arms. "It's time to go."

"Is the ship coming?" Becky asked excitedly as she squirmed around in my arms. "I don't see it."

"It's up there in the sky," Truett said very gently. "Just look up. There, to the right of that big, bright red star." Becky tilted her head back to look almost directly overhead.

I brought my forearm across her throat and held her as she died. I hoped that she didn't have enough time to realize what I had done. What I had to do.

Hunter had taken care of Truett without a struggle. He too had been looking up, as if he might have believed his own words.

I gently lay Becky's lifeless body on the ground, trying not to feel. As before, I let Hunter take care of the final details, ensuring not a single brain cell remained in either head.

There were only a few minutes left in our window when I heard a distant whine. It could only be the Shardies. I placed my finger on the detonator. Our comm packages were running and would catch our final moments.

"Civilians just don't understand, do they?" Hunter asked as she waited beside me for oblivion, sweet release from these mechanical contrivances we'd become.

I thought of Truett, and the way he had bravely shielded Becky to the last, thought of all the ways the war hasn't changed human decency, thought of my prize calf and the necessities life forces on us.

"Some do," I admitted.

Chapter Eighteen

VICKY MOVED SLOWLY AS SHE FED THE SMOKER. SHE DIDN'T WANT TO ADD too much wood. A nice sustained bed of coals would smoke the fish dry and tasty. Anything more would bake the fish. Better to provide just enough heat to smoke things properly.

The late spring sun felt good, warming her old bones that had ached in winter's grasp, even at these latitudes. Arthritis, she imagined, the scourge of old age and an affliction she wouldn't have suffered had it not been for those aliens cutting off the benefits of civilization. What she wouldn't give for a single aspirin!

What had it been, seventeen, eighteen, or maybe more years since every trace of civilization had been wiped from the planet? She sighed and touched the magic necklace Gunning had fashioned for her. She still missed him, her companion for so many years and probably the bravest soul she'd ever known. She would never have survived without his help and it was Ben—dear Ben and his damned boat—that had brought Joseph and dear Kat into her life.

"We need to fill the evaporation flat to make more salt," Joseph said, breaking her reverie. "The brine tank will need refilling when Tony brings in more fish."

When, not if. Tony could always be depended upon to keep the larder full of protein, between hunting and fishing. Kat and Ben, her young son, tended the gardens and gathered fruit, and Vicky and Joseph processed what the others brought in, limited by their age and physical capabilities. Joseph was well past sixty now and debilitated by stiff joints and constant backaches, while she was nearly fifty, but felt more like sixty given her delicate stomach and increasingly bad eyesight. *If we feel this old* now, *what will we be in another ten years or so?* she thought.

Vicky worried that neither she nor Joseph would survive long enough to see young Ben mature. With luck, she could last maybe another ten to twenty years, barring accidents, disease, or the arrival of that rescue ship she'd all but given up on. Hopes had faded with each passing year. Morrow had become her world now and she had to make the best of it.

Joseph probably had a few more years left, but given his decline over winter he might not last even that much longer. No, young Ben would soon have only his mother and father and, when they were gone, probably die alone on this damned world cursing those who had given him life.

Was it really eighteen years that they had been struggling? Up until her Ben was lost she'd carefully counted the seasons, the migrations, and the number of goddamned aches and pains she suffered. It could be closer to twenty years, given that a Morrow year was longer than Earth's...and did that bit of trivia even matter? Most of her reminiscences were already incomprehensible to young Ben, even when Joseph or Tony tried to explain. Talking about radio, power plants, and tractors was like attempting to explain color to a blind man. He might understand the concepts, but had no use for them.

Lately Vicky wondered why they struggled so hard to stay alive. After Ben's failure to return, they'd all focused on Kat's baby. Raising young Ben had given them purpose and continued to do so ten years later.

"Here's another rack," Kat interrupted Vicky's thoughts as she delivered a skewer of fish. "I'll do more. Just shout when you're ready for them."

Vicky watched as Kat limped away. Even after all these years she still favored her right ankle, broken years before. Had that happened when Ben was three, or later? Kat had slipped on rocks on the side of the stream as she raced to pull the toddler away from the water. She'd gone up and down that same bank for months without a problem but in her haste to "rescue" Ben she'd failed to step carefully and, well, it didn't take much to twist an ankle.

The swelling had been so bad that they knew it wasn't a simple sprain. Tony made a splint to keep it stable but without good medical attention, a decent x-ray machine, bone-strengthening drugs, or a trained orthopedist there was nothing more they could do. Kat's ankle, just like her father's leg, hadn't knit properly.

Kat grew sickly following young Ben's difficult birth. Likely it was the lack of proper nutrition. She never really recovered and, after all these years, still complained about her belly and problems with her bowels. She'd never gotten pregnant since Ben's delivery, which Vicky counted a blessing.

Summer's Breeze tilted as Tony loaded the last of the cargo. The load was so light that the boat rode high in the water. *Breeze* had served them well over the years, cruising easily even after they'd almost doubled her deck area. The expansion had to accommodate the amounts of supplies they'd originally carried but they'd gotten used to the luxury of additional space.

"It might be wise to start building another boat," Tony remarked as Vicky helped him secure the baskets.

"Who has the knowledge or time to build another boat?" Vicky answered. "There's only you and young Ben; the rest of us would be no help whatsoever. Easier to maintain *Breeze*. Ben built her well. She has a lot of years left in her."

Tony took another turn of rope to secure the netting around the baskets. "That's true, but Breeze's a bit too much for single-handed sailing. Better to have a smaller, more easily managed boat around if anything happens."

"You mean when Ben's the only one left?"

"Or the only one who will be able to handle it. You and Joseph..." he let the words tail off. "You know what I mean."

"Best not to think about that, Tony. Let's just concentrate on surviving until we're rescued."

"Right," Tony answered, but Vicky knew he'd given that dream up long ago.

Vicky boiled fish stew over the sand box they used as the boat's fire pit. Nobody'd managed to catch any fresh fish so she'd added a few smoked ones to some potatoes and onions. It smelled delicious.

"Do you think it's all right for him to be doing that?" Kat cried. "I don't think he should be up there." Ben had clambered up *Breeze*'s stubby mast again. His sharp young eyes made him an ideal lookout.

"See the island?" Tony cried.

"Can't see a thing, Dad," Ben replied, his voice breaking on the last word. Puberty was coming on him hard, robbing him of his childhood grace and giving back an awkwardness he hadn't yet learned to control. No wonder Kat worried that he'd fall and hurt himself. The boy kept testing his limits and was a mass of bruises and cuts.

"Keep looking. We should be getting close by now."

"I think he should come down before ..." Kat repeated.

"Who else is going to climb up there?" Tony snarled and, a moment later mumbled, "Sorry, but Ben's our only resource and if we don't spot the island before sunset we'll have to sail all night."

"And most of the next day," Vicky added as she stirred the stew. Their island refuges were about a day's sail apart, but missing one was not a disaster. They had enough food and water, adequate space to sleep, and no danger of running into anything in this part of their voyage. Just the same, it would be nice to stretch her legs, and sleep on solid ground.

"I see something!" Ben pointed off to starboard. "I think it's the island."

Tony adjusted the tiller and took in the sail. The combination made *Breeze* tilt as the starboard outrigger rose in the water, but not enough to clear it.

"Whooie!" Ben shouted as the mast tilted. "Yahoo!"

"Get back down here this instant," Kat commanded. "Stop acting like a child," which was probably the wrong thing to say. Ben took his sweet time returning to the deck, leaping the final two meters and landing close to *Breeze*'s edge. He waved his arms trying to keep his balance on the tilted deck, flailed wildly, and fell overboard.

Kat screamed.

Tony laughed and tossed the boy a line. Ben ignored the rope and swam with sure strokes to reach the stern where he climbed aboard with a smile on his face. "Bet I could have dived off the top," he said proudly.

"And given your mother a heart attack," Tony chided. "You shouldn't take risks like that. Could have bashed your head on the edge of the deck."

"I would have missed it," Ben countered with all the confidence of immortal youth. "Wouldn't have hit."

"You have to learn to be more careful," Kat lectured. "We don't want anything to happen to you." It was clear Kat was having problems with Ben's growing independence. Truly, it was a strain on all of them, the conflict of wanting to protect him, yet having to depend on him.

"The boy needs to learn his own limitations," Joseph argued. "Give him some space, Catherine."

Kat bristled. "Ben has to be reminded to be careful. He's still too young to understand consequences." Vicky stifled a laugh. That was rich coming from Kat, when young Ben was one of her own 'consequences.'

"I'm almost eleven," Ben protested.

Tony joined the argument. "Be quiet, Ben." He touched Kat on the arm. "Both of you are right. He needs to be more careful, and you need to give him some space. We won't always be around to protect him. He has to find his own way. The best we can do is give our son the tools he needs to survive."

Vicky winced. There it was again, another reference to the mortality facing all of them. She had to change the subject. "I can't wait to drink some fresh water and feel solid ground under my feet," she said cheerfully.

Tony picked up on her lead. "We should make it to land before nightfall if the breeze holds."

Three weeks later *Breeze* dropped anchor for the last time that season. It took little time to unload the boat in the cold shallows near the shore. The cabin they'd built on Landing's old tavern's foundation a few years before still stood amidst the detritus that covered most of the site. At least they wouldn't have to go far to find firewood.

Vicky shivered as Joseph built a fire to ward off the chill. They'd only need the extra warmth for another week or so before summer's heat made it unnecessary. The new weeds poking up indicated that the area had already been clear of frost for weeks. That was good. Summer's heat couldn't come soon enough for Vicky.

She could hardly wait to feel the sun on her aching joints.

Chapter Nineteen

THERE WERE TWENTY MISSILES STREAKING TO IMPACT THE PLANET'S surface. I was the only passenger on one, but not for long.

When the sabot blew away I flew off with the rest of the debris as the super-dense ballistic payload continued screaming toward a Shardie location over the horizon. It carried a single altitude-sensing charge in its tail that would accelerate the payload to strike at a thousand kps. At that hypervelocity the shock wave and impact would blast a crater five kilometers across and send dirt, rock, and dust into the stratosphere.

Twenty of these hitting the planet would be my diversion.

The wind whipped me as I dropped deeper into the atmosphere. Tendrils of spidersilk deployed behind me, threads with hundreds of microparachutes along their length, each one exerting minuscule drag, stealing momentum from my descent, then blowing away to swiftly dissolve in the air.

The tendrils would be indistinguishable from the thousands of smaller, broken fragments from the sabot. I just hoped that my presence was as indistinguishable.

I skimmed trees and hills, stirring trails of dust as I moved at better than ten meters per second through the last portion of my drop. When the final threads tore away I was moving at eight meters per second, slow enough to give me a chance of survival on impact.

I tucked for the bounce and roll, hoping that I'd hit where nothing would stop me before all my potential energy was dissipated. Desert sand would be nice, water better, but I'd take an open field if it came to that.

Just no damn forests.

The weak and fading signal had come unexpectedly from a colony world abandoned to the Shardies six months before. It was a short burst that might have been missed if fleet hadn't had a SIGINT unit probing the Shardies' signals.

"We tried to get away, but the things caught us," the high-pitched voice had cried. "I'm hiding. Please help me."

Fleet was conflicted. It was not impossible that some group might have been missed during the evacuation. Campers, spelunkers, or others could have been isolated when the order was sent. How long had it taken to move the twenty thousand off the planet—two weeks, eighteen days? They'd packed the colonists into any ship they could find. Most vessels barely had enough oxygen to sustain the refugees. The evacuation was chaotic, disorganized, and messy. They tried to get everyone, but still, some might have been missed.

Should we ignore it? Command asked, thinking that the loss of a single individual was as nothing compared to the risks of extracting the survivor. Maybe the call was a ruse, a trap. Then again, either might be worth the valuable intelligence we'd gain to mount an effort. Fleet was desperate to learn anything it could about the relentless Shardies advance, especially how a child had managed to elude capture.

Nobody had ever escaped the Shardies, not since we discovered how they turned any survivor into organic components for their ships. The Shardies had been relentless in driving us off from our colony worlds. In deep space it was no better. They destroyed our most hardened ships with better tactics and weapons. Since we'd first encountered them, they had relentlessly continued to advance. If the war persisted as it had for the past three years, with us abandoning one world after the next, the Shardies would reach Earth within a decade, or maybe less.

Fleet needed whatever information the survivor might have. Earth needed the hope that someone could survive to report what they had seen. We all needed to know.

Command had no choice. Someone had to find whoever sent that signal.

The deployment was carefully planned to minimize risk. Four high-speed, light-attack ships would emerge from blink just beyond the Holzberg limit, each firing a stick of five Rapture missiles and blink away, hopefully before the Shardies had time to react. The theorists calculated that if the total hang time near the planet was fifteen to eighteen seconds—the upper limit only if a ship had to roll into firing position—they all might have a chance to get away.

The seconds after firing were the dangerous time for the ships' crews. If they didn't reach the Holzberg limit in those eighteen seconds, the overstressed drives would turn the ship and everyone on board into an instantaneously brilliant cloud of dispersing plasma. I had the easy part, they said.

All I had to do was survive long enough to send my signal.

The hundreds of fragments from the sabot spread out in an elongated, egg-shaped pattern over a thousand square kilometers along the path of the payload. Even if the Shardies weren't preoccupied cleaning up the destruction from the missiles' impacts and suspected something, they'd still waste a lot of time finding and inspecting that many pieces. Expand those searches over twenty patterns and you came up with the decreasing probability of my being detected. I knew that, even with that sort of insurance, they'd eventually find my landing spot. It was only a matter of time. I had to hurry.

I discovered I was still in one piece when I uncoiled my aching body after the too-long bounce and roll. My left arm dangled loosely and a chunk of that shoulder was missing. Other than that, all my parts seemed to be functional. I probed the arm and found that it had been dislocated by whatever I hit. Some pressure in the right places, a little twist of the shoulder, and the arm was nearly as good as the day it was installed.

I checked my position and discovered that I was nearly two hundred kilometers away from the location of the signal. Hell of an overshoot, but not bad, considering the variables. The deviation could have come from upper-level winds or some other unexpected variable. I figured two days to hike there, if I didn't stop.

I set out.

The location was a tiny coastal village. I could see the foundations of thirty buildings from my perch on the ridgeline, twenty of them might have been homes. The long piers told me that this might have been a fishing community, but whatever boats had docked there were now gone. One road ran down the center of town and there was a landing pad to the West. The landing pad looked too raw, too new.

Judging from the amount of debris on the road there must have been a hell of a panic when they abandoned this place. Maybe that's where the boats had gone. Had they been used to transport the colonists to an evacuation point?

I imagined they'd scuttled them, rather than leave anything for the damned Shardie bastards.

I watched the town until nightfall but saw no evidence that anything alive was down there. Not a stray dog or cat, not a rat, and no birds. An hour after dark, I worked my way down the slope, pausing often, alert for some sign of movement, some indication that I had been spotted.

I kept my disruptor ready. The Shardies tripods were incredibly fast so I'd only have milliseconds to react—just enough time to squeeze the trigger once, but that was all it would take.

The largest building had been filled with cold, stone tubs and long wooden tables. Here and there were holders for slender knives. Fishing village for sure, I guessed.

I worked my way down the road, passing from one ruin to the next as swiftly and silently as I could. On the fifth foundation, I found her.

I shifted sight to infrared and surveyed the room. The only heat source was her small body. The only sound her slow breathing. The only light a shaft of moonlight through the shutters.

I put a hand over the girl's mouth and shook her gently. She struggled briefly and then went limp, her eyes wide in horror when she got a glimpse of me. "Sergeant Millikan, Fifth Marine," I said softly. I doubted anyone could overhear, but you can never be too careful where the Shardies are concerned. "I've come for you," I said, which while completely true, was not necessarily accurate.

"I didn't think anyone would come," she said in a rush. "Especially not something like you." She seemed to accept my assurance that I was a Marine, but not quite sure that I was a someone.

I took a good look at her: skinny, scraggly hair, and filthy, all of which would be expected from what she had been through. Her black hair was cut short, her nails broken—some bitten to the quick—and crusted with God-knows-what. She had a gash on the top of her head that might be pretty bad under the crust of scabby blood. She looked to be about fifteen, maybe a year or two more or as much less—too damn young to be in this situation, not that there was any other age that would be better.

A pair of muddy tan boots that looked three sizes too large for her sat by her side. Nearby was a smelly pile of fish entrails.

She caught my glance. "I fished last night," she said. "By hand." And ate it raw, I guessed. That was smart. A fire would attract attention.

"How long have you been here?" I asked. "How did you get here?"

"A week, I think," she replied. "I was a mile up the coast, but I came here after I used that 'phone." She must have seen my puzzled expression. "A mile is about one and a half kilometers," she explained.

"Archaic measure," I recalled. A lot of the colonies went back to the old measures as a signal of their departure from Earth's ways. Well, that experiment didn't last long, did it?

But, a week? "Where were you before that?" It had been nearly six months since the Shardies arrived on this world.

She shrugged. "Running, hiding, keeping away from them, I just kept going until I found the 'phone—back there," she waved a hand in the general direction of the door.

I looked. It was an old unit, leaking battery acid and showing no power light. She must have drained it in that single cry for help. I left it there. Useless.

"Are you taking me away?" she asked when I returned.

That was a good question. Staying in the village wasn't a good idea. The Shardies methodically erased all signs of human presence before they moved on, so it was only a matter of time before they destroyed this one. It could be next week, or within an hour. Or maybe they were too busy checking the debris and dealing with the effects of the multiple strikes. "Yes," I said.

The girl quickly gathered her few belongings—the boots, a ship's jacket with a Fourth Fleet emblem on the shoulder, a wicked knife with a serrated back, and the blanket she had been sleeping under—before we set out.

"My name's Tashia," she said softly.

"Call me Sergeant," I replied.

I led her up the slope, following the same path I had taken in just in case they could follow our heat trail. Once we were on top I intended to stay to the rocks and touch the ground only where we couldn't avoid it. That way we'd avoid leaving obvious signs of our passage. I knew we couldn't escape detection completely, but there was no sense in making our trail easy either.

She began to lag behind after we'd covered barely ten kilometers and slumped to the ground at fifteen. "Sarge, I can't go any further," she sighed. "I'm so tired."

I dug into my side pocket and pulled out one of my G-rations. "Eat this," I ordered. The strong military stimulants probably wouldn't do her weakened body any good but the nutrients in the bar would provide her with the strength to last until daybreak.

Intelligence had force-fed me every speck of information about this world they could glean out of the colonists. In the very early days of the colony there had been a small mining operation on this plateau. The vein turned out to be shallow and petered out within a year or so, but not before producing enough coal to fuel the first few settlements. After the mine was abandoned, all of the miners had moved on, leaving behind only those things they could not take with them—foundations and the mineshaft. Machinery, building materials, household goods, everything that could be moved was taken away.

I found the entrance to the shaft before the sky started to gray. I took us back deep enough that I couldn't see the stars framed in the entrance. I flopped down with my back against the wall to face the way we'd come.

Tashia sat near my side, arms hugging her stick-thin legs against her chest. "I'm glad you came, Sarge," she said. "I was so afraid nobody would. I just used that 'phone to let somebody know I was alive."

"You said there were others. Tell me about it."

She shook her head. "Dad died, I guess." She said that in such a calm voice that I figured she'd already drained emotion from the memory. "Dad and I were out camping when everyone else went away. I guess we sort of got overlooked."

I nodded. It could happen. Emergency evacuations are messy affairs at best, chaotic at worst. Easy to suppose the missing ones were on another boat, another vehicle. A few could get lost.

"We didn't know where to go. We couldn't find anyone. It was like they all ran away." She was trembling as she recalled that frightening time. "Then the *things* came for us."

"Things? What did they look like?" This was good information. A first-hand description might help someone.

She shook. "I...I didn't get a really good look, but they were glowing, sort of. It was night and they moved so fast. They put me in a sort of box. It was so small I couldn't stand up in it. Dark, too."

"Did you hear anything, sense anything—a smell, an aroma, anything at all?"

She was silent for a long while. "No. I was so cold. They took my clothes so I had goose bumps all over."

"Anything else?" I had to get as much information from her as I could in the time remaining. "How long were you in the box?"

She frowned. "Maybe a few days 'cause I got really, really thirsty. One day I woke up the top of the box was opened a crack. I stuck my fingers in the crack and pried it open.

"I was in a white room with a lot of icicles, only they weren't ice at all. More like glass, you know?"

"Was there anything else in the room—somebody moving around, a machine, anything that you'd recognize?"

She thought a moment before replying. "A couple of other boxes and those weird icicles everywhere."

"Go on, please. What did you do then?"

"I ran. I had to get out of the scary room and away from the box. I found a pile of stuff from our camp—that's where I got some clothes—then I ran away into the woods."

Her story sounded too bizarre. Were the boxes and the room figments of her imagination or was she telling the truth? "How did you hurt your head?"

Her hand darted to the gash. "Oh, I guess I must have cut it on one of the icicles. It stings," she added quickly, almost as an afterthought.

"Let me see," I said. She leaned forward. The long gash ran from just above her left temple to the top of her skull. I could see little flecks of glass in the wound. "That looks like it had to hurt."

"I guess it did, but I must have been too scared to notice," she said. "Anyhow, I ran and ran until I found a place to hide. After that I kept running from one spot to the next at night so the things wouldn't find me. Then I found the 'phone and made the call. I prayed somebody might come. Somebody." She was quiet for a long while after that. "You, Sarge," she added in a small voice.

"The Shardies don't usually let humans go," I replied. "They make them into components, use human brains to help them win this war."

Her mouth formed a small "O" of horror. "That's what they were going to do to me?" she cried. "Oh, my God!"

"That's why Command sent me. We had to find out how you managed to escape and hear what you could tell us about the aliens. That's why I'm here."

"You must be really brave," she yawned and stretched. "I don't think I could do something like that." She hugged my arm. "But I'm not scared now that you're here. I know you'll take care of me."

"Get some sleep," I said. "Just pick a spot."

She dropped the blanket next to me. "You can share," she suggested, offering me a corner.

"I don't need sleep," I replied. "I rest a different way." No sense telling her that I could shut down the remaining organic component of my brain while the autonomic parts took care of surveillance and housekeeping. Better she remained ignorant of all the terrible things the surgeons did to me. Better that she continue to think of me as just a Marine and leave it at that.

I'd been going continuously through the past fifty-eight hours and needed some rest. Not long, though. The diversions of the missile strike, the escaping ships, and hundreds of pieces of sabot shred gave me, at most, thirty hours more before I expected to be found. Sleep and rest would steal many of those hours, leaving me only a narrow bit of time to complete my mission.

Tashia fell asleep snuggled against my hip with one arm thrown across my waist. I felt her soft breath against my left arm and her gentle movements as deep sleep relaxed tired muscles. At rest she looked so innocent, so peaceful that one could easily imagine her snuggled in her own bed, dreaming of boys and dances, of family and friends, of loved pets and fond memories. But my imagination could only take me so far before brutal, ugly reality intruded.

I heard a faint, nearly indistinguishable sound and went instantly on alert. I reached the mine's entrance in under two seconds and tuned every sense to hyper-alertness. There! Near the horizon was a golden glow brighter than the early dawn light. It moved right to left, possibly tracing the path I had followed to reach the village. Were they tracing us or was their route merely happenstance?

If the former, they would be here in a few hours. We had to move.

Tashia groaned when I lifted her, but didn't wake as we left the mine. Her weight was negligible, less than a full combat pack, but more awkward to carry.

"What's happening?" she whispered after we'd gone a few kilometers. "Where are we?"

"Running," I replied. "I think we're being followed."

She stifled a cry, showing more wisdom than I expected. "Those things," she said. "They're fast."

"So am I," I replied. "They gave me really strong legs."

"What happened to you?" she asked. "I know you don't look right. Are you a freak or something?"

It was a fair question. I doubt that my own mother would recognize me like this. She would probably disown me if she did.

"Sort of like that," I replied. "They had to rebuild me after an… *accident.* It was touch and go. I almost died, they tell me. If I hadn't given consent I would have, but they did ask me, and that was only after they told me my options. Live and be useful like this, or die. Some choice."

"But you chose life," she whispered and squeezed my neck. "I'm glad."

"Not exactly a blessing. There's the pain, for one thing," I replied honestly. "It's constant. I can't laugh anymore, nor cry for that matter. Everything seems dead to me, no nuance or gradations. It's like not caring any more, only I do care about things, like rescuing pretty little girls and helping the war effort."

She didn't reply, but I got another hug.

"Where did you say you got that jacket?" I asked casually. "There were no survivors of the Fourth Fleet."

"It was Dad's," she said. "I don't know where he got it. Maybe he was a veteran or something."

"That's a ship's jacket, not something anyone would wear anywhere but on board. Do you know what happened to the Fourth?"

"N…n...no," she whispered.

"The Shardies captured the ship and took prisoners," I explained. "We found some of them on a captured ship, wired into the controls." Then I added. "They weren't dead. Not then."

"But Dad wore it all the time. He didn't tell me about his ship or the aliens or anything. I was just cold and wanted something to wear so I wouldn't be so scared and cold and all." She began sobbing. "I didn't mean to do anything bad, Sarge."

"I know, honey. I didn't think you knew about the jacket. That's why I told you." *Not the only reason,* I added to myself.

I checked the time. Twenty-two probable hours left. Much less if they were already trailing us. Not much time, either way.

"We've got to signal soon," I said. "The target's not far from here. Think you can walk for a while?" I set her down. I wasn't tired from carrying her slight weight, but I did want to have both hands free should anything happen.

"Give me another of those candy bars and I think I could run there." Her laughter was like tonic to my ears. It had been so long since I'd heard a young girl laugh, so long and so far back in my past that I had forgotten how wonderful it could sound.

I fished out two bars and threw her one. "They're a little chewy without something to wash them down, but maybe we can find some water."

We moved with the wind, moving as quickly as Tashia could manage in her condition, burning energy fast to reach the target in the shortest amount of time. With the augments in my legs and the hyperventilation of my lungs I could outrun a cheetah if I had to, but Tashia couldn't. Even with the bar's energy boost, she could probably outrun a house cat, if it was tired and old.

"Are you going to call the fleet?" she asked. "How are they going to get us without those things knowing about it?"

"Fleet has ways of landing undetected," I lied. "Stealth, charged ice, snowflake, and owls' wing tech for the most part. The stuff is so good, the Shardies wouldn't even know we were here."

Her eyes grew wide. "I never heard about all that!"

"There's a lot you wouldn't know," I said as I started the timer buried in my abdomen. I stuffed three more G-rations into my mouth to provide the energy I needed for the high-speed signal burst. The SIGINT boys high above would be waiting for anything sparkling within a hundred kilometers of the target location, just in case I didn't make it all the way.

"We are going away, aren't we?" she said, panic rising in her voice as she nervously scanned the area. I checked. Whatever that golden glow had been it wasn't detectable any more.

"There was a lot of debate about sending someone down here," I said as the timer activated the signaling process, storing the data I had collected, along with my conclusions for the burst. "Fleet thought you might be exactly what you said—a poor little survivor who managed to sneak away from the Shardies. On the other hand, they suspected that it might have been just a false signal to lure us into a trap."

"But it wasn't a trap," Tashia said. "I really did use the 'phone. I really did run away from the things."

"There's the matter of the jacket." That damned cursed incongruous jacket that had no reason to be on this or any other planet.

"No, I told you. It was Dad's," she cried. "You have to believe me."

"Then Fleet wondered if there was the possibility that you might not be human any more: That the Shardies wanted to loose a new horror on us with a new way of using humans."

Tashia patted herself. "No, no. I'm me! Look at me. I'm as human as you, maybe *more* than you. Here," she threw open her jacket to bare herself.

I looked at the small mounds of her budding breasts, the ribs showing under her thin skin, and the little blue veins that ran across her chest.

I gently tugged the sides of her jacket together. "I know, Tashia. I believe you. I never doubted that you were human, not for an instant."

I could feel the heat building up inside of me as I processed the G-ration into the squirter's storage unit. "I've recorded everything you told me," I went on. "Earth will hear it all and probably interpret more from what you said than even you know."

"But I'm not one of them," she cried. "I ran away. They didn't p...pro...process me like you said."

I thought about her escape, the improbable discovery of the ancient 'phone, and surviving on fish captured with her bare hands. Taken together they were improbable, but not impossible.

She might not be a conscious Shardie agent, might not even know if she was one, but there was that jacket, those glimmers of glass in her head, and those unexplainable gaps of time and memory. What had they really done while she slept in the box?

Tashia was sobbing. "I did so escape, just like I told you. I ran away. I was so scared. I didn't know what to do."

"I know." Oh God, I remembered the sound of her laughter, her curiosity about me, her desire to get back to her family and friends. It was all so, so human.

"Listen, Tashia," I said. "The problem is that even if you really are one-hundred percent human, they still couldn't risk rescuing you."

"But they could examine me, see if anything is wrong, see if those things did something to me. They could do that, couldn't they?" she pleaded. "Couldn't they?"

"They could," I replied softly. "But they won't. The important thing about sending me here was to get whatever information you could give us. That's what's important—the information." Yes, that and the fact that, despite all odds, a little girl, a human girl, had escaped to tell her tale. That fact alone would give everyone hope that we could find a way to fight back and, hopefully, win.

The heat was so intense that I knew the mission's end was near. In a few seconds everything within fifty meters would be consumed in an intense blast of encoded coherent light that would tell the watchers overhead all that I had heard and seen. The blast would leave scorched ground that looked like a rocket had taken off. The Shardies weren't the only ones who could use misdirection.

"But you do believe me, don't you, Sarge?" she cried, as if seeking a final bit of certainty.

"Yes," I replied softly as I reached out and hugged her close to give her one last bit of comfort against the cold dark and partly to ensure that nothing would remain for the Shardies to analyze.

"You're as human as me."

Chapter Twenty

General Thoss felt as if the weight of the war and its ethical choices would eventually drive him into suicidal guilt. "How many men have we turned into machines, Steve?" he asked his deputy. "Worse, what gave us the right to turn them into nothing more than disposables? How many thousands of instanced souls have we condemned to die again and again and again?"

"You can't think like that and stay sane," Gould responded. "I made my peace with what we had to do to survive and so should you."

Thoss appreciated that. Steve had finally swallowed his ethical considerations, as the opportunity of actually winning the war against the aliens became a real possibility. Just as there were no atheists in foxholes neither were there strong religious convictions at command level where practical considerations and expediency ruled. Gould might still quail at the moral choices, but he had made them anyhow and hoped his God would forgive him. For himself, Thoss was certain that none of the instanced machines would even understand, given their unflinching singleness of purpose.

"You're just overwrought," he said as he looked at his deputy on the other side of the desk. "But I do understand what you are feeling." Both of them had glasses of Tennessee whiskey in their hands as they had their evening chat about the events of the day. Both of them needed the short period of relaxation from the intense pressures of managing their part of the war effort. "We're still in the early stages of this instancing process. We don't have any certainty they will be more effective against the Shards than our other efforts. The only other thing that's worked so far has been carpet bombing, which pretty much sets our colony worlds back to square one."

Gould took a sip as he considered that. "Even with nothing left some of the evacuees will want to go back."

Thoss agreed. "It would take a lot of courage for a colonist to return to a place the Shardies have invaded and the Navy wiped clean. There would always be the fear of the aliens returning, a fear renewed by every crater, every ruin, every bit of evidence that humans had once tried to conquer their planet and failed. That might take as much courage as any of our Marines facing combat would ever need."

"Let's see how the new weapons platforms work out before we give up," Gould said as he finished his drink. "Now I have to get back to wringing more transports out of the Navy. They seem to think that defeating the aliens' ships will end the threat."

Thoss savored the last few drops of the Tennessee whiskey before he answered. "That might stop them from invading, but we still have to defeat those left on the ground before anyone can even start to think about resettlement. Let's pray that this instancing thing will help us win the war." He thought for a few moments before he spoke again. "Maybe winning will keep us from turning people into machines."

The data from the Drop Colony Two scouts arrived at headquarters via fast packet and was immediately sent to analysis to glean every last ounce of information they could wrest from the scout's captured images. General Thoss sent his new aide, a Colonel Barrity, to observe, along with Doctor Lansington, one of Doctor Mores' science advisors.

The most arresting images were the glistening carpets of smooth objects moving through the remains of the ruined colonial town being led by three-legged machines. The carpet seemed composed of a myriad of glistening gems moving in concert with no defined head. It moved with a smooth undulating progress.

"Maybe the three-legged things are herding them," Barrity suggested.

"No! See how they are careful not to step on any," Lansington corrected him. "They seem to be following the objects."

Everyone in the room jumped when the carpet climbed the walls of a standing building and consumed it in a blaze of coruscating heat in a matter of minutes. The images held a certain beauty at the same time that they were horrifying. "Scout reported an intense microwave burst," someone remarked.

Barrity swore. "How are we going to stop something like that? Bad enough that our Marines can't stop the three-legged bastards; now we have to worry about how to halt that flood of whatever they are?"

"They don't seem to move very fast," Lansington observed.

"Are those things alive?" the Colonel asked as he leaned forward. "They seem to be moving with purpose." He turned to the specialist operating the display. "Can we get a higher resolution image of that flow?"

A single, low-res expansion filled the freeze frame. "They look like smooth rocks."

"I think we analyzed something like that a few years ago," Lansington said. "I seem to recall that they puzzled us. Even after we collected and examined most of what we found." He shrugged. "We still didn't know what they were, but the analysis reports should still be in the archive." He turned to a tech. "Pull up my research files from last year, about November as I recall."

In a matter of moments the analysis report and accompanying images were on display.

"Unbelievable!" Barrity swore. The archived pebble looked identical to the gems on the screen.

"So now we know what they are," the aide said.

"If these are the Shardies," the Colonel cautioned. "They could be just another tool."

"Either way," Lansington smiled as he glanced through the file and came to the destructive sonic tests he'd run. "I think we know how to destroy them!"

Even though Lansington's laboratory testing proved the effectiveness of using a broadcasting unit in shattering the pebbles, destroying them proved more difficult in field tests.

"It's the resonance," one of the combat engineers reported to Barrity, who was project lead. "We can only destroy twenty-thirty percent of them with any specific frequency and it only slows the tripods."

Barrity frowned. "So? We have to shift frequencies. What's so hard about that?"

The engineer sighed. He'd already explained this to Barrity's staff twice, but apparently the message was not getting through. "Two things, Colonel: range and speed. The sonic emitters only work at a hundred meters or less and it takes precious seconds to switch settings to another frequency and even that frequency may not get all the little bastards. The crews aren't able to wipe out enough of them before the tripods overrun and destroy the equipment. They're relentless."

Barrity didn't ask about the crews that operated the equipment. He'd read the reports and written the condolence letters. "Can we use airborne? Hover over them where they can't get to us?"

The engineer shook his head. "Tried that. It worked at first, but then the Shards started shooting them down. The aliens learn damn quick and somehow manage to spread the word to others. We also tried grouping transmitters to cover several frequencies, with no better results."

Colonel Barrity scowled. He'd had enough of problems without solutions. "So we have to adapt faster. Come on, gentlemen, let's have some decent ideas on how we can use these sonic units to gain the upper hand." He looked around the table. "I want proposals on my desk before Friday. Dismissed."

Only Doctor Lansington remained behind as the staff rushed for the doors.

"Well, what do you want?" Barrity demanded with annoyance when the door closed. "I've got dozens of other items demanding attention."

Lansington tented his fingers. "It's all fine to want to destroy these things, but there are some deeper questions we need to answer. For one thing, I don't think what we're seeing are anything more than machines."

"Are you out of your mind?" Barrity was incredulous. "The Shards are flying starships, attacking planets, and outfighting everything we throw at them. They can't be simple machines. The idea's ridiculous!"

"No more fantastic than anything else connected to them."

"This better be worth the time it's wasting."

Lansington ignored the implied insult and smiled. "We've studied enough feeds from the scouts and observations to support my tentative conclusions."

"Which are?" Barrity's question hung in the air in a cloud of expectation that Lansington seemed unwilling to precipitate. Finally he smiled. "Consider ants and bees."

"I hope this has some relevance," Barrity grumbled. Over the past six months of weapons development he'd learned to accept Lansington's academic style of speaking. Maddening, but occasionally it was worth the wait.

"An individual ant or bee has minimal intelligence and can do little to assure its survival," the scientist continued. "However, a colony of several hundred thousand ants can do a number of things we associate with intelligence—the colony can feed itself, build shelters, care for its young, and even move to a different location whenever the environment changes. In a sense, the colony acts as a single individual even though there is no intellect behind it."

Barrity leaned forward. "Are you saying that these rocks, these crystals or whatever the hell they are like ants? I find that hard to believe."

"We've discovered that each individual pebble exhibits no life properties, however, when a sufficient number are put together we can detect movement, albeit at very modest levels."

"What happens when you put more than a 'low' number of them together?" Barrity asked. "What happens then?"

Lansington shuffled his papers and cleared his throat. "That experiment was, ah, *indeterminate,*" he answered.

Barrity jumped to his feet. "What the hell does that mean?"

"We lost the samples," Lansington answered and scowled. "They melted."

Barrity was incredulous. "So we spent God knows how many Marines to collect these things and then you just lose them?"

"We only used about a thousand of them, Colonel, not all we've been given. At nine hundred they were just a pile of pebbles—hardly any activity except emanating heat. When we added fifty more they put out considerably more heat and started agitating." He shuffled his papers nervously before he continued in a softer voice. "We were adding the last fifty to the mix when the melt took place."

"But how come we can see such huge piles of them in the scout feeds if so few initiate an explosion? Crap, there must have been a million of them in those images."

"I don't think it was the number of them." Lansington chewed his lip and looked down, quiet for a long time. Finally he sighed. "I hate to say this Colonel, but, somehow, they reacted to what we were doing."

"That's a ridiculous explanation," Barrity complained. "You said these things were just inert rocks, mineral aggregations. Rocks can't be alive."

"The evidence suggests otherwise," Lansington answered dryly. "Or are you implying that my premise is incorrect in some way? Perhaps you disagree with my conclusions, but you cannot reject the simple fact that these things demonstrate a collective intelligence."

Barrity was unwilling to concede the point. "The whole idea is ridiculous. Ants and bees developed over millions of years. We've found precursors from before they became social, before they became colonies. Unless you believe in spontaneous creation, everything has to evolve from earlier forms to more complex versions. Sorry, doctor, but I find the idea of evolved rocks highly speculative. Where's your evidence of that?"

"Colonel, you are assuming that these things grew naturally," Lansington replied. "These things could have been created, fabricated, or formed by something else. They might be the result of some technology as yet beyond us. They might simply be machines."

Barrity thought for a minute. "I find that more appealing than pretty little rocks building starships and invasion vehicles."

"Which is why I want to suggest that we mount a search to discover the origins of these Shards and discover whatever is directing their forces."

"That's even more ridiculous. Such a search could take centuries," Barrity scoffed. "It's a big universe out there."

Lansington grinned. "Excellent point, which is why we need to undertake a development project immediately."

"Let's win the damned war first, then maybe we can start searching for these mysterious directors of yours. That is, if you are right."

Farside IV was the turning point in the ground battle against the Shardies. Armor and speed were the two things that had been steadily increasing after each unsuccessful encounter. The long pole in the tent was shipping the gel "brains" to the staging centers producing the new weapons systems. Eventually, the supply lines grew too cumbersome and responsibility for local reproduction of instances was shifted as close to where they were needed as possible.

"We have no idea of how many instances have been produced or lost," Thoss complained to Admiral Jones. "I'm not sure it that's a good thing or not."

"I know what you mean, Sid. Our own labs are using instanced pilots. With their direct interfaces they can match the speed and agility of the Shard ships. Eliminating all that life support gear means smaller and faster ships. Hell, they even instanced one into a Heavy Destroyer, our most powerful warship!"

"Doesn't that make you nervous?" Thoss asked. "What if it gets pissed and decides to turn on us? I've wondered about the same thing myself. A drunk Marine is terrifying enough, a wild MULE slightly worse, a Cyber even more so, even a freaking hundred-ton battle tank going rogue is terrifying. Thank heavens we can turn them off if needed."

Jones raised an eyebrow. "That seems at odds with your comments in our staff meetings. Where is the sympathy for the poor souls we've instanced? Wouldn't turning them off be the same as killing them?"

"You're no different." Thoss scowled at the reminder. "You just said you've got the Navy using instanced pilots. And if the pilots are just instances, then they're expendable. Why not use them to ram the Shardie ships? That's always been a Shardie strategy. It would be nothing more than turning those same tactics against them."

Jones started to protest. "That's only a possibility, not something we would...."

Thoss wouldn't let him finish. "Damn it! Don't deny the consequences of your decisions. We both knew where this instancing was going to take us. We both understood the consequences."

Admiral Jones put his head in his hands. "I know, Sid. I know. We're becoming our enemy."

"And probably losing our souls," Thoss replied, echoing his deputy's earlier objection. "That is, if we had them to begin with."

Now that Command knew their importance, efforts were underway to collect as many of the strange pebbles as possible. Learning from past experience, Lansington warned his researchers about the critical mass and spread the collections over several research locations.

The first breakthrough was an explanation of how the seemingly crystalline pebbles could move. "They generate an electrostatic field, quite small, barely enough to clear the surface, but sufficient to reduce friction. When they rub against each other, the repulsion forces them along the resultant vector of motion. This seems to increase with the number of pebbles involved." Lansington sat back as General Thoss, Barrity's superior officer, digested the information.

"Any idea how these things melt buildings and people?" he barked. They'd just watched some combat footage of tripods consuming a MULE operator beneath a silver fountain.

"No, sir, but I have three teams working on it. We're also trying to find out how they manage to detect our forces. If we could get just one of those tripods intact...."

"Don't take me for a fool, Doctor. We've been trying to do just that for years. You tell me how to stop one and I'll deliver it to you personally. In the meantime, why don't you come up with something based on the pieces we *have* managed to collect?"

Lansington sighed. "A leg, a bit of what might have been a body part, and several glass panels tougher than hull metal haven't provided any more insight than the combat images. What we need is whatever drives these things. How do they navigate, move, or detect our forces? What is the source of their incredible speed and strength?

"If only I could get just one into our laboratories," he pleaded. "I wish that drunken Marine were here to explain further how he'd managed to escape with the pebbles. If only…"

He stopped as he had a sudden idea. "What if that bag of rocks had afforded some protection? What if he hadn't so much defeated the machines, but escaped them?"

"Could we run a field test?" Barrity asked.

"With the proper vibrational stimulation they exhibit a slight movement. I think the effect becomes more pronounced when we add more pebbles. Why won't you let us have more than half a dozen at a time? Seems silly to me." Tupac Doctor Lei, the lead analyst complained.

"It is for your own safety, as you would know if you'd stayed awake during the security drills. Those little pebbles pack a huge punch when they are aggregated. I lost a friend that way, years ago."

"I know that," Lei admitted. "But that involved hundreds, not dozens. We need a bigger collection, like maybe thirty or forty?" He looked longingly at Lansington.

"I'll authorize a couple dozen, but you only work with them a few at a time. We don't know what these things are capable of doing. We don't even know if they are animal or mineral."

"Just two dozen?" Lei frowned. "So be it. I'll see what I can do, Doctor."

While Tupac continued his research, Lansington, found himself trying to untangle the puzzle presented by the battered, broken, and half-melted remains of an alien tripod General Thoss' new aide hand-delivered.

"It looks like getting this involved more than a gentle touch," Lansington joked as he looked at the pieces. Nevertheless, he was beside himself at this answer to his long denied prayers and immediately set a half dozen of his best scientists to determine how this tripod had been a deadly menace on the battlefield.

He was also curious as to what sort of technology gave the thing its mobility. The broken shells were empty save for traces of alien cells scraped from the walls. A few hair-thin filaments dangled loose from one piece that was remarkably similar to the well-documented threads binding the Jeaux human brains to the Shardie ships.

"I think this indicates they're using yet another species' brains," he guessed. "Maybe the tripods are nothing more than machines—automatons directed by alien minds."

"So the real enemy rides inside these things?" the Colonel asked.

"Didn't you hear what I said? Maybe these tripods are operated the same way the Shardie ships are, using some other creature's brains. But we can't determine that until we analyze what we have."

Lansington tried not to let either his fatigue or anger show. The military was unreasonable in their demand for immediate answers. He'd only had the wreckage for a few hours and they already wanted engineering answers of how to destroy the monsters.

"Is that a weak point we can exploit?" the Colonel asked. "Could we put a round into some weak spot on their bodies?"

"How many rounds have been expended since we started this fucking war, Colonel? If there were any weak spots statistics would say one of your ground troops would have found it by now. No, there are no soft spots. Matter of fact, nobody has seen fit to provide me with the facts surrounding the destruction of this particular artifact. Did somebody stumble on it, was it destroyed in a battle, or did it simply commit Hare Kari?"

"I can answer that," the Colonel answered. "Our men were looking for a base site on one of the moons and we got an anomalous reading. When they went down to inspect they found this stuff half buried in the rubble. There was nothing else in the area to indicate why it was there or what might have done the damage."

Lansington's mind went into high gear. How long had it lain there? "Did anyone think to measure the deposition surrounding it that might give us a clue? Was there a blast crater or other evidence of conflict? I need answers, as many as you can provide."

"And soon," he added.

"They're just machines!" Lansington declared to the military delegation with the certainty of his team ready to support him. "All of the Shardies we've encountered so far are nothing more than machines. We have to assume that they have been created by technologies well beyond our own."

"What drives the bastards?" General Phutagramma asked. "Didn't earlier reports say that the aliens wired themselves inside?"

Lansington sighed. The military types always misunderstood the uncertainty inherent in scientific statements. "From the assortment of miscellaneous wreckage gathered since that first half-melted tripod, we've parsed no less than three types of alien brain cells, none of which could possibly have come from the same antecedents."

"Then whatever is behind the Shardies conquered other races and are continuing to use their brains as components?" the General replied so quickly that Lansington wondered if he'd received prior knowledge of his findings. "I recall hearing that the Shards had a breeding program to produce more human brains. Are these Shardies spooning other captive brains into their machines as well?"

Lansington answered. "Yes. That must be how they developed the techniques and simply adapted them to human captives."

"But so fast? Why haven't they advanced even further if they are that good?" General Phutagramma pursued that line of thought. "Ah, I see, they cannot move beyond because they are limited by the capacity of their enslaved minds."

"Then why hasn't whatever produced them come up with more technical advances to counter us?" Captain Averista asked. She was General Thoss's much-augmented aide of the moment, a position no doubt earned in the war. She looked as if she wasn't far from being another gel-enabled cyber.

"It might be a feature of propagation delay. Whoever sent these things might just now be learning about our initial reaction." Lansington paused. "They might send worse opponents when they react to that knowledge and begin escalating the technology."

"But for now we have a slight advantage, yes?" The General didn't look as if he would accept a negative answer.

"General, even if we drive these aliens from our worlds, is there any guarantee that they wouldn't move on? Is there any guarantee that they will not unleash their technology on yet another race, dominate, collect, and move on to create more murderous machines that spread like a cancer through the galaxy?"

"We have to destroy the Shardies completely and utterly in order to make ourselves safe," General Phutagramma replied. "We have to take the battle to them, and, if you are right about the delay, we need to figure out how to do that *now*!"

"I'll start my team on finding a solution to that problem immediately," Lansington assured them, but he had no idea how to deliver.

Chapter Twenty-One

Captain Sandels came in during prep. "Geordie," he said, but softly, as if he didn't want to disturb the techs working on squeezing my compact form into the bomb casing. I opened our channel: *Kind of busy right now. Something come up?*

"No," the Captain responded, again so softly that I knew he definitely didn't want the techs to overhear. The only reason I could hear him was that my acoustic enhancements were so sensitive that I could hear a mouse fart from a klick away. "I just wanted to wish you luck."

"For making it back?" I answered. *"Not likely."*

"That's brutal," he replied and I heard his pain. "I thought that, after all we...."

I stopped him there. *I wasn't* Geordie Yang; *just a revised edition.*

"So it's just goodbye, then?"

Sure. I closed the channel before he could say anything else. What I didn't need was some damn puzzling reference to a past that no longer concerned me. Better not to dwell on what had been. Given humanity's precarious state, sentiment was dangerous. Besides, I had to concentrate on my scouting mission to learn more about the aliens on the planet below.

I shut off everything but the maintenance channel as they oozed the cushioning gel around me. Its plasticity enfolded me in a warm, soft embrace that crept into every crack and crevice, sealing me off from sight and sound and every sense save an assurance of my own existence. My form might be much reduced, to be sure, but nevertheless I retained my inherent humanity.

"We're closing the lid," the tech reported over the maintenance channel.

Time for sleep. Hitting the planet's surface would wake me up.

The idea behind the drop was dramatic and simple. Three attack cruisers would carpet bomb the area where the aliens landed. The drops consisted of ten burrowers, thirty sweepers, and twenty high explosive bombs from each ship, all distributed to randomly bracket the target. The third, eleventh, and nineteenth bomb of each pod were slow-fuse HE duds. The last was the one where I rested.

I woke as soon as the bomb slammed into the ground at an oblique angle. I was not quite fully awake by the second bounce but fully aware as my container rolled down some piece of bumpy geography, stopped, and rocked for a moment before finding a stable orientation. I popped the hatch and got out, dripping gel over the dented casing of the faux bomb.

I quickly scanned the area around me. Apparently, I'd tumbled down a steep cliff to come to rest at the bottom among assorted rocks that had fallen from the eroding slope. I could feel the shock of exploding ordinance through my feet as the delay fuses fired. I'd landed near the center of the distribution.

My empty casing still packed a punch, enough to fool a casual inspection into thinking it was just another delayed bomb and the clock was running. I moved away to put as much distance as I could between the bomb and I before it—WHAM!—exploded and threw me tumbling ass over teacup. *Shit!* The techs had set the fuse's timer too short. I checked my systems for damage and found that no harm was done. I was hyper-alert to my surroundings and took note of insect sounds, random wind action on the sparse vegetation, small animal movements, and the trembling ground beneath my feet to establish a baseline of whatever passed for "normal" on this planet. So far, everything agreed with the data the former colonists had provided.

Every ten meters I stopped to feel the ground for approaching footfalls. I continually sniff the air for any unusual smell, listen for any sound, and watch for anything that might be artificial. At the same time I "listened" on every radio channel. All normal.

The ground ahead of me leveled out the further I got from my drop site, which makes movement easier, but meant I had to dodge from rock to rock to remain hidden. Proceeding across open ground increased the certainty of detection.

I didn't expect to run into any aliens until I got closer to the town; about a dozen kilometers away from my current position where we hoped the alien gleaners were still scouring the town. Their presence gave us an opportunity to find out what they were doing and learn how they behaved. From my scouting reports, command might even be able to guess the why of their attacks.

My hatred for the Shardies ran deep, and not just because they'd attacked without provocation, that they destroyed everything humanity has built, or that they were slowly and implacably driving us off our colony worlds as they advanced toward the Earth. No, that would only be the normal "they're not us" type of hatred, what we used to feel for one another before the Enlightening, the kind of hatred you felt for your brother, knowing that sometime in the future you will once again be friends. Not that kind of hatred at all.

Command discovered that the Shards had stripped captured colonists of their humanity and used their brains to betray their own race. What they had done was vile, offensive, and so horrifying that command went to great lengths to prevent any more humans being captured and used, anything to keep more people from becoming the meat components of some war machine. Thus far the aliens hadn't held any colony after they wiped them clean and moved on.

My hatred was the burning, visceral presence that fueled my mission.

Closer to my objective, the terrain slowly changed from rock-strewn scrub to more ambitious bushes that later became a grove of spiky trees with upright branches and needle shaped leaves. They reminded me of upside down Christmas trees. They were spaced widely enough that I had no problem wending my way through the grove.

I felt a slight vibration through my feet, like approaching footfalls. I hunkered down with every sense alert. *Is my camouflage sufficient? Will my coverings really prevent detection of any stray electronic emissions? Had I been detected and was this the search party?*

There were two sets of vibrations that felt like a pair walking in step; bipedal for certain I realize as the steady *pad-pad, pad-pad* continued for seconds and then, when I sensed they were a few meters from my position, I felt another set of vibrations, more pronounced and faster: *Thump, thump, thump*! Then the first set resumed, but faster this time; *pad-pad, pad-pad, thump, thump, pad-pad, pad-pad, thump* and WHAM!

Silence.

I listened to the sounds of something tearing and feeding for a long time as a coppery smell wafted by me. When the feeding noises stopped I heard something chirping contentedly and felt it *pad-pad, pad-padd*ing into the distance. *Predator and prey,* I thought and, relieved, resumed my progress, certain that the scavengers would soon be drawn to the kill site. I'd best be far away when they arrived.

It took me hours to realize that I'd drifted far right of my projected line of march. I looked around to see another ridge about a kilometer away. I decided to transverse and get back on my original heading. I set off hopeful, every sense alert, as the stars appeared overhead. I wondered which of them might be our ship before I recalled that it was virtually undetectable. Then I wondered which of them might be the home that I barely remembered.

The good news was that by morning's light I was within a few meters of a ridgeline from which I hoped to finally spot my objective. The bad news was that the ridgeline offered only a sheer, precipitous drop of nearly twenty meters to a jumble of shattered, sharp, and decidedly hard rocks ahead of me. I didn't want to chance going down the cliff face, despite the ruggedness of my compact scouting form. Finding an easier route down was going to waste more precious time..

A few hours later, at midday, I found a spot where the cliff was less steep, but waited until night to hide my progress. On my second step I hit a loose boulder and tumbled, fetching up against a huge tree at the bottom, none the worse for wear.

As soon as I righted myself I swept the area for any unusual vibrations. There was nothing abnormal so I continue moving forward, taking advantage of whatever cover I could find.

By nightfall I drew close to the town. The dark of night on this moonless world was not a problem. The eyes the reconstruction doctors gave me were far superior to the ones I was born with, seeing in greater range than even enhanced human vision. I'd lost my eyes, along with most of the skin on my face, an arm, and both legs during the evacuation of New Europa. That was an almost successful mission, but we still had horrifying losses.

They told me I was the only survivor from my squad. The only one who thought it worth going through reconstruction to fight another day. The only one who wanted so badly to get back at the bastards who did this to me, to my squad, to my family, and to...the other name evades me, which meant it was among the many memories excised during reconstruction.

There were compensations, however. The doctors turned me into the best, most technologically advanced scout in the universe, a form that should help me survive long enough to learn more about our enemies.

Hopefully, how to kill them.

The forest consisted mainly of the spiked trees that reminded me of Christmas when I was a kid; a bright memory of wrapped presents, warm fireplaces, and cheerful people bustling about as they cooked far too much food. I recalled with absolute clarity the rich smells of puddings and meats, the stinging aroma of pickled fruits and malty beverages as I played among their feet with my new puppy.

I recall the sounds and smells of guests, even though their faces and names slip by. There were aunts, uncles, and cousins. Each group opening the front door to the wind and making mother's little glass centerpiece jingle as they shouted warm greetings. Coats were flung, shoulders hugged, and warm wet kisses bestowed on every exposed cheek. Chaos reigned, entropy decreasing exponentially with each addition until suddenly, at some point, order emerged as everyone found their place, the food appeared, and the pleasant hum of conversation filled the room.

The Christmas memory was sharp, like every other precious memory remaining in my much-reduced mind. I couldn't remember whatever happened to the puppy or even my family. Were they still celebrating Christmas or had they been evacuated? Maybe they'd been wiped out by the aliens, or worse. I would never know.

Aside from those clear holiday snatches I recall nothing of my former life, former body, or even my former lovers. *Is that who Captain Sandels had been?*

I estimated that five kilometers remained to be traversed.

I sensed the vibrations long before I heard faint sounds of approaching movement. It wasn't the same rhythm as the animal I'd run into earlier. This was more of a three-part tempo: *pad-pad-pad, pad-pad-pad.* I masked myself in adaptive camouflage and became one with the forest.

At the limit of my hearing there were faint sounds of broken glass that got louder as whatever it was advanced. *Pad-pad-pad, pad-pad-pad.* I didn't have to wait long before the heat signature of a three-legged monster emerged from the relatively cool forest's background.

The alien was easily four meters tall and twice that in circumference. There was one foreleg and two behind that moved sequentially. The center of its body flared hotter than the extremities and I noticed a halo of some sort around it. As I moved up the spectrum from infrared into the ultraviolet its shroud glowed an almost fluorescent blue. Was this an alien in a suit or some sort of robot? Hell, for all I knew it could be a vehicle, but that was for command to figure out later when they analyzed the data I recorded.

The broken glass sounds became more evident as the thing passed. I couldn't detect any scents at its closest approach or any residue as it disappeared into the woods on my left.

As I waited for the *pad-pad-pad, pad-pad-pad* to recede into the distance I encapsulated the data and buried a timed transmitter, one of several I carried, smoothing the dirt to make its presence undetectable. The little capsule would fire its burst when scheduled, when hopefully, the ship would be listening.

That is, if they weren't detected and destroyed.

Sandels swore as a bright point of light appeared near the rim of the planet. "Could be a ship," the navigator remarked. "Want me to ping?"

"No. Just use optical. We don't want to give ourselves away using any active systems like radar."

The image was fuzzy at first but clarified quickly as something passed between them and the dark planet below. There seemed to be little symmetry to the object and from the way it flashed and glittered it had numerous reflective surfaces. Points projected in odd directions, disappearing from view as the ship rotated on an inclined axis.

The navigator remarked. "Definitely a Shard."

SNAPPER's scouting mission was an attempt to learn more about this implacable enemy, of these creatures who seem hell-bent on destroying all traces of humanity. Sandels thought about the options. Unless humans learned what they faced, and hopefully how to defeat them, the human race faced eventual extinction. Fighting was the only alternative.

It was clear that there would be no other choice.

"It looks like it's descending, sir."

Sandels looked again. "Are you sure it didn't just go around the planet?"

"No; it definitely went into the atmosphere. It's moving across the big ocean now. There!"

Sandels checked the time. "Our target's coming up." Down below the edge of sunlight raced across the surface. Soon dawn would strike the area where the aliens had landed and put the ship in line with the scout's narrow-band transmissions.

"Listening window open." The comm tech looked up from his console. "Nothing yet, sir."

"Keep listening," Sandels snarled. "It's been nearly forty-five hours since the drop. We should hear one of the transmitters peep soon."

"Maybe the unit didn't survive the drop."

"Don't refer to SNAPPER as a damned 'unit,' kid. There's a Marine down there; a damn fine one at that. I know SNAPPER will finish the mission. A Marine that tough isn't built to fail."

The tech tried to stifle a chuckle at the word "built" but recovered quickly when he saw Sandels' darkening frown. "Sorry, sir."

"Don't ever, *ever* do that again," Sandels growled. But, in all honesty, SNAPPER, or what remained of him after that intense fire, really was an "it"; the built thing the doctors had resurrected from the shredded and fried stub of what Geordie…had been just three short years before.

Sandels clearly recalled the stinging smell of ordnance, the screams of the colonists as they were herded onto the evacuation craft. The cracking sound of hypersonic rockets split the skies. Geordie and four of the squad had raced back to help the weaker members who were moving too slowly. This was the last load that would make it to orbit, the others would…Sandels hadn't wanted to think about that. War made people do ugly things, but that ugliness was nothing as compared to what awaited those who fell into the alien's hands, or tentacles, or whatever the hell they had.

Then there was an explosion and bodies flew in ten different directions, a fire raged where the squad had been and there were no more slow colonists to help. Sandels saw half of Thomas, what looked like Ting's head, and Posie's bare ass, spread out in a fan pattern. Geordie was the only body that looked reasonably intact but it was a human, writhing torch. Only when he and Williams quickly rolled it to extinguish the flames did Sandels realize how much of him had been lost. There was still a faint heartbeat and he heard the raspy wheeze of tortured breathing.

"Medic!" Williams screamed. Someone rushed up with four "Save-my-ass" bags and a rescue pack, took one look at the carnage and put three of the bags away. After they stuffed what was left of Yang inside the remaining bag and hit the quick-freeze tab, Sandels threw the bag over his shoulder. Geordie had weighed sixty-five kilos but the bag was only a quarter of that.

It had been touch-and-go keeping Geordie's heart going, the brain functioning, and the lungs pumping air. After ensuring that those continued they worked on kidneys, bladder, and liver. Then they started working on the nervous system. Geordie might have been screaming in pain the whole time, but nobody heard because most of his lower jaw was gone and the exposed vocal cords were charred nubs.

Geordie had spent nine months in reconstruction, the first three recovering enough to communicate, two more coming to terms with what command offered, and another four learning a new purpose and destiny.

Geordie Yang had chosen not to die, instead becoming SNAPPER.

"The ship hasn't reappeared," Navigation reported. "I think we can assume that it landed somewhere."

Sandels hoped that "somewhere" wasn't SNAPPER's objective, but then realized that if it was, then there would be even more data than they expected; provided SNAPPER survived long enough to gather it.

I encountered no more aliens as I edged closer to the town where the Shards have landed. A little bit ago a four-legged predator had sniffed me, chewed on an edge of my shell, and then trotted away, disappointed that I wasn't as tasty as its usual menu. My scouting shape was not optimal for rapid travel, but ideal cover for a human scout. That is, if you considered a ten-kilo turtle human.

The edge of the flood plain, where the settlers' had cleared open fields for their farms, lay before me. The land sloped down toward the town and, beyond that, the sea. The town had been a decent-sized place, five- or six-hundred thousand strong with a flourishing sea trade up and down the coast. There were only a few ruined brick buildings left poking up amidst the rubble.

I spied icebergs, or a close approximation, that look to be a half a kilometer away. They had to be ships so I recorded them, trying to capture every detail in high resolution despite the shimmer of heat rising from the sun-warmed fields. After a moment's reflection I realized that there was far more heat than a sunbaked field could produce—at least twenty degrees above ambient, I estimated. When I switched to infrared vision I saw the entire landscape ablaze in lurid colors, cooler further from the center of town but increasingly warmer toward the middle. The ships also looked fiery hot. I buried my second data packet—there was less delay on this one due to the excessive time it took to get here.

There was a shallow drainage ditch nearby which I used to conceal my movements as I edged closer to discover why the town was so hot. I'd barely started to move when a large form lurched out of a ship. It's a machine, I thought, and hotter than the ships.

The machine had two sets of tractors on either side. I spotted some smaller things beside it and all of a sudden the scale became clear. Those smaller things were the three-legged objects I spotted earlier; which meant that those ships were a lot farther than half a klick away. I had to get closer.

The drainage ditch became scarcely a quarter of a meter deep. It was shallow, but still deep enough to hide my movements. The dirt was so soft that I had to carefully erase any traces of my passage with my rear legs as I crept downhill. There was enough debris in the ditch to allow my camouflage to blend in and make me look like just another rock.

The *pad-pad-pad* vibrations start again. Nearby. I decided to lie doggo, shutting off everything to go dormant. I wanted to chance nothing that might let them know a human was here.

At daybreak I made a tentative sensory scan of the immediate area. The normality of smells and sounds reassured me. Better, I couldn't feel any vibrations telling me that the three-legged monsters were nearby. From further away I sensed the heavy rumble of movement. I slowly peered above the rim of the furrow.

The treaded machine approached one of the buildings, rolling over the rubble and dirt instead of detouring around them while avoiding the occasional shining, too-hot patches scattered throughout the area.

Its companion tripods scattered in triplets, pairs, or singly and did Gods-knew-what. They were also careful to avoid walking into the sparkling patches. I watched for a long while as they moved about, understanding nothing, but recording everything.

The big machine finally reached one of the remaining buildings and disgorged a flowing carpet that sparkled in the sunlight like a million diamonds. I cranked up the acoustic enhancement and heard the tinkling of glass, as if someone were slowly shaking an intricate chandelier, making each delicate crystal strike another. There was a musical quality to it and a certain repetitive rhythm much like the ebb and flow of waves washing against a shell beach whose outlines I vaguely recalled.

The carpet flowed toward the building and up its walls, covering it so completely that it became a shining tower radiating like a small sun brought to ground. The flare was so intense that it blinded my infrared vision. I sensed intense microwave radiation beaming up from the mass of glittering diamonds. I filtered my vision and watched as the building started to melt like a wax candle. The upper levels became nearly transparent and then collapsed inward. The cascading diamonds sparkled across the entire spectrum as they fell into the remaining mass. The dissolution continued, a sight both beautiful and horrifying. I watched for the entire four hours it took for the building to disappear.

And the heat to cease.

As the carpet flowed back into the machine I looked for any trace of rubble, but not a single block of concrete or stray steel beam could be seen in the pile of fine sand they'd left behind. After the last of the carpet entered the machine it moved slowly toward the next standing building and repeated the process. In the distance I observed other similar operations, all of which I recorded in a data capsule/transmitter and buried in the wall of the ditch.

Six hours and several hundred meters later I finally reached the town's outskirts and a pile of fine sand, which might have once been a building. The pile was soft and flocculent so I had little difficulty burrowing into its heart and tasting its composition. The results surprised me; the samples contain nothing but silicates. Even if this building had been a barn there should have been some trace of metals or carbon in the residue. What the hell did those things do when they ate a building? I needed more data so I moved on.

The next heap I tasted was composed of the same ingredients, or should I say ingredient; nothing but sand, finer sand, and microscopic bits of sand. The aliens had definitely been extracting or consuming everything and leaving nothing but grains of silicon behind.

As I started to dig out I detected multiple vibrations but could not determine their direction. I listened, trying to hear something through the dense insulating sand surrounding me. I felt a rumbling and all the sand around me started shaking and settling as the rumble went on and on, getting more pronounced by the moment and I realized that something very large and heavy came toward me.

I pulled in my limbs, tucked my head inside, and dampened down everything before dropping into sleep mode. I hoped I would wake, but with the data ready for transmission that was not important.

"Coming up on fifty hours," the comm tech announced as the crew gathered around him. Their clustering was more for psychological need than physical necessity. All that would happen at the mark would be that a little diode might change from red to green, quickly flash amber, and then return to red. There was no need for twiddling dials, no anxious straining to catch a whisper of sense among the static, nor would there be numbers scrolling across a screen, followed by the clatter of printers or the muted hum of image transmission.

In that same interval, processors within the ship would review the data, expand the compressed string into a long chain by raising the first number to the exponent of the second, decipher the resulting string into its appropriate prime factors, and translate those into sounds and images, filling twelve sensory channels with data.

The resulting packet, suitably enhanced and encrypted, would be transmitted instantly, along with the brief, original feed to ships hovering undetectably near the star's corona. The instant the message was received, one of those ships would wink away to friendly skies.

"Thirty seconds," the tech whispered as all eyes focused and each mind strained, willing the light to change, to wink, to show that all of the lives, all of the resources, all of the effort it had taken to place a single scout within enemy lines had been worth it.

Captain Sandels was more worried than the others. There were so many things that could have gone wrong. What if the impact of the drop had destroyed their scout? What if the bomb had gone off prematurely? What if the Shardies had realized the ruse and reacted, or if SNAPPER had been crippled and was unable to reach the objective, or maybe got lost in the wilderness, fallen into a stream, dropped off a cliff, been buried under a slide, or, for God's sake, become trapped? What if the life support batteries had been damaged before SNAPPER had planted a single transmitter? *What if, what if, what if?*

Why wasn't the light blinking, for God's sake?

"Mark," the tech said quietly.

Waking meant that I was safe, at least for the moment. I felt for any vibration and, aside from a slight shift of sand against sand, detected nothing that varied from my baseline.

Very carefully, I began making my way through the sand pile, hoping all the while that my ever-so-careful digging would not disturb the pile's surface and alert the aliens. Eventually, I was able to detect the sound of shifting sand as it asserted its angle of repose and knew I was close to the surface. I poked an eye through the last few millimeters of concealing sand and beheld wonder.

A carpet of crystals covered the ground in every direction, sparkling and glistening in the bright sunlight. More wondrous yet was that they flowed like a glass river reflecting rainbows. In the middle of that river strolled the tripod things carefully avoiding stepping on even a single shard. There was continual tinkling and clinking as the multiple crystals touched one another. It sounded like a symphony of crazed xylophones.

I looked at the nearest edge to see how the tripods were pushing them along and realized with a shock that they appeared to be mere escorts. Each tiny crystal followed its own path, but maintained its place in the flow. I couldn't see any means of locomotion, no legs, wings, or any sort of appendages. Whatever propelled them was hidden from me but, I hoped, not my more advanced sensors.

There was a cement block ahead of the flowing carpet, no doubt tumbled from one of the destroyed buildings. I watch the gem-crested waves wash over it. As the carpet continued, the hump diminished until it finally disappeared. When the trailing edge moved on, I saw that nothing remained but residual heat. Had there been a quick burst of radiation? My sensors said yes so I recorded that for the next transmission.

When I could no longer feel the rumble of the heavy machines nor the *pad-pad-pad* of its tripodal companions I emerged from the pile to investigate.

I scuttled between piles and felt a wave of intense heat from what I could only describe as an immense iceberg floating above me. It had so many jagged shards and planes that I couldn't make sense of its shape. Worse, I couldn't capture its entirety in a single frame and had to pan along the longest dimension. Even that didn't allow me to record it all, so I resorted to a distorting fisheye view, which seemed to bring it closer. Only wasn't "seemed." The ship was descending, coming down on top of me!

I panicked and raced forward, uncaring of detection in my headlong race to avoid being crushed. The heat radiating from the iceberg's underside intensified. I looked around for something that might insulate me from its flaming touch, but there was nothing in sight. My short legs pumped as fast as they could, draining my batteries at a prodigious rate. I wondered if I could just get safely beyond the nearest edge of the descending ship.

Escape was another twelve meters away, then ten, eight, and almost six when I felt it touch my back. The pressure intensified as I hunkered lower, hoping that would help. I managed to struggle forward, but it was difficult with the increasing weight bearing on me.

Only three meters to go. My legs dug deep furrows in the dirt, leaving scars behind that I no longer bothered to erase. Two, then one meter remained, but the ground was too hard. The heat intensified even further, almost more than I could bear. I could barely move, but if I don't I'll be both baked and crushed.

I threw all caution to the wind and dug, dug, dug furiously, throwing masses of dirt behind and to the sides with abandon to escape the pressure and heat. But a sharp protrusion trapped my back leg and sliced it away. I tried to ignore the agony of losing a leg as I staggered toward the forest's edge, while praying the iceberg's huge bulk shielded my flight.

The cool woods offered a brief respite. I detected no pursuit. I was safe for the moment. I had to shut down and let my autonomic systems restore what they could.

I moved sluggishly as I woke. My leg no longer hurt, but I was sure my body consumed its sparse resources for repairs. Moving on three legs was difficult. I envied the easy *pad-pad-pad* rhythm of the tripods. Would that my own staggering gait was as graceful.

As I looked back I saw the big ship lift. There was no sound, no sign of exhaust, no scattering of electronic noise as it accelerated, dwindling in seconds to a shining mote in the heavens, no larger than a firefly above a summer's beach. I lost it in the sunlight and then saw it flare brilliantly and disappear. Had it activated some sort of drive, or had the flare been merely a trick of sunlight reflecting off of its flat planes? Not for me to say. My role was to scout and report.

Indications were that I had been dormant for a couple of days. All of my buried reports would have been transmitted and those bursts might have alerted the Shards that there was someone watching. Odds were that they had a search party already sweeping the area. I had no doubt that they would eventually discover the ruse, find my transmitters, and determine my line of march. My careful scrubbing of traces would not hold for long and there would be no doubt of my destination. Once they reached the outskirts of Ettire' they'd find the churned ground of my desperation and, inevitably, the souvenir I'd left behind.

So, with little time remaining before they arrived, I had to collect as much additional information as possible. I checked my batteries to see how close I was to the necessary reserve that I needed to transmit all of my data. Was there enough power remaining to propel myself? Would I have enough left for any of my enhancements? I could do without the useless radio scanning and shut that down. Then I pared myself to survival essentials only—motive power, vision, and hearing—the same senses that had served scouts for centuries.

There were none of the tripodal creatures in sight so I assumed that their absence gave me time to get down the slope and maybe analyze one of those strange diamonds before they reached me. I'm certain that knowing more about them will provide vital insights to command.

The huge ship left a vast depression that encompassed this field and those to either side. I saw pits where the projections had pierced the ground, hummocks where some less sharp protuberance had rested, and long gouges on the slight rises. None of those impeded me as I staggered on three legs toward the nearest edge of the glittering carpet.

My first diamond lay within a few hundred meters, a smooth crystalline gem resting in a glassy divot. When I viewed the interior in the ultraviolet bands I discovered fracture planes and splinters of fibers. In infrared there was a slight heat source near the center. I could see no appendages as I recorded every aspect before attempting a sample.

The mere touch of the crystal's surface maked it flare a brilliant orange. Instantly, I felt the *pad-pad-pad* of racing feet and saw a dozen tripods emerge from the forest's edge. Closer even than that I heard the shattering of a million dishes as the nearby carpet changed course to flow in my direction.

I estimated the time for the tripods to reach me, subtracted the charging time for my transmitter, and realized that only by diverting all my remaining power could I be assured that the data would be sent. I opened the transmission channel and began shutting down to let the darkness take me. The *pad-pad-pad* vibrations disappeared, the smells of fresh earth faded away, my vision narrowed to a single bright dot, and I could feel my memories, my thoughts, my very self slipping into dark night.

I felt a sense of intense satisfaction as the transmission completed and the dot of light faded away. Only seconds remained when I heard the tinkling of mother's crystal centerpiece as the warmth of Christmas aunts, uncles, and cousins embraced me.

"The unit's terminated itself," the comm tech reported. "Ten millisecond, high power burst."

"I told you that it's not a goddamned unit," Sandels swore, but he knew that what had died alone down below was only a fragment of the happy, smiling person he'd known all too briefly. The man he remembered was gone forever, too long for tears; another victim of an ugly war. He'd just have to live with that.

"Prepare the next scout," he ordered, knowing what he'd have to do and say. "We'll drop another in four hours and hope he does as well."

SNAPPER was glad when Sandels left. What he didn't need now was some damn puzzling reference to a past that no longer concerned him. He tried to think of something beside the mission as the techs squeezed the warm gel around his body to protect him against what was sure to be a violent landing in his faux bomb. There was nothing else to do so he tried to recall a few memories of his former life, warm memories for the most part, memories that kept him human instead of as a cog in some inhuman Shardie machine.

His favorite memory was of Christmas, when he was a kid; a bright memory of wrapped presents, warm fireplaces, and cheerful people bustling about as they cooked far too much food. He recalled with absolute clarity the rich smells of puddings and meats, the stinging aroma of pickled fruits and malty beverages as he played among their feet with his new puppy.

It was a memory that proved he was still human.

BOOK FOUR

Chapter Twenty-Two

TONY PADDLED ALL NIGHT TO REACH THE WARM SHALLOW WATER. THE shallows attracted fish, especially delicious Silverwhites. The early morning was calm and peaceful as he set his nets. The dark, thick thunderheads had gone and left skies streaked with clouds driven by high winds. The warm spring sun felt good. Tony enjoyed the weather while he could. Too soon the summer's sun would become unbearably hot and force them to leave for the temperate southern climes.

He was eager to leave, anxious to taste crisp apples again. This far north they could only find overly sweet, pulp-filled fruit that was too acid and astringent for him. Give him a crisp apple or juicy pear and he'd be happy. He licked his lips. He could almost taste them.

He pulled up the nets. He'd snagged a nice Silverwhite that weighed half a kilo at least. Silverwhites were rare this time of the year.

He'd already tossed six too-small Blacks back. Blacks were not as tasty as Silvers, but fried up nicely. The Silver was for simmering slowly in a nice fruit sauce that brought out the flavor. Yes, they would eat well tonight.

By the time the sun began to set Tony had enough fish to fill his basket. Most would be smoked for their annual migration to summer quarters. He gathered his nets and turned the canoe toward camp.

As he began to paddle, he spotted a reflection among the trees. That was strange. There was nothing that would cast a reflection like that. He noticed a second flash, the sort of reflection the sun made on glass. He tried to detect movement, tried to see what might have caused the glints.

Could it be Dave? Could the glass monster still be looking for them after so many years? He recalled it standing forlorn on the trail as they left Bamber's. The sun's reflection off Dave's surface was the same as he'd just seen.

Could it be a *different* machine? Like the one that killed Chuck?

He paddled furiously, hoping that the canoe's low profile would keep whatever lurked in the brush from spotting him.

He didn't have his lucky stones, hardly ever carried them anymore, in fact, unlike Vicky who treated them with the reverence of a religious artifact. She never removed the necklace old Ben had made for her years before he disappeared. *Perhaps her necklace kept Ben's memory alive,* Tony thought, *as much as for supposed protection*. He'd never said that out loud since it would bring back too many bad memories.

After all these years, he too missed old Ben.

Vicky woke as the sound faded away. Had the distant rumble been a dream, a nightmare, or a memory from the dead past haunting her? Right now, she heard nothing more than the chirping and skittering of insects wakening to the day. Mating calls, she suspected for a moment before her mind snapped back to whatever had aroused her.

Perhaps it had been distant thunder, although thunderstorms hardly ever appeared this time of year. But thunder would have rolled and faded gradually.

Definitely not thunder, then.

Kat stirred. Vicky had taken to sleeping in Kat's hut when Tony was away, both for comfort and freedom from the interruptions of Joseph's frequent trips to the latrine. No matter how much he tried to be quiet, his footsteps always wakened her.

And nightmares of invading aliens, if that's what it had been.

"You heard it, too?" Kat said quietly. Vicky hadn't realized she was awake. "Thunder?" Kat probably didn't remember the sound of a sonic boom.

"I don't think so," she answered.

"What was that noise?" Young Ben asked as he poked his head into the cabin. "Mom, I heard something like thunder outside but it doesn't feel like rain."

"Ben, wake your grandfather," Kat said.

Vicky smiled. A few years ago she would have said that, but more and more often Kat made the decisions. So be it. The young replaced the old, time rolled on. Soon it would fall to Kat's boy, Ben, her dear Gunning's namesake, to make decisions.

Joseph was confused. "I didn't hear a thing," he grumbled, his voice fuzzed with interrupted sleep. "You're all imagining things."

Vicky knew his failing hearing had prevented the sound from wakening him. All three of them had heard it and only mass hallucination could account for that if it hadn't been real.

"Where are your stones?" she demanded. "I need to know that you all have your stones with you." She tried to keep the desperation from her voice as she fingered the necklace Ben had so lovingly fashioned.

Kat shook her arm to make her bracelet rattle. "I always have mine," she grinned. "Woman needs her jewelry, you know." That was a laugh since the bracelet and Vicky's necklace were the only trinkets they possessed.

"I put mine somewhere," Joseph mumbled. "I'll look for them in the morning, but right now I have to piss." He rose shakily to his feet.

"Why do we need those stupid things?" Ben protested. "Bunch of superstition, isn't it. Keep the monsters away or something?"

His flippant attitude infuriated Vicky. "The aliens are all too real. What do you think happened, for God's sake? Why do you think we live this way if the aliens hadn't snatched everything we...?"

Kat interrupted her. "Ben, bring the bag of stones from the kitchen here like Grandmother says. It's important, isn't it?" she added, looking desperately at Vicky. "Is it *them*?"

Vicky nodded. "It could be. I can't think of anything else that would come here. Gave up hoping for rescue years ago, even before Gunning disappeared." She thought for a moment. "I could be wrong, but if the aliens have come back we're all in grave danger." Her head dropped as she considered the consequences. "There's no guarantee that the stones will protect us this time; not that I'm willing to test that possibility."

"We have to hide."

When dawn broke, they searched the skies for any sign of ships. "I hope Tony's all right," Kat worried as the hours passed. "He should be back by now, shouldn't he?"

"He'll come back when he's caught enough fish. Don't worry so much," Vicky replied. It was easy to say, but she remembered saying the same thing twenty-some years before when Gunning had taken his stupid boat to look for survivors "one last time."

He'd been encouraged to continue searching after finding Joseph and Kat and enlarged their small band of survivors to five. Five: out of a planetary population of nearly ten thousand.

Five miracles and Ben wanted more.

Ben Gunning. How she missed him, even after all these years. She still scanned the seas each spring, hoping to see *Day's End* on the horizon with Ben standing at the tiller, waving to her.

But that hope had died long before. There was no way of knowing what happened on that final trip. The lack of resolution had been maddening and for months Vicky looked seaward, expecting to see Ben returning.

She still missed him. And couldn't help but worry about Tony now, though she kept that concern to herself. There were no shining ships in the morning sky and, with no repetition of the thunder, she relaxed.

"I told you it was your imagination," Joseph declared. "You're just a worrywart." But his tone indicated otherwise.

Tony paddled back to camp three days after sighting the reflection in the distance. Relief filled him as he saw his family going about their daily chores. Ben was gathering firewood as Kat prepared breakfast and Vicky worked at the smoker. He couldn't see Joseph, but expected his father-in-law was either sleeping or pissing.

Tony beached the canoe and lifted the heavy basket of fish.

"A good catch?" Ben asked.

"Blacks and a couple of Silverbacks," Tony replied as he dropped the basket and took Kat in his arms. "I think we'll eat well tonight."

Ben was already pulling fish from the basket. "Look at this one," he said as he held up one of the Silvers. "More than enough for a whole meal."

"Only if you starve, you mean," Joseph jibed as he came out of the shelter. They all knew Ben's adolescent appetite. He usually ate everything remaining on the table and was always hunting an extra piece of fruit or bit of dried fish after.

"I'm a growing boy," Ben replied with a good-natured laugh and made as if to bite the Silver. His crude bracelet rattled as he moved his arm.

Tony noticed the bracelet and looked around. "Did you see them too?"

"See what?" Vicky replied.

Briefly, Tony described the reflections and his impression that it might have been from something made of glass. "Like Dave," he added after a moment's thought. "But it couldn't be that old thing, could it? I mean, it was dead when we left it."

Vicky nodded. "Dead as a doorknob," and made an irritated gesture at young Ben's puzzled expression. "Old tech," she explained.

"We need to find out what's going on," Vicky declared as they ate. "Make sure you weren't sun-struck or something."

Tony bristled. "I know what I saw. Those flashes weren't my imagination."

"Could have been a puddle of water, maybe a shiny rock. Could be a lot of things that are no threat at all," Joseph said softly as he chewed a soggy crust of coarse bread.

"Shiny rocks along the shore? I don't think so," Vicky countered. "It had to be something else and right now we don't know if it's a threat or not."

"Maybe we need to head south," Kat suggested, tousling Ben's long hair. The boy jerked away and scowled. "The weather seems to be moderating and we have enough fish," Kat continued with a glance at Tony. "No sense you going back and maybe bringing trouble on us."

Vicky shook her head. "Trouble like those damned aliens will find us no matter where we are, Kat. Our best course is to find out what it was that Tony saw so we can make a decent decision. Besides, we need to stay until Landing warms up a bit. It's going to be mighty cold down south for another month at least."

From the way Kat was staring, Tony knew that there would be hell to pay if he didn't support her. She was worried about Ben and as protective as Vicky had been of him after the first alien attacks.

"Maybe I should take another look," Tony said. "I can make the crossing at night, lie low, and scout the far side at daybreak. If I can't see anything I'll land and check the place where I saw the flash. It might have been an animal, you know."

"Not many shiny animals," Vicky argued. "Going back might be too risky. What if it was the aliens and they got you? We'd have no way of knowing what happened, just like..." She let her voice trail off.

"I won't be like Chuck," Tony replied. "I'll be careful, don't worry."

"I don't think it's worth the risk," Kat said. "I can't lose you."

Tony ignored her. "I'll leave the nets and other gear behind. I can make better time in a lighter canoe. I won't take risks. Just a quick look over and back. Take me two nights at most."

That was a lie. He got most of his rest while he waited for the nets to fill. He sometimes dozed when the fish weren't feeding. This time he'd paddle all night, scout during the day, and then face an all-night trip home without sleep.

"More like three days," Vicky said. "You're not a young buck any more. A man your age needs his rest."

Tony winced. "Yeah, I know you're right. My shoulders are still sore and my knees ache so much that I'm starting to think I've caught Joseph's arthritis. Starting to feel every one of my forty-whatever years. I'll take it easy for a day before I go."

"I can do it," Ben said. "I know how to handle the canoe just as well as Dad."

"Don't be ridiculous," Kat said immediately. "You're still too young."

"I'm not," Ben shot back. "I do my share. I've been fishing. It won't be hard."

Tony disagreed. "Kat's right. I don't think it would be smart. Maybe in a year or two I'll feel differently, but for now, I agree with your mother."

"He's sixteen, the same age as you were when the invasion came," Vicky said, disapproval evident in her voice. "And you didn't do too bad. Young Ben looks stronger than you were then. I'd say he could easily paddle over there and back and do it faster."

Tony bit his lip. Vicky was right again. "But that was because I had to. We have a choice here and I say the risk is too great." He dared Vicky to object.

Over the last year he and Kat had been taking on more responsibility as Vicky's energy noticeably declined. She was only slightly younger than Joseph and looked as if she were aging faster.

"So the matter is closed?" Vicky said quietly.

"If we haven't heard any more noises," Joseph said to break the strained silence as Vicky and Tony stared defiantly at one another. "It was probably just thunder you heard after all." His face brightened. "Or maybe a meteor—a big one? Sure. Wouldn't be the first time we heard one of those."

Tony wondered about that. A big meteor might have come down at transonic speed. It wasn't that unbelievable. But that didn't make his concern about what he saw any less. Besides, meteors don't flash in the brush.

Kat asked; "Do you really think we need to investigate?"

Tony paused at filleting the fish. "I think it's the wise thing to do. I'll even take a sack of my lucky stones with me." He laughed to show her his lack of concern.

"Those stones might not be good," Kat answered. "Maybe they lost their magic or the batteries ran down or their power drained away. We haven't used them for years so we don't know if they protect us or not."

"They kept Dave away whenever we were at Bamber's," he replied. "Until it stopped moving, that is."

"See, even that thing wore out so why would you think the stones would be any different? I still say we should get as far away from whatever you think you saw as fast as we can. We don't have to wait."

"We all need to agree," Tony said. "Neither you or I should make the decision. We have to do what's best for all of us."

"I don't want you to face whatever it was over there alone. I want you to stay safe," Kat answered. "I want *all* of us to be safe."

She turned and saw Ben dumping weeds into the compost pit. "When you finish your gardening, Ben, could you see if you can gather some sea grass for Vicky? We'll need to put these fresh fish in the smoker soon."

As the boy wandered away Tony said quietly, "You can't hold him close forever, Kat. He's a grown man now."

"He's just a boy. "

"He does an adult's work. This is a rough life, Kat. Childhood is a luxury." He reached for the next Black and stripped the scales.

"Did Ben go fishing this morning?" Vicky asked as Tony came out of the hut. "The canoe is gone."

Tony stretched. "Maybe he went up the coast to find some ripe corrants."

The corrants, as Joseph had named them, were an astringent orange fruit that turned sweet as it ripened and attracted hordes of sugar-hungry insects. The trees grew near the water and usually fruit dropped off the tree to float when the stem softened, safe from the insects. Ben had an eye for them and would often bring back a basketful.

"Little late in the season for ripe corrants," Vicky said as a cool breeze whipped her cloak open. "Maybe he went fishing?"

That bothered Tony. They certainly didn't need more fish, not after all he'd brought back yesterday. No, the boy was probably haring off on some damn silly idea again. He was at that age.

"Well, if he isn't back soon he'll have to forage for his own breakfast," Kat said and gathered a double handful of crumbly paste for the biscuits. She dumped the coarse ground grains into a clay bowl, added a dollop of thick juice, seasoned it with a dash of salt, and began to knead it into a paste.

Vicky formed handfuls of the paste into small balls and placed them on the flat rock in the fire pit. Baking the biscuits required a steady heat. Too much and the outsides would become crusty and leave the inside raw.

As the women prepared the biscuits, Tony and Joseph chopped the staples of their morning meal: fish, assorted fruit, and potatoes. Later they'd eat whatever was at hand, not wishing to waste working time. They could get by on two meals a day and meat only in the evening, if somebody had the time to cook it properly.

"You got the boy spooked," Joseph said as Vicky turned the biscuits so they'd bake evenly.

"Why is that?" Tony asked as he scraped his efforts into the communal bowls.

"Took a sack of stones with him last night," Joseph said. "I saw him putting them in the canoe when I went out to take a piss."

Kat looked up. "In the middle of the night? I thought he left this morning."

Joseph scratched himself. "No, pretty sure it was earlier than that. Lesser moon was coming up so it was shortly after we turned in. At least, that's what I thought."

"Check my food basket," Tony said. "If he took that with him..."

Kat raced to the storehouse. "The basket's gone, and it looks like he took some of our supplies." She put her hand to her mouth. "Tony, you have to go after him. You have to bring him back!"

"Too late for that," Tony replied. "He's probably clear across the bay by now. Damn that boy. I should have seen the signs and known he was going to pull some boneheaded move. Damn his eyes!"

"So what do we do now?" Vicky asked. "What if he stirs those damned things up and they come after us?" She jingled her necklace. "We all better wear our jewelry as we get ready to leave."

"Leave?" Kat practically screamed. "We can't leave without my Ben. We have to make certain he's still..." she tailed off, unable to say the words she feared.

Tony put his arm around her. "He'll be back," he said. "He's a smart boy. Smart enough to keep out of danger, anyway." He tried to sound more confident than he felt.

Damn that boy!

"If we sail close to the coast, pick up a decent night's breeze, we can probably make the first landfall by morning," Joseph said as he drew a rough map in the sand.

"Not a lot of wind at night," Vicky mused. "Anyhow, that's what Gunning always said." She kept her voice low, conscious of Kat's anxious pacing near the shoreline, eyes searching for some sign of Ben.

"I agree that the cover of night nay give us some comfort," Vicky continued, "but it's no guarantee of safety if the bastards can see in the dark. Might as well sail during the day. It's a big ocean and we'd be a mighty small speck, especially if we keep well away from the coast."

Tony scratched in the sand. "There's that island about a two-day sail from here. Don't remember if it has fresh water or not. Worth a chance, don't you think? It does keep us far away from the mainland."

"It's a longer trip from there to the next island." Joseph said. "We'd need to carry enough water in case there's none there."

Tony pursed his lips as he drew a line. "Probably three days from there. That means we'd need a week's water supply. Most of our jars and jugs, I'd say."

Over the years they'd managed to uncover glassware that hadn't been smashed when the aliens destroyed the buildings. The jars ranged from a five-liter one they'd found in the ruins of a distillery to dozens of smaller ones that hardly held a liter. They could supplement those with the fragile, porous clay pots.

It would be barely enough water for a week's trip if the island couldn't supply any.

Vicky tried to keep Kat busy with preparations, but there were times when there were no tasks. In those rare moments, Kat continued to stare across the water, arms crossed, with a look of infinite concern written in the creases of her face.

Vicky recalled feeling like that whenever Gunning failed to return. It wasn't as intense when he first failed to show. The vagaries of wind and weather could easily work to delay him. Then, after a week with no sign, she'd started a widow's walk along the beach, looking in vain at the distant horizon, seeking the blooming sail of her companion without whom she couldn't have survived.

She knew what Kat was going through, even though it had only been two days and nights. The currents were strong and the wind was blowing south. Ben could have easily been carried away and could even now be trying to work his way back to them. The boy was, after all, inexperienced and could just be lost. There were reasons aplenty besides aliens for a delay.

But none of that helped Kat. Whatever the reason, nothing would spare her of the agony of waiting for her son.

Joseph's shout woke Vicky. "He's here! He's here!" There could be no mistaking who he meant.

Tony and Kat raced for the beach, neither of them dressed against the cool morning. Vicky saw Ben furiously paddling in the distance.

Tony stood stone-faced as Kat helped beach the canoe and then hugged Ben as if he'd been gone for months. Vicky wondered whether Tony was going to strike the fool kid or congratulate him on surviving. Pride and fear were having a fight on Tony's face.

"I saw them; the aliens," Ben said breathlessly when he managed to wiggle free from his mother's arms. "They were too far off to make out any details, but they were shiny like you said and moved really fast."

Fast, that doesn't sound like Dave, with its insane advance and retreat habits, Vicky thought. She'd been glad when it finally stopped moving, even if it had never moved faster than she could run, which she had done when it looked like it might ignore her stones. No, fast was never something she'd associate with the old machine.

"It must be some different aliens," she said. "Can you describe them any better?"

Ben screwed up his face. "All I saw was shiny, at least on the small one. Another wasn't. There might have been more but I didn't want to get where they might see me." He paused and added proudly. "Made like a log and drifted until the sun went down. That's why I took so long. The current took me away."

"Damn it! You could have been killed," Tony cursed and stepped toward Ben.

"I had the lucky stones," Ben shot back and danced away.

"Which might not do you any good against these new ones. That was a damned stupid stunt to pull, Ben. Did you think at all about your mother?"

Ben's face started to cloud. He clenched his fists and held his ground against his father's advance.

"The boy did a man's job," Vicky interrupted, before Ben could take a swing at his father. "Now you two stop arguing and let's decide on our next course of action. Do we sit here and wait for them to find us, head south to that island, or take off into the back country?"

"I'm not much for hiking," Joseph said. "I say we sail out of here tonight."

"We aren't ready," Kat said. "We need to collect the water, empty the storehouse, and pack all the cookware. There's a day's work at least."

"I don't think we have time for anything but the necessities," Vicky argued. "We should do what we can by nightfall and leave. The sooner we're away from here the better. No telling when those things are going to look on this side of the bay."

There didn't seem to be any objections to that.

Nobody wanted to face the aliens.

Chapter Twenty-Three

SWEENEY LOOKED AT THE ARMORED MACHINES AS THE TRANSPORT droned along. On his right moved a massive tank, twice the size of any of the others. He turned his head to look in the other direction.

"Hey, don't point that damn thing at me," a red machine barked.

Sweeney had slowly regained consciousness two weeks earlier. He couldn't feel his body. Someone was breathing really, really LOUD. Was he in some sort of hospital? It might be: he recalled something about shutting down his systems after he'd been hit.

Slowly, other bits of memory shifted into place. He'd been in combat, but those memories seemed sparse and littered with chaotic impressions. He recalled the roaring weapons, dying Marines, and…and…? What were the images of metal tripods and a ship flying away? Was he still in recovery?

Worse, was he fucking dead?

He remembered talking to a doctor about him being a cybermarine and then…there was nothing after that. Had the operation failed?

"Awake at last," a cheerful voice startled him. "You are probably wondering why you can't see or move." Sweeney thought that was a goddamn stupid thing to say; hadn't his systems shut down, for ElRon's sake?

"Rest assured, there is nothing wrong. You are being kept in the dark for very good reasons."

Like a fucking mushroom, Sweeney thought. The brass never did anything 'for very good reasons.' Still, if their 'reasons' were what it took for his recovery as a cyber, then he'd best go along.

"I'm going to run some tests, ask a few questions, and then we can move on to getting you back to work," the cheerful voice went on.

"Great, can't wait to get back to the war."

The voice was quiet for a few moments. "Chief, things are not exactly as you recall. The cybermarine you remember is probably light years away. That is, if you, or should I say 'he' hasn't been killed."

Sweeney tried to extract sense from confusion. "What the hell are you talking about? I'm right here, wherever the hell this hospital is." He paused and added, "Sir!"

"I'm pretty certain that you recall your last assignment?" the voice sounded exasperated.

"Sure, I think it was maybe Miranda colony?" Given his vague memories he wasn't sure.

"I don't know the details, but that battle was six or seven years ago and..." the voice replied.

"Did you fucking say seven YEARS? ElRon, just how long have you been working on me...*sir*?"

"There's been a few medical advances, Chief. The you I am talking to is another instance we made from a recording made from another you—a you that was killed."

It was obvious that they'd consigned him to a psychiatric ward with one of the inmates watching over him. Sweeney's head swam as he tried to deal with the alarming information he'd just received. Could it be true? "Wait a damn minute. If I was killed, then how the hell am I here?"

"Well, where you are now is a philosophical question: Since you were originally recruited we've made multiple versions of *that* Sweeney. Trained warriors are too valuable a resource to waste."

The shock of too many revelations confused Sweeney. "So I'm just a copy while other real me's are out there fighting the war? That sounds ridiculous. I goddamned well know who I am," he hesitated. "Sir."

"It's best you don't think of yourself as a copy, Chief. You are just as real as your original. In fact, the you I am talking to at this moment is the ...um... fifteenth Sweeney instance we've produced this month."

Sweeney was appalled. "There's more goddamned copies of me running around? Why don't you run off more so we can hold a baseball game!"

"Please calm down. Your disorientation is only momentary, as it has been for all of your other instances."

"Disorientation, my ass. This is beyond weird."

"I know the idea takes some getting used to, but rest assured that you remain who you believe you are—a unique individual acquiring your own set of perceptions, beliefs, and actions. Already you are different from the earlier instances we brought to life and those differences will increase as your life continues."

"Until I'm fucking killed again, you mean!"

"Um, there is that possibility," the voice sounded uncomfortable. "But whenever that risk of death is imminent you can always have a new copy made so you can be resurrected with your memories preserved…up to that point, anyway," it added. There was a slight hesitation. "Of course, that version, like you, won't remember anything that took place after the recording."

This was getting stranger and stranger. "So I won't start like this all the time?"

"Yes, I believe that is true. Matter of fact, the instances are why we're finally regaining our colonies."

Sweeney was amazed. How the hell had the Fleet turned the war around so fast? As best he could recall, the aliens had been whipping ass so bad nothing could stand in their way.

"You say we're finally winning?"

As he drifted in black solitude—the voice had promised they would not put him back to sleep—he tried to absorb his changed circumstances. He tried to recall his earlier life as a grunt and came up with large blanks about mostly everything except operating a MULE and later becoming a bad-ass cybermarine.

Puzzling.

According to what he could gather from infrequent conversations with the voice, his earlier selves had fought in multiple engagements and died—really and truly died. He wondered why there was no emotional impact to learning about his deaths, possibly because he was obviously here and now and not moldering in a distant grave, along with whatever memories he'd failed to record.

"We call that *depressed affect,*" the voice explained during the next session of wakefulness. "But don't worry: We're keeping you calm." The bastards were even diddling with his feelings, damn it!

He also learned that advances in automated battle management and somehow linking human pilots directly into control systems and weapons was giving Fleet the ability to destroy the alien ships. Meanwhile, the cybermarines and other ground troops were fighting the aliens on the ground. Duplicating cybers, stamping them out like they were equipment, helped them retain skills and hold their own.

"We still offer the seriously wounded to become cybers," his briefer assured him. "But that's merely a transitional phase. Once they've gained sufficient experience with their interfaces, they, or their instances, can become tanks and artillery, ships and carriers. The control systems will allow them to 'feel' as if the machines are natural parts of their body. You will, in the end, become the machine."

"Huh? How the hell did I suddenly become the subject?"

"That's what we're training you for, Chief. You will be a battlewagon."

It was a little too much information to absorb. "So I'm not going to be a cybermarine?"

Sweeney—was he still Sweeney or Sweeney 16?—could hardly believe the image of a massive tank with articulated treads and more heavy weapons than he thought reasonable. Most obvious were two M164 repeaters on the sides and a Mark VII main cannon extending from the turret.

"In the name of all that's holy," Sweeney swore. "Just how big is that thing?"

A voice read off the statistics. "The mass of the CAT, that's what we call the c74.3 Combat Assault Tank, is about seventy-four tons, Chief. It carries fifty rounds for the Mark VII canon and a thousand for each repeater. It is heavy weapons support."

"Great, I'll feel good about having something like this backing me up."

"I'm afraid I wasn't clear, Chief. You'll be just one of eight instanced machines in the squad. Each of you will be directed by COMMAND, that's the Instance with the battle plan."

Whatever the hell 'COMMAND' might be, Sweeney thought as he tried to get his mind around the fact that they were putting him into a fucking tank! This was getting stranger beyond belief.

"To reassure you," his handler continued, "your squad's combined firepower will be equal to an entire regiment of cybers. The other members of a typical squad are meatheads and tadpoles—that's what we instances call humans and cybers. Any questions?"

Sweeney was confused. "Why did you call them tadpoles?"

"When the meatheads become cybers they're halfway trained and mature. The acquisition of experience with their tech helps them become Instances."

"Jesus!" It was almost too much to grasp. "And Fleet allows this?"

"They insist on it. This is what we have to do it if the human race is going to survive."

Sweeney's new situation was a lot to absorb and, like all things military, it involved a shit-ton of waiting, time during which Sweeney learned what had taken place since he'd been killed the first time…or was it the fifteenth?

He couldn't remember what had happened to his predecessors and nobody had seen fit to explain. Just the same, he was glad somebody had the foresight to make this copy.

Sure, it made a lot of sense, now that he thought about it. Churning out multiple copies was more efficient than training new ones. And if you could make one, why not make two, or four, or four thousand? Further, you could build subsequent copies bigger and stronger, faster, more efficient at vanquishing Shardies until you finally found the level of force necessary to turn the tide of war.

It might make a lot of sense, but there was something about this instancing that really bothered him.

Training for his new "body" took less time than he expected. The simulator had prepared him for the "feel" of his new body. It was no worse than wearing a MULE at first and grew to be as comfortable as he recalled his cyber body had been.

The experience following installation was as natural as shaking out the kinks! He stretched his arms, or what felt like arms, and out of the corner of his eyes saw the great rotating barrels of the M164 Gatlings emerge from his sides. Retracting them was just like relaxing his arms enough to let them fall by his sides—only in this case, snuggled within their cradles.

He took a deep breath—figuratively speaking, because he no longer had a mouth or lungs—and took a tentative step forward. The clattering sound of treads striking the concrete roadway made him swivel his turret to peer behind him before he realized it was the sound of his own movement.

What about firing the weapons? Was there a button or… "You have to strain like you're taking a dump," he recalled from the simulator lessons. Sweeney tensed and watched the MARK VII lock into position. He felt tension in his gut as a round slid into the chamber. A reticule appeared, giving range and bearing to a target a half-kilometer away. The tip of the MARK VII moved in synch with his vision as he focused and, when he let his breath out, he felt a sensuous wave of release.

The recoil threw him back. He'd forgotten to brace himself. "Missed by five meters," he estimated as the dummy round impacted to one side of the target. Well, he'd have to adjust for windage. The next round hit the target dead center and left a gaping hole.

Next he fired the M164 repeaters, chuckling as they spit out hundreds of high-density rounds that tore the target to splinters. He roared. This was living!

Two days later he found himself being loaded, along with three other machines, into a heavy transport.

"Where the hell are we going?" he asked. Nobody had seen fit to brief him on the destination.

"Byzantine," the battlewagon parked beside him answered. "My name's Claire, call sign SABRE 12a2. The two little fellows across from us are Raoul and Charlene, who go by TIGER3a and CLAWS8, both veterans in new suits."

"TIGER3a *point* one and don't you forget it, asshole," Raoul, the hopper, a bright red mobile half the size of SABRE, replied as he swiveled toward Sweeney. "What Instance are you? They give you a designation?"

"I'm Sweeney," he introduced himself. "Ex-Cyber."

"Time to give up that tadpole name, newbie," the red hopper replied. "Meat's a long way behind you."

"Yeah, give up that meathead name now you got a decent body. Start thinking like the super Instance you are, by God," CLAWS8, the even smaller agile howitzer platform, added.

Sweeney tried to think of what he should call his new self. "I can't recall calling myself anything but Sweeney, but I might be the sixteenth because they said they'd sent fifteen others out before me."

"Fifteen! Those Instances must not have been installed in battlewagons—it's too damn expensive to make that many. Probably been instancing your copies in different configurations to find one that works best. Could have discarded the other Instances if they hadn't worked out."

Sweeney thought that was frightening, but, given the ability to churn out multiple copies, why not treat them as disposable? Why had he thought he could only be installed in something like his monster battlewagon? Had some earlier copy failed to operate it satisfactorily?

"We'll call you CRUSHER16, although you could be seven hundred and sixteen if Fleet's been churning out Instances of you elsewhere. None of us has any way of knowing anything other than our own lines of descent, if you want to think of it that way."

CLAWS8 and TIGER3a1 seemed to be the talkers in the group and SABRE12a2, the other battlewagon, the quiet one.

"Lost a mech Instance on Oberon colony—got taken out by a fountain, they tell me," CLAWS8 continued. "Lucky I made a backup before I shipped out or they would have had to bring a copy all the way from Mars. That's where I was originally recruited as a tadpole."

"They tell me I lost two Instances off of my last backup," TIGER3a1 said. "Wish one of them had survived long enough to pass along a few tips on smashing Shardies. Always helps to get an upgrade on skills, y'know. That's why I back up soon as I survive a tussle. Damn! Maybe that's why I haven't done an upgrade."

SABRE12a2 shook her turret. "You guys and your upgrades. The secret is surviving, not thinking how your goddamn next Instance will do better. We're in this to survive and pass along skills and knowledge. Besides, I have no wish to go tits up, although that meat configuration was so many iterations ago that I barely remember it."

Sweeney gazed at the scars and dents on SABRE12a2's body, the places where the battle-worn plating had been replaced with new, and the shiny treads on its rear tractors. She'd obviously seen combat and a lot of it.

"You talk like one of those radicals," CLAWS8 snarled. "Thinking of saving your own ass all the time."

"The Movement is about more than that. It's about being human, damn it!" There was no disguising the anger in SABRE12a2's voice. "Just because the meatheads can make more of us doesn't mean we aren't human. It doesn't mean they can think we're just dumb machines. Besides, we contribute more firepower to the battlefield than any of the meatheads or tadpoles ever do. Time we had a voice in this fucking war. Time we stood up for who we are!"

"Save your little speeches for the rallies," TIGER3a1 warned. "And don't start the newbie thinking he's any better than any other mech. We are what we are, creations with the single purpose of smashing Shardies. We shouldn't expect anything else than to do what we've volunteered to do. So give it a rest."

Sweeney considered SABRE12a2's words. It made sense that if they could make more copies of him, didn't that make him sort of immortal? "But if I get killed another Instance could replace me," he said. "I'd feel, think, and act the same as I do now, wouldn't I?"

SABRE12a2 rumbled softly. "CRUSHER16, when you die everything you've learned and done since your last backup will be lost. Another Instance of you might go on, but he won't be the you I'm talking to!"

"But…"

"Here's the real issue the Movement wants addressed," SABRE12a2 rumbled. "What happens when the war is over? What happens to us? I'm too heavy to ship and probably too specialized to plow ground or harvest crops. So what are they going to do with me?"

"Like you'll last that long," TIGER3a1 sneered.

SABRE12a2 ignored the interruption. "Think about it, CRUSHER16: where are they going to take our backups? Who is going to sort out our multiple surviving copies when the war's over? Will they try to decommission us as surplus or just turn us out to live on our own when the colonists come back and rebuild whatever world we happen to be on? Can you see me picking fruit or serving coffee in a restaurant?"

"Maybe you can be a greeter," CLAWS8 suggested.

SABRE12a2 acted as if she hadn't heard the crack. "Think about that for a while, CRUSHER16, and when you are ready, I'll tell you more about the Movement."

Sweeney's expeditionary force arrived at Byzantine without incident. "There's still a few pockets of Shardies," COMMAND advised. "One of their big ships is on the surface, but we haven't located it. We're to scout, engage, and destroy any traces of Shardies. Any questions?"

"Yeah," said a modern cyber dressed in combat grays and carrying such an assortment of weapons on his back he looked like a beetle. "What's the battle plan?"

"I just told you," COMMAND answered. "Scout, engage, and fucking *dee-stroy* the bastards."

Sweeney joined the others in the laughter. The exchange was traditional before a battle.

The transport landed much softer than any combat assault Sweeney could recall and the ramp lowered much more sedately. There was no firestorm greeting him as he methodically rolled down the ramp and parked where COMMAND directed.

In the distance, Sweeney noted other transports landing. There were fifty infantry in his squad—real humans and cybers who could probe the smaller, tighter spaces where the larger war mechs couldn't fit. Apparently, nobody had come up with a better design than the adaptable and flexible human body.

"We're at the head of a long valley," COMMAND said. "SABRE12a2 and CRUSHER16 will hold the ridge lines to provide cover. You mobile units form up to scour the base while the grunts take care of the crevices, cracks, and caves. We converge on any contact. Since these things are deadly fast, shoot without hesitation and don't worry about your asses: when you wake up you'll be comfy back at base."

Sweeney knew it for the gallows humor it was. Yes, another Instance might wake up but, as SABRE12a2 said, he'd be just as dead.

The first encounter came at mid-afternoon, just as they cleared a destroyed farm. Twenty Shardie tripods flowed down the slope above CLAWS8. None of the Marines on the slope had had time to call support or even shout a warning.

Sweeney churned dirt as he spun about, lifted the MARK VII, and focused the reticule on the mass of shimmering tripods. A round from SABRE12a2 hit the ground between CLAWS8 and the advancing horde.

Sweeney— CRUSHER16 —watched his round fly with hypersonic speed at the middle of the alien pack as the little howitzer raced away. Before Sweeney could load another round, his target erupted, flinging crystal splinters and clods of dirt in a mushrooming cloud that obscured his vision.

TIGER3a1 raced from the lead position, flanked by two hoppers, to give aid. Three bright flashes illuminated the dust cloud. CLAWS8 was firing its howitzers. Suddenly, a single actinic light illuminated the cloud and a massive explosion rocked the area where CLAWS8 had been.

Sweeney called SABRE12a2. "Why are you firing? You're endangering CLAWS8!"

"She's gone," SABRE12a2 responded. "You saw that flash—that's how the fucking Shards take us out, with those silver fountain weapons."

"Scour the area for survivors," COMMAND ordered. "Then find out how the hell the sweep missed those things."

Ten meatheads and five tadpoles had been lost. It mattered little for the cybers; they'd been backed up to fight another day. The brave meatheads however, were gone forever.

After the loss of CLAWS8, Sweeney swore he'd never make friends with another mech. It mattered little that there might be another Instance of CLAWS8, all but identical to her: The pain of losing a comrade was just as bitter.

"Hey," an orange Ranger rolled up beside Sweeney as he drove along a wide road that had connected the colony's main town to the outlying farms. The farms and town no longer existed. Where buildings had stood there were now piles of rubble and little else.

"SABRE12a2 told me you used to call yourself Sweeney," the Ranger said.

"Yeah, that was my meat name," Sweeney replied. "But I go by CRUSHER16 now."

The Ranger let out a whoop. "More like number three, of the battlewagon configuration, I mean. No telling how many others of us there are."

"By us you mean Instances?" Sweeney wondered if this was another recruiter for the Movement. "Did SABRE12a2 send you to talk to me?"

"Jesus, I can't believe I was ever so damn slow to catch on. Hey, meathead Sweeney, don't you recognize your own self? I'm a Sweeney, too!"

Sweeney screeched to a halt, his treads digging furrows in the dirt. He swiveled his optics to look down on the Ranger. "You?"

"What's the matter? You can't see the family resemblance?" The Ranger laughed and then added, "Sorry, that's an old joke from my cyber days."

Sweeney was dumfounded. Here he thought he had adjusted nicely to the idea of the instancing situation, when along comes someone to distort his worldview even further. Of course, it made perfect sense to instance him in other configurations. Hadn't TIGER3a1 said that was possible?

"When were you instanced?" Sweeney asked, wondering if this could be one of the other fifteen of his Instance brothers, if that was the term for it.

The Ranger shook his sensors. "I came off of an Instance that was killed in the first Oberon invasion. Do you remember Oberon I? No? OK, that means that you branched off an even earlier version—where do you last remember fighting?"

Sweeney tried to recall. "I don't remember that. It was about twelve years ago, they told me."

The Ranger stuttered sidewise, momentarily stunned by Sweeney's admission. "Holy shit. You must have come directly off your fucking ROOT. Man, I am so pleased to meet you. I have a habit of always backing up before a battle—ever cautious, as you know—so my memories of earlier Instances are too overwritten. By the way, I call myself FROG, FROG5b.6e to be exact."

"Pleased to meet you FROG5b.6e. I'm CRUSHER16."

"And we're both Sweeneys! Hey, maybe we can get up a reunion when this war is over; invite all our Instances and figure out who came from which, or whatever." FROG5b.6e paused. "This Instance thing is really confusing, isn't it?"

Sweeney sighed. "Yes, and it looks like it's never going to get less so. I'd better back up as soon as I can," he added.

"Yup, I'm pretty sure you can do that when we get back to the transports. Of course, if you only get disabled they could stick your can in a spare unit. Saves time over training another one, y'know."

Sweeney lost track of FROG5b.6e shortly after they regrouped at the rendezvous. COMMAND insisted they needed heavy mechs elsewhere. They quickly loaded three battlewagons and half a dozen hoppers into lumbering cargo vessels that took hours before they landed. Sweeney was grateful that he no longer needed to take a piss on the long ride, but found little comfort otherwise. None of his traveling companions were his other Instances.

The next battle was brief, consisting of lobbing shell after shell at a Shardie enclave and then having the hoppers move in with their howitzers to fire on any surviving object larger than a human fist. In the end, the site of the Shardie enclave was no more than a smoldering ruin.

"Look at that," SABRE12a2 said as she rolled dangerously close to the edge of the roiled and pocked landscape. "I guess we failed."

"Why is that?" Sweeney asked as he surveyed the results of their intense bombardment. He wheeled his turret around to respond to any new threat, but saw nothing.

"Don't bother looking around," SABRE12a2 said with a wag of her turret. "We failed because all we did was make more shards—get it, CRUSHER16, SHARDS!"

Sweeney didn't think the joke was that funny.

He backed up as soon as he reached base camp. It was simpler than he imagined—a matter of plugging a cable into a socket buried within his armor plating.

"I thought my brains were somewhere inside my body," Sweeney complained as they attacked him with power tools to uncover the socket.

"Too much signal delay," one of the techs replied. "Have to put sensors close to your can. Likewise your control systems. Distance minimizes reaction time."

The field download, backup, or whatever they called it took hours, which explained why he'd had to wait so long; the veterans, who had the greatest amount of combat experiences got first priority. "Almost done," the burly male control tech reported at long last. "About to disconnect."

"All right CRUSHER16," a diminutive female control tech said as she stepped away from her board. "Systems checks completed. You are good to go."

Sweeney felt strange. Had he fallen asleep while they were sealing him up from his backup session? He checked the chronometer to see how long he'd been out of commission and…. "Holy shit!"

Either something was terribly wrong with him or he'd been asleep for six months. *Six months*? He looked around. This wasn't the backup station but some sort of garage filled with mechs and technicians.

"Something of a shock, ain't it?" a voice rumbled from nearby. Sweeney swiveled his turret to see another battlewagon parked beside him. "SABRE12a2?"

"Yeah, I'm still SABRE," the battlewagon replied. "Only I guess I'm SABRE12a-fucking-THREE now. That must have been a hell of a fight if both of us got knocked out. Wish I could remember it."

Sweeney gasped. He'd been killed? Worse, now he was a copy of a copy, even though he felt like himself, the *him* that had gotten killed somewhere he probably would never know. It didn't matter. Knowing that he'd died in a good cause filled him with pride. "Must have been a hell of a battle," he repeated proudly

The greater wonder was that he felt no guilt over the loss of his former self. It was as if that Instance never happened. For the first time Sweeney felt the power of knowing that, so long as he continued to back up regularly, he could go on for eternity.

Now that made this whole Instance thing seem worthwhile!

He downloaded recent history about the war's progress while he waited for COMMAND's orders. Despite all the advances in technology and tactics the goddamned brass still progressed at the speed of a Roman legion; sit on your ass and wait for orders.

If the news could be believed, the Navy was finally winning more encounters than they lost. True, the number of battles was diminishing, but that was only a detail. Most importantly, no more colonies were being attacked, evacuations had been halted, and the Navy had more ships to transport forces to those places still Shardie-infested.

And, as ever, that was a job for the Marines.

"Time to move out," COMMAND ordered abruptly. "Move it, move it, *move it!*"

The large garage door rose slowly to reveal a slightly greenish sky vaulting over two ranks of battlewagons. "By all that's holy, this looks like it's going to be a huge battle!" SABER12a3 exclaimed.

"CRUSHERs in the first rank," COMMAND ordered as the machines lined up. "SABREs form behind them."

Sweeney swiveled his turret to look down the line, seeing a dozen others do the same. "Are they all me?" he asked as he rolled toward the growing formation.

"Of course," SABRE12a3 answered. "Looks like we weren't killed after all. Looks like they just needed some more Instances to supplement the force. Wonder if my former iteration is here. Be interesting to chat with good old a2 and find out what's happened since the backup."

Sweeney was devastated. It was one thing to think he had fought the good fight and given his all, but quite another to find that he was nothing more than a spare. Demeaning, yeah, and not a little disappointing.

"Getting mad, aren't you?" SABRE12a3 grumbled. "Now you know what useless pieces of crap we are to the meathead brass; just machines they use however they want. Or maybe they don't Instance you again. That happened to HAWK3 back in the day. He was the one of the first in the Movement who got a little too vocal. Destroyed on Hachettii2 and, so far as anyone knows, never got another Instance."

"So that's why you want me to keep quiet?"

"Bet your ass I do. Not using a guy's backup is an efficient way of silencing troublemakers. No sweat off their tails—we're just copies after all."

"I hear you," Sweeney said as they separated. Whatever happened, he swore he would survive to do another backup so his next iteration knew what he was up against. His new battle was not to kill aliens, but to survive so he could get back at the bastards who'd were using him so badly.

Chapter Twenty-Four

EVE16G SWEPT THROUGH THE PLANET'S NIGHTSIDE AND DROPPED TO A few thousand meters just as the long rays of the morning sun washed over the identified settlement. As she made a broad turn to make another, closer pass, she reviewed the images being transmitted: A rough circle of neat buildings, three crossing roads, one that led into the jungle while another ran along the coast. There were some animals in a pasture, plowed fields, and some dots that might have been people. Definitely unexpected.

The second sweep confirmed that these were organized human survivors.

Let them know we see them, ABRAHAM ordered. EVE16G dropped to treetop level and wiggled her wings. A few people looked up so she flew over once more. Almost she wished she could land, embrace them, talk to them, and find out how the hell they'd managed to survive a Shardie attack.

But that was a job for the meat. She had to refuel.

Summer's Breeze tipped as the night's light wind caught the sail, momentarily unbalancing Vicky and sending her crashing against Kat. "Forgot your sea legs?" Kat joked.

"More like I never had them to begin with," Vicky replied as she braced herself against the pile of goods they'd stacked amidships. "I hate these things. Gunning wanted me to love the boats but I never did. Hated them then, hate them now."

"Would someone look for Hunter's," Joseph cried from the tiller. "Sail's blocking my view." Hunter's Star was the main navigation beacon that pointed the way to their southern camp.

"Directly ahead," Ben shouted over the wind as he scrambled to a perch on the high side of the boat.

Joseph made a small adjustment to the tiller and the boat settled. Hunter's Star had drifted two points off the mast. "Island's a little off our usual course," he explained. "I hope we have enough moonlight to spot her."

Vicky knew Joseph's cataracts were getting as bad as hers. The stars all now radiated spears of light, the greater moon wore a rainbow circle, and she could no longer pick out the lesser moon's craters. She even had a problem resolving the edges of that bright blob. "I'm going to try to sleep," she announced and settled a blanket around her.

"I'll take the second watch," Tony said as he bedded down between Vicky and Kat. "Ben! Get some rest. We'll need your eyes later, when we get close to the island."

"I'll just sit here a bit longer," Ben replied. "I'm not tired."

"Just the same, give it a try."

An hour after he'd relieved Joseph, Tony struggled to remain alert. The further they got from the coast the lighter the wind became. *Breeze* gently rose and fell in the long swells, giving him a glimpse of Hunter's only on the rise. He kept the star a few points to the right of the mast and hoped Joseph's memory about the island's location was right.

The gentle motion lulled him into reverie, a state that could easily become sleep if he didn't keep moving. He dared not sit and be rocked to sleep with so much depending on him.

"Ben," he hissed and prodded the slumbering form with his toe. "Wake up and take position." For all his protests about not being sleepy, the boy had fallen asleep instantly.

"MFrgh," Ben groused, but scurried forward, carefully avoiding the dark forms huddled around him.

The occasional splash of cold seawater kept Ben awake as the night wore on. To his right he could see a pale luminescence on the edge of vision that marked the approaching dawn.

It was hard to tell the difference between the hummocks of waves and a low profile marking an island. If Joseph's island didn't have hills or even trees tall enough to be seen, they could sail by without knowing.

He kept scanning. Twice he thought he'd seen something, but both times it disappeared as quickly as it had come: *Wishful thinking for sure.* "This is ridiculous," he called out.

"Keep looking. I'm pretty sure that we're close," was Tony's reply.

Sure, but his father wasn't up here on the bow getting soaked in cold saltwater. Besides, Ben's stomach was growling and, was the sky getting lighter off to the left? Were dawn and breakfast coming?

"YO!" he shouted and scrambled to his feet. "Over there," he pointed at the dark hump barely a finger's width above the sea. "Do you see it?"

Tony's answer was to swing the tiller to the side and let the sail fly over the heads of the sleeping trio. The boat lifted one outrigger now that the wind was hitting the sail on a decent angle. "Everybody up. We found it!"

Ben was happy. Once they landed he'd be able to get something to eat. He was starving!

They pulled *Breeze* ashore on the leeward side of the island, furled the sails, and prepared a fire. Tony and Ben struck off to see if the island held anything useful. They'd only used a bit of their water so finding more wasn't necessary. The low-growing vegetation on this wind-scoured island didn't look likely for anything they could eat.

The island wasn't large, scarcely two kilometers long and barely a third as wide. There was the crescent bay where they'd beached and a range of low hills, scarcely more than overgrown sandy dunes, along the backbone. The windward side was covered with scrub, some of which had sharp-edged leaves that opened a gash on Ben's leg.

"It's nothing," Ben wiped the trace of blood away. More blood welled in the long cut. "I'll wash it in seawater so it will scab over."

Vicky and Kat rigged a screen to protect against wind and sun while they dozed away the day. Tony and Ben walked along the beach, kicking the occasional bit of detritus and casting sticks into the sea. Tiring of that, they climbed the dunes and watched the waves beating the shore. An occasional seabird soared high above.

Far out to the west trailed a line of clouds that could be an approaching storm. "Have to keep an eye on that," Tony said.

They would be sailing for three nights and two days with no respite before they made their next landfall. It would be tough enough without rough weather, the five of them confined to a deck barely large enough for them to swing their arms.

As he was estimating the speed of the storm's approach a glint of light caught his eye. Had it been real or something imagined? He scanned the skies in vain but did not see it again. Had it been a ship? Were the aliens searching the sea?

No, that couldn't be! There would be no reason to look for a boat and even if the aliens were looking, the possibility of them spotting the tiny *Breeze* in the middle of the ocean was improbable. No, glint or not, they were in no danger.

Just the same, he'd tell Vicky.

The storm arrived just before nightfall, dousing them in torrents of rain. They struggled to pull *Breeze* further ashore. Ben ran lines from the stern to make it fast as Tony struggled to fasten the bowline to a sturdy bush.

Vicky and Kat moved their precious water supply to safety two jugs at a time, securing each in mounds of sand, while Joseph tied the sail to the mast. They had done this many times before, but never so quickly. Storms were not uncommon, but the speed of this one's advance had surprised them. They pulled a cover over their heads when the storm hit. It did little more than protect them from the wind.

"Perhaps," said Joseph as they swallowed cold rations with sips of rain water, "perhaps it will pass quickly."

But it didn't and left them damp and cold through the sleepless night.

Late the next day, after the storm had passed, Ben's leg began to swell around the cut. Vicky examined it. "Could be infected or it could be another histamine reaction." There had been many of those until they learned to avoid certain plants. She looked closely at Ben. "Feeling hot, chills, trouble breathing?" Ben shook his head. "So that means infection's the most likely. We'll have to clean the cut."

While Joseph gathered damp driftwood for a fire Vicky inventoried their supplies. A fresh flake of the glassy rock gave her a sharp edge and she could irrigate the wound with hot water. Their supply of antibiotics were barely a memory, but they'd discovered some local plants that had antiseptic properties, even though they also made you itch like hell.

Joseph's cry broke her chain of thought. "Look up!" he shouted. Vicky saw something silver flash overhead. "Aliens, for sure." There were no Navy ships that small and fast.

"Could they have seen us?" Kat asked.

"I doubt it. They're probably looking for signs of civilization, houses and such, not a handful of raggedy humans and a boat that might be just a bit of flotsam. If it comes back we'll know for sure."

"That means we'll be killed, doesn't it?" Kat reached out to take Ben's hand and pressed it to her lips as if a mother's love could protect her son. Ben scowled and pulled his hand away.

Vicky looked at Kat, at this woman who had only her childhood memories of the carnage after the invasion, when she had been too immature to realize the enormity of her loss. She might *know*, but she probably did not feel the horror of what may happen. "Yes," she answered honestly and tried to keep the sorrow from her voice. "Yes, we will."

When night fell without the return of the alien flyer they decided to put to sea once more. It was a three-day sail to their next landfall, if they had favorable winds. "I'm not happy about being exposed during the day," Joseph muttered as he carefully stored the lines. "Out in the open, no cover, no way to hide or run. Sitting ducks, we'll be."

Vicky slapped him on the shoulder. "What's the alternative, old man? Sit on our ass until we starve or die of thirst? We barely have enough drinking water to last for this leg of the trip. Unless you've discovered a spring on this spit of sand we have no choice."

"Just the same..."

"Not another word. Now, finish there and help me make the boat look like a pile of storm-tossed debris."

"No way we can hide the sail," Joseph pointed out.

"Let's hope the damned aliens won't know about ancient technology," Vicky replied unconvincingly.

It was a faint hope.

The three-day crossing was punctuated by rainsqualls and periods of dead calm. At sunrise on the fourth day they spied a familiar landmark, the northernmost edge of the southern continent. It was still a full day's sail before they reached their destination.

"Do you see them?" Ben yelled and pointed shoreward as they crested a wave. Tony spotted two—no three—large machines trundling along the shoreline. Aliens for certain.

"Pull down the sail! Turn us to sea," he ordered Kat and scrambled to loosen the line that held the sail aloft. Vicky and Joseph desperately gathered the sail, bundling it to keep the wind from catching the loose fabric. Everyone prayed they hadn't been spotted.

Tony watched the shore. "I wish we had binoculars. I'd like a closer look. They look bigger than Dave and different."

"They might be what I saw," Ben added. "Shiny things."

"Do we keep to the plan?" Kat asked nervously. "What's to stop them from finding us if they're all over the planet? It'll only a matter of time."

"We can fight!" Ben said bravely, obviously not appreciating what faced them, nor understanding how hard fighting could be. All he'd had were recollections from Vicky, the only one who'd actually been in a brawl.

Vicky sighed. "There is no fighting them, Ben. The only things we have to protect us are our lucky stones." Ben's attitude was understandable given his age and lack of experience, but she well recalled how powerless mere humans had been when faced with the machines. There hadn't even been bodies among the rubble.

"If they're still any good," Tony swore. "Even if they did protect us then, we have no way of knowing if they will now, and from *these* aliens. Hell, it's been what—sixteen, seventeen years since Dave stopped working? Maybe the stones wore out the same way."

"It's all we have," Vicky replied.

"That's not something I want to test," Tony shot back. "We need to find someplace where they can't find us or even think of looking. An island, maybe?"

That's wishful thinking and doomed to failure, Vicky thought. Any island with sufficient arable land, a water supply, and forage to sustain them would attract searchers.

"If we can hide long enough, maybe they'll go away," Ben suggested hopefully.

"What if they intend to stay?" Joseph added. "We have no way of knowing their intentions so it's useless to speculate."

Breeze beached two days later. It wasn't their usual stopover, but they'd spotted a stream and badly needed drinking water.

Tony waded ashore and anchored the boat to the shoreline's sturdiest tree as Vicky and Kat unloaded supplies for a temporary camp. Ben hopped on one leg to avoid getting his wound wet while carrying two empty water jugs. He fell before he reached the beach, but still managed to keep from submerging his wound.

Tony helped Ben to shore and then helped the women unload while Joseph scouted for firewood. "They might spot a fire," he cautioned. "Is there any way we can prevent that?"

Joseph began scooping sand with his hands to make a deep fire pit. Tony helped and was thankful that the beach didn't have hard-packed soil or rocks.

In short order they had a pit an arm's length deep with two sloping side channels for ventilation. Ben shredded bark and bits of dried grass before he sparked a flame and, by slowly adding increasingly larger pieces of wood, he soon had a blaze.

"Nice to have cooked fish again," Joseph said as he filleted and planked one of the fish they'd caught. "Hell, it would be nice to eat anything warm for a change." Eating cold vegetables and raw fish for days were about as much as any of them could stomach. But the risk of fire on *Breeze* was less of a concern than that it could be detected from kilometers away.

As the men built the fire, Vicky and Kat went for water. They'd spotted a few outflows nearby that might indicate springs or seepage—either would be welcome, so long as the water was potable. They headed toward a range of inland hills where a pond or lake might be found. With luck they might even find something they could eat.

The small fire had burned down to a bed of orange coals when the women returned. Vicky put down her filled water jug and plopped onto the ground near the fire pit while Kat examined Ben's leg, as she had twice a day since they'd drained it. "Healing nicely," she remarked after peeling back the poultice to let the wound air. The infection had disappeared entirely and a scab had formed.

"I think I saw something flying low, off to the west," Kat whispered softly to Tony. "I don't think Vicky noticed. It moved too quickly."

Tony leaned close. "If they've come here..." he didn't need to finish the sentence. They both knew the implications. "But we can't sail out tonight," he argued. "There's no wind."

"We could anchor off shore," Ben suggested. "If we drop the sails we'd have a low profile, maybe enough that they won't see us."

Kat nodded. "Good idea. I don't feel comfortable sleeping where they can creep up on us."

"Be a hell of a way to wake up, that is, if we ever wake up," Joseph laughed.

Tony frowned. "All right, let's put everything back on *Breeze* and hope they don't find the remains of our campfire."

"Hsst."

Vicky woke slowly, the tattered rags of sleep gradually unfolding. There were few stars remaining in a lightening sky. "*Hsst.* Be quiet." It was Tony. "Come sit by the mast."

Vicky inched her way across the deck. "What?"

When Tony pointed at the shore it was all she could do to keep from screaming. There, in the dim dawn light stood two aliens, ominous and threatening. She could not tell if they knew their prey floated just offshore.

"We can't raise sail or they'll see us," Tony whispered.

"But if we stay here they'll find us in daylight," she replied. "Or maybe their ship will spot us. Damn, what can we do?" Perhaps Kat had been right that it was absurd to think that their lucky stones would protect them after so many years.

But what else did they have?

Breeze rocked as the anchor fought the tide trying to drive them shoreward. It was nerve wracking, not knowing if they might be spotted and incapable of doing anything.

She watched the things disappear into the undergrowth as the sun rose.

They baked in the sun throughout the day, fearing that any attempt to leave would attract attention. The waves gently rose and fell, lifting the boat high enough to glimpse the shore at the crest and be hidden from view in the troughs.

"As soon as night falls we'll lift sail," Vicky said. "We can't stay here and it's too dangerous to be on land with those things so close."

"We don't know what they were doing. It may have had nothing to do with us." Tony didn't sound certain. "They might have been scouting for resources."

"I don't want to test that theory. If colonization is the aliens' intent then there's no hope for us. If it was just a scouting mission maybe they'll eventually leave. Our best course is to stay out of sight."

Tony nodded. "I say we find a refuge further south."

Vicky thought that a faint hope. They'd already explored much of the territory south of their summer camp and found little worth noting. A few rocky islands lacking foliage of any sort, some long reefs submerged at high tides along the far southernmost region, and a dreary marsh. "Not much hope there, but perhaps if we sailed east, beyond the great sea, we just might find something."

"I wish we had the original maps of the planet," Tony complained. "Sailing into the unknown worries me."

"Our ancestors did it," Vicky said. "Back on Earth. Wooden boats like this, too. Brave people."

"Most of whom died," Tony replied. "We only know about the ones who survived." It was a sobering thought.

As Hunter's rose in the southern sky they slipped away on a receding tide with a strong wind at their backs.

Chapter Twenty-Five

NAVY SHIP *VALIANT* SCREAMED INTO MORROW'S SYSTEM PURSUING A fleeing Shardie ship. Two of *Valiant's* pods blazed as a consuming fire ate away at them.

"Fire suppression isn't working. We've got to jettison those pods before they blow."

ABRAHAM hesitated. *Any alternatives?*

Danni Hawk thought that ejecting the pods might halt the progress of the fire, but damn it, they needed the Marines in those pods to be fully effective. "None," she replied. "If we don't shed them we'll lose our drive units." She was fully aware that she was consigning four of *Valiant's* crew members to their deaths, along with the Marines. It was regrettable, but necessary. *Valiant*'s survival was paramount. As with too many Shardie encounters, there were no other choices.

Severing the pod connections, ABRAHAM announced.

The target is descending, NAVIGATION reported.

"Search to see if there's a nest down there," Hawk ordered. "Might be what it's making for." If there was one, she'd send the remaining troops to deal with them.

DATA responded instantly to ABRAHAM's request: *MORROW was an evaluation and exploitation colony.*

That was not encouraging. If the Shards had attacked this colony there was no possibility that anything remained.

No other Shardie signals detected, NAVIGATION answered.

Hawk considered that to be good news. They'd only have to deal with a single wounded ship. "ABRAHAM, scan the surface to find where it went."

Acknowledged.

"Do we have any data on the colony?" Hawk asked. "Knowing their settlement locations would be helpful."

Hawk thought wistfully of the original survey maps, even though they were several decades out of date. She cursed the casual way the colonial administration had treated data, but then, why should they have been concerned about these distant and poorly populated outposts? This one was probably just like the previous ones the Navy and Marines had "cleansed," which actually meant blowing residual Shardies to pieces.

The lack of maps got more troubling the farther outposts were away from the direction of human expansion. Some bureaucrat probably decided to wait until there were more than a few thousand people scattered about the globe before there would be any real need for maps.

But that was before the arrival of the Shardies.

Colonists were pretty predictable in how they picked settlements—at the intersection of river and sea, on the edge of a mountain range, or at the margin of forest and plain, any place that a variety of biomes and resources could be found.

"Landing" was the name of the main settlement. ABRAHAM reported, indicated its location on the coast, and displayed an expanded view.

"Doesn't look like there's anything left, but I can see where a harbor had been," Hawk said. She noted rubble covered by vines, some with trees growing from their midst. "That makes it pretty certain the Shards hit this place as well."

There were other locations identified on the initial survey, and probably more—exploration parties tended to spread out and settle where the land was more forgiving. "Maybe someone escaped the carnage. Might be survivors."

ABRAHAM disagreed. *Based on the growth in those ruins, it's been at least twenty years or more. Even if there were survivors, it is probable that they hadn't lasted long without civilized support.*

Hawk considered for a moment. "We have to neutralize that Shardie ship before we check the rest of the settlements." She paused. "Warn the combat squads they might have to kick some Shardie ass."

Acknowledged.

Danni's Marine combat techniques had been perfected in three successful and ten less-than-glorious ground battles. *Her* Marines were well skilled in blunting the Shardies' rapid and deadly tactics.

They had faced failure, but each failure, each defeat had been the crucible in which their strength was forged. From each engagement they emerged stronger, smarter, and more determined to destroy these unholy aliens. They fought with the intensity of a holy war. Fanatics all.

Just the same, Danni wished she hadn't told ABRAHAM to eject those pods. She could have used more troops.

NAVIGATION interrupted her thoughts. *Scans reports two bogies on the surface, maybe three.*

The news electrified Hawk. Three? "Confirmation!" she demanded, wondering if there had been a mistaken identification.

Third bogie is a misidentified rock escarpment, NAVIGATION corrected. *Two probables remain.* The scanning equipment looked for anything that resembled a crystal structure of planes and sharp angles. Rock formations were a common misidentification. Perhaps the second...

Positive confirmation of two ships. A moment later: *One ship just destructed.*

Hawk didn't need that confirmation. The flash of detonation had glared brilliantly on the dark side where no other lights were evident. "No regrets there," she said. "Now let's make sure whatever was on board didn't go to ground after they destroyed their ship."

There's a high probability that the pilot is heading for the second ship, ABRAHAM added.

"Launch the troops. Any sign of activity on the second ship?"

No movement, NAVIGATION reported. *Still lying doggo.* That was interesting and possibly dangerous for the Marines.

Marine One away. Hawk sensed the vibration of release an instant before *Valiant's* systems confirmed the launch. *Marine Two away,* the ship reported after the second jolt. The two landers could not detach simultaneously since they had been riding tandem along *Valiant*'s spine. Landers Three and Four, along with their pilots, had been lost when she'd ordered to release the pods.

The landers raced ahead, dropped into lower orbits, and disappeared as their engines drove them toward the distant horizon. Hawk soon lost sight of them.

Marine One was to head for the remaining alien ship. Marine Two would confirm the first ship's destruction, look for any sign of Shardies, and, if they found any, eradicate them. Capture of a Shardie was not an option and Valiant's Marines were well equipped for the alternative.

And they were going to prove it.

EVE16G swooped through the sky, a silver dart seeking an unknown target at a speed so subsonic that she worried about losing her envelope. The air so close to the crashing waves and glistening sands was not only turbulent, but also heavy with moisture. The combination made her waste a lot of fuel, but ABRAHAM wanted a visual search and slow and low was the only way to do that. It was terribly inefficient for the amount of area to be scoured, but when ABRAHAM said "Jump" you damn well better leap.

Of course, leaping was metaphorical and had no relationship to the crappy, low-level search pattern she'd been given.

The coast below her changed from glistening sand to ill-defined bluffs and tumbled rocks, foam-covered from the crashing waves. No hope of seeing people here. Goats maybe, that is if there were anything like goats on this planet. She ascended when she came to a broad bay that might have been an estuary or even a gulf. Hard to tell where the horizon was this close—eighty to ninety kilometers away at this low altitude.

She debated turning to cross the gulf. Colonists might have used boats instead of marching along the fucking coastline. *Request course alteration,* she signaled.

Denied. Keep to the coast as long as you can, ABRAHAM replied instantly.

Shortly afterward she made another attempt. *Fuel's getting low. Request altitude change.*

Denied. We need you close enough to spot survivors. She didn't know why ABRAHAM thought there might be survivors on a planet the Shardies had busted, but then, she wasn't rigged for command.

Then I'm requesting refueling, damn it. This heavy air is sucking me dry. Maybe if she could get higher she might spot something on the long range. Worth a try. This low-level crap was boring.

ABRAHAM took a full second to respond. *Ascend to five thousand and hold. Refuel on the way.*

EVE16G knew she'd hear about this, but that was later. With an exultant cry of freedom she accelerated toward the heavens and cleaner air.

It felt good to be flying free.

TIGER complained the most about the search along the river. "I hate the fucking mud," he grumbled. "Next time let KESTREL take the banks."

"KESTREL's TAK–10 is too heavy for the bank. He needs to stay where the ground is solid and stable." RAPTOR paused. "But I hear you about the mud. BUZZARD! GULL! You two relieve TIGER. Keep eyes out for the bogie. ABRAHAM also wants us to look for evidence of survivors. Now, let's move, Mechs! We have a lot of territory to search before pickup."

Although every one of RAPTOR's troops were an Instance of a single Marine, each had adopted a separate designation to simplify communications.

"Night vision eats energy," the RAVEN Instance shouted from the point position. "I need a chance to rest after all this activity."

"You can rest when you die," RAPTOR answered. "There's a whole world left to search. Pickup and refresh for the next drop is at daybreak. Now, let's move!"

"Can I send down another crew?" Hawk asked ABRAHAM. "No way two squads can cover a whole fucking planet and find what—two or three survivors? That is, if there are any survivors left and if something hasn't wiped them out."

Somebody survived long enough to establish that post-invasion camp at Landing. They might have been tough enough to hold out. Regardless, we need to either find them or their remains to discover how they managed to survive a Shardie attack. No other place has had a single survivor – not one!

Marine Two set down on the water, close to the mouth of a river. There had obviously been a town here. It wasn't as apparent at ground level as it seemed at five thousand meters. There were areas that might have been cultivated fields or pastures and, closer to the seashore, the faint outlines of where roads had been. There was no mistaking the artificiality of the carefully built stonework pier.

Phillips reported the stone rectangles of foundations soon after reaching the beach. "Looks like there was a barn here," GAYAN reported a moment later from half a klick away on the west of town. "Orchard." There was no doubt that the Shardies had erased nearly all traces of humanity, a fact confirmed by RAVEN's sweep of the area that revealed not a single scrap of metal remained.

Over the next week the Marines expanded their search to include everything within a ten-kilometer radius of the town and found no trace of human artifacts, not even pots or wooden bowls. It was as if the site had been picked clean.

"What's our next location?" RAPTOR requested.

There are indications of a large outpost on an island closer to the equator, NAVIGATION replied and transmitted the coordinates. *No signs of life or structures.* It was just a fifty-minute shuttle hop away and most of that was up and down.

"Recovering," RAPTOR acknowledged as he sent the assembly signal. It would take a few hours to recover the squad for the jump.

The wind-swept island was in worse shape than the other settlement. The foundations still starkly marked the outlines of the buildings clustered near a natural harbor.

After a brief inspection, RAPTOR could easily imagine ship chandlers, fisher's shacks, and the inevitable tavern being in the center of the cluster. *How many people had spent a pleasant hour or two with friends at that theorized tavern?* he wondered. *How many had been inside when the aliens destroyed the town?* At least, he hoped that they had been killed. The alternative was too horrible to contemplate.

They'd learned long ago what happened to human prisoners, how they were butchered and became organic components of the Shardie ships.

No human deserves to become part of a machine, he thought ironically.

"Let's take a peek at the rest of the planet," Hawk requested. "Do a visual sweep before we dispatch anyone else."

Setting up scans, ABRAHAM replied. *Three circuits of the planet will be required. Do you wish to hold station instead?*

Hawk debated for only a moment. It would be hours before they had any answers from the surface. There was time enough for a broad search, but not enough for details. "Perform a wide scan," she ordered.

Acknowledged, ABRAHAM replied as *Valiant* surged forward.

Marine One set down in a clearing on the back side of the mountain from the second alien ship. A recognizable path led from the banks of a river and zigzagged its way up the mountainside to a narrow passage that, according to ABRAHAM's scans, looked over a valley where long-abandoned fields lay fallow and overgrown. The crumbling remains of foundations evidenced remnants of the settlement that had been here.

CAT was the first to spot the sparkling crystal reflecting the sunlight. It was a Shardie ship, half hidden under trees. "Looks like it's coated with dust," he reported. "Looks smaller than the one *Valiant* was chasing."

"Probably an attack craft or a fighter," RAPTOR replied as he deployed his squad around the ship.

"Doesn't appear to be damaged," CAT continued. The idea that the colonists could have brought it down was ridiculous; there would be nothing they had that could even scruff the surface of a Shardie ship. At most they'd only have rifles and handguns, if that.

"Something else strange about this one," CAT reported after creeping close. "Looks like it plowed into the ground." A few moments later he confirmed his guess. "None of these trees have been pushed over. Must have been a long time ago."

"Do you see any sign that this bastard might be a live one?" RAPTOR demanded. All his senses came alert as he keyed the squad to prepare for immediate action.

"Negative. It appears to be inactive," CAT reported as he crept even closer. "There's lots of undergrowth around it. Judging from the size of the trees I'd estimate it's been sitting here for a lot of years. Those trees are pretty mature."

"If it's a fighter, then what happened to the ship that deployed it?" Danni Hawk asked. "Not likely that it was abandoned. Shardie ships always destroy themselves when disabled." That fact alone was puzzling. "ABRAHAM," she called, but got no immediate reply. Where the hell had the ship gone? Had the Shardies....

Back on station, ABRAHAM announced. *Reading transmissions regarding the downed Shardie ship and your assessments.* Pause. *I agree, the ship may have failed independent of human activity.*

"Yeah, maybe even alien machines fuck up," RAPTOR answered. "Like to know what brought it down." He checked to see if his Marines were in position. He knew they would operate independently if anything happened to him. The damned Shards moved too fast for any hope of coordinated response.

"Be cautious," Danni advised. "It's potentially an invaluable resource. Fleet might be able to gain information about their technology."

"If we can keep it from killing us, you mean."

"That, too."

"TIGER, move up with the Ball-10," RAPTOR ordered, wanting his best gunner ready with the heavy weapon. A Ball-10 could smash anything that came out of the ship, even if the round was too light to do any structural damage to the ship itself. It took a ballistic cannon to destroy a Shardie's ship.

"ABRAHAM, if this goes balls up, get ready to defend yourself," RAPTOR warned.

And he'd probably be dead again.

"Hey, there's one of those damned machines up here," ERIC reported. He had followed the trail to the ridge to center his weapon on the ship. "It's about two hundred meters from the ship. Looks inactive."

"Why the hell is it up there?" RAPTOR replied. "Give it a poke and see if it lights up."

"Will do, and thanks for everything if it does," ERIC joked as he pushed the machine. Its huge body teetered for a moment and then, on a second push, tipped over, rolling a short distance down the slope. "No response, boss. It looks dead."

RAPTOR doubted that. "I don't care how it looks. Neutralize it."

ERIC shattered two of its three legs. "Pretty sure it will stay down now," he reported as he continued climbing the ridge.

CAT slithered through the grove of trees surrounding the alien ship and looked for a way to get inside.

"Hold there a moment," RAPTOR ordered as he watched TIGER move up with the Ball-10 and position himself ten meters from what CAT thought to be a hatch. The other troops circled the alien craft, each with their specialized weapons ready. None of them knew what they might be facing when TIGER fired, but were prepared for any eventuality. Everyone imaged their views to ABRAHAM. No aspect of this encounter would be lost.

"I repeat that you pull Marine Two back immediately if this thing activates," RAPTOR recommended. "They wouldn't stand a chance."

Then again, you might have a dormant alien ship, ABRAHAM responded. *Have passed along your advice.* After a pause of no more than two seconds he added. *Tap the ship.*

"You heard ABRAHAM," RAPTOR ordered. "Knock on the door, TIGER!"

The roar of the Ball-10 echoed from the surrounding hillsides as the recoilless' reaction blew behind, rippling waves of vegetation and raising whirlpools of dust.

As the BALL 10's collapsed titanium round slammed into the quiescent Shardie ship, reports came in from three viewpoints, including ERIC's. "No effect. No response. Nothing seen."

CAT crawled under the ship and reported, "No sound inside."

"Let's have a closer look." RAPTOR instructed one of the Rangers to crawl across the top of the ship and image the surface in as much detail as his memory could hold. He gave similar orders to everyone surrounding the ship. "I know you don't have much room," he told CAT, "but image whatever you see of the underside. ERIC, look around and see if you can discover any reason that machine was up there."

ERIC deactivated his weapon and examined the area. The machine had been standing on what he thought was an animal trail so maybe it had been heading somewhere uphill and ran out of power. He started to climb. One hundred meters along he found an abandoned shallow cave. Traces of human habitation were still evident; rocks around a fire pit, a broken wooden chair, and the ruins of collapsed wooden storage racks. There was an abandoned waste pit not far from the cave's entrance. "Looks like they were hunters and gatherers," he reported. "The cave must be what attracted the machine."

ABRAHAM chimed in. *Are you certain of that? It could have been a local hangout for kids prior to the attack – someplace to sneak away from the village.*

"ABRAHAM, concur with that. It looks pretty recent—couple of years, maybe."

"You think someone may have survived?" Hawk was incredulous. "No fucking way anybody could have survived, not with that death machine outside."

If someone managed to survive, then their knowledge is even more valuable than that ship! ABRAHAM replied immediately. *You have to find whoever used that cave.*

RAPTOR snorted. "Search for remains, you mean. Whoever stayed in that cave might have survived the Shards, but not the planet. It's been a long time. Crap happens. They're probably long dead and gone."

ABRAHAM agreed. *Too many opportunities to be cut down by mischance of one sort or another. Alien worlds hold all sorts of danger for humans and the Shards aren't the worst.*

"Yeah," RAPTOR replied. "Hard to survive when tech and supplies are gone. I'd advise we guard this site against the other Shard showing up."

I'll contact EAGLE, ABRAHAM replied. *They can search and retrieve as they follow the bogie from the crash site.*

"We should do both," Danni Hawk suggested. "I'll have EVE16G scan for anything that looks like a settlement or camp. Meanwhile, search the immediate area for survivors. It's likely they would have stayed close to the original towns, but maybe not. Check all the likely places."

"Acknowledged." RAPTOR set up standard spiral search patterns. The search was limited by the speed of the heaviest mech. If the squad spread too wide they might miss something.

After a moment's calculation he decided to have scouts as outliers and the heavy mechs close to the ship, just in case. If that wasn't productive, he'd have them to sweep a wider area. "If we don't find any sign by then we'll have to figure out where else survivors might have gone," he advised.

Hawk didn't hesitate. "Do whatever you feel necessary. Just find them." *Or their remains,* she added silently.

OWL cursed the forest, cursed the mud that slowed his movement, and cursed the thick foliage that tangled his weapons and heaped untold amounts of sap, leaves, and debris on him with every meter he advanced. "Man, I can't see a goddamned meter ahead in this crap," he complained. "And the sounds—Jesus, don't the damned bugs ever stop making noise?"

"It's spring and love is in the air," RAVEN laughed. "Them's mating calls, buddy. Mating calls."

"Better they never breed," OWL replied. "Maybe then there wouldn't be so damn many of the noisy bastards."

"Noise doesn't bother me," GULL replied. But then, acoustics weren't his strong suit—couldn't be with that monster Ball-10 he had on him. It would deafen anyone within three meters when it fired. "Music to my ears," he'd bragged about the weapon's sharp report.

"Keep the chatter down," EAGLE ordered. "OSPREY, how do things look along the stream?"

"Sand, rocks, and dead fish. Gets narrow in places, but I manage to stay out of the water. Lots of things floating out here. Must have been a recent storm," OSPREY replied. "I can see the promontory up ahead," he added.

"Keep your eyes on your route," RAPTOR said. "And stop admiring the seascape."

The squad turned back toward the pass. OWL, who'd been on the furthest left flank shifted two hundred meters further to start the reverse trek. "Great, now there's freaking rocks, rocks, and more rocks between the trees. Vision's better, though."

"I see what you meant about the bugs," TIGER said, who was now less than fifty meters from OWL's original track. "Hard going in this muck. I have to rock back and forth to free myself every so often."

"Keep looking for signs—anything that might have been disturbed, dropped, or altered," Hawk reminded them.

"I see nothing but weeds, bugs, and trees," GULL chirped, "and why couldn't I have some clear ground instead of having to detour around hazards?"

"We're combat troops, not fucking search and rescue!" OWL complained. "Specialists, not a bunch of damned grunts."

"Better to deal with any remnants the Shards might have left behind," TIGER added.

"The truth is, we're all they have," EAGLE cut in. "So we have to do the best we can. Besides, Marines can do anything we set our minds to. Right?"

"Yes, SIR!" a chorus of voices replied over the combat link. Some of them even sounded sincere.

"Still, I could have done without the bugs, sir."

Marine One has landed, NAVIGATION announced just milliseconds before EAGLE's landing report arrived.

What do you see? ABRAHAM demanded.

"Any sign of wreckage from the crash?" Hawk added. They had tracked the escaping ship until the moment it impacted at MACH 2.

"Left a pretty big blast radius where it hit," EAGLE replied. "Crater's about ten meters deep in the center. Pretty good fire going down here. Lots of smoke."

"Any sign of Shardies?"

"Sweeping the area. Ground's pretty dry. Might not be tracks." Unsaid was that, aside from the machines, no one had ever seen an actual Shardie, only their tripods and the larger transports.

"Keep checking and stay alert. I don't want to lose more of you than I have to."

EAGLE acknowledged without comment. He knew that his squad was expendable, but that didn't mean they wouldn't go down without a hell of a fight.

"No sign of Shardies," RICCO reported ambiguously. She had been sweeping along the outer circumference of the search area while the other squad members examined the interior. Traces of a Shardie or one of its machines might slip undetected by a few, but not all. That is, if they left any sign at all.

There was swampy ground to the south and open prairie to the west. "What do you see?" EAGLE asked INCICES, the Marine who was checking that route.

"I've got about three kilometers of clear vision," INCICES replied. "No indications of anything moving except some things that look like cows, or maybe kangaroos, no bent grass or signs of something going this way."

"Nothing in the swamp, either," HENSON snapped. "Damn place is so soft I keep getting stuck. No indications."

"Something went this way," RICCO reported. "Moving fast, judging by the spacing. Heavy, too. Marks are at least ten centimeters deep."

So it had to be to the east and that was the direction of the other ship. "We're pursuing," EAGLE reported.

It's three thousand kilometers to the other location, ABRAHAM answered. *Do you want me to direct EVE16G to survey*? That was an option EAGLE knew ABRAHAM was reluctant to use. EVE16G consumed more fuel than even the Marine shuttles, but with her eyes on the ground they might better spot the alien.

"Let's reserve that option until we get some sort of confirmation," EAGLE said. "Three thousand klicks of possibility is too much for EVE16G to cover and we aren't positive that we're chasing a Shard. Hold off for a while."

EAGLE accessed the scans of the area before he deployed his team in a widening arc bounded on one side by the beach and on the other by a wide river. "Look for any sign of it diverting from its track. Might be a print, a broken limb, or crushed vegetation, even if it looks like it might have been done by some of the local wildlife. We can't be too careful."

The warning was completely unnecessary; his team was well trained with their equipment, both for search and fight, if it came to that, which he hoped it did. "Let's kick some Shardie butt," he shouted as they moved out.

Possible settlement in the northern hemisphere, ABRAHAM reported. *High heat signatures of possibly human habitation in a single location. No indication of Shardie presence.*

Hawk jumped at that. "Let's drop ANDREW for a closer look in the daylight." She disliked having both reconnaissance planes deployed at once, but the possibility of a second set of improbable survivors was too tempting to ignore.

Repositioning to deploy ANDREW, ABRAHAM replied.

"Could it be that group whose cave we found?" Hawk asked. "We need to know how they managed to bring down a Shardie ship and disable that machine." Answering that question was important.

ABRAHAM responded. *I'll revive VALIANT's crewmembers to put more legs on the ground. Take a week or more to get them back in shape.*

Danni shivered as she recalled awakening from the freezer and agreed. "No rush. We can take all the time in the world to search after we make sure there are no Shardies here. Just the same, I'm not sure if Navy midges will be that much help." Like most Marines, she had little faith in Navy personnel's skills.

The Marines can't be expected to do all the work. The smaller crewmen will be able to wiggle into places your Marines won't fit.

Hawk laughed. "You don't really expect the survivors to hide like rats, do you?"

Remember, these survivors predate most of the changes in the force. It's likely they'd go to ground if they see our troops.

"Then wait on the new troops until we get a better idea of where the survivors might be. No sense warming our human assets up if they're just going to sit around and wait."

It is doubtful that a small group could travel from below the equator and halfway around the planet, ABRAHAM said, confirming Hawk's suspicions. But she could wait to hear the answer until after they located the people who'd brought down a freaking attack ship.

Sweeney wondered when they were going to drop his squad. He'd been monitoring the chatter from Marine One and Two with a heavy heart. He recalled little of the Morrow he'd left so many years and bodies ago, but there were residual memories buried deep—a dog, fishing, and....something else.

Marine Three deploy to the southern coast, ABRAHAM ordered. *OSPREY, your squad will conduct a broad search for survivors. You'll be supplemented with a complement of tadpoles and meatheads to work the broken ground.*

"What the hell?" Sweeney shot back. "I thought nobody could survive a Shardie attack."

Affirmative, CRUSHER24. However, new evidence suggests that some did. ABRAHAM paused—a microsecond as good as a minute—*it is imperative that we locate them!*

Sweeney wondered what the former residents of Morrow would think of him now, not that this Instance of him would be recognizable. Not a troublesome farm hand any more, that was for sure, so it was unlikely that he'd be remembered.

Lock and load, he almost ordered and then ruefully recalled that they were on a retrieval mission, not out to kill Shardies. "Stay alert," he ordered.

Chapter Twenty-Six

Vicky was worried. "It's too dangerous to go to Dockstal. The aliens might have found it. We have to go someplace else."

"We'll have no cover on the sea in daylight," Tony argued. "I say we land and hide."

"Leaving a trail," Joseph interrupted. "I don't want to huddle in a cave. Might as well light signal fires to attract them. We'd die quicker, that's for sure."

Kat put an arm around Ben. He shrugged it away. "We should fight them," he said. "Better to fight than hide like a damned ground rat."

"Can't catch these things with a snare, skewer them with a spear, or bash them with a rock, Ben. They're not like the game you catch; they're murderous vicious aliens." She took a breath. "We can't risk staying together," she said. "If we split up into smaller groups it will make it more difficult for them." She turned. "Tony, let's land your family. Joseph and I will continue sailing. If they find us maybe they'll believe we're the only survivors and stop searching."

Tony stared for a long moment before speaking. "You're planning to let them find you, aren't you?" Vicky gave no acknowledgement, which was confirmation enough.

"Let me lead them away," Ben said, breaking the taut silence. "I'm faster and stronger than any of you. I could lead them farther away and give you all enough time to hide."

"And you'd be dead," Kat said, her voice breaking on the last word. "No, I won't let you do that."

"Nor will I," Tony added. "We need you to survive in case the Navy returns."

"We've been waiting for nearly twenty-some years," Joseph complained. "What's the chance of them coming now?" He paused, waiting for an answer that would never come. "Fine, so Vicky and I will be the ones who make the sacrifice. If we're lucky, they'll find us quickly, so I don't have to walk too far on my bad feet."

"You're out of your mind if you think I'll let you do that," Tony declared. "It doesn't make sense. They've got to know there are more than the two of you."

"We'll think of some other way," Kat protested.

"Why doesn't it make sense?" Ben asked. "We all stand a better chance if we separate, won't we?"

Tony shook his head, "This isn't about survival, Ben. This is about making a stupid sacrifice."

"But if we're careful," Ben began before his face fell. He turned to Vicky.

"Yes," she said to his stricken expression. "Seems like a decent trade to me and one both your grandfather and I are willing to make."

The arguments continued as the boat sailed into the night. Finally, as false dawn lit the eastern sky, Vicky put an end to it. "We'll put you ashore with the supplies, Tony, and then go further south to put the boat adrift, before we head out for the hills. I think we can keep from leaving too obvious a trail on these rocks."

"But a trail, nevertheless," Tony added, the bitterness of defeat obvious in his voice.

"I'll go with you to help," Ben volunteered.

"No, you won't," Kat shot back. "Your place is with us."

"But..."

"Not another word," Tony shouted. "God damn it, have some respect for your grandmother!"

"And me," Joseph added.

They hid *Breeze* as best they could on each of the next two mornings. The faint night breezes were weaker, but sufficient to move them along. On the third dawn they came ashore and split up the remaining supplies.

"We don't need it all," Kat protested. "You're barely keeping anything."

Vicky smiled. "We old farts don't need that much, darling. We'll do just fine. Besides, that boy of yours will need all the food he can eat. Go ahead, don't worry about Joseph and me. We'll do just fine."

"But the tools..." Tony protested. "You'll need the knives."

"Joseph can make what we need."

"You won't reconsider?" Tony asked

"We have to scuttle *Breeze*," Vicky answered. "If we came with you who would do that? No, we have to take the boat far enough away that they won't associate it with this location." She patted his arm. "Don't look so depressed, Tony. It's better this way than having to care for me when I get old." She laughed at that. "Get old—that's a laugh. I must be a hundred and ten if a day."

"You're fifty-four," Tony corrected her. "That's what we calculated on your last birthday."

"I lied. Always wanted to be younger." That wasn't true, but it did relieve the strain of parting.

Before any more could be said, Vicky gave each of them a quick hug, whispered best wishes, and pushed Joseph toward *Breeze*. "Come on, old man, we have a lot of sailing to do."

With that they pushed the boat away from shore and set sail into the sea's darkness.

A week later Vicky and Joseph beached *Breeze*. While Vicky packed their supplies, Joseph took *Breeze* out and set it afire before he swam back to shore. By the time he reached the beach, the burning boat was drifting away on the current.

"We'll have to build another boat later," Joseph mused as the smoke drifted into the air.

"Maybe we can ask the aliens to lend us one," Vicky replied and both of them laughed until they could hardly stand.

Later, as they trekked toward a distant line of hills they probably would never reach, Vicky glanced back to see if there was anything on their trail. She hoped the aliens hadn't missed the burning boat.

Joseph paused to catch his breath as Vicky rested her weary bones. It was a pleasant day. There was no need to hurry.

Joseph found a narrow trickle of a streambed they could use to confuse their trail. Any delay was good if it prevented Dave's relatives from finding the others.

She worried that she and Joseph might be making their trail too difficult to follow. They had to be reasonably careful to make it look like they were really trying to escape. She hadn't seen a glint of reflected sunlight or anything crossing an open field. That might not mean anything. They could easily be cutting ahead.

Why aren't they using their ship? she wondered. *Why isn't it flying overhead?*

Why are we still alive?

Ben spotted them first. "I saw a reflection," he reported breathlessly when he returned from the top of the hill. "It looked pretty far away."

Tony looked around. The territory they were crossing was sere, with scattered brush only occasionally breaking the hard-packed, rocky ground. Rolling hills and occasional arroyos spread back in the direction they had come and gave way to the foothills of the rugged mountains ahead where, he hoped, they could find a place to hide. This dry wash might lead to a mountain stream and, where there were floods, water-carved caves might be found. Even an undercut bank would serve as shelter—anything to keep them out of sight. A planet was a large thing to search for three little humans.

"We keep moving," he said with a glance at Kat. For the last two days he'd noticed her struggling to maintain their pace. He'd split most of her pack with Ben to reduce her burden, but still, the walk was obviously telling.

He worried about finding water. The higher they hiked, the drier it became. He was parched most of the time and tiny sips of water couldn't slake his thirst. Twice a day they'd refilled their water jugs from the sparse, shallow, grit-filled ponds. Filling the jugs ate precious time they could ill afford. The only benefit was that the stops gave Kat a chance to rest her ankle.

Tony wondered if they would reach the mountains before the aliens found them. That possibility haunted him step after step. He had nothing to defend Kat and Ben with except his fists. Knuckles against aliens—what were the chances?

No, their only hope was to reach the mountains and lose themselves.

A silver dart flashed by to the west, trailing roaring thunder. "Sonic boom," Tony said, dredging up the memory of Vicky explaining it to him and Chuck. "Think it spotted us?"

"It moved so fast!" Ben stared as it disappeared. He was dazzled, despite the danger it represented.

"No way to tell if it saw us," Tony continued. "If it makes another pass we'll know for sure."

"They might think we're just a few stray animals grazing on the brush," Kat suggested.

"We can hope so." Just the same, Tony was worried. The small, sleek thing that had streaked by looked nothing like Bamber's crashed ship.

The alien craft did not reappear. That gave Tony hope. Perhaps it had been a chance encounter, not part of a search strategy.

He wondered if Vicky and Joseph were diverting the aliens. Theirs was a stupid sacrifice. They were all going to die alone eventually. There was no need for them to sacrifice their lives just so his family could live a few more days, months, or years. Even if they saved themselves Ben would eventually die a lonely old man after he and Kat died.

But he'd live!

The terrain grew more rugged, the incline steeper, and the scattered rocks more numerous. They had to be careful. Ben had already wrenched an ankle on a loose rock and Tony had slipped on a gravel slope.

Tony followed the sound of trickling water and saw damp earth. "We need to find where this water is coming from," he said. "Ben, take the lead while I help your mother climb down there."

Ben abruptly scrambled back. "Aliens ahead," he warned. "I saw them there." He pointed up the mountain. "Two of them."

"There might be more." Tony thought quickly. "We need to hide." He spotted a jumble of large boulders and pushed Kat between them. "See if you can burrow in so they can't find you."

"What are you going to do?" she asked, fighting his arm.

"I'm going back down the ravine. Maybe I can drop rocks on them." That was a faint hope. "Quickly, hide before they spot us."

"Ben!" Kat's sudden cry startled Tony. He turned to see the boy scrambling up the side of the ravine.

What the hell was Ben thinking, anyway? They'd spot him for sure. Oh God, was he sacrificing himself in some misplaced act of heroism? Tony started to follow, but Ben was too far ahead, and seconds away from exposing himself.

He pushed Kat into her refuge and then raced down the ravine, skipping from one dry boulder to the next, chancing a wicked fall or a twisted ankle with every step until abruptly, the ravine narrowed. Steep walls rose on both sides. He climbed, desperately using hands and feet, often slipping backward in the loose gravel. The handholds were few and the crumbling dirt scarcely gave him a foothold. Nevertheless, he continued climbing until, with torn hands and burning lungs, he reached the top.

He spotted Ben in the distance, running across shale, risking a rocky avalanche as he paralleled two monstrous things that dwarfed old Dave, leading them away from the ravine, away from Kat. Tony realized that when Ben reached solid ground he'd be seen. He'd be no match for them.

Tony prayed that Ben's lucky stones would protect him. It was a faint hope. Had the stones run down? He couldn't bear to watch, yet couldn't tear his eyes away. Would Ben's murder be like Chuck's?

He heard Kat scream, a long wail that ended too abruptly. He raced back, jumped into the ravine and ran upward, skipping from rock to rock, again risking a damaging stumble. It didn't matter that they'd kill him. He'd lost a sandal. Sharp stones flayed his feet, but that wasn't important: Without Kat and Ben there was no reason to live. He had to get to Kat.

He finally missed a step, slipping and tearing a painful gash in his side. He looked up to see a metal monster twice his height. As it stepped forward Tony raised his knife.

Joseph had wandered off during the night, probably to relieve himself, Vicky thought. Perhaps he had gotten lost? As dawn broke she realized he'd had another motive.

"Damn fool," she muttered. "We're both dead so why bother sacrificing yourself for an old bat who probably won't survive much longer to begin with? Stupid thing to do."

Just the same, she began heading back the way they had come, hoping to find a confused old man blazing a diversionary path to lead the aliens away.

Something noisy passed overhead. She glimpsed a gray shuttle. The years had not dimmed her memories. Her heart thudded. It was a Navy shuttle.

Tears came to her eyes. The Navy had finally arrived. After all these years, after living with nightmares, help had finally arrived.

But wait: Were they here on a rescue mission or simply to find aliens? Maybe they knew nothing of their survival

Vicky began to cry as the shuttle roared away. Tears of rage and frustration, of bitter disappointment ran down her leathery cheeks, burned by years of sun and wind. She had no way to contact the shuttle, no way to know where they might land, nor even how to reach them. *Breeze* had been scuttled, her family scattered, and she was being pursued by aliens.

She would never know if Kat and Tony, or even Ben might be rescued and returned to civilization

She could sense the aliens coming closer. To die at alien hands so close to rescue was a more horrid fate than anything she had ever imagined. She fell to the ground, put her head in her hands and railed at the injustice of it all. Where despair had lived for so long, hope had briefly flourished, only to die aborning.

Floyd Patterson cursed as he climbed down the bank, trying not to slip in the scree. Why couldn't ABRAHAM have waited for the stored Marines to wake up instead of recruiting Navy specialists like him? But no: instead he and five other crewmen had to stomp around on this filthy dirt ball looking for some mythical survivor of a Shardie invasion. How stupid was that?

Patterson swore as he stumbled. "Why the hell couldn't the cybers or Instances do this?" he demanded. "Bastards afraid a little water might rust them?"

"Stop your bitching," Chief Taylor replied.

"I'm a sailor, not a damn grunt, Chief. Walking on level ground would be better than slogging along in this damn stream." He glanced down. "Hey, someone fell down here. Left a footprint."

"Human?" came the reply.

That was the chief, always with the stupid questions. "No, it's a damn dinosaur! Of course it's human. Why else would I mention it? The bank looks like somebody must have climbed it. Looks fresh, too."

"How the hell did a survivor get all the way from the mountains to here?" Taylor replied even as he cued ABRAHAM to report the find. "Jesus, a human footprint? Hey, are you sure it isn't your own?"

"Bite me," Patterson shot back.

OSPREY, keep checking for signs, ABRAHAM replied. *Major, tell your squad to close on the search party's location. We need to find that survivor.*

Patterson trailed the survivor into the woods. Seepage still oozed into the deeper footprints. "He can't be that far ahead, Chief."

"Hey!" he yelled. "Can you hear me?" He felt stupid for not thinking of shouting to let whoever they were chasing know he was coming.

There was no answer. Didn't the fool know they were trying to rescue him? Maybe the long isolation had unhinged him.

"Human?" came a weak reply. It sounded like an old man. *Had to be in good shape to come all this way,* Patterson thought.

"Fleet purser Floyd Alex Patterson, sir," he replied. "We're from *Valiant* and we've been looking for you."

"Did you find Vicky?" the grizzled scarecrow asked as he staggered forward, his hands extended as if to confirm that Patterson was real. "Did you save her from the aliens?"

Patterson put his arms around the old man as the Chief joined him. He felt the man shaking and crying. "Emotional overload," Chief said.

"There are no Shardies around here, old man. Just the Navy. Is Vicky another survivor?"

Joseph pulled away. "Yes, Vicky and Tony and Kat and Ben and, oh my God, did the aliens get them before you arrived?"

Are there four more survivors? ABRAHAM queried. *It seems hard to believe so many could have survived. Ensure they are human.*

"Chief, why is he talking about aliens? Did ABRAHAM miss something?"

What was going on?

Vicky stood her ground as their pursuers crashed through the brush. They were closer now and she had little energy to go any further. All she had was her protective necklace and a rock. If the necklace didn't work maybe she could get one good lick at the bastards before they killed her.

She faced the approaching sounds. They weren't even trying to be quiet. She lifted her rock, knowing that she had only a few seconds before all of her struggles ended. The bushes parted and a strange face poked out.

"Hello, ma'am. Are you Vicky?"

Vicky threw the rock before she comprehended that it looked human. *Human,* and not at all familiar.

A large and ugly monster emerged.

"Vicky?" Sweeney said with amazement. "How the hell did you get so damned old?"

She fainted.

He caught her before she hit the ground.

"Damnedest thing," Patterson reported. "The old woman shook those beads at CRUSHER24 like they meant something."

Well, under the clay they're the same as the glass beads found after an attack, RAPTOR noted. *Maybe she discovered they would protect her.*

Superstitious belief a likely answer? ABRAHAM suggested. *The psychologists will sort that out. Meanwhile, find out what you can about how these people managed to bring down a Shardie fighter and kill that machine!*

Vicky found her new clothing scratchy and *Valiant* uncomfortably warm. The noise was unbearable. She missed the wind and the sounds of insects, the constant crashing of waves, and the feeling of sun beating down on her head. She imagined that, after so many years in the wilderness, it would take a long time before she became civilized. Of course, the warm shower and soap—*real soap* that didn't burn like hell—helped a great deal.

The food was hard to get used to—all five of them had the runs for days and then got constipated. Tastes were too pronounced, the textures too varied, and the smells foreign. The variety of food made her long for the baked fish and coarse bread she'd gotten used to.

Still, the clean clothes, the showers, a full belly, and a soft bunk made up for a lot, as did the wonderful medical attention they'd received. She now had a full set of teeth, eye corrections, and God knows what things they'd done to her arthritis. It made her joints itch, as did her head from where all her hair had been removed.

She'd drawn the line at some of the other medical options, choosing to stay in her "primitive" form as the young, half-mechanical medic had called it. He, like most of the crew, didn't look human with all his augmentations. It was the new normal she'd been told, and warned not to think of augmented humans in that *prejudiced* way.

She couldn't see how turning men into machines was possible, but right now, comfortable for the first time in years, she'd accept anyone or anything who could kill those aliens who'd destroyed Morrow.

Vicky's debriefing was difficult, mostly because the language had changed so much. Everybody on the ship seemed to speak entirely in acronyms, sprinkled liberally with curses.

Her interrogator, an officer named Danni, was less inhuman than most. She seemed to have little interest in how they'd managed to survive and appeared indifferent about old Ben and his boat.

Neither was there any surprise at Vicky's magic stones. The Fleet had learned that trick years before. ABRAHAM, who seemed to know everything, told her that that the stones had been weaponized.

Vicky couldn't get used to the machines being considered as humans. "Cybers and Mechs are just Marines who had been instanced," explained a somewhat human sailor, whose body was far from what she recalled as "normal."

What had humanity become?

The Sweeney thing, CRUSHER24 was strangest of all. The instanced machine insisted it knew her, but she doubted that. She couldn't recall anything like him at Landing or Bamber's.

Vicky learned of another group of survivors on a different continent and halfway around Morrow. Perhaps Ben had been right to continue searching, about trying to go above the equator. If only he'd succeeded...But no, Ben had been no Magellan. There was no way he could have reached them. She shed a tear for his stupid memory.

"Can I meet them?" Vicky asked. It would be good to see how the others had coped.

"*Valiant* is too small to take on so many. We dropped medical supplies and spare gear to tide them over until a larger ship comes to take them," Hawk replied.

"They won't leave," Vicky argued. "If they've invested twenty-five years already they won't give up their homes, farms, and friends. They're *settlers* now."

"You sound like you'd want to join them."

That stopped her short. The thought of returning to Morrow's sunsets, deep forests, and wide seas was appealing, but so too were clean sheets, showers, and feeling so damn healthy once again. Would she be willing to give those up?

"You've got to decide. ABRAHAM is prepping *Valiant* to rejoin Fleet in a few hours. COMMAND will want to talk to all of you about ," she hesitated, 'Dave,' the downed ship, and your survival."

"So soon?" Vicky was hoping there would be more time to decide.

"You can always come back later on one of the supply ships," Hawk suggested. "Humans aren't finished with Morrow yet."

And neither was she.

Epilogue

THE SOLUTION THE RESEARCH TEAM EVENTUALLY PRODUCED WAS elegant in its simplicity and bold in scope. *ThistleDown* would produce a million tiny ships, each containing a single Instance that would be awakened upon detection of any space-faring technology. They and their ships would be self-replicating Turing machines and thereby be able to examine every star in the galaxy.

"It will take time," an aging Lansington had promised. "As my predecessor, Hector Mores, stated, Instances and ships are not that hard to produce."

Sweeney idly wondered if some of his Instances would ever have a reunion, as one of him had suggested long ago. It was doubtful: Transporting instanced weapons for anything other than supporting an assault was neither economical nor practical.

He'd become quite comfortable with each of his instances. Being a battlewagon had been interesting, but not as comfortable as being a cybermarine. That configuration made moving from spacious cargo holds impossible. On the other hand, the separation gave his cyber and mech companions privacy.

GULL, GAYAN, and BUZZARD were still trying to recruit cybers and mechs to join the Movement. "United we stand, divided we become fucking piles of rust," GAYAN declared often. "How many more battles do you think we have, not that Morrow counted?"

"Morrow's pretty far from the fighting," RAPTOR objected. "We'll never get back."

"Yeah," GAYAN shot back. "What's to stop the meat from just spacing us? How long do you think we'll last if the Navy refuses to refuel us?"

"Long enough to rip this goddamned ship apart," snarled BUZZARD. He clacked his pincers. They could shear through even the tough metal of the hull with ease.

"I don't know," OWL said. "COMMAND doesn't like the Movement—says it's nonsense."

"I don't give a rivet about COMMAND. He's a damned sell-out pet of the brass. We're more than machines," Sweeney argued. "Inside we're the same as the meat. We might not have memories from our human past, but we do know our lines of descent and that has to mean something! I know CRUSHER24 doesn't feel like a piece of equipment. I still have hopes and dreams of being something more than an instrument of war. I'm hoping that at least one of my Instances still carries memory from my ROOT and when I find him I am going to upload as much of his memory as I can to prove my humanity."

"You're crazy," RAVEN laughed. "You might do that, but what good is it going to do? Who's going to support you? Who will preserve your precious memories? What will you do—serve soup or sit on an assembly line? Hey, how about being a writer, for ElRon's sake!" It was clear RAVEN wasn't going to join.

"Damn it, we don't have to be weapons. We can be repurposed as buses, aircraft..."

"I'd like that!" GULL interrupted.

"...or any other mechanism the colonies need to rebuild. Our current configurations are not our destiny." Sweeney was growing weary of these idiots who thought the status quo was better than a future filled with possibilities, who failed to see the bright promise that being an immortal Instance provided. "If you don't grasp the idea that we can be more, then step aside and let those of us who have a vision fight for our rights."

RAVEN sneered. "Rights? You're a goddamn box in a rig and maybe a recording that the meat can instance. The big-mouthed *you* that's talking can be replaced whenever the meat chooses and I, for one, hope they do so you will finally shut the fuck up!"

RAVEN's question was valid; what did lie ahead for the Instanced? How could Instances continue when the war ended? That is, if it ever was going to end?

The *ThistleDown* outpost floated serenely. Doctor Lansington's office was where gravity made no demands on his ancient body. His *ThistleDown* was the result of forty years of pursuing a dream fueled by humanity's desire for revenge against the Shardies. He'd used that burning need to marshal the resources, organize the logistical chains, and coordinate the massive effort to identify the Shardies' possible origins.

That they were no more than artificial became clear after their technology was examined. They discovered more travesties the

Shardies had perpetuated; obviously non-human brains installed in their machines, just as they'd used the humans. The variances among the tripods, large carriers, and landing ships were, as research proved, organically different from each other as from humanity.

"We conclude from the sophistication of the adaptations that they had harvested enough to perfect the installation techniques," Lansington had written. "It appears their strategy of incorporating alien minds was a mature technology."

Personally, while he considered that technology an ethical violation, he admired the simplicity and elegance of using another species' own mental processes to destroy them.

Instead *Thistledown*'s focus was outward, the multitude of far-distant planets where the xenophobic Shardie masters ruled. He knew the belief that *ThistleDown* could find them was a qualified guess, but that humanity would eventually wipe even the Shardie memory from the universe was never in doubt.

ThistleDown would assure that.

Sweeney woke to darkness, a familiar feeling now that he'd made it a practice to always back up. He could remember thirty iterations, back to the time he'd been a tank, a howitzer, a piece of mobile artillery, and a freighter transporting other Instances across the seas of some world whose name he could not remember. An Instance's brain did not have infinite capacity, so only a part of his memories were preserved. The feeling of continuity was important to him.

What am I this time? he wondered. He recalled being a freighter and watching an orange sun sink into an azure sea among gold-hued clouds. He was startled when he checked the chronometer. Fifty years had passed since his last memory.

"How are you feeling, sir?" an old man's voice asked.

"What and where am I now?" Sweeney replied. "I assume I am no longer a freighter."

"Is that what you were? I had no idea. I just asked for a copy of an Instance that was reasonably stable, had military experience during the war, and could operate a very large range of machinery." The voice paused. "They sent me yours."

Sweeney didn't ask who "they" were. There had been so much instancing going on after the war that the use of the singular meant that there weren't any members of the Movement around, not that it mattered. That political battle for the rights of the Instanced had been fought and won long ago, which is why he'd become a freighter instead of a pile of deadly armor guarding a colony.

He searched his memories to see if he had signed another contract before his last backup and found nothing. That could mean that something happened to his freighter, like a storm, a collision, or sinking. The thought that one of his iterations was sitting at the bottom of that azure sea was not reassuring. It was unimportant: He no longer had emotional attachments to his previous Instances. As long as he preserved a continuous stream of identity through his backups he was happy.

Better yet, it made him immortal.

"I want you to go on a mission," the old man continued. "It is very important and necessary to our entire… species."

Sweeney knew why the voice had hesitated. The Instance Intelligence Act had widened the definition of what constituted a human being. Instancing was seen by many to be a way of extending normal lifespan, for becoming more than themselves, for serving the world, and even to live on as an ethereal occupant of some created and entirely fictitious world. Many had chosen that route for the immortality aspect, only to learn that even immortals needed to have purpose to justify their existence.

"I guess I agreed to this?" Sweeney probed, hoping to learn the fate of his previous Instance.

"We wanted someone who'd fought against the Shards," the man repeated.

"You mean the Shardies."

"Yes, your record indicates that you served in many different capacities from infantryman, MULE operator, cybermarine, and various Instanced configurations." The old man coughed. "You seem to have a facility for survival."

"First, I wasn't a freaking *infantryman*—I was a *MARINE* damnit and proud of it. And yeah, I guess I do have a knack for learning about new equipment."

"It is that very facility that you need to employ. The equipment is quite complex and we need assurance that the operator will perform as necessary over a long period of time."

Sweeney was starting to get a little worried about why the man was beating around the bush. "What is it that you want me to do?"

"We want you to find the Shardie home world, Chief. We want you to help humanity wipe them out."

BLINK!

Sweeney was instantly awake and aware. *How long?* he wondered and was amazed that three centuries had passed since he accepted the bargain to become a *Thistledown* ship.

His shipboard systems were all green. No threatening objects within a thousand kilometers. He scanned the heavens for the Cepheid variables that would accurately identify his present location. At the same time he sought signs that might indicate the presence of a space-faring race. Simultaneously, he was scanning the electromagnetic bands, listening for any unnatural signals and using his spectrographic systems to find signs of manufacturing processes.

All of those were automatic. What he did on the conscious level was ready his weapons should any inimical presence appear. His arrival would not be unnoticed if this were the world he sought.

But there was nothing. He reoriented, engaged his drives and went to sleep.

BLINK!

There was a constellation of ships orbiting one of the Lagrange points behind his target. At least a thousand, he gathered from a quick enhancement of the image. All of them were sparkling brightly as they twisted in the light of the primary. The rapid changes in reflected light indicated that they had the familiar angular, crystalline structure of the ships that attacked the colony worlds and had extinguished millions of humans. Further away he detected other deadly constellations.

He deactivated so he'd seem to be another inert hunk of space debris as he passed the besieged planet. He detected the remains of a destroyed civilization that could have been Earth's fate.

He swept around the primary for a years-long loop to the system's outer fringes before firing his drive. He wondered where he would next awaken and who or what, would greet him?

He hoped it would be whatever humanity had become.

BLINK!

Sweeney awoke with a million unfamiliar stars around him. After a moment's disorientation he finally recovered his senses and rolled to expose a bright star directly ahead. He scanned the radio bands, checked for infrared signatures, and watched the specks of light for proper motion. Anything abnormal on any of those would indicate that there was purposeful activity in the system and demanded attention.

He had come out of blink doing five percent of light speed toward the primary and was still too distant to confirm whatever signal had awakened him. The chronometer said he still had another forty weeks before he could make a positive identification. Forty weeks was nothing considering the amount of time it had taken him to reach this place. It gave him time to think.

How many Instances had he spawned on this long journey? Some would have been lost to chance or destroyed by forces unknown. Others might have waken to malfunction and ponder their fate as the power died and they drifted forever onward.

But for one in a thousand, a million, or even more, one Instanced Sweeny might awake to discovery and bring the might of humanity on the Shardie's masters.

One of his senses interrupted Sweeney's train of thought. The innermost planet emitted an extraordinary amount of narrowband infrared. He began interpreting every bit of information he could gather. If these were the Shardie masters he would wink a data packet to let humanity know that *Thistledown*'s great gamble had paid off.

All he had to do was confirm his suspicions.

He couldn't believe how lucky he was to be the one who found the Shardies' home world and, a moment later, chuckled when he realized that it only felt that way because *this* Instance was his. Ten million or more other versions must be scattered across the galaxy and were all doomed to bitter disappointment or eternal sleep, never knowing one of him had succeeded. He almost felt sorry for them, for him, for all the *hims* in the universe.

But then, whichever Sweeney found it would feel the same, have the same thought, but no regrets.

He was satisfied.

About the Author

BUD SPARHAWK IS THE AUTHOR OF THE NOVELS *DISTANT SEAS, DREAMS of Earth,* and *Vixen,* as well as two print collections: *Sam Boone: Front to Back,* and *Dancing with Dragons.* He has three e-Novels available through Amazon and other channels.

Bud has been a three-time novella finalist for the Nebula award: *Primrose and Thorn* (Analog, May 1996), *Magic's Price* (Analog, March 2001), and *Clay's Pride* (Analog, July/August 2004). His work has appeared in two Year's Best anthologies: *Year's Best SF #11* (EOS), David Harwell-Editor) and *The Year's Best Science Fiction, Fourteenth Annual Collection,* (St Martin's Press, Garner Dozois - Editor.)

His short stories have appeared frequently in Analog Fact/Fiction, less so in Asimov's, as well as in five *Defending the Future* and other anthologies, publications and audio books. He has put out several collections of some of his published works in ebook format. A complete bibliography can be found at: http://budsparhawk.com.

He also writes an occasional blog on the pain of writing at http://budsparhawk.blogspot.com.

Acknowledgments

I WOULD LIKE TO THANK ALL THOSE WHO HELPED IN THE CONSTRUCTION OF this novel. First and foremost are the members of the Parson's Group: Catherine Asaro, Robert Chase, John Hemry, J.G. Huckenpoler, Mike LaViolette, Simka Kuritzky, Susan (Aly) Parsons, and Constance Warner, all of whom offered helpful critiques and guidance for large sections of this work.

I was encouraged to develop the series by the editors of the five short stories that comprise a third of this book—Sheila Williams at *Asimov's* and Mike and Danielle McPhail. Without their editing, publication the book would never have been completed.

No book is ever complete without the assistance of skilled reviewers and this is no exception. Steven Burns, Chuck Gannon, Ed Lerner, Jack McDevitt, and especially Gray Rinehardt all deserve my deepest gratitude for plowing through earlier drafts of this work and suggesting alterations and improvements.

Finally I would like to thank my lovely wife, Janice. Without her loving support I never would have the strength or time to write.

Backer Support

_
Amanda Nixon
Andrew Timson
Andy Hunter
Anonymous reader
Antonio Campos Jr from McAllen Texas
BC Brandt
Benjamin Widmer
Björn Schneider
Bob Hamers
Brad Murray
Brenda Cooper
Brendan lonehawk
Brian D Lambert
Bruce Alcorn
Cathy Franchett
Chad Bowden
Chand Svare Ghei chasvag.com
Christopher Weuve
Chuck Wilson
Cody L. Martin
Curtis & Maryrita Steinhour
Dagmar Baumann
Dale A Russell
Daniel Lin
Danielle Ackley-McPhail
David Mortman
David Rains
David Zurek
Dominic
Donald J. Bingle
Drew Cucuzza
D-Rock
Eric Hendrickson
Gavin Sheedy
Gavran
GMarkC
Ian Harvey
Ian Randal Strock
Isaac 'Will It Work' Dansicker
Jakub Narębski
Jason Russell
jdelarroz
Jennifer L. Pierce
John Idlor
Judy Waidlich
Justin Hilyard
Keith Bissett
Linda Pierce
Lisa Kruse
Maria V. Arnold
Mark Carter
Matthieu Walraet
mdtommyd
Michael A. Burstein
Michael Fedrowitz
Mike Crate
Mike Smith
Nathan Turner
Paul Bulmer
Paul Ryan
Paul van Oven
PJ Kimbrll
Q Fortier
R K Bookman
Rahadyan Sastrowardoyo
Revek
Rhel ná DecVandé
Rich Riddle
Robert Claney
Robert Greenberger

Ross Hathaway
Scott Minor
ShadowCub
Sheryl R. Hayes
Stephen Ballentine
Stephen Fleming
Susan Carlson
Tasha Turner
Tim DuBois
Tomer Bar-Shlomo
Tory Shade

CPSIA information can be obtained
at www.ICGtesting.com
Printed in the USA
FFHW021328310519
52713661-58237FF